T0304992

COFFIN ISLAND

KATE ELLIS
COFFIN ISLAND

PIATKUS

PIATKUS

First published in Great Britain in 2024 by Piatkus

3 5 7 9 10 8 6 4 2

A CIP catalogue record for this book
is available from the British Library.

ISBN 978-0-349-43317-2

Typeset in New Baskerville by M Rules
Printed and bound in Great Britain by
Clays Ltd, Elcograf S.p.A

Papers used by Piatkus are from well-managed forests
and other responsible sources.

Piatkus
An imprint of
Little, Brown Book Group
Carmelite House
50 Victoria Embankment
London EC4Y 0DZ

An Hachette UK Company
www.hachette.co.uk

www.littlebrown.co.uk

In memory of John Fry – *you'll never walk alone*

1

The storm on Monday night was more violent than usual. It battered St Rumon's Island relentlessly for several hours and the wild wind snatched the flagpole from the church tower and dislodged a couple of stone tiles from the roof of Coffin Hall before dying down in the early hours. However, the lighthouse, now automated, survived unscathed.

By ten o'clock on Tuesday morning, everything appeared to be more or less back to normal, as though the storm had never happened, and the sea was calm when the Reverend Charlotte Jennings, known to the worshippers in the five parishes under her care as the Reverend Charlie, crossed from the mainland in the little motorboat she'd been lent by a generous parishioner. In her former life in an inner-city Leeds parish she'd had nothing to do with boats, and at first the short journey had terrified her. After some expert instruction in handling the boat, her confidence had increased, but given the choice, she still preferred to walk to the island along the causeway that emerged at low tide.

The crossing took less than five minutes, and as Charlie headed for the jetty on the church side of the island, she noticed that the storm had brought a small section of cliff down onto the shingle beach below, exposing tree roots and fallen rocks. She cut the engine and let the boat drift while she shaded her eyes to peer at the damage. The stone wall marking the boundary of the churchyard lay a few yards away from the cliff edge, and she sent up a swift prayer of thanks that it seemed to be undamaged. She'd often feared that the erosion of that particular piece of coastline would worsen one day and send coffins and their sleeping occupants tumbling onto the shore and into the fierce waves.

She was about to resume her short journey when she spotted something flapping at the foot of the cliff: a piece of purple cloth caught by the breeze. She fired up the engine and steered the boat towards the island, and when she came as close as she dared, she dropped the anchor and removed her shoes to wade to the shore, hoisting her skirt out of reach of the lapping waves. As soon as she reached the beach, she scrambled towards the scrap of garish cloth, which stood out incongruously against the rock and earth dislodged by the storm.

She could see yellowing bones amongst the fallen mess – and two skulls: grinning death's heads with bared teeth. Her fears that human remains would one day fall from the top of the cliff had been realised, but she needed to stay calm. This had to be reported and dealt with in a respectful, prayerful manner.

She was about to return to the boat when the breeze shifted the purple material to one side, revealing something beneath. She edged towards it. Surely nothing could be worse than the shattered bones and grinning skulls she'd already seen.

But she was wrong. The half-rotted face of the corpse wrapped in the purple floral shroud would be imprinted on her memory for years to come.

2

DCI Gerry Heffernan enjoyed the short voyage to the island on the deck of the police launch as the clouds scudded across the spring sky. The sea was a little choppy, but he stood on the prow in the sharp breeze like a ship's figurehead, breathing in the salty air.

He turned to his colleague, who was sitting quietly with his eyes shut.

'You all right, Wes?'

'I'm fine,' DI Wesley Peterson said bravely. Unlike the DCI, who'd once served in the Merchant Navy and now filled his leisure time with outings on the thirty-foot yacht he'd restored after the death of his wife, Wesley wasn't keen on boat trips, and he couldn't wait to set foot on dry land.

'Soon be there.' There was a hint of sympathy in the DCI's voice, as though he understood.

Over the years, Wesley had seen suspects underestimate Gerry, mistaking the overweight, scruffy man with the thick Liverpool accent for a fool. Wesley himself always dressed smartly and spoke with a public school accent – or dead posh, as Gerry put it – although he had similarly experienced suspects misjudging him because of the colour of his skin. Despite their apparent differences, even the chief super admitted they made a good team.

Once the launch docked at the jetty, Gerry leapt off the rocking boat first and held out his hand to steady Wesley, who grasped it gratefully as he stepped off. They wasted no time in making their way along the shore to the place where part of the cliff had tumbled onto the narrow strip of shingle. A couple of officers were there already, looking as though they were waiting for guidance.

'No CSIs yet?' Gerry said as they neared the site.

'They're on their way, sir,' one of the uniformed constables said sheepishly, as though he was afraid the DCI would blame him personally for the delay.

It was Wesley who stepped forward, assessing the situation.

'I always thought nylon sheets were the work of the devil,' said Gerry as he joined Wesley gazing down at the corpse. 'Especially purple ones.'

Wesley nodded in agreement. He was too young to remember the days when such bedding was ubiquitous, but he was an intelligent man with a good imagination.

'Should we wait for the CSIs and the doctor, or shall we take a peek?' said Gerry.

Wesley shook his head. 'I don't think we need to worry about disturbing a crime scene. The body obviously came down with those other bones when the cliff collapsed. They'll have to be dealt with as well, but it looks as though they might have come from the churchyard.'

He glanced at the sheet, imagining what it contained. All they could see at the moment was a head that reminded him of an unwrapped Egyptian mummy: discoloured flesh, dusty brown hair still clinging to the skull and teeth bared in the semblance of a growl.

Gerry put on his crime-scene gloves and squatted down, flipping the sheet aside to expose part of the corpse's left side. 'The clothing's pretty much intact, which should help with the ID – and there's a ring,' he said.

'The sheet and the state of decomposition suggest that this isn't a historic burial. But those others definitely look old.' Wesley pointed to the yellowed bones nearby. The fall had separated skulls from femurs, pelvises from ribs. It was a tangled mess. 'I think it might be best to get Neil to have a look at them.'

'Good idea,' said Gerry. He'd come to know Wesley's old university friend well over the years, and he had to admit that Neil's expertise had often come in useful when the services of a reliable forensic archaeologist were required.

'He's digging on the site of a new housing estate near Dukesbridge, so he's not a million miles away. I'll give him a call.'

Neil answered quickly and Wesley told him he needed someone to have a look at some old human remains. He asked him to get over to St Rumon's Island as soon as he could. When he ended the call, he saw that Gerry had flicked the sheet back into place so they wouldn't have to look at the corpse any longer.

'Let's wait for the team,' the DCI said. 'In the meantime, I'd like a word with the woman who called it in.'

'The Reverend Charlie. I've heard my brother-in-law talk about her,' Wesley said. His sister's husband, Mark Fitzgerald, was the vicar of Belsham near Neston but he also had responsibility for several neighbouring parishes. 'According to Mark, she's quite a force of nature.'

'With any luck she'll be able to give us a name for our dead body.'

'Not sure about that. As far as I know, she's only been in the job six months. Besides, I don't think this is a conventional interment. Sheet from the second half of the twentieth century. No coffin. I think we've got a suspicious death on our hands. Either that or it's an illegal burial.'

The sun had just emerged from behind a large grey cloud, and Wesley shielded his eyes, scanning the mainland for the arrival of the team. Sure enough, a couple of patrol cars and a van had drawn up on the strip of concrete behind the sandy beach thoughtfully provided by the Heritage Trust to serve as a car park.

'Here's the cavalry,' said Gerry. 'Let's go and have a word with the Reverend Charlie. I take it she's at the church.'

'That's where she said she'd be.'

'Do we know much about this island then?' Gerry asked as they made their way along the shore towards a set of stone steps leading up to the top of the cliff, fortunately still intact after the storm. 'Strange, but I've lived in south Devon for years and I've never been here before.'

'The inhabitants must be very law-abiding,' said Wesley with a smile.

'Well, it's about fifteen miles from Tradmouth, and it isn't as famous as Monk's Island five miles further up the coast, with its posh art deco hotel, so tourists probably give it a miss. Also, it's only accessible via a causeway at low tide, so the rest of the time you have to get here by boat. No picturesque sea tractor like Monk's Island.'

'I looked at the Ordnance Survey map before we set out. I know it's called St Rumon's Island, but when I spoke to Neil just now, he said the locals sometimes call it Coffin Island.'

3

Gerry raised his eyebrows. 'You're joking?'

'I'm not. I noticed on the map that it's shaped a bit like a coffin; I'm guessing that's the reason for the alternative name.'

'Is there much here?' Gerry asked, looking round.

'The map shows a church, a pub, the ruins of a priory, a large house, ten cottages and an unmanned lighthouse. I've done a bit of research.'

'Good. What did you find out?'

'The pub's called the Hanging Monk, and only four of the cottages are occupied all year round. The rest, including the former lighthouse keeper's accommodation, are used as holiday lets. As for the big house, it's owned by an author called Quentin Search – he's quite well known, I believe. The church, St Rumon's, used to belong to the priory and is still used by people from the village of Midton, just across the water. I looked up St Rumon. He's a Devon saint.'

'You *have* done your homework.'

'I was a Boy Scout in my younger days,' said Wesley with a self-effacing grin. 'I like to be prepared. Seriously, I can't claim all the credit. When we got the call to come here, I asked Ellie in the CID office to find out all she could about the place.'

'That was quick.'

'She's good,' Wesley said, appreciating their recent recruit's efficiency. 'Also when I spoke to Neil, he told me he'd been contacted by an amateur archaeology group from Millicombe. They asked for his advice because they want to investigate the site of the priory. Apparently all that's left of it above ground is the church, a few ruined walls, parts of the pub, and the house where the prior used to live before the place was shut down by Henry VIII.'

'Is Neil going to be digging here?'

'No. He's tied up at Dukesbridge, so he'll have to leave St Rumon's Island to the archaeological society. He thinks it might prove to be more interesting than the Dukesbridge dig, but the developers are paying, and money talks.' Wesley checked his watch. 'He said he'd be here soon to have a look at those bones, though.'

'There's never an archaeologist around when you want one.'

They climbed the steps, Wesley leading the way, and once at the top they found themselves at the edge of a churchyard filled with lichen-covered headstones. The number of graves suggested that there had once been a thriving community on the island. But life must have been tough for the fisherfolk who used to live there, particularly in the winter months.

It was promising to be a pleasant spring day, and it was hard to believe the previous night had witnessed a violent storm. However, as they walked, Wesley saw that the weather had left its mark in the form of fallen branches and a flagpole blown down into the churchyard. The church itself, a sizeable stone building with a stubby tower, appeared undamaged, but it must have survived many storms over the centuries and witnessed many a maritime disaster on the rocks beyond. He could see telltale signs that it had once been considerably larger; scars of demolition had been left on the ancient stones where sections of the building had been removed, possibly by the islanders in need of building materials.

As they walked Wesley halted every now and then to read the inscriptions on the headstones beside the path. Some were illegible, weathered by time, but amongst the few he could read were memorials to drowned sailors. The previous inhabitants of St Rumon's Island had made themselves responsible for burying dead strangers who had come to grief on the sea; their act of Christian charity.

Gerry led the way to the church porch, where they found the weathered oak door unlocked. The interior of the building surprised the two detectives. They had expected it to be bleak and neglected, but instead the aisle was carpeted in red and the old pews and brass memorials were gleaming. Sunlight streamed in through stained-glass windows, casting colourful patterns on the scene, and there was a faint whiff of wax polish in the air.

The Reverend Charlie was standing with a group of people of varying ages. Wesley counted nine in all. She was a small, stocky woman wearing a knee-length skirt and a bright red jumper with a dog collar peeping from the neck. Her brown hair was curly and untamed and there was a benign but determined look on her round freckled face.

She detached herself from the group and walked over, her hand outstretched in greeting. 'You'll be the police.'

'Is it that obvious?' said Gerry.

She laughed. 'No. I was expecting you.' She studied Wesley for a few seconds. 'You wouldn't be Mark Fitzgerald's brother-in-law, would you?'

'Guilty as charged.' It was hardly surprising the local clergy knew each other's business – and the fact that the vicar of Belsham's wife, Maritia, a doctor of Caribbean descent, had a brother who was a DI in Tradmouth CID was probably common knowledge.

She gave him a beaming smile. 'Mark told me you used to be an archaeologist back in the day.'

'I studied the subject at university. Archaeology has a lot in common with detective work. Piecing together the clues.'

'Which goes to prove what I've always thought – nothing is ever wasted,' said Charlie. 'Millicombe Archaeological Society are keen to do some digging here. They're interested in what's left of our priory.'

'Yes, they contacted a friend of mine, Neil Watson. He's got some fancy title now, but he's what used to be known as the county archaeologist.'

'Well, if he wants to come here, he's welcome to have access to the church whenever he likes,' she said as though she meant it. She turned to look at the assembled group, who were listening in with interest. 'Let me introduce you to my champing guests and their colleagues. They're all bell-ringers.'

'Champing?' Gerry sounded puzzled.

'Short for church camping. It's very popular. Matt and Julia are champing here in the church and the others are renting a couple of holiday cottages on the island. They're all from up north, apart from Jack, who's local.'

'Up north?' said Gerry eagerly, as though he was hoping to find some fellow Liverpudlians.

11

'North Cheshire. They arrived yesterday to tackle five peals on our bells.'

'Peals?' He frowned.

'A peal involves ringing for three hours non-stop. I'm told it's something only expert ringers do, but I'm a little vague about the details. We have eight bells here in good condition, so I was delighted when Matt contacted me.' She lowered her voice. 'We have a few faithful ringers who come over from the mainland to ring for our Sunday-morning service. They do their best, bless them, but they're hardly experts. Jack is the only one who rings locally – by locally, I mean at St Luke's, Cranton, just along the coast.' She nodded towards one of the ringers, a lanky man in his fifties with thinning hair. 'I'm looking forward to hearing some really impressive ringing sounding out over the island again. Although not everyone approves.'

'I wouldn't have thought the bells would disturb many people round here,' said Wesley.

Charlie looked as though she was trying to come up with the most tactful way to answer. 'There is one person on the island who doesn't approve of the church making itself known.'

'Really?'

'I think I've said enough, Inspector. I've only been here for six months, and you learn which battles to fight and which to leave well alone.'

'So you don't know anything about the burial you came across?'

'There haven't been any burials in this churchyard for decades, as far as I know. And besides, burials nowadays are all in decent wooden coffins – or those lovely willow baskets that have become popular lately. I've never seen anyone buried in a purple floral shroud.'

Satisfied that the vicar couldn't provide them with any helpful information, Wesley and Gerry turned their attention to the bell-ringers, who were standing round awkwardly in the chancel. The northern group had only arrived the previous day, but even so, during an inquiry into a death that might be suspicious, everyone had to be interviewed and eliminated.

Wesley studied the ringers: an athletic-looking pair in their forties who looked as though they might be in charge, a fresh-faced young couple who were holding hands, and a tubby man with faded red hair flanked by two strapping teenage boys, probably his sons judging from the family likeness. The man Charlie had pointed out as Jack, the only local ringer, stood a little apart from the others next to a woman of around his own age. Neither of them looked as though they quite belonged.

'When did you all arrive on the island?' he began.

'Late yesterday,' the man in charge said. He was tall, with a shaved head and a concerned expression. 'I'm Matt Evans, by the way, tower captain of St Olaf's in north Cheshire, and this is my wife, Julia – Julia Partridge. This outing to Devon was my brainchild. It was me who contacted the Reverend Charlie.' His words sounded like a confession. 'The prospect of ringing five peals on an island appealed to our band, so here we are.'

'You're actually sleeping here in the church?' said Wesley pleasantly, wanting to put the man at his ease. 'It was pretty stormy last night.'

'Matt and I are the only ones staying here,' said Julia. She was slim, with long ash-blonde hair and tight denim jeans.

'It's surprisingly cosy.' She looked at the others. 'Eddie and Ruth are renting one of the cottages on the island, and Simon and his two lads are renting another.' She smiled at her husband. 'Matt and I thought champing would be fun.'

Matt nodded enthusiastically, and Simon's teenage sons looked a little envious, as though they wished their father had opted for more adventurous accommodation. From the keen expressions on their faces, Wesley guessed that they were enjoying the excitement of being involved, however tentatively, in a police investigation.

It was time for the others to introduce themselves properly. There was Eddie Culpepper, a tall man in his twenties with dark wavy hair, his small, pretty fiancée, Ruth Selby, together with Simon Good and his two student sons, James and Andrew. They were all fellow ringers from Matt's tower in north Cheshire, and it was clear the seven knew each other well.

The last to make his introductions was the local man, Jack Beattie, who was there with his wife. Maggie Beattie was blonde, with the prematurely lined features of someone who spent too much time on sunbeds. She wore a short leather skirt and looked a little out of place amongst the keen visiting ringers in their jeans and matching sky-blue polo shirts with the words *St Olaf's Ringers* printed on the back. The Beatties were both in their fifties and lived in Cranton on the mainland. Jack, as Charlie had mentioned, was a regular ringer at his local church, although he seemed eager to point out that Maggie had never touched a bell rope in her life.

He was the more chatty of the pair, and he revealed that when someone from the northern group had dropped out because of illness, Matt Evans had put out an appeal to local towers via the bell-ringers' grapevine for someone to make up the numbers. Maggie had decided to come along to keep her husband company amongst the northern strangers. The Beatties seemed to be an unremarkable couple, but Wesley kept an open mind as usual.

'We're planning to attempt our first peal today,' said Matt. 'We're aiming for five in all – one a day. Norwich today. Bristol tomorrow. Then London and maybe Glasgow the day after, finishing off with Cambridge if all goes well.' He saw that Wesley and Gerry were looking puzzled at the mention of these geographically diverse cities. 'They're different methods. An interesting variety of changes. Completing a peal is the ringers' equivalent to running a marathon,' he added by way of explanation, before changing the subject. 'So what exactly is going on here?'

'The recent storm caused a landslip, which brought some bones down from the graveyard. But it also brought down a burial that appears to be recent; an unexplained death.' Wesley deliberately didn't use the word 'murder'. 'I take it none of you know anything about it?'

The ringers shook their heads as expected. Gerry thanked them all for their time and wished them luck with their peals before turning to go. But Wesley made no move to follow. 'Has anyone been to the pub here?'

'The Hanging Monk,' Matt said quickly. 'We went there last night after we arrived. All of us apart from Jack and Maggie, that is.'

'We might go again tonight,' said Eddie Culpepper. 'Celebrate our first peal ... if we manage to get it.'

Matt suddenly looked worried. 'It is OK for us to go ahead with our ringing, isn't it? We've come a long way.'

The DCI said he didn't see why not, and Wesley noticed

an expression of sheer relief on Matt Evans' face. None of the group seemed concerned with anything other than achieving their bell-ringing goals. Wesley knew true passion when he saw it. Only Maggie Beattie didn't appear to share the general enthusiasm. Wesley saw her glance in the direction of the door, as though she longed to be somewhere else, and he couldn't help wondering why she'd decided to come.

As they walked outside into the spring sunshine, Gerry checked his phone. 'Better get down to the beach. Colin and the CSI team have arrived.'

Journal of the Reverend Thomas Nescombe

May 1573

This is a true and perfect account of the strange and terrible occurrences I have witnessed since my arrival in this parish. I feel compelled to make a record, for many would give no credence to my words, but God will be witness to the truth of them.

The name of this place is St Rumon's Island, but I have heard the islanders call it Coffin Island. I was informed by the bishop who sent me here that the name refers only to the island's shape. Yet I suspect it is thus named because a coffin is the only means of escape from this dreadful place. I knew nothing of the island before I arrived to take up the post of vicar three weeks since, but now I freely acknowledge that being banished here to this wild place must be punishment for some sin I cannot in all honesty remember.

Nearby, across a narrow stretch of water, is the parish of Midton, a village filled, so I am told, with honest folk. But at full tide the island is cut off from the mainland, and some say this makes it a kingdom apart. It is home to some seventy souls, most of whom make their living from the sea. I heard before I came here that the folk of the island know little of the law, which made me fear that I would be preaching to the air were it not for our queen's insistence that all should attend church on Sundays or pay the penalty of a fine. And yet they seem just as other folk, good and bad, so I must not be swift to judge.

I have visited some inhabitants of my new parish but they do not invite me into their homes, as though they are concealing fearful sins and fear my judgement. I must gain their trust and convince them that I am not only their vicar but also their friend.

The church itself is large, as it once formed part of the priory that was here before our queen's father, King Henry, destroyed such establishments. It is said the monks still haunt the island, mourning their lost home. I myself have seen no evidence of such unquiet spirits, but fisherfolk are prey to superstition. I have always believed that people can be won over to the word of God with patience and the assurance of His love.

It is the man regarded as lord of this island, one Elias Anselmo, who causes me the most concern. I am told the manor house once served as the prior's quarters, but its present incumbent is reputed to be a wicked man whose chief delight is consorting with the Devil. I fear that with such an adversary, my work will not be easy.

Yesterday I summoned the courage to call at the house, hoping that I would be received there as custom dictates. When I knocked at the door, a sullen man I took for a servant informed me that Master Anselmo was not at home. Later I discovered this to be a falsehood, for I saw him looking from an upstairs window: a cadaverous figure with long grey hair who bore a strong resemblance to the man I had taken for his servant, as though they might be brothers. I consider it *my duty to try again, to attempt to acquaint myself with the only other gentleman of learning on this island. Yet I fear my efforts might be in vain.*

When I walk about the island in the day, I come across men and women going about their business, mending their nets and tending to their small strips of land. There are sheep here too, scrawny beasts quite unlike the fat livestock I have seen on other Devonshire farmland. There is an inn that was once the priory's guest house, but I have not yet ventured inside. It is called the Hanging Monk, and the host, Cuthbert Sellars, seems a good man who attends church each week with his family. His eldest daughter appears to care for her siblings, as I understand her mother is in poor health. As for the priory itself, it lies in ruins, and the local people use the stone for their own houses, so that with each passing year there is less and less of the once fine building left above the ground.

By day all seems well on St Rumon's Island, but after midnight I hear strange sounds outside my bedchamber when honest men should be in their beds. I have on sundry occasions looked from my window and seen lights, and when I asked the churchwarden about this, he said that some islanders light fires to warn ships of the dangerous rocks round about. I asked him why the fires were not lit every night if they were so efficacious in preventing disaster. He had no answer for me.

My wife says she will be driven mad by this place, and she told me last night that perhaps the old rules concerning the marriage of clerks in holy orders were right after all. We have been married only three years, yet I fear she regrets her choice. I know she longs for a child, but we have not yet been blessed, although we both pray for it.

4

The purple sheet had been drawn back to reveal the gruesome remains: a half-rotted corpse dressed in tattered clothing – a skirt of some kind and a cardigan, now reduced to rotting shreds.

Dr Colin Bowman squatted down to examine the body. Over the years Wesley had worked with him, Colin had occasionally been unavailable, and Gerry had never been entirely comfortable with any replacement. The DCI was a man who liked the familiar. Wesley, on the other hand, tried to be more open-minded.

'We're dealing with a female,' Colin said as he looked up from his task. 'I can't give you a cause of death yet, but I'm sure things will become clearer at the post-mortem. Four o'clock in Tradmouth?'

'That'll do nicely, Colin,' the DCI said. 'How long do you reckon she's been there?'

'Hard to say, but I'd guess about a year, give or take six months or so.' He thought for a moment. 'That sheet looks as though it's from the 1970s, but I'm certain she hasn't been here that long.' He smiled as though he'd just remembered something amusing. 'I remember my aunt had sheets

20

like that, only in a hideous orange. She told my mother you didn't have to iron them.'

'Who on earth irons sheets?' Gerry muttered. Wesley looked at him and nodded. He and his wife, Pam, had no time for that sort of thing either.

The CSIs had arrived and had started sifting through the debris that had fallen with the corpse in the hope that it might contain some clue to her identity, perhaps even a murder weapon if they were lucky. Others had begun work at the top of the cliff some twenty feet above their heads.

Wesley's phone rang and he saw Neil's name on the caller display. When he answered, Neil said he was stuck in a meeting with developers but he'd be there as soon as he could to look at the bones.

'I'd really like to spend time on that island with the Millicombe Archaeological Society,' he added before he rang off. 'Ruined priory – just up my street, especially as this Dukesbridge dig's turning up very little. Trouble is, commercial digs take priority.'

Wesley could hear the frustration in his friend's voice. He suddenly realised it was coming up to midday and he was hungry. Perhaps when Neil arrived they could grab something to eat in the Hanging Monk.

'All this sea air's giving me an appetite,' said Gerry as though he'd read Wesley's mind. 'If you've recovered from our little voyage, let's seek out this pub and see what's on offer.'

They left Colin and the CSIs to their work. The plan was for the undertakers to bring their van across the causeway at low tide to pick up the remains, and Gerry observed that in half an hour the water would have receded enough to expose the narrow road. Wesley had a vision of the van being swept away if the raging water rushed in unexpectedly, but Gerry, who knew about such things, assured him that the undertakers would have plenty of time to carry out their grim duty.

Wesley texted Neil to say they'd be in the pub, but Gerry suddenly changed his mind. 'Why don't we pay a visit to the big house? Coffin Hall, it's called. Didn't you say it was owned by someone called Quentin Search?'

'Yes. Apparently he's an author of some kind, but I don't know the name.'

'Nor do I, Wes. No doubt he'll tell us all about it when we get there.'

Wesley messaged Neil again to inform him of their slight change of plan, saying they were going to see Quentin Search. Had Neil ever heard of him?

Neil's reply was immediate. *I've heard of him all right. He calls himself an alternative historian with a mission to expose the lies of the archaeological establishment. He's been publicising some sort of conference about his work – a symposium, he calls it. I posted something unflattering about his unscientific nonsense on social media and he wasn't a happy bunny. If I were you, I wouldn't believe a word that man says.*

5

'What did Neil mean by unscientific nonsense?' Gerry asked as they approached the house. It was built of the same stone as the church, and like the church was squat with an air of solid permanence, as though it had always been part of the landscape, withstanding gales, invading armadas and all the other disasters history had thrown at it.

'No idea,' Wesley replied. 'I'm sure he'll tell us more when he gets here.'

'Intriguing. Don't you think this place is a bit creepy?'

Wesley didn't reply, although he thought Gerry was right. He'd sensed a strange atmosphere on the island, but he'd put that down to the fallen bones and the half-decayed body in the sheet triggering his imagination.

As they crossed the courtyard, he noticed a small van parked around the corner of the house, presumably driven there at low tide. There was a name on the side: *S. Helivant Plastering and Building Services*. He nudged Gerry's arm and nodded towards the vehicle.

'Looks like Mr Search has got the builders in.' He looked up at the building. 'A place like this must need a lot of upkeep.'

Gerry raised the lion-head knocker in the centre of the studded oak front door and let it fall twice. When there was no answer, he knocked again. It seemed an age before the door was opened by a man in a plaster-stained boiler suit that must once have been blue. He was in his thirties, average height, wiry and clean-shaven, with fair wavy hair and a mouth that smiled readily.

'Are you looking for Quentin?' His accent was local and his manner friendly. 'He's in his study, but he doesn't like being disturbed.'

'I don't think that applies to us,' said Gerry, holding out his ID. 'And you are?'

'Scott. Scott Helivant. Plasterer and builder.' The man hesitated, the smile still fixed to his lips but his eyes betraying a new wariness. 'Er . . . I'll let him know you're here.'

'Before you do, maybe you can answer some questions for us,' said Wesley. 'I don't know whether you're aware that a section of cliff near the churchyard collapsed onto the beach during last night's storm.'

'No, I didn't know that. I drove over at low tide so I haven't been down that way.'

'The damage revealed three burials. We think two are old. But there's a more recent one that we're treating as suspicious.'

Scott raised his eyebrows. 'It's a churchyard. There'll be lots of bodies in there.'

'According to the vicar, there hasn't been a burial there for decades, and this one appears to be fairly recent.'

'I live on the mainland. Don't know nothing about the churchyard.'

'But you're a frequent visitor to the island?'

'I do work for Mr Search from time to time and I've done

plastering in a couple of the holiday lets, but I wouldn't say I'm regular.'

Wesley caught Gerry's eye. They'd probably learned all they were going to learn from Scott Helivant. 'You were going to fetch Mr Search for us.'

'So I was.' Scott grinned. 'If he's not away with the fairies.'

Before Wesley could ask what he meant, the plasterer vanished into the depths of the house, leaving them standing on the doorstep.

A figure approached along the hallway: a cadaverous man with long grey hair and a hooked nose. Wesley thought there was something theatrical about him, like an actor playing a role, and he guessed he was younger than he appeared.

'Scott said you wanted to see me. What is it?' the man demanded accusingly. 'I'm rather busy.'

Wesley explained politely why they were there, hoping Gerry wouldn't chip in and say something inappropriate. He could tell the situation needed careful handling if they were to get anything out of Quentin Search.

Search assessed them for a few moments, as though he was wondering whether he could safely send them away without repercussions. Eventually he must have decided that antagonising the police wasn't the wisest course of action, and he invited them in, walking ahead and leaving it to Gerry to shut the heavy front door behind him.

'You'd better sit down,' he said once they reached a drawing room with heavy oak furniture and dark panelling.

The two detectives sat down on a pair of well-worn leather armchairs. The spring sun shone through the diamond-pane windows, casting intricate patterns on the stone-flagged floor.

'I really don't see what this body has got to do with me. I'm in the middle of preparing the keynote speech for my symposium,' Search said, as though he imagined they'd be impressed.

'Sorry if we've interrupted your train of thought. We're interviewing everyone on the island as a matter of routine,' said Wesley. 'Does anyone else live here?'

'My daughter, Ginevra.'

'Her mother?'

'Ginevra's mother is abroad. My partner, Jocasta, lives here, but she's gone to Tradington. There's a lot to prepare before the symposium this weekend.'

'I'm sure there is. How old is your daughter?'

Search let out an irritated huff. 'She's eighteen, if you must know. Although I don't see how that's relevant.'

'We'd like to speak to your partner when she gets back. And to your daughter.'

His face clouded. 'I'd rather Ginevra wasn't disturbed at the moment. She isn't well. She's lying down.'

'Very well, but we'll need to send an officer round to take her statement. And your partner's.'

Search gave a theatrical sigh. 'As you wish, but nobody here knows anything about your burials.'

'What kind of sheets do you use in this house?' Gerry asked bluntly.

Search looked at him as though he'd gone mad. 'The normal kind – if that's any of your business.'

'Not purple flowery nylon ones?'

'Certainly not.' He sounded affronted at the very suggestion.

Wesley took a deep breath before carrying on, asking routine questions. But Search claimed he had seen nothing and knew nothing.

'How long have you lived here, Mr Search?'

'*Professor* Search. I bought the house five years ago because of its history. It dates from the fourteenth century and originally served as the prior's lodging when there was a Benedictine monastery on the island. After the dissolution in the 1530s, it was sold to a local landowner, then later bought by Elias Anselmo, a follower of John Dee.' He looked down his nose at Wesley. 'You won't have heard of him.'

'He was Queen Elizabeth's adviser and astrologer, involved in alchemy and the occult.'

'DI Peterson's got a degree in archaeology,' said Gerry with what sounded like paternal pride.

Search gave Wesley a look of distaste. 'In that case, you will have heard of Lyonesse.'

'The legendary lost land said by some to be located around the Scilly Isles. Yes, I've heard of it.'

'For centuries the stories have been wrong – or should I say, they had the location wrong. I have proof that St Rumon's Island is part of the ancient kingdom; a high point in the landscape that survived the disaster that destroyed Lyonesse. There were half a dozen churches in Lyonesse, and St Rumon's is the only one still standing – that's why the priory was built around it. All those other church towers are now hidden beneath the sea, and they say that under certain conditions, you can still hear their lost bells. For ten years now I've been conducting research, and my latest book proves beyond all doubt that Lyonesse still lies beneath the waves.' He lowered his eyes modestly. 'You may be aware of my book about Atlantis. It was a bestseller.'

Wesley was starting to understand Neil's attitude. Like

most reputable archaeologists, his friend dealt in hard facts, not magic and legends.

Gerry stood up, thanking Search for his time. Their host made no attempt to show them out, but as they reached the door, he spoke again.

'The people of Lyonesse were well known for their wickedness, you know. To them, murder was an everyday occurrence, and their spirits still haunt this island and influence events. I know that for a fact.'

Wesley saw Gerry roll his eyes. 'Let's get out of here,' he whispered.

6

'I wouldn't trust that man if he told me the sea was wet, Wes.'

Wesley didn't reply. He was busy wondering how much Neil knew about Quentin Search. Normally he had little time for publicity-seeking authors encroaching on his area of expertise.

They made straight for the Hanging Monk and had just started to eat their sandwiches when Wesley received a message from Neil to say he was running late and he'd meet them on the beach in half an hour. Once they'd finished lunch, they wandered back to the site of the cliff fall to find that Colin Bowman had left. The CSIs, however, were still hard at work on the beach and the clifftop above and they'd probably be there some time.

It wasn't long before Neil and his second in command, Dave, arrived to deal with the bones, and Gerry left Wesley with them, hurrying away to see how the CSIs were getting on. Neil was wearing the shabby combat jacket he always wore when working, and Dave, the smaller man, sported his customary Indiana Jones-style hat like a badge of office.

'Wes, good to see you,' said Neil. 'How did you get on

with that old fraud Quentin Search? If you ask me, he's a bad man.'

'You mean he's one of these rogue archaeologists who makes a fortune from spouting a rubbish theory and writing a bestselling book about it? I can see how irritating that might be.'

'It's not just that. I've heard things on the archaeological grapevine.'

'What sort of things?'

'Well, his wife walked out on him, not that I blame her, and now he's shacked up with his assistant. And I've heard that he thinks nothing of stealing other people's research. Calls himself a professor, but I have it on good authority that he bought his professorship from a dodgy website in the States. He's made some outrageous claims about the archaeology of the Devon coast, and last week I put him right about a few points on social media. He responded by calling me a narrow-minded representative of the archaeological establishment who refuses to acknowledge the brilliance and originality of his research. In the end it got quite personal. If you ask me, he's just trying to stir up a bit of controversy to get publicity for his ridiculous books.' Neil shook his head. 'Let's have a look at these bones then.'

Wesley would have liked to find out more, but there was work to do. He led the way to the site of the rock fall, and after assessing the situation, Neil and Dave concluded that the disturbance caused by the landslip ruled out any possibility of learning anything from the context of the burials. They began placing the bones in plastic containers, making great efforts not to get the individuals mixed up. Their work was as painstaking as that of the CSIs, and

Wesley watched for a while, fascinated. Once Neil had finished, he looked up.

'Word has it that there's another body, wrapped in an old sheet, and you're treating it as suspicious.'

'That's right. Colin Bowman says she might have died as recently as six months ago.'

'I wondered why all those people in white suits were buzzing round like wasps at a picnic. I knew it couldn't be anything to do with the bones we're dealing with; all the signs are they've been there for centuries. What's the story then?'

'We're working on the theory that someone buried the recent body thinking it would lie there with your old bones at the edge of the churchyard, undisturbed for eternity.'

'Best place to bury a body is in a graveyard amongst all the other burials,' said Neil. 'Like hiding a tree in a forest.'

'Until the weather decided otherwise.' Wes glanced at his watch. 'Sorry, Neil, I'd better go.'

He headed to the landward side of the island to rejoin Gerry, and was pleased to discover that the tide was out, which meant they could walk back to the mainland. As they made their way towards the causeway, the church bells began to ring. The first peal had started.

They heard a cheerful voice calling their names and stopped to let the Reverend Charlie catch up. 'I've just been talking to the archaeologists,' she began breathlessly. 'They've assured me the remains will be treated respectfully.'

'Of course,' said Wesley.

'And Dr Watson's a friend of yours. How nice. He mentioned some unpleasantness with our most prominent resident,' she added meaningfully. 'I do think social media has a lot to answer for. And as for that poor daughter of his . . . ' She looked at her watch. 'I'm sorry, I have to rush. Parish meeting.' She paused. 'It might not be very Christian of me to say this, but I don't think Professor Search is a very nice man.'

When they reached Midton, Wesley looked back at the calm sea and noted that the water had begun encroaching on the causeway.

'Just in time,' said Gerry. 'Come on, Wes. We've got an appointment with Colin at four.'

7

They retrieved the car from the car park in Midton, and as Wesley drove back to Tradmouth, he couldn't help thinking of what Neil had told him about Quentin Search. He knew very well that archaeologists, like many other close-knit professional groups, loved a bit of juicy gossip. And who better to gossip about than a man they all regarded with suspicion and perhaps even a little envy. But the Reverend Charlie had expressed similar misgivings, and even after such a brief acquaintance, Wesley was inclined to trust her judgement.

They reached Tradmouth at 3.30 and called in at the police station before walking along the river to the hospital. Wesley concentrated on the scene to his left: the yachts skimming over the shimmering water in the spring sunshine and the pleasure boats carrying early tourists up and down the river. He strained to hear the amplified commentary drifting across the water, anything to take his mind off his appointment at the mortuary. He viewed post-mortems with trepidation, even though Colin was genial company and always offered tempting refreshments in his office once the gruesome business was over. The pathologist kept a stock of the best tea from Betty's in Harrogate, and organic biscuits from the king's own estate at Highgrove; the sweet after the bitter and a treat Wesley knew Gerry always looked forward to.

They arrived at quarter to four and took their place behind the screen to watch the proceedings from a distance while Colin gave a running commentary into the microphone above the table. The sight of the half-rotten corpse made Wesley avert his eyes. He came from a family of doctors; his father was an eminent surgeon, recently retired and awarded a knighthood for his services to medicine, and his mother and sister were both GPs. However, he knew he'd never have had the stomach for their chosen profession.

'Well, gentlemen,' Colin began. 'I can confirm this is a woman, probably in her fifties. Five foot five, and her hair appears to have been brown, although I'll send samples for testing in case it was dyed. Judging by the state of decomposition, I'd say she was interred around a year ago, but I can't be exact about that, of course.'

'What killed her?' asked Gerry.

'Patience, Gerry. I'm not a magician.'

Colin worked on in silence for a while before he spoke again. 'There's no indication that she's ever had children, and as for cause of death, I can rule out shooting, strangling and stabbing.'

'Poisoning?' Wesley suggested.

'I'll send samples off for a tox report.'

It was another five minutes before the pathologist exclaimed, 'Ah ha!'

'What is it?'

'I've found something in the windpipe that might be

relevant. A tiny feather stuck halfway down. Very easy to miss,' he said as he extracted the object with a pair of tweezers and placed it carefully in a kidney dish.'

'Does that mean she was smothered?' Gerry could hardly curb his impatience.

'I can't think how else a feather could have got in there. And there are other indications of suffocation.'

'A pillow or cushion over her face, then?'

'You know I never like to commit myself until I'm absolutely sure, but I'd say that was highly likely. I'll need to do more tests, of course.'

'What about her clothing?' Wesley asked. 'Is there anything to tell us who she was? A name tape, for instance?' He knew he was clutching at straws, but miracles did happen occasionally.

Colin turned to the tray containing the stained clothing taken from the corpse. It had been photographed *in situ* and was now awaiting examination by the forensic lab. 'She was wearing a floral skirt, a light-coloured blouse and a cardigan. Fortunately the man-made fibres have withstood the elements, just like the nylon sheet she was wrapped in. Buttons and zips have survived well too, and there are labels in the clothing that might clean up in the lab, but if they were bought from a chain store that might not be much help. There's a ring as well. Gold.'

'A wedding ring?'

'She was wearing it on the third finger of her right hand. Although in some countries the wedding ring is worn on that hand, I believe. I thought I'd keep the best for last. The ring is engraved with leaves – quite an unusual design. And there's an inscription inside. Two letters. KL.'

'Just one set of initials?' Wesley was surprised.

'That's right.'

'I suppose it gives us somewhere to start,' said Gerry.

Wesley knew the boss always looked on the bright side.

Journal of the Reverend Thomas Nescombe

May 1573

When I first met my wife, Anne, I thought her a sweet and gentle woman. Her late father was a minor canon at the cathedral in Exeter, and was forced to conceal the fact that he had a wife during the reign of Queen Mary, who returned the land to the Roman Catholic faith. During those years, Anne's mother became skilled in the art of secrecy, and she still betrays little of what she thinks or believes. She lives now with her other daughter, Elizabeth, who married a merchant of Tradmouth; her family prospers greatly there from the trading of wine and wool. They have a grand house in the middle of the town, and it is said that one day my brother-in-law will be mayor.

Whenever Anne visits her mother and sister, she is reminded of the difference between Elizabeth's situation and her own. And how could she not feel envy and dissatisfaction when she is a poor clergyman's wife on this wild little island, while her sister lives like a duchess in a fine and wealthy sea port, made richer in recent years by plundered Spanish gold? Her sister has three bonny children, reminding her of her own failure. Sometimes I wish she would not visit so often.

I sit here in my humble vicarage praying for guidance, for I have heard talk that Elias Anselmo dictates what happens in this place and commands the island as though he were its king. Worse still, people say that he conjures demons, and as the island's priest, and the Lord's servant, I feel it is up to me to challenge any wickedness.

Anne went out yesterday saying she was taking victuals to the poor. She carried nothing with her, so I did not believe she was speaking the truth.

8

Neil Watson was clearing up at the site of the cliff fall, having arranged for someone from the university to pick up the bones and take them back to the lab to be examined properly. He'd been joined by the Reverend Charlie, who asked him about the archaeology society from Millicombe who'd contacted her about organising a dig on the site of the old priory. He assured her that he'd already been in touch with them and that he was keen on their proposal, although he was fully occupied with his Dukesbridge dig at the moment.

But the reverend wasn't one to take no for an answer. 'They'll do all the work,' she said. 'All they want is a bit of advice from an expert.'

She gave him a hopeful look and he hesitated before replying. The unexcavated priory was a tempting prospect, especially as the dig on the site of the new housing development wasn't producing much of interest. In the end he found himself saying, 'I'll contact the organiser again – see how I can help.'

'Bless you, Dr Watson. Bill will be thrilled.' With that she hurried away.

Neil had stuck to the rules and erected a screen so that

the fallen bones on the beach would be treated with respect rather than becoming a spectacle for rubberneckers. But to his surprise, Quentin Search had let himself into the screened-off area to watch the proceedings, behaving as though he was supervising the work. His arrogance when Neil asked him to leave was breathtaking, and he began lecturing the two archaeologists.

'You really have no idea what you're doing, do you. I suggest you attend my symposium this Saturday if you want to learn the truth. This island was once part of a great land and those bones obviously belong to early inhabitants of Lyonesse.'

Neil decided it was time to be firm. 'I really must insist you leave, Mr Search.'

'Professor Search to you.'

He looked at Dave, who rolled his eyes.

'You're a fool, Watson,' Search went on. 'You've failed to acknowledge the greatest archaeological discovery of all time when it's under your very nose. Once it becomes public, your bogus career will come to an ignominious end.'

After his spat with Quentin Search, Neil felt the need to call Wesley. The police should know what the man was really like – and who was in a better position to dispose of a body on the island than the self-appointed lord of the manor?

But his personal feelings and prejudices were hardly evidence, and he wasn't inclined to waste his friend's time on speculation. He took out his phone and scrolled through his messages, and realised he had a number of notifications. To his horror, he found that Quentin Search had been posting about him on social media. *The so-called County Archaeological Unit is headed by Dr Neil Watson, a man who wouldn't know the truth if it reared up to bite him. Dr Watson is a fraud who knows nothing about real archaeology. My new book,* Lost Truth Island, *will debunk all the self-styled experts' pet theories and prove them to be liars, particularly Dr Watson, who is doing his very best to conceal the truth from the world.*

He stared at the words, horrified. It seemed that Search had singled him out as a representative of the hated archaeological establishment, and as soon as he'd become aware of his presence on the island he'd decided to launch a personal vendetta against him, probably in the hope of garnering publicity for his latest book.

He'd seen enough. He held out his phone to Dave, who was arranging bones in their new plastic resting place. 'Look at this.'

Dave stopped what he was doing and read the post, swearing under his breath as he did so.

Neil was used to dealing with awkward characters in the course of his work, but Quentin Search beat the lot. He was sorely tempted to help out with the Millicombe society's dig, if only to annoy him.

When they returned to the station at 6 p.m., DS Rachel Tracey stood up to greet them. Wesley thought she'd been looking tired ever since she'd returned to work a month ago following her maternity leave. But that was hardly surprising. Her husband, Nigel Haynes, had a farm to run, with all the long working hours and pressures that entailed, and Wesley knew that being a farmer's daughter herself, Rachel often helped out. However, that afternoon she seemed revitalised and eager for news.

'What's the latest?' she asked. 'Is it murder?'

'Colin thinks the victim was smothered, but he won't

commit himself until he's done more tests. We've no ID for her yet, though. Can you arrange for someone to go over every missing persons report in the area for the past five years?'

'We're working on it as we speak. I've already taken a couple of possibles in to the boss.'

'Thanks.' Wesley had missed her while she'd been on leave, and was grateful that she was back. 'Everything OK?'

She smiled. 'Freddie slept through last night, so I'm firing on all cylinders again.'

'Delighted to hear it.' He remembered the time when his own children were young. The teenage years that had now hit his son, Michael, brought problems of their own.

'Let me know as soon as you have that list of missing persons, won't you.' He hesitated. 'It might be a late one tomorrow, so if you need to get off ... '

'It's OK. Freddie's with Nigel's mum.'

'You're lucky to have a doting granny looking after him.'

She smiled. 'My problem is how to stop his two grannies fighting over him. But I suppose that's a good problem to have.'

'Even so, don't stay too late. Seven thirty start in the morning.'

Rachel returned to her desk and Wes hurried to Gerry's glass-fronted lair in the corner of the open-plan CID office. He found the DCI slumped in his creaking executive leather swivel chair, the buttons of his shirt straining over his ample stomach.

Gerry grunted a greeting. 'Rach dumped these on my desk. Misper reports for the appropriate period. One's a teenage girl with family problems. Don't think that fits our mystery corpse, do you?'

Wesley shook his head. 'According to Colin, the woman in the purple sheet was well beyond her teenage years.'

Gerry began to rifle through the pile of papers in front of him. In the end he found what he was looking for and pulled it from the pile, holding it aloft theatrically, like the Lady of the Lake wielding Excalibur. 'Got it,' he said, before putting on his reading glasses and studying it with a frown. 'Woman believed murdered. Body never found. Do you remember a man called Bryan Dearlove, who went missing just over a year ago?'

'I recall the name, but I didn't deal with the case because I was on leave at the time.'

'Well, one day last May, Dearlove went sailing. His boat was found drifting in the English Channel, abandoned like the *Mary Celeste.*'

'He fell overboard and drowned?'

'That's what everyone assumed at first, but there's more to the story. Dearlove was having an affair with a woman he worked with – Deidre Charlton – and she disappeared a few days before he did. Her husband reported her missing, but she wasn't classed as vulnerable so finding her was never a priority. They both worked for a firm of solicitors. Dearlove mostly dealt with conveyancing and Charlton was a legal secretary. After they disappeared, an audit was done and a considerable amount of money was found to be missing from the firm's client account. It was assumed that the pair of them had siphoned it off, but by the time the loss was discovered, there was no trace of them.'

Gerry gave Wes a meaningful look before continuing. 'It was thought they'd run off together, but a couple of days after Dearlove vanished, his wife, Barbara, received a letter from him that must have been posted in Tradmouth before he embarked on his fatal voyage. In it he confessed to killing Deidre during an argument the previous week. He had helped her steal the money but then found out that she was planning to go off with it and leave him to take the blame. He lost control and killed her. In the letter, he said he was going out in his boat to commit suicide because he was full of remorse and couldn't bear the disgrace of going to prison. Murder-suicide was the verdict. Deidre's body never turned up, and our unidentified woman on St Rumon's Island could be the right age.'

'In that case we need someone to ID her.'

Gerry stood up. 'Let's see if her husband's still around. Hopefully we'll be able to get this wrapped up within the next twenty-four hours, then we can all go home and put our feet up.'

Wesley said nothing. He had an uneasy feeling that things wouldn't turn out to be quite that simple.

9

One of the team tried the number they had for Steven Charlton several times, but there was no answer. As it was getting late, Gerry decided they should all get a good night's sleep and make an early start the next day. In the great scheme of things, he reckoned a few hours wouldn't make much difference, especially as up till now the case had been regarded as stone cold.

Wesley agreed, but he did wonder whether this was influenced by his desire to get home to Pam and the kids; to enjoy a leisurely meal and a glass of red wine.

As he walked home up the steep, narrow streets heading away from the heart of the ancient port, he thought about the body in the purple sheet. Gerry seemed convinced that they already had a name for her, and for her killer. He hoped the DCI was right.

A journey seems short when your mind's fully occupied, so it didn't seem to take long to arrive at his modern house in a small cul-de-sac of similar dwellings perched on the hill above the town.

His heart sank when Pam came out into the hall to meet him and whispered that they had a visitor. Her mother, Della.

Wesley had once described his mother-in-law as a human hurricane: wild, unpredictable and liable to bring chaos in her wake. She wore her grey hair either long or pinned up in an untidy bun, favoured flowing ethnic scarves and involved herself in whatever New Age or artistic endeavour currently took her fancy. Her latest enthusiasm was the novel she was working on, although Wesley suspected she talked about it more than getting down to the hard graft of actually writing the thing. His own parents in London were the exact opposite: reliable professional people full of good sense. But he put up with Della because she was Pam's mother and his children's grandmother, although she had a horror of being called Nana or Gran. To the children she was Della; she considered herself far too young to be known as anything else.

He fixed a smile to his lips and took a deep breath before entering the living room, where Della was holding court with a glass of wine in her hand. Thirteen-year-old Michael and eleven-year-old Amelia were listening entranced.

'Wesley, I was telling your darling children about the offer I've had from an agent. She's quietly confident my book will be a bestseller.' She turned back to her grand-children. 'Della's going to be famous, darlings. You can boast about it to all your friends at school. It'll make up for your father being a representative of the oppressive state.' She never missed an opportunity to take a swipe at Wesley's chosen profession. He'd given up arguing long ago.

He saw the children exchange a look. They were at the age when they didn't want parents or grandparents to draw attention to themselves and the slightest deviation from the boring caused acute embarrassment.

'That's great, Della. Congratulations,' Wesley said unconvincingly. He could smell good things wafting from the kitchen and he suddenly realised he was hungry. He and Pam exchanged an unspoken signal and he followed her out of the room.

'What time's she leaving?'

'She's on her third glass. After you've eaten, why don't you offer to walk her home?' She gave him an apologetic smile. 'Sorry, love, but I think it's the only way we're going to get the evening to ourselves.'

Wesley sighed. 'I was hoping to put my feet up, then have an early night.'

'I heard about all the excitement on the local news. Mystery body on St Rumon's Island – or as the press are calling it, Coffin Island. I've lived in south Devon all my life, apart from when we were first married and you were working in the Art and Antiques Unit at the Met, but I don't think I've ever actually been there.'

'It's a bit off the beaten track. Not much of interest apart from a ruined priory, and there's very little of that left to see.

'So what happened?'

'The storm on Monday night caused part of a cliff to collapse and some old bones were brought down from the graveyard. Trouble is, we found a more recent body amongst them. Colin Bowman thinks she died about a year ago, so we're treating it as suspicious. I called Neil in to deal with the old burials. He's working in Dukesbridge at the moment."

'If he's not going to be far away, we should invite him round.'

Wesley was glad Pam had suggested it. She had a busy

part-time teaching job and he was cautious about imposing on her free time. 'If that's all right with you.'

'Knowing Neil, he'll invite himself anyway. Seriously, it'd be good to see him. And he said something about Michael joining one of his digs in the school holidays, so that needs to be arranged. Fingers crossed Michael doesn't lose interest in the meantime. You know what kids are like.'

She sat with him while he was eating, catching up on the day's news out of Della's earshot. Twenty minutes later, he was escorting his mother-in-law down the hill to her flat in the middle of Tradmouth, trying to convince himself that a post-dinner stroll would do him the world of good.

They walked in silence for a while before Della spoke. 'Pamela mentioned St Rumon's Island. I know somebody who's there at the moment. Her name's Maggie Beattie.'

Wesley stopped, suddenly interested. 'I think we came across her.'

'Her husband's a bell-ringer. Real enthusiast. Rings bells for hours on end apparently,' she added with a sneer.

He remembered the local man who'd volunteered to make up the numbers when the ringers from up north found themselves a person short. He'd been surprised that Maggie Beattie hadn't stayed at home if she didn't share her husband's interest. Unless the couple were inseparable and went everywhere together.

'We spoke to Mr Beattie. Just routine.'

Della huffed, disappointed not to hear a tale of police brutality and the persecution of innocent bell-ringers.

'How do you know Mrs Beattie?' he asked.

'She's just joined my creative writing group. She's working on a fantasy novel about a lost civilisation. Not my cup of tea, but each to her own.' A knowing look appeared on her face. 'Mind you, I suspect I know why she's gone to the island.'

'Why's that?'

'Let's just say there's an attraction there. His name's Quentin Search.'

'What do you mean?'

'I've said too much already. I'm not a grass.'

Irritatingly, Della remained silent for the rest of the journey. Wesley was baffled by what she'd told him. He was curious to know more about Maggie Beattie – and her relationship with Quentin Search.

10

Wesley lay awake half the night mulling over Della's revelation. He wasn't sure whether she was implying that Search and Mrs Beattie were having a relationship or if she was just making mischief by dangling the suggestion in front of him.

When he arrived at the station the next morning, Gerry was in his office getting ready for the morning briefing.

'Anything new come in?'

'Nothing more from local missing persons, but we're contacting other forces in case they have any likely candidates who might have been visiting the area. And we're waiting to see if there's a DNA match on the database. Our first port of call will be Deidre Charlton's husband, but I suppose we should keep an open mind. Belt and braces.' Gerry sighed. His initial certainty about the corpse's identity seemed to be fading a little, and Wesley agreed.

Devon was a popular holiday destination, attracting people from all over the country and beyond. There were a number of holiday lets on the island and it would take painstaking routine work to follow up each booking and make sure that everyone who'd stayed there was accounted for.

'She was obviously buried by someone who knows the island. If they're not local, it might be someone who stayed there a while ... or more than once.'

Gerry studied the pile of witness statements on his desk and pulled one out. 'The landlord of the Hanging Monk has been spoken to. He's only been there nine months, so I don't see him having anything to do with it. He plans to make the place into a gastro pub, you know – a destination, he called it. He wants to put St Rumon's Island on the map.'

'What about the other residents?'

'There are several inhabited cottages on the other side of the island from where the body was found; two were bought a couple of years ago by young families into self-sufficiency.'

'Tough living in a place like that in winter – cut off from the mainland every high tide,' said Wesley.

'True, but each to his or her own. The officers who spoke to them didn't think there was anything suspicious, but we can't rule anything out at this stage. The other two cottages are owned by retired couples who bought them initially to use in the summer months but now spend most of the year there. None of them admit to knowing anything about the burial, but all their stories are being checked out. The rest of the properties on the island are holiday lets, and someone's tracing everyone who's stayed there over the past couple of years. Our priority at this stage has to be giving the victim a name.'

'We can send local TV an image of the ring and hope someone knows who KL is. Could be the victim – or the person who gave her the ring.'

Gerry shrugged his large shoulders. He looked weary, and a little dishevelled. He'd been looking that way since his partner, Joyce, had moved out to start a new life, claiming she wanted to travel before she became too old. Wesley suspected this had been triggered by the news that Alison, the daughter Gerry hadn't known existed until she'd turned up on his doorstep a few years ago, was relocating to Devon from Liverpool and wanted to move in with her long-lost father. Joyce had moved out just as Alison had taken up residence. Gerry had welcomed Alison's arrival, as had his son, Sam. His other daughter, Rosie, however, didn't share her father and brother's delight at the arrival of her new-found half-sister.

'Alison OK?' Wesley asked, hoping the reunion wasn't beginning to pall.

But Gerry's face lit up in a wide grin. 'She's great. Got herself a job as a receptionist at Sam's vet's surgery and she's really enjoying it . Sam's persuaded her to apply to train as a veterinary nurse. She loves animals. She's talking about getting a dog. You've no regrets about getting Sherlock, have you?'

'Absolutely not. He's one of the family now.'

Wesley was struck by the fondness in the boss's voice whenever Alison was mentioned. He'd met her himself and liked the straightforward young woman. Even though Gerry had had no contact with her until she was an adult, he could see similarities between father and daughter, blood being thicker than water.

'Have you heard from Joyce?' he asked.

Gerry shook his head, and Wesley found it hard to gauge his feelings about his former partner, the woman who'd shared his house and his life for several years. Before he could ask any more questions, however, the DCI rose from his seat. 'Time to address the troops.'

Wesley stood beside Gerry as he gave the morning

briefing and allocated tasks: continuing the trawl through missing persons reports; tracing the jeweller who'd supplied the ring and discovering the significance of the initials KL; discovering the origin of the sheet and the victim's clothing; dental records and anything else anyone could think of. Gerry explained that Colin Bowman thought the victim had probably been smothered with a cushion or pillow, which meant they were definitely investigating a murder. With that, he told them to get on with it. He wanted the culprit locked up and charged by teatime. This produced a titter of laughter. They all knew the boss well enough to tell when he was joking.

There was one job the DCI kept for himself and Wesley, and that was the visit to Steven Charlton, Deidre Charlton's husband.

Journal of the Reverend Thomas Nescombe

May 1573

I was returning from the church when I encountered Elias Anselmo in the company of the taciturn servant, who trailed behind him like a kicked dog. Once more I saw a resemblance between the two men in build and age, but I did not enquire whether they were related.

When Anselmo saw me, he stopped and waited so I had no choice but to greet him civilly. I had resolved to pay another visit to the hall, but my own cowardice had prevented me. Perhaps this meeting was intended by fate. The Lord does indeed move in mysterious ways.

'Nescombe. I wish to speak with you.' He addressed me as one would a lowly servant rather than a learned man in holy orders.

'Indeed, sir,' I replied, and waited for him to explain himself.

'Attend me at the hall in an hour.'

With that, he walked off with the servant following in his wake. I had been summoned. And it was a summons I felt I must obey.

*

Arriving at the hall, I felt a thrill of fear. The island rang with tales of evil and ungodly deeds, but I had dismissed this as the idle talk of poor ignorant folk. And yet there was something about the place that made me doubt this judgement. I had never encountered true evil before, although I have preached on the subject often enough, warning my flock against the snares of Satan. Now I wondered whether I was about to meet it face to face. Or whether this strange island was causing my mind to conjure demons that do not exist.

The door opened before I could knock and the servant led me into the great hall, a gloomy chamber with filthy rushes strewn over the stone floor. A fire burned in the massive hearth at the end of the room, but it threw out no heat. I sat myself on the bench beside the long oak table and awaited my host, uttering a silent prayer for protection.

The servant left me alone, and it was a full fifteen minutes before his master deigned to appear. To my surprise, he wore a long cloak embroidered with moons and stars and other symbols of the occult. There was a sly smile on his lips, as though my presence amused him.

'Reverend Nescombe. You obeyed my summons, came here at my whistle like an obedient hound. Good.'

For a while I said nothing, taken aback by this humiliation. I am no faithful dog and I will not be commanded as such. I stood and bowed, preparing to take my leave with some dignity.

'I pray you, do not leave, sir. Do not take offence at my jests. I am unused to society and must be forgiven. You deal in forgiveness, do you not?'

'I do, sir. Forgiveness and salvation.'

'But my own path to everlasting life is not yours.' He paused, looking at me as though he was seeing into my very soul. Then his thin lips turned upwards, but his eyes were cold. 'I was once as you are now. I came to this island as a novice monk at the priory. You cannot help but see the ruins of that life all around you.'

'And yet you rejected the path of righteousness.'

His laugh was bitter. 'What righteousness did I witness when Master Thomas Cromwell's men came to eject us from our home? They stripped the altars, smashed the images and used violence upon the brothers. When the prior defied them, they hanged him and left his corpse to rot as a warning against disobedience. Did you know that?'

I told him I had heard some such thing.

'It was then I realised that evil men regard goodness as weakness.' He paused. 'And that even the weakest and most harmless of men might be tempted into betrayal and evil by the offer of riches. So at the peril of my eternal soul, I made the decision to follow another path. Come with me and I will show you things that will amaze you.'

I am ashamed to say that I felt afraid. I should have trusted in the Lord, but somehow the presence of Elias Anselmo fuddled my mind to such a degree that all thoughts of Our Saviour were banished at that moment.

Without a word, I followed him into the bowels of that house with a feeling of dread.

11

To Gerry's bitter disappointment, just as they were about to set off, he was summoned upstairs by the chief superintendent, who wanted him to bring her up to date on their progress. As he left the office, he grumbled to Wesley that so far there wasn't much to report. The body was still unidentified, although the disappearance of Deidre Charlton seemed to be their most promising lead, and hopefully it wouldn't be long before they could make an arrest. Unless Bryan Dearlove had been responsible, in which case the culprit was dead.

Wesley admired Gerry's optimism, and as the DCI wasn't free, he asked Rachel to go with him to visit Deidre's husband.

'What do we know about him?' she said when he told her his plans.

Luckily he'd looked up the details of Deidre's disappearance, so he had the answer at his fingertips. 'The Charltons moved here from London because he got sick of the rat race and wanted to start a vineyard. That all came to nothing, so he opened a vegan café in Neston instead. Deidre became the main breadwinner. No children. Steven Charlton reported his wife missing, then a few days later

Barbara Dearlove received the letter from her husband confessing that he'd been having an affair with Deidre and that he'd killed her after a row and was intending to commit suicide. Neither body was found.'

Rachel nodded. 'Have you got the ring found on the body? Charlton might be able to identify it as his wife's.'

Wesley held out the small clear evidence bag containing the ring. For the first time, he was struck by how small it was; an adornment for a dainty finger.

Rachel hurried over to the coat stand in the corner of the office and pulled her jacket off the hook. She had an eager look on her face, as though she couldn't wait to escape the tyranny of her computer.

First they called at Steven Charlton's café, the Noble Veg. It was a small establishment off the main high street in Neston and was busy with people enjoying their morning coffee. The young man behind the counter sported a variety of piercings and a man bun and asked them politely what they'd like. When they showed their ID, he looked shocked, then guilty. But Wesley had seen many law-abiding citizens react like that when the police came calling.

'Steven's at home,' he told them. 'He won't be in until later.'

'Thanks, we've got his address,' said Wesley, doing his best to sound unthreatening.

Rachel drove the two miles to Steven Charlton's cottage in a small village outside Neston: little more than a handful of houses, including a Methodist chapel that had long since been converted into a desirable dwelling. It was a true backwater, and Wesley, who'd lived in the area a while, had never had reason to venture there. Even for Rachel, who'd grown up locally, it was *terra incognita*.

'Some people like peace and quiet away from civilisation,' she said as though she'd read his mind. Then she added, 'Maybe Deidre craved a bit of excitement.'

'Your parents' place is pretty isolated.'

'True, but there's always plenty to do on a farm, and the farming community's close-knit. If you came to live in a place like this after London without knowing anyone, you'd probably go mad.'

Wesley suspected she was right. In his experience, she usually was.

Steven Charlton greeted them in his pyjamas, as though he'd only just got out of bed. He was in his late forties, bald, with a snub nose that gave him the appearance of an overgrown baby. There were bags beneath his pale grey eyes as though he hadn't slept well.

Wesley held up his ID. 'DI Wesley Peterson, Tradmouth CID, and this is DS Rachel Tracey. May we have a word?'

The man suddenly looked alert. 'Is this about Deidre? Have you found her?'

Wesley didn't reply. They followed Charlton into a cluttered living room. The dust caught in the sunlight streaming through the dirty window told of neglect, or indifference. Perhaps once his wife walked out on him, he'd decided he couldn't be bothered.

Wesley handed the ring to Rachel. Breaking bad news was one of her talents. She could always radiate gentle sympathy when the occasion required.

'Do you recognise this ring, Mr Charlton? Take your time. No rush.'

Steven Charlton took the evidence bag as though he feared it would be red hot to the touch. Wesley watched his face and saw relief.

'I've never seen it before. Why? Where did you find it?'

'Are you absolutely sure?'

'Absolutely.'

'We found it on the body of a woman who died about a year ago – around the time your wife went missing.'

Steven shook his head. 'Well, it's not Deidre's. It's far too small for a start. She had quite plump fingers.'

'There are initials engraved inside, KL. Do they mean anything to you?'

Another shake of the head.

'Do you mind telling us what happened when Deidre disappeared? We've read the file but there might be something you've remembered since.'

Steven sighed. 'It was just over a year ago. We hadn't been getting on well for some time – in fact we'd been leading separate lives – but it still came as a shock when she didn't come home one day. I went to the police and reported her missing, but they didn't do much; said she was an adult so she could do what she liked. Then I heard that Barbara Dearlove's husband had gone missing around the same time, and later they found that money had gone missing from the firm's client account.' He hesitated and looked away.

'Dearlove sent his wife a letter saying he'd killed Deidre and was intending to kill himself. I didn't even know they'd been having an affair and I felt stupid for not noticing the signs. But Deidre was good at covering things up: her out-of-control spending and the way she lied about giving up smoking.' His voice began to shake. 'Maybe her and her fancy man were scared they'd get caught. Maybe it all got too much for him and he snapped.' He looked up. 'This body – is it her?'

'I'm sorry. We're not sure yet,' said Wesley. 'Can you give us the name of her dentist?'

'She went to a man in London. Had five implants – cost a bloody fortune. She was always vain about her appearance. Loved her designer clothes.'

Wesley caught Rachel's eye. At the post-mortem, Colin had noted some old fillings but no implants, and the remnants of clothing certainly hadn't borne exclusive labels. It was beginning to look as though they weren't about to get a name for their corpse after all.

'Do you have the dentist's details?'

'No. I just know he charged a bloody fortune.'

'Have you anything of hers? A toothbrush or hairbrush?'

Steven shook his head. 'I threw everything out. Couldn't face looking at it.'

'Had she any relatives – siblings perhaps?'

'No. Her parents died years ago and she was an only child. She always used to say she was alone in the world.'

They apologised for disturbing him and left.

'Well, that rules out a DNA comparison,' said Rachel, disappointed, as they walked back to the car. 'And what he said about the dentist seems to suggest the body isn't hers. Can we cross her off our list of possibles?'

Wesley stopped, the car keys in his hand. 'I'm not sure. Did you see the way Charlton avoided looking at us? What if he was lying about the ring and the implants?'

'Why would he?'

'Perhaps it wasn't Bryan Dearlove who killed her.'

Rachel had to acknowledge that Wesley might be right.

12

Neil was still furious, the sort of anger he normally only experienced when he caught a greedy developer destroying a valuable ancient site. He told Dave he was leaving him in charge of the Dukesbridge dig because he had something else to do on St Rumon's Island. He left his car in Midton and walked across the causeway at low tide.

As soon as he'd finished checking the site of the fallen bones, still cordoned off by police tape, he walked to the other side of the island, marched up to the front door of Coffin Hall and raised the lion-head knocker. As he waited, he couldn't resist studying the building's historic features. Definitely medieval with sixteenth-century alterations, particularly the windows and chimneys. It had been part of the monastic building complex that had once dominated the island. After the dissolution, it had become the manor house, and for centuries the church and the manor would have been inextricably linked. Although he couldn't imagine Quentin Search having any time for the likes of the Reverend Charlie. People like Search fancied themselves at the centre of the universe – no room for the Almighty.

For a while there was no answer, then just as Neil was

about to give up, the door creaked open to reveal a man in a stained boiler suit with plaster dust in his hair.

'Yeah?'

'I'm after Quentin Search. Is he in?'

'Nah, mate. He's gone to Neston. Something about his book.'

'You're working on the house? It's listed, isn't it? Grade Two?'

The man folded his arms, ready to waste some time now his employer was away. 'Yeah. The powers that be are a fussy lot, but I'm used to working with lime plaster and all that. Scott Helivant's the name. That's my van.' He nodded towards the vehicle parked on the cobbles a few yards away. 'If you want any plastering or general building done, I'm your man. I'd give you my card but I don't have any on me at the moment.'

'Thanks, mate,' said Neil, adopting the affable blokeishness many men assume when they're talking to mechanics or tradesmen. 'Anyone else live here?'

'There's Jocasta, and Search's daughter, but she's a bit odd. Reads a lot of books,' Scott said, as though reading was some strange eccentricity. 'Mind you, she likes a drink down at the Monk and she will speak to the peasantry which is more than her old man does.'

'Who's Jocasta?'

'Search's fancy piece. Calls herself his assistant. She's got a flat in Neston too. I've done some work for her there. Nice place overlooking the river.'

The way he said it made Neil wonder whether his relationship with Jocasta hadn't always been strictly professional.

Scott stepped out of the front door and looked up at

the house. 'I couldn't live in a place like this. It'd give me the creeps.'

'Didn't it used to be part of a monastery?'

'Yeah. I heard something about monks.' He shook his head. 'It should have been pulled down years ago in my opinion. Build something nice and new. All mod cons.'

Neil tried his best to conceal his horror at the suggestion. 'No chance of that. It'll be protected,' he said, resolving to double-check the listing once he got back to the office. Sometimes historic buildings slipped through the net.

'My dad always said it was a money pit,' Scott continued. 'Guess he was right, but ours not to reason why, eh.'

Neil's initial fury had subsided during his conversation with the plasterer, even if he felt disappointed that he hadn't managed to glean any information that might discredit Quentin Search in some way. The history of the place intrigued him, though. He'd been putting off contacting the Millicombe Archaeological Society because of the Dukesbridge dig, but he told himself it would do no harm to arrange a meeting with the person in charge.

Wesley said little during the journey back to Tradmouth. While Rachel steered the car along the winding B roads, he was busy thinking about their encounter with Deidre Charlton's ex-husband. Could the man have been lying? Surely he would have kept something of hers that might provide a DNA sample. The fact that he'd been so eager to erase all trace of her presence said a lot about their relationship. Once they'd located Deidre's London dentist, the question would be answered once and for all. But he knew these things took time.

Gerry looked crestfallen when Wesley reported that Charlton had failed to identify the ring.

'If we continue to draw a blank, Neil has contacts who might be able to arrange a facial reconstruction,' Wes told him.

Gerry grunted in agreement. 'Good idea, but let's hope it won't come to that because I don't know whether the budget can take it. Unless his contact is willing to do it for mate's rates.'

Wesley recalled something Neil had told him in passing. 'He said the old bones that came down with the landslip must have been buried outside the boundary of the church-yard. Unhallowed ground. Suicides maybe – or outcasts from society.'

'Poor buggers. It would have been a fishing community in those days, I suppose.'

'Along with a bit of smuggling.'

'Smuggling's always gone on round this coast – still does,' Gerry added. 'Drugs. People. With all the little marinas and inlets, it's far too easy.'

Wesley couldn't argue with that. But he couldn't see how it would help them identify the woman in the purple nylon shroud.

The phone on Gerry's desk rang, and after the DCI's curt 'hello', Wesley saw his expression soften. 'Take him to our nicest interview room and tell him I'll be down in five minutes. And give him a coffee,' he added before ending the call.

'What was that about?' Wesley asked as the DCI rose slowly from his seat.

'Someone downstairs wants a word with a detective – an American gentleman, the receptionist said. He wants to talk to us about his missing sister. Said he was watching the TV breakfast news this morning and heard an unidentified body had been discovered.'

'And he thinks it might be his sister?'

'We won't know until we talk to him. But he told the receptionist that her name is Karen Liden. KL. Coming?'

Wesley didn't need asking twice. This might be the lead they'd been waiting for – and sooner than they could have hoped.

They found the man sitting on a grey sofa in the interview room normally reserved for witnesses and victims; quite different from the spartan, windowless rooms where suspects and wrongdoers were interrogated under caution. There was a mug of coffee on the table in front of him. Gerry's instructions had been carried out.

'Good afternoon, Mr Liden. I'm DCI Gerry Heffernan and this is DI Wesley Peterson. I'm told you want to talk to us about your sister.'

The man was in his mid forties, heavily built, with neat dark hair greying at the temples. He wore a pink polo shirt under a blue bomber jacket. 'It's not Liden,' he said. 'It's Shultz, Carl Shultz.' He hauled himself out of the low sofa to shake hands.

'What can we do for you, Mr Shultz?'

He took a photograph from his pocket and placed it on the coffee table in front of them. 'I signed up to an ancestry website and gave a sample of DNA so they could trace my relatives. You can make some surprising discoveries when you start these things, but I got a hell of a shock when I found out I had a sister I didn't know existed. Well, a half-sister, I should say. Seems when my mom was a teenager she came here to the UK to work as a nanny, and to cut

66

a long story short, she found she was pregnant. She kept it secret all these years, but I guess DNA never lies. Before she passed away, she admitted it was true. I asked her if it was OK to contact the woman and she said yes. Anyway, Karen emailed back and told me she'd been adopted by a couple up north and she lived there for a while. Manchester, I think. Know it?'

Gerry nodded. 'It's a couple of hundred miles away.'

'She said she was widowed, no children, and three years ago she decided to take early retirement from teaching and move here to Devon. Make a new start.'

'What part? Devon's a big county.'

Shultz took out his phone. 'South Devon, she said. A place called Dukesbridge. Two years back, she sent me this picture, but that was the last I heard from her. I'm taking a year's sabbatical, so when I planned this trip a few months ago, I sent her a message suggesting we meet up. My mother – our mother – passed away last year and I had pictures I wanted to show her. I would have liked to get to know her properly. She never replied to my emails. I kept trying, but ... I have no other relatives, you see, Inspector. And I hoped ...'

Wesley saw how upset the man was and felt for him. 'I understand.' He waited for Shultz to carry on.

'I went to the address Karen gave me in Dukesbridge, but the couple there said they'd bought the flat eighteen months ago from a Mrs Liden, though they never actually met her and they had no idea where she was now. Nice couple. They invited me in for a cup of tea.' He gave a weak smile. 'I went to the local library as they suggested and the staff there were very helpful and looked at some register they had – the electoral roll, I think it was called – in case

67

she'd moved locally, but her name wasn't on it. Then I heard on your TV news this morning about this unidentified body being found – a woman who'd been dead a while – and ... well, I just wondered ... '

Wesley picked up the photograph, obviously a selfie. In it, a middle-aged woman wearing a blue cagoule who bore a slight facial resemblance to Carl Shultz was standing in front of a church porch. She was slim and athletic-looking with short brown hair peppered with grey. He looked for signs of the ring, but her right hand was in the wrong position.

He passed the picture to Gerry. 'Does that porch look familiar to you?'

Gerry studied the image with a frown. 'Could it be the church on St Rumon's Island? Mind you, one old church porch in Devon looks much like the rest.'

'I can see some notices,' said Wesley. 'So if we can enlarge it enough to read them ... '

'I've got it on my phone,' said Shultz. 'Maybe that'll help.' He found the picture and passed the phone to Wesley.

'I was right. One of these notices definitely says "St Rumon's Services". But all this proves is that Karen Liden visited the island at some point. You say she sent this two years ago?'

'That's right. When I heard about the body, I thought I should let you know that I hadn't heard from Karen even though she was so keen to keep in touch initially.'

'Would you be willing to give a sample of your DNA?' Wesley asked.

The answer was a nod.

Journal of the Reverend Thomas Nescombe

May 1573

I was led into a low chamber with stone walls. The stench of rot and decay assaulted my senses, and I knew at once this was a place of death. The candle Anselmo held in his gnarled hand cast flickering shadows onto the dank walls, making them appear like living things.

'You preach the resurrection of the dead, do you not?'

'I do indeed, sir.'

'You may preach it but soon I will have the power to bring it about. Thanks to my powers, I will raise the dead and they will walk among us here on this very island.'

I looked into his eyes and saw the fire of belief. He imagined in his heart that what he had just claimed was the truth.

'That, sir, is impossible. Only God has power over life and death.'

He gave me a pitying smile. 'Come with me.'

He led me into another chamber, his candle guttering so I feared for a moment that we would be plunged into darkness. Then the flame suddenly brightened and I was faced with the vision of a high-ceilinged space lined with niches containing unlit lanterns. A table stood at one end laden with bottles, jars, cauldrons and pestles.

But when I looked down at the floor, I saw the strangest thing of all. Inscribed there were various arcane symbols; the sort of symbols I have been informed are used to summon the Devil. I felt a sudden chill.

'Your wife has seen this place,' Anselmo said almost in a whisper. 'She thought it very good.'

'That cannot be so,' I said, my heart beating fast, for I felt afraid.

'I speak the truth. She has asked for my help and I have promised to give it.'

His words plunged me into despair. I thought I knew Anne. I thought her a true and dutiful wife. Yet I feared this place had seized her very soul. I hurried from the house, for I could not face being there another moment.

13

A sample of Carl Shultz's DNA was taken and Wesley explained that it would be sent off to the lab for comparison. He didn't clarify what it would be compared with; that was left unsaid. It seemed tactless to talk about the unidentified decaying corpse that may or may not be the man's long-lost half-sister. If the dead woman did prove to be Karen Liden, it would mean Carl Shultz would never truly get to know the close relative he'd found through the wonders of science. To Wesley, this seemed sad, possibly even tragic. But then he told himself that Karen Liden could be anywhere; that she might have had cold feet about establishing a relationship with the half-brother she'd never met from the other side of the Atlantic Ocean; that she'd moved away and chosen to sever all contact.

They told Shultz they'd be in touch as soon as they knew anything, and he returned sadly to the Castle Hotel, an establishment in the middle of Tradmouth that dated back centuries. Wesley and Pam had been for meals there and he'd heard good things about the accommodation, so at least Shultz would be waiting for news in comfort.

He asked Trish Walton to find out as much about the retired teacher as she could. If Karen was out there somewhere alive and well, they didn't want to waste valuable time and resources.

They retired to Gerry's office while the team beavered away outside, making calls, typing into computers and studying Gerry's scribbled comments beneath the photographs on the incident board that took up almost all the far wall of the room.

'Let's go over what we've got,' said Wesley, grabbing a sheet of paper to create a list. 'Get our thoughts in some sort of order.'

'Excellent idea,' said Gerry, donning his reading glasses. 'Start at the beginning. Between six and eighteen months ago, someone buries a woman at the edge of a churchyard on an island that's only accessible at low tide or by boat.'

'Which suggests she was killed on the island. Surely it wouldn't be easy to bring a body over.'

'Not impossible, though,' said Gerry.

'We're still trying to trace, contact and eliminate all the people who've stayed in the island's holiday lets over the past couple of years. All the permanent residents have been interviewed but nobody appears to know anything. Although that author who lives in the manor house wasn't exactly co-operative. Neither was his partner when the officer called round to take their statements.'

'And we have to ask ourselves why.'

'Agreed. There's a daughter, but they said she was in bed ill and she didn't know anything anyway.'

'Believe them?'

'No reason not to, but I'd still like someone to have a word. Then there's Deidre Charlton. Bryan Dearlove posted a letter to his wife confessing to murdering Deidre and saying he was going to kill himself out of remorse. Neither body was ever found.'

'The timing of Deidre's disappearance fits perfectly with our burial.'

'However, her husband claims she'd had expensive dental work, which doesn't match our corpse.' Wes paused. 'Although I thought he could have been lying to put us off the scent.'

'Anything else?'

'Karen Liden was definitely on that island at some point. There's no doubt that photograph Shultz showed us was taken at the church. Her initials match the ring too.'

'We've taken a sample of Shultz's DNA, and once we get the results back from the lab we'll know for certain.' Gerry stood up suddenly and slammed a fist down onto his paperwork. 'I hate all this waiting.'

'My parents always taught me that patience is a virtue, Gerry.'

'I'd like to pay Bryan Dearlove's widow a visit.'

'Think she'll know anything she didn't already tell us when her husband vanished?'

'We won't know unless we ask.'

Barbara Dearlove lived near the medieval parish church in Bereton, some half a mile inland from the wide expanse of Bereton Sands. Her home was a chocolate-box stone-built cottage. She and Bryan had moved there from Birmingham; they'd had no children or family ties, and had been attracted by the prospect of a slower pace of life. Bryan had taken a job at a firm of solicitors in Neston, while Barbara helped out at a café in Tradmouth. On the surface, they'd led an idyllic life.

Until Bryan became infatuated with his colleague and began an affair.

The glazed front door opened to reveal a thin middle-aged woman.

'Hello, Mr Heffernan. Thank you for coming,' she said before ushering them inside anxiously. What Gerry's mum would have called a bag of nerves. 'Are you here about the report I made?'

'What report?' Gerry sounded puzzled.

'I thought there was someone in the garden yesterday evening and I called the police saying I was sure I had an intruder. A nice young constable came round half an hour later but he didn't find anything.'

'Sorry, love, that wouldn't have been passed to us in CID. We're here about something else. A woman's body has been found. This is DI Peterson, by the way. Don't think you've met.'

She gave Wesley a wary nod, as though she suspected he might be an imposter who'd just tagged along out of curiosity.

'Do you think this body is hers? That Deidre?'

'We're not sure yet. Sorry,' Gerry said gently.

Barbara led them into a tiny low-ceilinged living room filled with furniture that seemed too large for its surroundings. She slumped down on the sofa. 'I was wondering whether to ring you, Mr Heffernan, but my neighbour said it was probably a hoax.'

'What was?'

She walked over to the mantelpiece, where a letter stood propped up in pride of place like an invitation to a wedding or a posh function. She held it out to Gerry. 'It arrived in the post this morning.'

Gerry glanced at Wesley before putting on a pair of crime-scene gloves to examine the letter. The envelope bore a Cheltenham postmark, and it had been posted first-class two days ago.

'Know anyone in Cheltenham?'

Barbara Dearlove shook her head.

'Recognise the handwriting on the envelope?'

'No. But it definitely isn't Bryan's.'

Gerry took the printed letter from the envelope, put on his reading glasses and read it out loud. '"I think you should be aware that your husband Bryan might not have drowned as everyone thought. You need to take care. Remember what happened to Deidre Charlton."'

He looked perplexed; he had never been one for hiding his emotions, and always joked that he'd be useless in a poker game. He passed the letter to Wesley, who read it carefully, looking for hints that it was a hoax. But it was the last two sentences that worried him. The anonymous letter contained a veiled threat. No wonder the woman was scared.

'The constable couldn't find anything, but I was sure there was someone outside last night.' There was a note of fear in her voice.

'Tell us about it,' said Wesley.

'When I closed the curtains, I thought there was some-one there – just a movement in the bushes.'

'Could have been an animal?' Gerry suggested. 'One of the local cats, or a fox?'

She sounded unconvinced. 'It's not only that. Over the past week I've been getting phone calls. The phone rings and the caller says nothing.'

'They could be scam calls,' said Gerry. 'I get them all the

time, but I can see why that might be unsettling. Know what I think, love? I reckon someone's playing a cruel trick sending this letter. I know Bryan's body never turned up, but the currents round that part of the coast can sweep bodies away to the French coast – or more often they're dragged down to the seabed, never to surface unless a trawler brings the bones up years later. Enquiries were made at the time and no trace was found of him, or the woman.'

'But what if he is still alive, Mr Heffernan. What if my dead husband's stalking me?'

14

Maggie Beattie had waited for her husband in the relative comfort of the church while the second peal was being rung. But as soon as the ringing was over, he had headed off with the others for a well-earned pint in the Hanging Monk – a reward for their efforts. He'd asked her to go with them, but she knew they'd be talking about ringing. Besides, she'd noticed the northern lot looking at her curiously, as though they were wondering why she'd bothered to come. They had no idea that being there, ostensibly to support Jack, gave her the perfect excuse to be closer to the man who'd started to play such a major part in her life.

The ringers were planning to eat at the Hanging Monk at seven, and she'd promised Jack she'd join them there later, which gave her time to make her visit.

It was a fine spring day and it was hard to believe that a destructive storm had hit the island only a couple of nights before. She felt the warmth of the sun on her face as she walked away from the church towards the sparse ruins of the old priory in the neighbouring field. There wasn't much left above ground, just a stone arch and some low walls. The locals had taken most of the stones for building, until only the church, the pub and the big house remained – and this was where she was heading.

She'd read all Quentin Search's books, some several times over. There was the one about a Trojan called Brutus arriving in Devon to found Britain, only according to Search, Brutus hadn't come from Troy but from another galaxy, which explained his special powers. Then there was the one about alien spaceships being buried beneath St Michael's Mount in Cornwall and Mont Saint-Michel in Brittany, communicating over the ages via invisible ley lines.

Yesterday she'd heard Quentin – she thought of him now as Quentin – on the local radio talking about his latest book, which was about a lost land off the Devon coast, drowned by the sea centuries ago and long forgotten. She'd seen adverts for the series of talks he was due to give at Tradington Hall near Neston – a symposium, they called it. And in the radio interview he'd mentioned that the book contained irrefutable evidence that St Rumon's Island had once been a great and powerful city at the centre of a vast lost kingdom. She hadn't mentioned the symposium to Jack because she knew he'd scoff, but Quentin's writings fascinated her, and she couldn't help admiring the way he debunked the staid thinking of the archaeological establishment.

She'd recently become an author herself, a member of a writing group dominated by a woman called Della Stannard. Della boasted that the novel she'd been working on was going to be a bestseller, but Maggie feared her own early efforts lacked the necessary polish to guarantee immediate acceptance by a publisher. But if she could actually meet Quentin Search, she could ask him for some advice – maybe show him her work in progress. Although the idea made her a little nervous. He must be such a clever man.

When she'd let slip to the writing group what she was planning, Della had asked – although ordered was a more appropriate word – her to invite Quentin to come and talk to the group. Maggie doubted whether she'd be brave enough. The last thing she wanted was to make a fool of herself in front of her hero.

When she reached the house, she saw two vehicles parked in the cobbled courtyard outside: a newish Range Rover and a builder's van. Quentin Search was having building work done just like ordinary mortals, and she felt a thrill at the thought that she'd been given a glimpse, however brief, into the great man's private life.

The builder emerged from one of the outhouses at the side of the house and gave her a smile. 'Can I help you?'

Suddenly she lost her nerve. Maybe this wasn't such a good idea after all. 'No thanks.'

She began to hurry away, but when she reached the gate, she heard a voice. 'What are you doing here?'

She spun round, her heart thumping in her chest. What *was* she doing there? She wasn't sure how to answer.

'I'd like to speak to Quentin,' she said, trying to stop her hands from shaking.

Wesley sat at his desk, abandoning any hope of getting home at a reasonable time. He trawled through witness statements, searching for something, anything suspicious. At that moment they had two possible names for the victim in the purple nylon shroud; two middle-aged women who'd gone missing without trace at about the right time. Deidre

Charlton, whose lover had confessed to her murder. Then there was Karen Liden, who'd been traced by her long-lost half-brother from the States two years ago and shortly afterwards seemed to vanish off the face of the earth. The team had been making efforts to find Karen, just as Carl Shultz had before them, only with better resources. But so far they'd drawn a blank.

The phone on Rachel's desk rang, and after a short conversation she turned to him. 'I've been looking into Bryan Dearlove's extended family, just in case they could shed some light on that anonymous letter his widow received. He has a brother called Greg who lives in Bristol, but Barbara said she hasn't spoken to him since Bryan's disappearance. I sensed there was some ill-feeling there. We asked the local police to go to the address she gave us, but they came back with the news that Greg Dearlove moved out six months ago. I'll try to find out where he's gone.'

'Thanks, Rach. Keep trying.'

Fifteen minutes later, Wesley heard Rachel's phone ring again, and as the conversation ended, he noticed that she was looking pleased with herself. She then made another call and when she rose from her seat and rushed across to him there was no mistaking the look of excitement on her face.

'I've got details back from one of the holiday letting companies we contacted. We're still waiting for the others.' She thrust a sheet of paper in front of him. 'Look at this. The smaller of the two cottages attached to the lighthouse was rented for the weekend fourteen months ago. Look at the name.'

'Mr and Mrs Bryan Dearlove.'

'Paid for with Bryan's company credit card no less. Then

I rang Barbara Dearlove and asked her about it, but she knew nothing and she's never visited the island. She said Bryan went away on business quite often.'

'And we can guess what sort of business that was,' said Gerry when Wesley and Rachel delivered the news to him a few moments later. 'It means that Bryan Dearlove knew the island. And he'd know where to bury a body.'

Journal of the Reverend Thomas Nescombe

May 1573

I took my place opposite Anne at the dinner table as our maid brought in our repast. My wife looked demure, not like a woman who would consort with one such as Elias Anselmo. It was then I realised that he had been mocking me, making me doubt my own wife. Such men relish stirring up distrust and hatred. But on this occasion he had failed.

'I went to the hall today,' I said, watching her expression carefully, for although I knew she was blameless, Anselmo had sowed a bitter seed of suspicion in my mind. And such seeds can grow and flourish if unchecked.

'You saw Master Anselmo?'

'Have you met him?'

She shook her head but avoided my gaze.

'They say he is a magus, a magician who summons Satan himself,' I went on.

'Country people will say anything.'

'He was once a monk at the priory. Did you know that?'

'I have heard talk of such a thing. They say the prior was hanged for defying the king's officers. They say that nothing grows in the place where his body hung.'

'It is not fitting for my wife to listen to silly tales,' was the only reply I could think of. Her story and what I had seen at the hall had disturbed me. To think that I preach in the very church where that unfortunate prior ministered to his flock. No wonder I sense evil about this place.

That night sleep would not come and I lay awake with my eyes closed. In the small dark hours I heard Anne rise from our bed, and some time later I heard the front door shut quietly. I rose and looked out of the window. My wife was wearing her cloak and was flitting through the ruins of the priory like a spectre, running in the direction of the Hall.

15

As Wesley arrived home that evening it was already grow-ing dark, and when he let himself into the house he found that they had a visitor. Neil was in the living room talking earnestly to Michael about archaeology, and Wesley was delighted to see that his son was listening transfixed. Any distraction from the phone and computer games that increasingly dominated his leisure time was more than welcome. He and Pam did their best to restrict that sort of thing, but they felt like King Canute trying to hold back the tide, especially as they both had challenging jobs and lacked the time or energy to place their son under constant surveillance, however much their parental instincts told them it might be wise.

'I've signed Michael up for the dig in the summer,' Neil said as soon as Wesley walked into the room. 'It's going to be an exciting one. Wartime plane that crashed on Dartmoor.'

One look at Michael's face told Wesley that his enthu-siasm wasn't feigned out of politeness. 'Fantastic. You'll enjoy it.'

'Ever miss life in the trenches, Wes?' said Neil. 'Any regrets about joining the forces of oppression.'

Wesley laughed. 'You sound like my mother-in-law.'

'You talking about Della?' Michael said, keen to join in with the banter. 'She's a bit crazy, but who'd want a boring grandmother. She says her book's going to be a bestseller and when she makes a lot of money she's going to buy me a new iPhone.'

Pam had entered the room and looked sceptical about her mother's claims.

'Haven't you got any homework to do?' she said in her best teacher voice. Michael grinned at Uncle Neil and slunk from the room.

'I haven't told you the main reason I'm here,' said Neil once the boy was out of earshot.

'I thought this was a social call,' said Wesley.

'Half and half, I'd say. Mixing business with pleasure. And before you ask, I can't have more than one glass of wine. Dave and I are camping near the site of the new housing estate for the duration of the dig, so I'll be driving back in half an hour.'

'Camping,' said Pam, surprised. 'That's risky in early May.'

'We've found a decent campsite and we've got good sleeping bags,' he said bravely before changing the subject. 'I spoke to the person in charge of the Millicombe Archaeological Society before I set off. We had a good chat about St Rumon's Island and I'm meeting him tomorrow morning. Luckily a few of their members have been on digs previously, so they should know what they're doing. The priory hasn't been excavated before and I'm quite excited about it, as is the Reverend Charlie. I just wish I could be more involved – if only to annoy Quentin Search.'

'What's the latest on the bones from the beach?'

'They're being carbon dated. Talking of human remains, that's the main reason I'm here. I went to see Colin Bowman and made him an offer he couldn't refuse. One I'm sure you'll approve of. I've got someone at the university lined up to make a facial reconstruction of your mystery lady in the purple shroud. Colin's given permission for her to come to the mortuary and scan the head and whatever else she does. Then you can release the image to the media.'

Wesley's spirits lifted. This could be just what they needed to move the investigation forward – and all without putting a hole in Gerry's budget.

'Brilliant. I was going to suggest it, but you've beaten me to it.'

'All part of the service.'

Pam brought Neil his ration of wine. Wesley thought it was the least he deserved. Soon they'd know what their victim from St Rumon's Island looked like. And once they did, he was confident that someone would give her a name.

Jack and Maggie Beattie had been invited to join the bell-ringers for an evening meal in the Hanging Monk. They'd accepted to be polite, but Maggie was feeling the strain. She'd told Jack about her earlier visit to the home of Quentin Search and her meeting with Search's daughter, who'd actually deigned to speak to her. But Jack's reaction to her exciting news had ruined everything. Once again he'd scoffed at Quentin's books. 'Why do you bother with that rubbish?' he'd said. 'Search is nothing but a charlatan, with his crazy theories about legends and aliens. I spoke to one of those archaeologists who were dealing with the rock fall and he said the man's a complete fraud. I bet he laughs at the likes of you.'

Maggie thought his words were cruel. And inaccurate. Quentin would never mock his devotees.

She sat silently in the corner of the pub while Jack and the others chatted on about the peals they'd rung and towers they'd visited all over the country and beyond. Jack accused her of being obsessed with Quentin Search, but in her opinion he had obsessions of his own.

'You're quiet.' Julia Partridge's voice made her jump. The northern tower captain's wife seemed a nice woman, and at least she made the effort to speak to Maggie – the non-ringer, the outsider. Even so, Maggie felt she couldn't share her thoughts, because Julia was bound to think she was stupid. Jack was always telling her that if other people found out about her enthusiasm for Quentin Search and his theories, they'd regard her as an idiot.

She gave a weak smile. 'I'm a bit tired, that's all.'

Before Julia could answer, there was a commotion at the bar and they all looked round. The young woman Maggie had seen earlier at the gate leading to the Hall – Quentin's daughter – had staggered in obviously the worse for drink. Her long fair hair looked as though it hadn't seen a brush that day and her skimpy white dress was too insubstantial for the cool spring evening. She was arguing with the landlord. 'You've got to serve me. Don't you know who my father is?'

'I know only too well, my lover,' the landlord said patiently. He was a big man but there was a gentleness about him. 'But I'm not serving you in that state. Why don't you go home. Go to bed.'

'Sexist pig,' the girl said in a drunken slur. 'I could report you.'

'Go home, Ginevra.' The landlord's voice was firm. 'Your father will be worried.'

'He doesn't give a damn about me,' she shouted before making her way unsteadily to the door. She was almost there when she swung round, nearly losing her balance. 'Everyone thinks Quentin Search is so wonderful, but actually he's a complete bastard.' She paused and drew herself up to her full height. 'Why doesn't anyone ask him what happened to my mother?' They all watched as she swept out.

Maggie sat for a while in stunned silence. Seeing Quentin Search's daughter in that state made her feel quite sick. Surely her hero would never harm anyone. After all, he was a remarkable man.

16

After his single glass of wine, Neil had driven back to his tent. Wesley couldn't help thinking of the recent storm that had brought down the cliff, and the bodies, ancient and more modern, with it. If Neil and his fellow archaeologists were intent on camping out, he hoped the weather would prove kinder from now on.

When he arrived in the CID office the next morning, Gerry was waiting in his lair, his anorak slung on the back of his chair. Joyce had insisted that he buy a new one to replace the disreputable one he normally wore. But Gerry had never been comfortable with the replacement, and as soon as Joyce had moved out, he'd reverted to the one he described as his 'old friend'.

Wesley stood beside the DCI as he gave the morning briefing to the team. The quest for a missing person who fitted the description of the unidentified corpse was continuing, but so far Deidre Charlton seemed to be their most likely candidate, especially since the discovery that Bryan had stayed on the island, presumably with Deidre – or enjoyed a dirty weekend, as Gerry put it.

When Wesley announced that Neil had arranged for a facial reconstruction, the news was greeted with noises of approval and the mood in the CID office suddenly turned more optimistic. They'd soon know the identity of the woman in the purple sheet for certain. And once they did, Gerry was confident that the riddle would finally be solved.

After the briefing, Wes followed Gerry to his office, where the DCI sprawled in his executive leather chair, surveying the piles of paperwork on his desk with distaste.

Wesley broke the amicable silence. 'How are things?'

'If you mean Alison, we're getting on like a house on fire.' There was a long pause. Then Gerry lowered his voice as though he was about to make a confession. 'To tell you the truth, Wes, I was a bit relieved when Joyce left. She was always trying to get me to change my ways, and I know it was wrong, but I couldn't help comparing her with Kathy.'

'That *is* wrong, Gerry.'

'I know, but I couldn't help myself and she never measured up. Nobody could.'

Wesley said nothing. Since Kathy was killed in a hit and run accident, she'd taken on the mantle of a flawless saint, all domestic rows and irritating habits forgotten in the perfection of death. He knew it happened. And he understood. He'd never met her, but he had a mental picture of Gerry's late wife. A nurse, small, dark and pretty; the perfect mother and the perfect spouse.

After getting the personal stuff out of the way, they began to focus on the case; on the facial reconstruction and the origins of the hideous sheet. There were too many possibilities. They needed something definite to narrow them down.

There was a commotion as Gerry's door opened to reveal DC Rob Carter standing on the threshold. Rob's partner, Harry, had passed away at New Year, and the previously cocky young DC had been weighed down by grief ever since. Gerry had treated him with surprising thoughtfulness and told him to take as much time off as he needed, but Rob insisted that he wanted to keep working. Wesley had learned long ago that anyone who thought Gerry Heffernan was an insensitive old-style copper was way off the mark. When he himself had first arrived in Tradmouth, Gerry had welcomed him warmly and made it absolutely clear that he wouldn't tolerate any hint of racism towards the first black officer in the department.

Now Wesley was pleased to see a keen look in Rob's eyes, and he hoped he was witnessing the first signs of recovery. But he knew these things couldn't be rushed.

'I've got a number for Bryan Dearlove's brother, Greg,' Rob said breathlessly. 'I called him and he says he has information but he'll only speak to the detective in charge. He won't let the locals take a statement and he insists it's something he won't discuss over the phone.'

'Where is he?' Wesley asked, hoping it wouldn't be too far away.

'Cheltenham. He sold his house in Bristol six months ago and bought a flat there.'

Wesley felt as though a piece of the puzzle had just slotted into place. He turned to Gerry. 'The anonymous letter Barbara Dearlove received was posted in Cheltenham.'

'You're right, Wes. We can't ignore this. Call this Greg and say we're on our way, and we should let his local station know too, out of courtesy. It's supposed to be very genteel up there, so they won't have much to do,' Gerry added with a laugh, knowing his last statement was ridiculous. People thought south Devon was a haven of law-abiding tranquillity; he could have told them otherwise.

91

He checked his watch. 'We can do it there and back in a few hours. And the chief super's on about the overtime budget again, so it suits me to get out of her way for a while. Rach can manage here.'

'You can't avoid the chief super for ever,' said Wesley.

'I can try. Let's get going.'

The traffic on the motorway was mercifully light, and they made good time to Cheltenham. Wesley drove through the Regency town, passing pleasant parks and rows of tall cream stucco houses of delightful eighteenth-century proportions. The sat nav guided them to Greg Dearlove's flat, which occupied the entire first floor of a grand house in the middle of a Georgian terrace. The front door opened a couple of seconds after they rang the bell, as though the man had been waiting for them.

Wesley had seen photographs of Bryan Dearlove, and his brother was very like him, only slimmer and with more hair. In his spotless chinos and cashmere sweater, he had the quietly prosperous look of a successful professional man.

The living room of the flat had probably served as the main drawing room at the time the house was home to a single wealthy family. It was beautifully proportioned, and a large Persian cat had spread itself out on the velvet sofa. Greg picked the animal up so the police officers could take a seat. It wasn't pleased and gave a resentful hiss before stalking off disdainfully, tail in the air.

Greg sat down opposite and Wesley saw that he looked troubled. They didn't have to wait long to find out why.

'I wanted to speak to you face to face rather than giving a statement to some twelve-year-old constable fresh out of training. I hope it's not inconvenienced you too much.'

'Not at all,' Gerry lied, glancing at Wesley.

There was a long silence while they waited for Greg to go on.

'Would you like to start at the beginning?' Wesley said gently as the cat re-entered the room and made straight for the visitors, rubbing up against his legs. Luckily he was used to cats; his own, Moriarty, was equally demanding.

'I received a phone call out of the blue last week. I didn't recognise the number, and when I picked up, the caller rang off without saying anything. I assumed it was one of those scam calls you get from time to time. But the third time it happened, the person on the other end said my name. Said, "Greg, is that you?" It sounded very like Bryan's voice, but the call was cut off before I could say anything.'

'You didn't think to tell the police,' said Gerry.

'I couldn't be absolutely certain it was him.' There was a long pause. 'Bryan's four years older than me. We were never particularly close, but he's my brother. If he's still alive and in trouble ...'

'Did you send an anonymous letter to Barbara?'

'I thought she should know, that's all. Barbara and I never got on, to tell you the truth. In fact we haven't spoken since Bryan's death.'

'But why anonymous?' said Gerry. 'I don't understand. Why didn't you just pick up the phone and tell her?'

'I wouldn't have known what to say. And I don't think she would have believed me. Besides, I feel really awkward about the way Bryan treated her – having that affair, then ... Guilt by association, I suppose. It was easier to take the coward's way out and do it anonymously. If Bryan is still alive ... and I can't be sure that he is ... ' He looked Gerry in the eye. 'I never thought my brother was capable of murder, Chief Inspector, but if he can do it once, Barbara might be in danger.'

'Have you had any more calls since you sent the letter?' Wesley asked.

Greg shook his head.

'What do you know about the woman Bryan was alleged to have killed? Deidre Charlton.'

'I never met her, but I know he was besotted. The last time we spoke, he told me he intended to divorce Barbara so he could be with Deidre. I made my disapproval quite clear.' He hesitated. 'I got the impression that Deidre pulled the strings, and I'm not sure whether I would have liked her if I'd met her.'

'Do you know anything about your brother going away for the weekend to a cottage on St Rumon's Island?' Wesley asked.

'I wasn't privy to that side of my brother's life.'

'Do you really think he's still alive?'

'I didn't think he was ... but now I'm not so sure.'

Wesley found himself feeling a little sorry for the man, who'd been plunged into a murder case against his will. People couldn't choose their relatives – or control how they behaved.

'The body of a woman was found on the island where we believe your brother and Deidre Charlton rented a cottage shortly before they disappeared,' said Gerry. 'Deidre has never been found, and the body was buried around a year ago, which fits with the date it's believed she was murdered. Our pathologist thinks she might have been asphyxiated. Is it possible that your brother killed her then went into hiding, laying a false trail so everyone would assume he was dead?'

Greg Dearlove buried his face in his hands. Then he looked up. 'I've really no idea what's going on. I just wrote that letter because I thought Barbara should be aware. That's all. I've told you everything I know.'

'What do you think, Gerry?' Wesley asked as they got into the car to drive back to Devon.

'I think Bryan killed Deidre Charlton. And I really believed he'd killed himself, but now I'm considering the possibility that he abandoned his boat, faked his own death to escape the consequences of his crime and is still alive somewhere.'

'But why risk surfacing now when he's got away with murder?'

'Only he can answer that.'

'Unless it's a hoax and someone wants Greg to believe he's still alive – the person who really killed Deidre Charlton ... and maybe Bryan too,' said Wesley.

Gerry didn't answer.

Journal of the Reverend Thomas Nescombe

May 1573

My wife returned two hours later and slipped into bed beside me. I pretended to be asleep, for even if I had attempted to question her, I knew I would not have learned the truth.

The next morning we broke our fast but she said nothing to me, and her silence made me fear that what I imagined had come to pass: that my wife, Anne, had come under the spell of a wicked man; a man who, unlike myself, had abandoned all virtue and goodness. At that moment I had nobody to guide my actions but the Lord, so I left her with the servants and went into the church to pray.

At first I thought I was alone, but after a while I heard a muttering from the chapel to my right. It was a small chapel dedicated to Our Lady with a fine wooden screen concealing the interior. The screen had once been decorated with depictions of saints and angels, but during the reign of our queen's late brother, Edward, these paintings had been defaced, scratched out with hatred until only sad faint traces of their painted visages remained. I am a faithful servant of the Church and yet I never shared King Edward's intense loathing of sacred images: the idea of such bitterness towards holy things makes me uneasy.

After a while I rose from my knees and approached the chapel to learn the identity of my companion in prayer, thinking it might be a soul in need of comfort and advice.

I was surprised to see kneeling before the little altar the man who keeps the island's inn. Cuthbert Sellars is a large man of some forty summers who has always welcomed me into his home and treated me with respect. He must have heard my footsteps, for he turned his head as I entered the chapel.

'I do not wish to disturb your prayers,' I said as he rose from his knees. There was a worried look on his florid face.

'Reverend, I wish to speak with you,' he said.

I nodded my assent and sat on a bench. If he wished to confide in me, it was my bounden duty to hear him. I begged him to proceed.

'My wife is sick. I fear she is near death, and my children grieve for their mother.'

'I will pray for her,' I said earnestly. 'And will visit if it will bring her comfort.'

'It will, Reverend.' There was a long pause before he spoke again. 'Reverend, I fear there is evil on this island.' He fell silent once more, as though he was gathering his thoughts. 'I was born in Midton and my father sent me as a boy to the priory, where I learned to read and write, for which I must thank the brothers. The prior was a good and holy man, but this made him unworldly, and he didn't comprehend the wickedness that went on beneath his nose.'

'King Henry's commissioners came to root out such things,' I said.

Cuthbert Sellars shook his head. 'The king wanted only the riches the monastic houses contained. The commissioners were little interested in true sin. There were some who used the Priory of St Rumon for their own purposes.'

'Do you speak of Elias Anselmo?'

The man looked uncomfortable. 'He was a novice, but it soon became clear that he hated the priory. He mocked the other monks, even mocked the Mass. The prior challenged him but he was too gentle a soul to understand what a threat Brother Anselm truly was.'

'That was his name? Brother Anselm?'

Sellars smiled. 'He changed it. His given name is Anselm Perch and he is the younger son of a gentry family from the north of the county. They no doubt sent him to the priory in the hope that he would mend his ways.

'But their efforts failed?'

Sellars smiled again, a bitter smile. 'You speak truly, Reverend. For Anselm Perch is a betrayer and a murderer and I will not have him in my inn. The same goes for that servant of his, who was always his creature, even at the priory.'

17

There was no way of identifying the bones that had tumbled down the cliff on St Rumon's Island, no handy metal coffin plates engraved with the names of the deceased, but at least the remains had now been properly arranged, and it was plain that they belonged to two men of similar height and build. The archaeologists' painstaking investigation of the collapsed soil had revealed the existence of a few heavily corroded shroud pins, suggesting that the bodies had been buried without coffins; low-status burials from centuries ago sent into the afterlife wrapped in linen shrouds. They had been interred outside the boundaries of the churchyard. Neil knew that executed criminals, suicides and unbaptised children were once denied access to hallowed ground. As the burials were both adults, it was the first two possibilities that concerned him.

He'd left the Dukesbridge dig to meet Bill, a representative from the Millicombe Archaeological Society, to discuss plans for the coming weekend's activities. They would dig test pits and were anticipating some exciting finds. Neil said he would like to lend a hand but couldn't promise anything. He added jokingly that he was hoping for some gold sovereigns lost by the brutes who came to evict the monks from their home. When Bill nodded earnestly, Neil realised he'd taken his words seriously.

He was still intrigued by the bones they'd found, so he called the Reverend Charlie, who'd offered to dig out the parish burial records for him. She'd sounded proud of the fact that they went back to 1597, when the first Queen Elizabeth had ordered that records of baptisms, marriages and burials should be kept by each parish in parchment registers. Earlier records, kept in a more haphazard manner, had been copied into the new registers, the state's tentacles reaching as far as St Rumon's Island, and Neil was eager to see whether the burials outside the churchyard had been registered. And if any details still existed of the individuals involved.

The records she'd promised to show him weren't the originals; they were far too fragile and precious to leave in an ancient building on a windswept island. Copies had been made by a previous incumbent before the originals were placed in the archives in Exeter, where Annabel worked. Neil still wasn't sure whether to think of Annabel as his partner, because their relationship was on and off and they each had their own flat. After Annabel's brief and disastrous marriage and his own relationship with fellow archaeologist Lucy, which had fizzled out when she decided that she preferred the archaeology of Orkney to a permanent partnership with Neil in Devon, the arrangement suited both of them.

At times he envied Wesley's domestic stability. Neil had gone out with Pam at university before she'd chosen Wes, and part of him still wondered what might have been if things had worked out differently, although this was something he hardly liked to admit to himself. And he'd certainly never share these thoughts with Wesley. He valued their friendship too much.

Charlie told him to meet her as soon as his talk with Bill was over, and as he walked down the path to the church to keep the appointment, he heard the bells ringing. It seemed the visiting ringers never stopped. When he reached the porch, the heavy door opened and a girl shot out as though the Devil himself was after her. But the person who emerged from the church next looked nothing like the Evil One.

'Ginevra, are you alright? Wait, please.' The Reverend Charlie was shouting so loudly her voice could be heard over the clamour of the bells.

But Ginevra disappeared from sight. And Neil saw that Charlie was looking worried. 'Who was that?'

'Quentin Search's daughter,' she replied. 'She came into the church but as soon as she saw me she ran.' She paused. 'I'm sure something's troubling the poor girl. I just wish I could help, that's all.'

Wesley felt their brief trip to Cheltenham hadn't been a complete waste of time. They'd found out more about Bryan Dearlove. And Bryan's own brother was starting to consider the possibility that he hadn't died in the sea as everyone thought. But could he really have fooled them all into believing he was dead?

Gerry seemed happy during the journey, and when Wesley asked him why, he said, 'I reckon Bryan killed Deidre Charlton, buried her in that sheet and fled the country. Then for some reason he got cold feet and tried to contact his brother. An alternative scenario might be that

101

Deidre's husband got sick of her playing around and killed her. Crime of passion.'

'If that was the case, why would Bryan fake his own death?'

'Bryan said in his letter that Deidre planned to trick him out of his share of the money. What if that was a lie? What if he killed her to get his hands on the whole lot? Thieves falling out? Or perhaps when Steven Charlton killed Deidre, he threatened to kill Bryan as well for having a fling with his missus, so Bryan escaped abroad – maybe with a new ID. Perhaps he was secretly glad of the chance to get away from Barbara.'

Gerry looked uncharacteristically pleased with his theories, and Wesley didn't like to burst the boss's bubble while he was in such a good mood.

They arrived at the police station in the middle of the afternoon. In their absence, the team had been hard at work under Rachel's supervision, and as soon as they entered the office, she stood up to greet them.

'Any luck with Deidre Charlton's dental records?' Wesley asked.

'We're still contacting London dentists. There are a lot of them.'

Gerry looked disappointed and muttered something about budgets. Wesley heard him give a dramatic sigh before he marched away into his office and closed the door behind him.

'Boss doesn't look pleased,' said Rachel as they watched him go.

'He's got a couple of pet theories and he hoped to have one of them proved by now. He'll huff and he'll puff for a while, but he'll get over it.'

Wesley and Rachel exchanged a conspiratorial look.

There'd once been an attraction between them, but by unspoken agreement, nothing had come of it. He had Pam and she had Nigel. Anything else would lead to complications and unhappiness. What had happened to Bryan Dearlove and Deidre Charlton was proof of that.

'Anything come in while we've been out?'

'We've heard from more holiday let owners and we're still going through the list of people who stayed on the island at the relevant time. All the permanent residents have been double-checked. Nothing suspicious so far.'

Wesley thought for a moment. 'What do we know about Quentin Search?'

'Only that he's famous.'

'And controversial. He's the self-appointed arch-enemy of the archaeological establishment. Comes out with all these far-fetched ideas and turns them into bestselling books. Neil's not his greatest fan.'

'What is it they say? Never let the truth get in the way of a good story. If Search is making a fortune out of it, Neil's probably jealous,' Rachel said with a smile.

'Search was living at the Hall at the time our unidentified woman was killed.'

'He's been interviewed. He said he knows nothing and there's no reason to think he was lying.'

'I still think we should speak to him again.'

'Is that because your friend Neil doesn't like him?'

Wesley didn't answer. Perhaps Rachel was right. Maybe he was just prejudiced. But there'd been something about the man he didn't trust.

His phone rang. It was the lab with the news that the DNA results for Carl Shultz had come through.

*

103

Seeing Quentin Search's daughter in the pub the worse for drink the previous evening had given Maggie Beattie a jolt. Then earlier she'd seen the girl enter the church then dash straight out like a frightened creature as soon as the vicar greeted her. But in the end she told herself that Ginevra Search's behaviour didn't necessarily reflect on her father. All families had their troubles. In fact it made her hero more human.

The others had rung the bells in the tower for almost three hours non-stop, and now they'd returned to the pub to celebrate the completion of their third peal. Maggie had promised to join them again later, but for now she settled down to reread one of Quentin Search's earlier books, perched on the priest's chair in the chancel, which was considerably more comfortable than the pews. The others were welcome to their draughty tower and their post-peal ringing chat. She was more interested in Search's discoveries: facts and ideas that turned history upside down. Things those in power didn't want you to know.

The vicar woman had been in earlier with that scruffy archaeologist who'd been called in to deal with the bones that had fallen onto the beach. They'd acknowledged Maggie but hurried to the vestry as though they had urgent business. Now that they'd left, and without the sound of the bells above, the peace of the empty church was blissful.

The sound of the heavy church door shuddering open shattered the silence, and she placed her bookmark in the pages, irritated by the intrusion. When she looked up, she saw two dark figures walking along the aisle, and for a few seconds her body tensed. Until she recognised one of the newcomers and relaxed.

'Hello,' she said. 'I didn't expect to see you here.'

The pair came to a sudden halt and stared as though they'd only just realised they weren't alone.

18

Neil was supervising the opening of a new trench at the Dukesbridge dig when he heard Dave's voice.

'Have you seen this?'

He swung round and took the phone Dave was holding out. He couldn't quite believe what he saw on the screen. His own name was there beside his photograph and the word FRAUD in stark capitals.

'It's all over social media,' said Dave. 'On Twitter and all the rest. It says you're trying to stifle the truth and you're afraid of being shown up by someone who's researched deeper into the subject than you have. Calls you an intellectual coward, whatever that means.'

'Who posted it?' Neil was still staring at the phone in horror.

'The Friends of Lyonesse, whoever they are.'

'I can take a guess. I think this is another of Quentin Search's pathetic attempts to drum up publicity for his ridiculous book.'

Neil read aloud, his anger making his voice unsteady. '"Dr Neil Watson, the so called Heritage Manager (Archaeology and Historic Environment) for the county, has obstructed my vital research every step of the way, demonstrating that the powers that be hate original thought and new discoveries. There is proof that as late as the eleventh century, Lyonesse was a fertile, prosperous land later destroyed by a terrible disaster. In 1270, a priory was founded on the island to pray for the souls of those lost in the tragedy. But it wasn't until the late sixteenth century that the magus Elias Anselmo uncovered the lost truth. Now Quentin Search is in possession of that truth, and he reveals all in his latest ground-breaking book, *Lost Truth Island*. A book that has rocked the archaeological establishment to its foundations."'

'There you are, Neil, you're the powers that be. Who would have thought it? And he's rocked us to our foundations. How about that?'

'It's not funny, Dave. This is close to libellous. Pity I haven't got any money to sue him.'

'The advert below this crap for his symposium is a big giveaway. I'm sure you're right about it being a publicity stunt.'

'In that case we have to fight back.'

'What do you mean? Do you want to attend the symposium?'

'I think my time would be better spent finding out more about this Elias Anselmo.'

'What about the excavation here? And the local society digging test pits at the priory over the weekend? You promised to look in and give them some advice.'

'True. And I want to know more about those bones from the rock fall. I'd like to hear what the university lab have to say before they're reinterred. You never know, we might be able to link them with this Anselmo character while we're at it.'

'Search wouldn't like that at all.'

Neil's lips turned upwards in a mischievous grin. 'I know.'

Jack Beattie sensed that his wife was growing tired of hanging about while he was ringing. One of the northerners had joked that she was a bell-ringers' groupie. It wasn't meant unkindly, but Jack was glad Maggie hadn't been there to hear it.

She hadn't joined them for a meal at the Hanging Monk as arranged, so he called her phone. When there was no answer, he headed straight for the church to see whether she was still there.

There was no sign of her, and he was rather concerned. She couldn't have gone home because she didn't drive, so she must be somewhere on the island. He left a message asking her to call him back, but after half an hour had passed, his worry increased. It was obvious that the other ringers thought he was fussing for nothing, but eventually he persuaded them to begin a search.

They began at the lighthouse and walked the perimeter of the island, peering into the windows of the empty rental cottages and asking everyone they bumped into whether they'd seen her.

'It's low tide, so she might have walked across to the mainland,' Matt Evans said. 'Her battery might have died. Or she can't get a signal.'

Matt's wife, Julia, had been listening in to the conversation. 'I noticed she was reading a book by that author, Quentin Search. Doesn't he live here at the Hall? Maybe she's gone exploring. We'll go up there and ask if anyone's seen her. You wait here.'

Matt and Julia hurried to the Hall and knocked on the

door, but there was no answer. They were about to give up when the builder emerged from around the side of the house, heading for his van.'

'Nobody's in,' he called across to them. 'They've gone over to Tradington. Something to do with that conference.'

'Have you seen a woman? Small, brown hair, glasses?' Matt asked.

'Why? Have you lost her?'

Matt didn't like the smirk on the man's face, so he didn't answer. When the couple rejoined the others, they all decided to return to the church in case Maggie had decided to come back.

While they were walking down the path through the overgrown churchyard, Jack tried Maggie's phone again. As Matt opened the church door, they heard a tinny ringtone somewhere in the distance.

'That's Maggie's ringtone,' Jack said, his eyes widening in alarm.

Without another word, the ringers began to look for the source of the sound.

'It's coming from over there.' Matt Evans rushed to the small door that opened onto the steep, narrow spiral staircase leading to the first-floor ringing chamber. He spotted the phone on the stone floor, half hidden beneath a shelf filled with old hymnbooks.

'Could she have gone up to the ringing chamber for some reason?' Julia asked, trying to keep her voice steady.

The ringers climbed the staircase in single file, but when they reached the chamber where the eight bell ropes hung like nooses in a circle, they found it empty.

Jack looked at the door leading to the bell chamber itself. 'She wouldn't have gone up to the bells, surely.'

Matt led the way upwards, but still there was no sign of Maggie.

Julia took Jack's arm. 'Better let Matt check the roof. We'll go downstairs and wait.'

Jack hesitated before doing as he was told.

After a few minutes, Matt came rushing down the steps, his face ashen. 'She's at the foot of the tower,' he said. 'Looks like she fell.'

Julia's hand went to her mouth in shock. But she knew they had to act quickly in case Maggie was still alive, injured and in need of help.

She and Matt instructed their fellow ringers to look after Jack before hurrying out into the churchyard, where they found Maggie Beattie lying in undergrowth at the bottom of the tower. Her injuries looked extensive, and Matt knew even before he felt for a pulse that it was too late to do anything for her. She was dead.

Journal of the Reverend Thomas Nescombe

June 1573

Yesterday my heart soared with joy, for Anne told me that she is with child. I had almost abandoned hope that we would be blessed, but now I rejoice.

And yet her night-time walks disturb me. I summoned the courage to question her, but she tells me that she likes to walk in the night air when she cannot sleep and the reason for her stealth is a reluctance to wake me. I wish to believe her and yet I cannot forget Elias Anselmo's claim that she has seen his strange chamber. Cuthbert Sellars told me of the man's past wickedness and I believe the innkeeper is an honest man. Anselmo is a sinner – and such men are liars.

Today I was in good spirits as I visited the poor of the island. I am now received without suspicion in most cottages, and I suspect Sellars has spread the word that I am to be trusted. Mine host is a respected man at the heart of the village, and if he is seen to be my ally then surely folk will be won round in the end.

I attended Sellars' wife, Agnes, who appears to have recovered her strength after her illness but still keeps to her bed, cared for by her family, and was pleased to see that my prayers for her have been answered. Then I visited the mother of one of the fisherfolk; an old lady with flesh wizened as an ancient apple left too long before eating. She knew she was close to death and asked if I was the priest come to give her the last rites. I surmised that her mind was wandering back to the days of the old faith, but I prayed with her and I think this gave her comfort. The cottage was a poor dwelling and the fisherman was mending his nets alongside his wife while their children played upon the shore.

I wended my way home, passing the inn again. I thought the Hanging Monk an ill name for such a place. Perhaps Cuthbert Sellars named it so in memory of the prior he had described as a holy and unworldly man. I saw a girl emerge from the doorway and knew her to be Sellars' eldest daughter. She greeted me with a smile and thanked me for visiting her mother.

Her name is Talitha, and in spite of her stained apron and rough hands, she is the most beautiful creature I have ever seen.

I made the discovery four nights after my visit to the fisherman's cottage.

In the quiet hours of the night I was awoken by the sound of a door closing, and I saw that my wife was no longer beside me in the bed. This had not happened for three weeks, and I had hoped Anne's nocturnal wanderings would stop now that she was with child. I lay for a while until I could no longer contain my anxiety. Then I put on my clothes, careful not to wake the servants, and let myself out of the house.

On previous occasions I had seen Anne from the window wandering through the ruins of the priory. But this time there was no sign of her, and a feeling of terror gripped my heart.

I prayed that my worst fears would not be realised as I walked towards the Hall.

When I reached my destination, I saw lights in the windows. Elias Anselmo – once known as Anselm Perch – was awake and I could not stop myself creeping like a thief to the nearest window to peer in. I thought nothing of the dignity of my position. I needed to know whether my wife was consorting with a man I knew to be evil.

A stone mounting block stood against the wall, and I climbed onto it in order to see better. I leaned towards the window, hoping I would not be spotted, and the sight I had dreaded met my eyes.

Anne was there, kneeling before Anselm Perch like a supplicant, and he was placing something in her outstretched hands. It was then I heard the dogs barking, so I jumped off the block and fled as though the Devil himself was after me.

19

'So the DNA's not a match, which means our unidentified body definitely doesn't belong to Karen Liden,' Gerry said as soon as Wesley walked into his office. 'That leaves Deidre Charlton, but we're having no luck with her dental records, and thanks to her husband chucking out her possessions and obliterating all trace of her, we've no DNA for comparison.'

'Have you told Shultz about the results yet?'

'I gave him a call. He was disappointed, but I've advised him to file an official missing persons report.' He gave a despairing sigh. 'Karen Liden appears to have vanished off the face of the earth.'

'Nobody vanishes off the face of the earth.'

'Unless they're buried underneath it. I keep thinking of that ring with the initials KL. Karen Liden fitted the bill so well.'

'Well, they say DNA never lies.'

Gerry thought for a moment. 'Unless the ancestry website got it wrong and Carl wasn't a match with her after all. There might have been some sort of mix-up. I'll get someone to contact them to see if it sometimes happens. And even if they haven't made a mistake, I'm still curious to know what's happened to Karen Liden.'

Wesley hesitated. 'I know we both feel sorry for Carl Shultz because he's come all the way across the Atlantic to track down his long-lost relative, but if it has no bearing on our case, we can't waste valuable resources trying to trace Karen. After all, there's no real evidence that she's come to any harm. Is it any of our business if she's decided to go AWOL?'

'Getting one of the DCs to make a few phone calls won't take up much of the budget. And if she's a missing person ...'

Wesley knew the boss was right, but he felt obliged to play devil's advocate because the chief super would ask exactly the same questions. 'So we try to find her?'

'That's what I promised Carl Shultz. In the meantime, he's talking about hiring a private detective.'

'Can't do any harm. As long as he or she doesn't get in our way.'

Gerry reminded Wesley of a deflated balloon as he sank into his leather chair. 'Oh Wes, we're no nearer identifying the victim, never mind the murderer. We've gone through all the missing persons reported in the area and beyond and come up with nothing. No middle-aged women who haven't been accounted for.'

'Apart from Deidre Charlton. We keep coming back to her.'

The phone on Gerry's desk rang and he answered with a weary 'What is it?' After he'd listened to the reply, he sat up straight and pressed the speakerphone key so that Wesley could listen in.

'It's on St Rumon's Island, where that body was found, sir.' the constable on the other end of the line said nervously. 'At the church. A woman. It looks like an accident.'

'Have we got a name for her?'

Wesley sat on the edge of his seat, hoping it wasn't the Reverend Charlie.

'Someone said her name was Maggie Beattie and she's got something to do with the bell-ringers. The police launch had to attend because it's high tide.'

'Has the area been sealed off?' Gerry barked impatiently.

'Yes, sir. And the pathologist's on his way.'

'We'll be right there.'

He ended the call and stared at the phone. 'Well I wasn't expecting that.'

'Remember what Neil told me about people calling St Rumon's Island Coffin Island?' Wesley said. 'Looks like it's beginning to live up to its name.'

20

Julia Partridge took a tissue from her pocket and dabbed away the tears that had started to form in her eyes. 'If any of us had known she was likely to wander up there ... We were so focused on achieving our peals that we never gave poor Maggie a second thought.' A look of horror appeared on her face. 'You don't think ... you don't think she might have done it deliberately?'

'We're not sure yet, but you mustn't blame yourself,' was the only thing Wesley could think of to say, though he knew this wasn't much comfort.

He was standing on the south side of the church, well away from where Colin Bowman was conducting his examination of the body. He glanced up at the squat tower from where Maggie must have fallen. He could see the CSIs up there in their white crime-scene suits, edging round the splintery base of the flagpole, which had been broken in the storm.

Julia continued, as though she needed to get the guilt she felt off her chest. 'After we finished our third peal, we went to the pub to celebrate. We asked Maggie to come with us but she said she'd rather stay in the church reading her book and join us later for something to eat. Maybe we shouldn't have left her on her own, but she insisted.'

'So she was alone in the church?'

'Yes.'

'And the door to the tower roof was unlocked?'

'I think so. At home, Matt's very strict about who has access to the tower, but I suppose being on an island makes people a bit careless. There aren't any kids around to wander up there, so no one thought it posed a risk. Poor Maggie. We should have insisted that she came with us.' She thought for a moment. 'Jack and Maggie only live a few miles away, so to tell you the truth, I'm not really sure why she chose to come with him. She didn't seem the sociable type. Quite shy really.'

'We'll need to talk to Jack. Where is he?'

'He had to identify ... the body and now he's in the vestry with Matt and the Reverend Charlie. She came over as soon as she heard. She's been incredible.'

Wesley sensed that Julia was reluctant to end their chat, but he had things to do so he thanked her and walked round the church tower to the centre of the action. The area had been taped off and a tent had been erected over the body. Gerry was already in his crime-scene suit watching Colin go about his work. Wesley had a word with the crime-scene manager and struggled into his own white suit before heading to the tent.

'Ah Wes, there you are.'

'The dead woman's husband is in the church. We should have a word with him.'

'Right you are. As soon as Colin's done his bit.' Gerry turned to Colin, who was squatting next to the body. 'Well, Colin, what's the verdict? Do you think she might have been pushed, or are we looking at an accidental fall or a suicide?'

Colin peeled off his gloves and scratched his balding

head. 'Some of the injuries are consistent with a fall from a great height.' He glanced upwards. 'But . . . '

'But what?'

'Sorry, Gerry, I won't be able to tell you more until I've had a better look down at the mortuary.'

Wes looked at Gerry. 'I've been talking to Julia Partridge, one of the visiting ringers, and she told me that Maggie was shy and that she preferred to stay reading in the church rather than going for a drink with the others. They're all expert ringers apart from her, so she probably felt left out.'

'She must have known what it would be like,' said Gerry. 'She could have stayed at home. Why did she decide to come?'

'Dr Partridge was puzzled by that too.'

'No hint that Jack was dallying with one of the other ringers and she wanted to keep an eye on him?'

'The Beatties only met the northern ringers a couple of days ago, and there's no suggestion they knew each other before.' Wes thought for a moment. 'Della mentioned her, you know. They're in the same writing group. She thought Maggie might have come to the island because of Quentin Search.'

Gerry looked surprised. 'You're saying she came here to see him?'

'Jack never mentioned that, but we need to find out.'

They were interrupted by Colin. 'It's getting late, gentlemen. Post-mortem first thing tomorrow?'

'That'll do nicely,' said Gerry.

'I hear you're . . . er . . . no longer with Joyce. I only met her once. Nice woman.'

Wesley watched Gerry's face as he answered. He'd

hardly said a word about how he felt about the break-up, almost as though he was keen to put his time with Joyce behind him.

'These things happen,' he said nonchalantly. 'And Alison's moved in. My daughter,' he added proudly.

Wesley listened to the boss chat with Colin about Alison's new job and how well she was settling in, while the photographers recorded the scene and the CSIs gathered evidence before the light faded. It might turn out to be an accident or suicide, but they couldn't take the risk of missing something vital.

'Right, Wes,' Gerry said when Colin started packing up his things. 'We've put it off long enough. Let's have a word with the dead woman's husband.'

Wesley walked a couple of paces behind the DCI, preparing himself mentally for the coming encounter with grief. Jack Beattie was bound to be in shock – unless he'd already known about his wife's death. Unless he'd been responsible.

They found him in the vestry, seated by a large desk in the centre of the square room lined with dark oak cupboards. The Reverend Charlie had drawn her chair close to his and had a comforting arm around his shoulders, while her head was bowed in sympathy, or maybe prayer. She looked up and spotted the two detectives, and whispered something in Jack's ear. He nodded and took a shuddering breath before standing up, steadying himself on the desk. He seemed to have aged ten years since they'd first met him.

Gerry left it to Wesley to step forward. He'd always claimed that he was better than his boss at the sympathy stuff. It was Rachel who, because of her experience with family liaison work, usually dealt with grieving relatives – but Rachel wasn't there.

'Mr Beattie, I'm so sorry for your loss,' Wesley began. 'Do you feel up to talking to us?'

Jack nodded, and Wesley pulled up another chair, one of a pair probably used by happy couples to sign the marriage register. Once they were settled, Gerry chose to watch while Wesley asked the questions.

Jack Beattie spoke in a low voice, so quiet that Wesley had to lean forward to hear what he was saying. He told much the same story as Julia. They'd rung a peal of London, then repaired to the Hanging Monk to celebrate with a pint or two. He had asked his wife whether she wanted to join them but she'd said she wanted to finish her book in peace and she'd come later to eat.

'Why did Maggie choose to come to the island if she didn't intend to join in with the ringing?' Wesley asked.

'Because she knew *he* lived here.'

Wesley glanced at Gerry. 'Are you talking about the author Quentin Search?'

'Yes. I wish she'd never heard that man's name.'

Jack fell silent, and Wesley waited, hoping the man wouldn't be able to resist filling the vacuum. Eventually his patience was rewarded.

'She started reading his books about a year ago. She read them over and over again, then began doing her own research on the internet. She became obsessed with those weird conspiracy theories of his. I said he wrote a load of nonsense, but ... '

'Do you think she might have gone to Search's house to try to speak to him?'

There was another long silence before he answered. 'I

121

suspected that was the reason she was so keen to come with me. She's got . . . had tickets for this symposium he's doing at Tradington Hall.'

'Were you going with her?'

'You must be joking. In my opinion, Search is a con man. Maggie and I got on well before he came into our lives.'

'She never tried to come to the island to see him before?'

'We live three miles away and she didn't drive. Besides, she was quite a shy person.' He thought for a moment. 'I don't know whether she would have had the nerve to venture to his house. And I don't suppose she would have told me if she did.'

'Do you have children, Mr Beattie?'

He shook his head. 'We have a dog. Benny. He's a cockapoo.' He smiled at the thought of his pet, now his sole companion. Then the smile vanished as though he'd remembered something important. 'He's with the dog minder today. I'll have to pick him up. She's having him tomorrow as well. We're ringing Glasgow major.'

Gerry raised his eyebrows. 'You intend to carry on with your ringing after what's happened?'

Jack looked at him as though he'd only just noticed he was there. 'The others planned this visit over six months ago and they've travelled a long way. Surely we can carry on as long as it doesn't interfere with what you're doing? Besides, it'll help to take my mind off what's happened.'

'We'll have to see,' said Gerry. Wesley knew he was hedging his bets. If Colin and the CSIs concluded that Maggie Beattie's death was a tragic accident or suicide, it would do no harm if the ringing went ahead, even if, in his eyes, it seemed inappropriate. On the other hand, he wondered how on earth the bereaved husband would have the stomach for it.

122

He knew his next question would be sensitive, and he found himself wishing that Rachel was there to take the burden off his shoulders.

'Mr Beattie, did your wife have any ... medical problems?'

'She was as fit as a fiddle.'

'Did she take any medication at all? For depression, for instance?' He felt awkward about this particular line of questioning, but it was something he needed to ask.

Jack looked up sharply. 'You want to know if she might have decided to end it all. Well the answer's no. She was looking forward to that symposium. I've never seen her so excited about anything. Even the writing group she's in.'

Maggie had been a member of Della's group so Wesley hoped this might be another possible source of information, provided Della would co-operate.

'What was she writing?'

'Fantasy, inspired by that man Search.'

'Might she have wanted to discuss her writing with him?'

'I'm sure she'd have loved to, but as I said, she was quite reserved.'

Wesley was tempted to observe that people could be unpredictable, but he stopped himself.

'Can you think of any reason why Maggie would have climbed to the top of the church tower? Had she talked about looking at the view?'

Jack shook his head. 'Not that I remember. But I have been rather preoccupied,' he said sadly. 'When you have an absorbing pastime like ringing, it can become ... all-consuming.' He put his head in his hands. 'Maybe if I'd spent more time with her ... '

'You invited her to the pub,' said Gerry. 'You did your best not to leave her out.'

123

'Yes, but she didn't know the others and we talked about ringing most of the time, while her only interest was Quentin Search and his mad theories.'

'Is there anyone we can contact for you?' Wesley asked. 'Someone you can stay with tonight?'

'My sister lives in Newton Abbot, but ... '

'One of my officers will call her if you give us her details,' said Wesley.

Jack seemed reluctant. 'I've got the dog to consider, and if you say the ringing can go ahead, I'd like to stay and finish our peals.'

Wesley caught Gerry's eye. It seemed Maggie Beattie wasn't the only one who was in the grip of an overwhelming obsession.

'It's up to you, but the offer's there. If you think of anything else, you will let us know, won't you, Mr Beattie?' said Wesley as he stood up.

'Of course. When will I be able to arrange the funeral?'

'We'll let you know as soon as possible.' He didn't like to mention that the post-mortem was planned for the following morning.

'Perhaps I should give the go-ahead for the ringing, Wes,' said Gerry once they'd left the church. 'If Maggie's death turns out not to be suspicious, at least it'll take that poor man's mind off things.'

Wesley saw his point. 'OK by me. Where are we off to now?'

'Quentin Search. We need to find out whether the dead woman went to see him. Maybe he upset her. Some people take it badly if they discover their idol has feet of clay.'

Journal of the Reverend Thomas Nescombe

June 1573

I waited on the lane, and when my wife left the Hall, I followed her. How could I not? I was concerned for her well-being, especially as she was now carrying the child I had longed for since we married. I kept my distance so that she would not know I was there and she led me through the priory ruins towards the cliffs. There was a full moon, so I could see her clearly, and I was prepared to come to her aid if she did anything that might harm herself or the babe.

I watched as she stood upon the clifftop, her head held high. She was speaking words that I could not hear, for a stiff breeze had begun to blow, and when she raised her hand, I saw that she was holding something. I edged closer until I could hear what she was saying, but it made no sense to me. She was waving what looked like herbs or flowers, and with each movement of her arm, the wind became fiercer, so that I pulled my cloak around me. I could only conclude that she was summoning a storm.

The wind stirred the waves into a frenzy. She was shouting now in some strange language, throwing the herbs into the churning sea.

Fearing that the storm she had conjured might blow her off her feet and down the cliff, I rushed forward to grab her. She had appeared to be in a trance, but at my touch, she screamed and struggled against me. I held her fast.

'Do not stop me. I'm summoning them.'

'Who?'

She stared at me as thought she had just awoken from a bad dream, and I knew that she had indeed been under some kind of spell. Then she suddenly collapsed to her knees.

'The people of Lyonesse. Their spirits must be freed.' She began to weep, and I put my cloak around her shoulders and led her home.

21

Wesley and Gerry were greeted at the Hall by the builder, who appeared to be packing up for the day. When he told them Search had gone to Tradington, Gerry looked like a child who'd woken up on Christmas morning to find an empty sack at the bottom of his bed. He had never been good at hiding his feelings.

Quentin Search had already been interviewed as a matter of routine and had denied knowing anything about the body in the purple sheet. But because of his connection with Maggie Beattie, they needed to speak to him as soon as possible.

However, their plans were thwarted when they drove to Tradington Hall, an arts centre housed in a beautiful medieval building a mile outside the town of Neston. They found the staff arranging chairs in the lofty oak-panelled main hall and were told that Quentin Search had left twenty minutes before, heading with his publicist to an unspecified bookshop, where he'd agreed to sign their stock of his latest book. The man was proving elusive.

'I'll ask one of the uniforms to let us know when he gets home,' said Gerry, checking the time. 'We might as well get back to Tradmouth. Until Colin and the CSIs have done their bit, we won't really know what we're dealing with.'

Wesley's phone rang. It was one of the CSIs who'd been on the tower roof.

'Thought you'd like to know that we haven't found anything suspicious up there. No sign that anyone had been there recently and certainly no evidence of a struggle. The only thing out of place was the broken flagpole, and I'm told that happened in the storm a couple of days ago.'

Wesley thanked the man and rang off, then told Gerry what he'd said.

The DCI thought for a moment. 'If it was an accident, surely there'd be some indication on the tower roof that she tried to save herself.'

'Unless it was suicide.'

'Sadly, it looks that way.'

'We need to speak to Quentin Search. If he said something to her that drove her to it ... And we need to find out more about her life. What was the marriage really like, I wonder. Perhaps if we speak to her friends and wider family—'

Gerry shook his head. 'If it turns out to be suicide, it's a tragedy but not really a matter for CID. Don't let yourself get emotionally involved, Wes. I know what you're like.'

Wesley knew the boss was right, but he couldn't help thinking of the quiet woman he'd met when they'd first arrived on the island; the outsider in the group of enthusiastic ringers who'd sat in the church immersed in Quentin Search's fantasies while the others cheerfully pursued their passion. The thought of her last days filled him with sadness. Hundreds of years ago, it was said that people could die of melancholy. Could that have happened to Maggie Beattie?

The light was fading as they drove back to Tradmouth, and when they reached the CID office, Gerry checked to see whether anything new had come in on the unidentified body in the purple sheet. Frustratingly, there was nothing. As Colin Bowman was performing Maggie Beattie's post-mortem first thing the following morning, Gerry ordered everyone to go home and get some rest. Rachel was still at her desk, making calls and buried in a pile of paperwork, and the DCI stood over her until she'd packed up and left.

'She's been working too hard since she got back from maternity leave,' he said as soon as Rachel was out of earshot.

Wesley knew his heart was in the right place, but he told him not to let Rachel hear him saying that; in this day and age, such a sentiment might be construed as sexist.

Gerry's answer was a snort of derision. 'I'd be a bad boss if I didn't look out for the people in my team.'

Wesley, as usual, could see both points of view.

When Wesley arrived home, he found that Della had turned up again and Pam had retreated to the kitchen, leaving her mother alone. The children were nowhere to be seen; he assumed they were in their rooms getting on with their homework. For once, he was glad to see his mother-in-law.

'I'm not staying long, Wesley,' she began. 'I've got a writing group meeting tonight, but I need to talk to you first.'

'Actually, I wanted a word myself.'

'I saw on the internet that Maggie Beattie's been found dead.'

'We haven't released her name to the press yet. How did

you find out?' he asked, partly relieved that he hadn't had to break the news.

'Things get round on social media,' said Della with a smug half-smile on her lips. 'I wonder if she was murdered because of the book she was writing.'

Wesley took a step back. 'What do you mean?'

'What if someone was afraid she knew something and was about to reveal all in her book?'

'Is it that sort of book?'

'She read out bits to the group – we all share our works in progress – and as far as I could gather, it's about an ancient civilisation that lives beneath the waves and emerges every now and then to kill "the dry ones", as they call them.'

'Doesn't sound as if she was about to give away anyone's darkest secrets.'

'Who knows? She never said how she intended to develop the story. She'd only completed the first three chapters.'

'Can you tell me anything about her? Did she seem worried about anything?'

Della shrugged. 'Not that she ever mentioned to us. She seemed quite a private person really. Shy.' Her eyes lit up. 'Come along, Wesley. Tell all. Was she murdered?'

Wesley gave an exasperated sigh. He couldn't rid his mind of the image of Maggie Beattie's battered body, and the look on the face of her distraught husband. He hoped Della wasn't regarding her death as entertainment and appointing herself as an amateur sleuth. 'There's no evidence that Mrs Beattie's death was suspicious, and if I were you, I'd keep the speculation to yourself. It's not helpful and it could be distressing to her husband.'

'But—'

'No buts, Della. I'm serious. You wouldn't want to

upset her family, would you?' He'd always found his mother-in-law irritating, but now her hunger for drama made him angry. 'Look, I've have had a hard day. Perhaps it's best if you leave.'

'If you're going to be like that, I'll keep my thoughts to myself,' she said haughtily as she made for the door. When she reached it, she turned. 'But you might like to know that Maggie was intending to contact the author who'd influenced her writing. Someone in the group suggested that if she was going to be near his house, she should go there and ask him to come and speak to us. We never imagined she'd pull it off, of course, because he's quite famous and she was a bit of a mouse. But she messaged the group yesterday to say she was going there to speak to him.'

'She actually met him?'

'No idea.'

'I take it this author is Quentin Search?'

'That's right. If I were you, I'd have a word with him.'

'He's already on our list,' said Wesley, frustrated by their failure that day to pin down the author. Perhaps they'd have more luck tomorrow.

'I'll leave you to it then,' Della said with a hint of sarcasm, before flouncing out, doing her best to make a dramatic exit but spoiling the effect when she caught her flapping coat on the door handle.

At 7.30 the next morning, Wesley and Gerry met at the station before walking along the embankment to the hospital. It was another fine day and the river was busy. A fishing boat was chugging back to port to unload its catch, and yachts that had been laid up for the winter were skimming across the water as their owners made the most of the spring weather.

'You wouldn't think that storm only happened on Monday night, would you, Wes,' said Gerry as they walked. 'If we didn't have to work, I'd be out in the *Rosie May* today. Perfect sailing conditions.'

'I'll take your word for it.'

'Alison's keen to come sailing with me, you know.' He smiled fondly. 'Chip off the old block. Did I mention she's persuaded me to join a shanty group that meets at the Tradmouth Arms?'

'Shanty group? You mean sea shanties?'

'That's right. I already know a lot of them from growing up in Liverpool.'

A mental picture of Gerry in a striped jersey belting out bawdy songs with a pint in his hand flashed across Wesley's mind. It didn't seem too hard to imagine.

'Trouble is, I'll only be able to join in when we're not busy. Let's hope Colin says there's nothing suspicious about Maggie Beattie's death.'

When they arrived at the hospital, they made straight for Colin's office. He was typing into his computer, already gowned up, ready to get to work.

'Ready, gentlemen?' he said, before leading the way to the mortuary.

Wesley and Gerry stood behind the glass screen listening to Colin's commentary, awaiting his conclusions. They both thought they knew what those conclusions would be: Maggie Beattie had fallen from a great height and died from multiple injuries.

But Colin had a shock in store. At one point during the procedure he exclaimed a surprised 'Hello, what's this?'

before falling uncharacteristically quiet. Then he resumed his commentary into the microphone and Wesley heard the words 'contusion' and 'blunt instrument' together with 'hyoid bone' and 'signs of asphyxiation'. When it was over, he left it to his assistant to finish off and turned to face the two detectives. 'I've come across something unexpected. Let's have tea in my office.'

When Colin had finished pouring the tea, using a strainer, milk in last – he believed in doing things properly – he sat down, a worried look on his face.

'From my initial cursory examination at the scene, I'd expected to find injuries consistent with a fall from a great height. I didn't like to say too much during the post-mortem because what I found was so unexpected, but now I'm certain I wasn't mistaken. The woman in the mortuary was strangled. The finger marks around her neck are quite clear, even though the killer tried to cover them up by administering a beating post-mortem to make it appear as though she'd fallen from the church tower.'

'So it's murder then?' said Gerry, sounding surprised.

'It's murder all right, Gerry. No doubt about that.'

22

Wesley and Gerry walked in silence back to the station. They hardly noticed the spectacle of a cruise ship arriving up the river, escorted by tugs and watched by fascinated locals who'd gathered on the embankment to stare at the huge vessel manoeuvring its way between the moored yachts and the ferries that were plying to and fro across the water. The shocking news that Maggie Beattie had been murdered meant that the two detectives were oblivious to anything but the case. She had been the victim of a vicious attack while her husband was enjoying a cheerful drink with his fellow ringers. And the killer had mutilated her body to conceal the real cause of death.

The CSIs had been alerted and had returned to the scene. Only now their focus was the churchyard rather than the top of the tower. A call to Gerry an hour later confirmed that they'd found a spade propped up against the wall at the west end of the church next to a wheelbarrow, not a place they'd bothered to search before. There were stains on it that looked like blood, and it was being taken to the lab for examination. There were also signs of disturbance nearby; it looked as though the victim had been killed there and transported to the spot beneath the tower in the wheelbarrow. The path beside the church was concrete, so the wheels would have left no tracks. It had been a clever piece of misdirection.

Back in the CID office, Gerry assembled the team for a briefing. Rachel looked shocked, and Paul Johnson, sitting beside Trish Walton, his fiancée, shook his head in disbelief. Only DC Rob Carter showed no emotion as he sat at the desk he'd bagged by the window overlooking the Memorial Park and the river.

'We need to re-interview everyone on that island,' said Gerry. 'Rach, can you organise that? From Colin's estimated time of death, the tide was high when she died, which means the island would have been cut off. Either our killer came by boat or he was already there, which narrows down our list of suspects. I want everyone's whereabouts checked and double-checked.'

'One person wasn't there,' said Wesley as he followed Gerry into his office once the briefing was over. 'Quentin Search was in Tradington.'

'So we were led to believe, but we need to make sure.' Gerry glanced out of the office window. 'I'll give that job to Rob. Your mate Neil wasn't on the island at the time, was he?'

Wesley shook his head. 'He's at his dig near Dukesbridge. But he says he's going to visit the island when the priory dig starts tomorrow.'

'What's the progress with that facial reconstruction he promised for the body in the sheet?'

'It's being done as we speak.'

Gerry put his head in his hands. Then he looked up. 'With this new murder, we might have to put the purple-sheet body on the back burner for a while.'

'I don't agree, Gerry.'

'Why's that?' Wesley could hear a note of irritation in the DCI's voice. But he had to say what he thought.

'I know the victim in the sheet died a while ago, but don't you think that two suspicious deaths on the same small island might be linked?' He paused, gathering his thoughts. 'And it feels like Quentin Search is the connection.'

'What about the other residents of the island? The landlord of the pub?'

'He hasn't been here long enough to have anything to do with the older case.'

'The people in the cottages?'

Before Wesley could answer, Paul Johnson appeared at the door.

'Come in, Paul,' said Gerry. 'Don't stand on ceremony. What can I do you for? Please tell me you've made an arrest and the culprit's waiting for us in the interview room ready to make a full confession.'

Paul gave a nervous smile. 'Sorry, sir. We've got a lead on the sheet the body was wrapped in. It's a style manufactured in the 1970s.'

'The decade that taste forgot. I guessed as much as soon as I clapped eyes on it. Anything else?'

'It was a line sold at Beriam's – the old department store in Morbay that closed down in the nineties.'

Gerry let out a sound that sounded like a growl of frustration. 'Don't suppose anyone's still got their sales records from fifty years ago?'

'Not that I know of, but my nan knows someone who used to work there in the seventies. She was manageress of the home textiles department. She's almost ninety, but according to Nan, she's still got all her marbles.'

'Would she be willing to talk to us?'

Paul grinned. 'I think she'd be more than willing. I think she'd be delighted.'

'Good work, Paul. We'll pay her a visit.' Gerry hauled himself out of his chair. 'It might be wise to set up an incident room on the island so we don't have to keep travelling to and fro.'

'I'll get someone to see to it.'

'And there's one thing we need to do before anything else, Wes. We've got to break the news to Jack Beattie that his wife was murdered.' Gerry paused. 'Besides, I was always taught that the partner should be viewed as the prime suspect until proved otherwise.'

'Beattie was in the Hanging Monk with the other bell-ringers when his wife died. That's seven impartial witnesses, not counting the bar staff and any other customers.'

'People nip out – make a phone call, answer a call of nature. I don't think we can rule him out just yet. And by all accounts his wife was obsessed with Quentin Search's particular brand of nonsense. He might have got sick of her going on about it and finally snapped.'

Wesley couldn't disagree with that.

They grabbed their coats, left Rachel in charge and set off back to St Rumon's Island. They had to see Jack Beattie. And they needed to have a word with Quentin Search.

23

They found Jack Beattie at the church, sitting beside the Reverend Charlie in the front pew. Some interviewing officers would have viewed her presence as interference, but Wesley was glad she was there, a quiet, comforting presence, there for the bereaved man if he needed support.

The other ringers were nowhere to be seen, although the sleeping bags and camp beds belonging to the champers, Matt Evans and his wife, were still in place at the far end of the nave. Wesley imagined the visitors had made a tactful retreat to the Hanging Monk, shocked by the unexpected turn their ringing adventure had taken.

Gerry left it to Wesley to tell Jack that Maggie's death was being treated as murder, and the new widower's reaction was to shake his head in disbelief. 'I don't understand. Everyone loved Maggie. She never harmed anyone in her life.'

From experience, Wesley knew this was always said about murder victims. Nobody cared to speak ill of the recently dead.

'Can you tell us everything that happened since you arrived on the island?' he asked. Jack would have gone over this in the statements he'd already made, but the detectives needed to hear it again, alert for any deviations from the original story or small things he'd only just remembered.

He told them how he'd met up with the northern group on Monday, and the visitors had left their cars on the seafront in Midton before walking across to the island at low tide. He'd left them to settle into their accommodation in the church and the rented cottages, then joined them for a couple of hours at the Hanging Monk, just to be sociable. On that occasion, Maggie had stayed at home. Their ringing challenge began on Tuesday. Maggie had come over to the island with him, but she'd done her own thing while they'd been ringing in the tower. She'd seemed happy enjoying some peace and quiet with her book.

'You told us she was obsessed with Quentin Search,' said Gerry.

Jack considered the question for a moment. 'It was OK at first, just an interest in his books and theories. She'd always been a keen reader, but after a while his were the only books she'd read, and if anyone dared to say they were nonsense, she stopped talking to them. She fell out with one of our neighbours because of it. She'd seen the posters for Search's talk, and when she made a joke about it, Maggie was furious.'

Wesley caught Gerry's eye. 'How did the neighbour react to that?'

'More in sorrow than in anger, as the Bard once said. She said she was worried about Maggie – thought she might need help.'

'Was your neighbour right?' said Gerry sharply. 'Did Maggie need help?'

'I was afraid it might get to that stage, but ... You never like to think things are out of control, do you?'

Wesley nodded. It was easy to bury your head in the proverbial sand where a loved one was concerned. When Pam had been diagnosed with breast cancer a few years ago, he'd been in denial for a while until he came to terms with the diagnosis and realised she needed his support. But Jack's problem was far more sensitive and nebulous. When did a keen interest turn into an obsession? And when did an obsession become a danger?

'I understand she told her writing group she intended to call at his house,' said Wesley. For once, Della had told him something useful.

Jack glanced at the Reverend Charlie, who was sitting perfectly still, listening intently. 'She didn't mention it to me. But then she wouldn't.'

'Did you know Search has been waging a campaign on social media against Dr Neil Watson, an archaeologist who's been challenging his theories?'

Jack looked up. 'You told me Maggie was attacked with a spade. Archaeologists use spades, so perhaps this Dr Watson wanted to punish Search and my wife got in the way. Have you considered that?'

Wesley was lost for words. The possibility that the friend he'd known since his student days could be involved had never occurred to him, and the very suggestion came as a shock.

Gerry nudged his arm as though he'd read his thoughts. 'Dr Watson's not on our list of suspects.'

'Then perhaps he should be. Perhaps Maggie was collateral damage.'

Journal of the Reverend Thomas Nescombe

February 1574

I have not written in this journal for many months. Not since that terrible night when I found my wife casting spells on the clifftop. She said nothing of it afterwards, even when I questioned her about Lyonesse and what she knew about such things. I asked her why she had visited Elias Anselmo, but she swore she had never been to the Hall and had never spoken to Anselmo alone. I knew she was lying because I had seen her with my own eyes. She had tried to summon the spirits of Lyonesse and I had interrupted her.

And yet after that night she seemed to reach a new state of contentment, and there were no more wanderings in the night. We were happy, and with the help of Cuthbert Sellars, who is now my loyal churchwarden, I feel I have won the trust of the island people. I have even joined them at the Hanging Monk on occasions. There are times when I can almost believe that Elias Anselmo does not exist.

Anne is great with child, and we must prepare for the babe's arrival. She is tired and spends much time in her bed, resting. All was peace until last night, when I heard a knock upon the door. I answered thinking it would be some villager in need of my help and prayers, but when I opened the door, I saw a cloaked figure there. As he stepped forward, I realised it was Elias Anselmo.

He pushed past me, asking where Anne was. His manner was most aggressive, as though he had some right to see her. But I barred his way.

'My wife is resting. Her time is near. What business have you with her?'

He smiled, the smile of a skull; of death triumphing over the living. 'Did you not wonder why she was never with child before she visited my house? My business, sir, is that of one who is responsible for her happy condition.'

The horror of his words struck me like an axe blow. Evil was on the island. And it had wormed its way into my very bed.

24

Wesley and Gerry walked towards Coffin Hall.

'You don't seriously think Neil could have anything to do with this?' Wesley asked as the Hall came into view.

'Not really, but we have to treat him like anyone else.'

'I accept that,' said Wesley. 'But I know for a fact that he was with his team near Dukesbridge at the time of Maggie Beattie's death.'

'Without fear or favour, remember, Wes. No such thing as mate's rates as far as a murder investigation is concerned, but I take your point. I think we can eliminate Neil from our enquiries. What do we know about these bell-ringers from up north?'

'Only that they're from north Cheshire, just south of Manchester, and Jack was recruited to make up the numbers when someone dropped out of the trip. I want to know whether any of them have a connection to this area – or to the victim. Although we can probably rule out Simon Wood's teenage sons, James and Andrew.'

'Not necessarily; they're both strapping lads. But I tend to agree with you. According to the DC I've just spoken to, they've all retreated to the Hanging Monk again, sulking because the Reverend Charlie's asked them to postpone the peal they had planned for today out of respect.'

Gerry made a call to the incident room. The northern ringers were to be interviewed again and new statements taken. Any possible links with the area or the dead woman were to be noted, and the DCI was to be informed as soon as possible.

'What about the Reverend Charlie? Do we treat her as a suspect?'

'Can you really imagine her strangling a stranger and battering the body with a spade? On the other hand, I suppose we need to eliminate her from our enquiries as well.'

When they reached the Hall, they were in for a disappointment. According to the builder, who was heaving bags of dry plaster out of his van without any obvious effort, Search had gone off on his travels around the bookshops of Devon again. Jocasta had gone with him, and the daughter was out, whereabouts unknown.

He himself had seen a woman answering Maggie's description, but when he'd told her that Quentin wasn't there, she'd left straight away. He had no idea what she'd done after that.

'We can ask one of the team to let us know when Search gets back,' said Gerry as they walked away. 'In the meantime, I'd like to speak to the lady from Beriam's. If we can find out where that sheet came from, we might make some progress.'

Normally they would have delegated the visit to Mrs Rita Miller, former manageress of the textiles department at Beriam's department store, to a more junior officer, but Gerry saw it as an opportunity. Fresh air and a change of scene did wonders for clearing the head.

'I'm not sure what she'll be able to tell us after all this time,' said Wesley as the car ferry chugged slowly across to the opposite bank of the river, where they'd pick up the main road to Morbay. 'Is this really a good use of our time?'

'Don't be so pessimistic, Wes. Never underestimate the accumulated knowledge of an elderly lady.'

'You're hoping she'll be Morbay's answer to Miss Marple.'

'You never know. Besides, it's a lovely day and we need a break.'

Mrs Miller lived in a block of sheltered flats on the outskirts of Morbay, and Paul Johnson had rung ahead to warn her of their visit. She'd told him she was looking forward to it. When they arrived at the front door, she buzzed them in and told them to walk straight down the corridor to their left and look for Flat 12. Her instructions were clear and concise. A good omen.

She was a sprightly ninety-year-old, small and bird-like with perfectly coiffed silver hair and sharp eyes. After the introductions were made, she offered tea, which they accepted gratefully. Once the china cups were placed before them, along with a plate of biscuits, she sat down opposite and studied them closely.

'Well, gentlemen. I was told you wanted to ask me about a sheet.' She tilted her head to one side, strengthening the impression of an intelligent bird, alert for predators or underground worms.

Wesley took out his phone and brought up a picture of the sheet the St Rumon's Island corpse had been wrapped in. 'I believe Beriam's used to stock this particular line,' he said.

Mrs Miller donned a pair of reading glasses and studied it closely. After a few moments, she removed her glasses. 'I remember the pattern well because I thought it was hideous. Although one never questioned a customer's taste, of course.'

Wesley guessed this woman was probably as tough as many police officers he'd worked with, so there was no point in protecting her from the gruesome facts. 'Have you heard of a place called St Rumon's Island?'

'I heard on the radio that a body was found there and the police were treating the death as suspicious,' she said. 'I'm guessing it was wrapped in this sheet – am I right?'

'Spot on, love,' said Gerry, a note of admiration in his voice.

'I like to keep abreast of the local news, and it was such an unusual story. This line was stocked back in the 1970s.'

'We have reason to believe the burial was a lot more recent than that.'

She raised her eyebrows. 'So either someone was still using it, which after all this time I find hard to believe, as it wasn't one of our more expensive and well-made lines. Or it had been stored somewhere. An attic, perhaps.'

'I know it's a long time ago, but I wonder whether you remember anyone who bought this bedding,' said Wesley. 'I suppose all the sales records are long gone.'

The old lady's lips formed a triumphant smile. 'Now that's where you're wrong, Inspector. When I retired from Beriam's in the 1990s, I kept some of my old purchase books from the sixties and seventies as souvenirs because they weren't needed any more. Silly really, but that department was my little kingdom. My late husband was in charge of the china department, and we were never blessed with children, so Beriam's was our life.'

146

Her eyes turned to a black-and-white wedding photograph on the mantelpiece: Rita as a bride in white, and her tall, thin husband in a suit with a carnation in his buttonhole. No doubt all their colleagues had been invited to the festivities.

'My Bert passed away soon after he retired. Heart attack.'

'I'm sorry,' said Wesley.

'Don't be. We had a good life. The worst thing is seeing Beriam's as an empty shop. All those happy memories gone.' She sighed, a faraway look in her eyes. Then she pulled herself up straight, suddenly businesslike. 'I'll get those books for you.'

She rose to her feet, pushing herself up carefully with her hands on the arms of the chair, her sole concession to age.

'Hope I'm like that when I get to ninety,' Gerry whispered once she'd left the room.

They waited in silence for her to return, and when she appeared, she was carrying four ledgers. They looked heavy, and Wesley hurried over to give her a hand.

Once the tea things had been moved out of the way and the books had been placed on the coffee table, the reading glasses went on again. 'I remember that particular pattern was called Purple Haze Floral Dream,' she said. 'More of a nightmare if you ask me, but it was the height of fashion back then. Was it a single or a double?'

'A double,' said Gerry.

She began to leaf through the first ledger, stopping whenever she came to the sale of one of the sheets. Wesley made a note of the name and address of each purchaser. Fortunately there weren't many. As Mrs Miller pointed out, it wasn't a popular line and it had been discontinued pretty

147

quickly, so only two of the ledgers she'd produced were of any relevance.

They already knew that Beriam's had been the only local outlet for this particular item, so there was a good chance that the name of the purchaser would be on their gratifyingly sparse list. Of course it was possible that the sheet had changed hands a few times since then, sent to a charity shop or jumble sale. But the initial purchase was a good place to start.

As Wesley scanned the list, one name stood out. He pointed it out to Mrs Miller, who put on her glasses again.

'Oh yes. Of course I remember Mrs Wallace. She was one of our regular customers. She bought a pair of sheets for her teenage daughter, who liked that sort of thing. She was such a nice lady; no airs and graces. You wouldn't think she lived in ... well, I can only describe it as a manor house.'

Wesley passed the list to Gerry. 'Notice the address. St Rumon's House. St Rumon's Island.'

Gerry frowned. 'We never came across anywhere called St Rumon's House.'

'Mrs Wallace was very chatty; not snobbish like some. She told me once that when she moved in, she changed the name of the house because it was far too gruesome. I remember her saying that she'd told her husband she couldn't possibly live in a house called Coffin Hall.'

As Wesley drove back to Tradmouth, Gerry called the station. He needed someone traced. And quickly.

25

Half an hour later, Rachel called back with news. 'I've found the Wallaces. The father, Edmund Wallace, died fifteen years ago, but the mother and daughter are still in Devon. The daughter, Sarah Rowdon, runs an animal sanctuary on Dartmoor and her mother lives with her. Want me to give her a call?'

Wesley hesitated. Did he really need to speak to the people who used to live at Coffin Hall? The burial they were investigating dated from long after their time on the island. On the other hand, according to Rita Miller, ex-employee of Beriam's department store, the sheet wrapped around the body had probably once been their property. That was something he couldn't ignore.

It was three o'clock by the time they arrived back at the station to find the team still hard at work. Gerry gave orders that all the other customers who'd bought similar bedding were to be traced as well, even though the St Rumon's Island link seemed the most promising.

But Wesley wanted to speak to Mrs Wallace face to face. If she or someone connected with her had decided to dispose of a body on the island she must have known well, the old sheet might have been used. It was a long shot, but he needed to know. Gerry was busy, so he approached Rachel's desk.

'I'd like to go to Dartmoor and speak to the Wallaces,' he said. 'Fancy coming with me?'

Rachel nodded eagerly.

Wesley's spirits lifted as Rachel drove across Dartmoor. From the passenger seat he could gaze out of the window at the passing landscape. The land was green with new life. Lambs trotted by their woolly mothers in the fields and the sun was shining. At that moment it was easy to forget the world of crime and murder.

They drove along winding roads past stone-built villages and through the vast open moor, where lofty granite tors reared up like spindly church towers in the landscape. Eventually they came to a wooden farm gate on the fringe of a tiny hamlet. Beside it was a flaking sign: *Yarmtor Animal Sanctuary*. Wesley got out and opened the gate.

After navigating down a long and bumpy track, they parked in front of a plain bungalow, probably built in the 1950s before planners became fussy about the sort of architecture they allowed in a national park. It was surrounded by enclosures and outbuildings, some brick, some wood. An assortment of animals grazed in the surrounding fields: sheep, donkeys, goats and horses. They could hear barking coming from a new-looking barn behind the bungalow.

A woman emerged from the front door with a smile on her face. She was tall and athletic, with no-nonsense short grey hair.

'Mr and Mrs Meadows? You've come to see the new puppies. They're all beautiful, so it's going to be hard for you to choose between them.' She sounded excited at the prospect.

Wesley looked apologetic as he showed her his warrant card. 'I'm sorry, we're not here about the puppies. Mrs Rowdon?'

'That's me. What's this about?' She looked worried, racking her brains in an effort to recall some long-forgotten misdemeanour that might be of interest to the police, and failing.

'We'd like to ask you a few questions about your former home on St Rumon's Island. And your mother too, if she's available. Nothing to worry about,' he added by way of reassurance.

'You'd better come in,' she said, leading the way into the bungalow, which appeared to be furnished with a hotchpotch of second-hand furniture. Wesley found it hard to imagine any of it in the ancient stone house on St Rumon's Island.

She led them through to a utilitarian living room, where a trio of aged Border collies had made themselves comfortable in dog beds on the floor. An imperious cat gazed down at them disdainfully from the back of the sofa, and a wizened elderly lady sat in an armchair in the corner, a Zimmer frame set in front of her like a cage.

'Mother, these are police officers. They want to ask some questions about St Rumon's House.'

'That was a long time ago,' said the old lady in a surprisingly firm voice. 'Another life. Do take a seat if you can find one. If there's a dog there, tell it to get down.'

'Thank you,' said Wesley, perching on the edge of a chair covered with a blanket coated with dog hairs. It was clear the woman couldn't see or she'd have known the dogs were elsewhere. She stared ahead, but he could tell that her brain was still sharp. 'We've spoken to someone who used to know you. Rita Miller, from the textile department of Beriam's department store in Morbay.'

A smile lit up Mrs Wallace's face. 'Beriam's. It was such a lovely shop. And they served delicious afternoon teas in their café on the top floor. Do you remember, Sarah?'

The daughter nodded dutifully. 'I remember.'

'This was in the days when we had money and lived in the big house,' Mrs Wallace said wistfully. 'Six years ago, my husband passed away and I discovered that he'd made some rather unwise investments, so I was forced to sell the house and its contents and move in with my daughter here. Sarah's husband had died the year before, so she was running the sanctuary on her own. And now she's got me to care for as well.'

'Come on, Mother, you're a great help, and I'm not entirely alone; we have lots of volunteers helping out.' Sarah turned to Wesley. 'This sanctuary was my late husband's life's work, Inspector. I'm continuing it in his memory.'

She smiled fondly and Wesley found himself warming to the pair in a way he hadn't warmed to Quentin Search, the new occupier of their former home. The suspicions that had flitted through his mind when he'd learned of their connection with the sheet now seemed a little foolish. It was hard to believe either of these women could be capable of murder, but he knew he had to keep an open mind.

'I'm sure you're doing a brilliant job,' said Rachel. Wesley had noticed that she'd been assessing the condition of the animals they'd seen with a professional eye. She was a farmer's daughter and now a farmer's wife, so she knew her stuff.

'I take it we're not suspected of any crime, so what do you want to ask us?' said Mrs Wallace.

'It's about a sheet. A purple nylon one.'

Sarah looked puzzled, and Wesley turned to her mother. 'Mrs Wallace, according to Mrs Miller from Beriam's, you bought a pair of similar sheets for your daughter back in the 1970s.'

The old lady looked as though she'd just remembered something pleasant. 'Do you know, I'd forgotten all about that. You went through a phase of loving purple when you were a teenager, darling. Remember?'

Sarah laughed. 'Don't remind me.'

'That's right, I bought some bedding for you. A pair of purple nylon floral sheets. Absolutely hideous, I know, but that was the latest fashion and it was what you wanted. Heaven knows why.' Mrs Wallace chuckled.

'What happened to the bedding?'

'Why are you asking?'

Mrs Wallace was an intelligent woman, and Wesley knew there was no point in sweetening the bitter truth. 'A few days ago, part of the cliff on the church side of St Rumon's Island collapsed onto the beach during a storm. A couple of old skeletons came down, and archaeologists are dealing with those. However, one burial was obviously far more recent. The body is that of a middle-aged woman, as yet unidentified.' He saw the two women look at each other, mystified. 'She was wrapped in a purple nylon sheet, identical to the pair you purchased in the 1970s, though we believe the body had only been there a year or two – long after you moved away.'

Sarah went over to her mother and sat on the arm of her chair, cradling the old woman's shoulder. 'This is a bit of a shock,' she said. 'To think that my old bedding might have been used like that. It's horrible.'

'I suppose you want to know what we did with it,' said Mrs Wallace firmly. 'Well, I can tell you. It was left behind with everything else at St Rumon's House. Now reverted to its former name, Coffin Hall, I believe. I changed it for obvious reasons.'

'Are you sure? You didn't get rid of it at an earlier date?'

'I'm part of the wartime generation, brought up to keep things in case they came in useful, Inspector. Old sheets make excellent dust sheets, so I kept it in the attic, along with the rest of the worn-out bed linen I'd accumulated over the years. When I moved here, Sarah told me there was no room for all my junk, as she calls it.' She touched her daughter's arm.

'It's true, Inspector. We just don't have space here, so it was all left at the house for the new owners to deal with.'

'You met the new owners?'

Mrs Wallace nodded slowly. 'I did indeed. He's quite famous now, you know. Quentin Search. His wife was a peculiar woman. Kiara, her name was. Hardly said anything when they came to look round.'

'She looked as though she was on drugs to me,' said Sarah bluntly. 'Mind you, I wouldn't blame her. I wouldn't fancy being married to that man. Talk about thinking you're the centre of the universe.'

Rachel had been listening intently while Wesley asked the questions. Now she spoke for the first time. 'Mrs Wallace, did anyone else have access to your house while you were living there? Guests, or tradesmen, for instance.'

Even though she couldn't see, Mrs Wallace looked

towards her daughter for guidance. 'Do you remember anyone, darling?'

'I can't think of any guests we didn't know well. Certainly nobody you'd class as untrustworthy.'

'Indeed not.'

'You must have had a few tradesmen in over the years in an old house like that.'

'There was a painter and decorator who worked for us. Nice man. He passed away a couple of years before we moved and we never bothered with decorating after that. And there was a man who mended the central heating – he was from a firm in Neston – and a glazier who mended a broken window.'

'Anyone else?'

'A builder from Dukesbridge worked on a damp patch in the kitchen passage.'

'When was this?'

'Shortly before I sold the house,' said Mrs Wallace. 'Five years ago, perhaps.'

'Could he have got hold of the sheet somehow?'

'I wasn't watching him all the time. People don't like being watched while they're working, do they? It's possible he could have found the sheet and used it as a dust sheet. I really can't remember.'

'Can you recall his name?'

'He was called George,' said Sarah. 'But I don't remember his surname.'

'Would you have details of his invoice – and the payment?'

Wesley saw the old woman's face redden. 'I paid him cash. He said he preferred it.'

'Oh, Mother,' said Sarah.

'Can you describe him?'

'He was in his sixties. Bald. Smallish. Rather grumpy – hardly a cheerful soul. He came round asking whether I needed work done, and I knew I had to get the damp seen to before I put the place on the market. He had a young man helping him, as I remember.'

'Really, Mother, you should have asked me before—'

'You were so busy with this place, I didn't like to bother you.'

Sarah shook her head and squeezed her mother's hand. When she asked if there was anything else they needed to know, Wesley said there wasn't and told them they'd been very helpful.

'Now all we've got to do is track down a builder called George,' said Rachel as they were driving back.

'I suppose it's as good a place to start as any.'

26

When he returned to the CID office, Wesley sat down on the chair at the visitor's side of Gerry's cluttered desk. The DCI seemed preoccupied as he looked up and gave him a nod of acknowledgement.

'Rach and I have spoken to Mrs Wallace who used to live at Coffin Hall – or St Rumon's House, as it was then,' Wesley began.

'Sorry, Wes, I was busy thinking about Karen Liden. What did she say?'

'She confirmed the sheet was probably hers.'

'Do you have her down as a suspect?'

Wesley suppressed a laugh. 'She's suffering from macular degeneration and she walks with a Zimmer frame. Besides, I can't see her as the murdering type.'

'If I had a fiver for every killer I put away whose friends and relatives said that, I'd wouldn't be here, I'd be sunning myself on a yacht in the South of France.'

Wesley allowed himself a chuckle. 'I take your point, Gerry, but I don't think it applies in this case. She sold the house to Quentin Search and his then wife Kiara five years ago and moved in with her daughter on Dartmoor. Search bought the house and all its contents – including the junk stored in the attic. And Mrs Wallace confessed to being a hoarder who never threw anything away.'

'Including old bedding from the 1970s?'

'Exactly.

'We definitely need another word with Mr Search. You don't think he's trying to avoid us, do you?'

Wesley shook his head. 'Someone's checked. He's doing the rounds of the bookshops in the area. Apparently his publicist arranges it all.' He grinned. 'If Neil's to be believed, Quentin Search has horns and a tail and eats kittens for breakfast.'

Gerry chuckled. 'He's not a fan then.' He checked the time. 'I reckon he should be home by now. We need some straight answers about that sheet.'

'What about George, the builder Mrs Wallace mentioned?'

'I'll ask someone to try and trace him, but without a surname . . .'

They drove back to Midton, and after a short journey on the police launch to the island, they arrived at Coffin Hall. Search's gleaming black Range Rover was parked in front of the main door, but the builder's van had gone.

The woman who answered the door was tall and slim. She wore a long Indian cotton dress and her dark hair was caught up in a chignon, just the elegant side of casual. It was difficult to assess her age, but Wesley guessed she was between thirty-five and forty-five. Younger than Search, but not young enough to be his daughter.

'Is Mr Search at home?' he asked politely after he'd introduced himself and Gerry.

It was hard to gauge the woman's feelings about two senior police officers arriving on her doorstep as she stood aside to let them in.

'I'm Jocasta Adams. We've all given statements and I'm sure nobody has anything to add.' There was a note of irritation in her voice.

'There's been a development since then, madam,' said Gerry. 'A woman was found dead near the church yesterday. Perhaps you've heard about it. Or maybe you've been aware of an increased police presence on the island.'

'We've been out most of the time, publicising Quentin's new book and preparing for the symposium tomorrow. Besides, we're not privy to local gossip.'

'We still need to speak to Mr Search . . . and you, madam. And anyone else who lives here. Just routine.'

She pressed her lips together impatiently and walked ahead of them into the drawing room.

Quentin Search was scrolling through his phone as they entered, and when he looked up and saw them, he made no effort to hide his annoyance. 'I've already told you, I don't know anything. This is ridiculous. This is harassment.'

'We've come about another matter, sir,' said Wesley. He went on to tell Search about the discovery of Maggie Beattie's body.

The man nodded smugly. 'I told you on your last visit that this island was known for its wickedness, so it is hardly surprising if that wickedness extends to murder.'

'You're not saying this woman was murdered by spirits,' said Gerry, unable to keep the mockery out of his voice.

'Spirits influence the behaviour of the living, Chief Inspector. A former occupant of this house, Elias Anselmo, raised spirits in this very place. If you come to my symposium this weekend, you'll find out the truth the archaeological establishment don't want you to know.' He gave Wesley a sideways glance, as though he was expecting him to raise an objection.

'Thank you, sir,' said Gerry. 'But we're a bit busy right at the moment. What we haven't mentioned is that the dead woman, Maggie Beattie, was a great fan of yours, and she had a ticket for your symposium. Her husband says she was quite obsessed with your books and he suspects that she chose to come to the island because of you. Your builder told us she called here.'

'Well if she did, I didn't see her.'

'If you were out, maybe she came back – wanted a book signed?' Gerry produced a photograph of the dead woman provided by her husband and thrust it in front of Search's nose.

'No,' said Search after giving the photograph a cursory glance. 'I've never seen her.'

'What about you, Ms Adams? Do you recognise this woman?'

When she was shown the photograph, Jocasta shook her head. 'I've been with Quentin,' she said quickly. 'If this woman hoped to see him here, she chose the wrong time. Besides, we value our privacy. Like any celebrity, he attracts fans, but you can't pander to them or your life wouldn't be your own. I'm sorry, we can't help you.' The finality of her words served as a signal that she wanted them out of the house.

But Gerry wasn't giving up. 'We'd like to speak to your daughter. She might have seen Maggie Beattie when she came looking for you. Does anyone else live here? Do you have any staff?'

Search exchanged a look with Jocasta. 'Ginevra never mentioned this woman's alleged visit to me. As for staff, there's a woman who comes in to clean twice a week, but she's on holiday at the moment.'

'Can we speak to Ginevra now?'

There was a silence, as though they were concocting an excuse.

'No,' Jocasta said. 'She's resting, and I don't want to disturb her. She hasn't been well. And she's already made a statement.'

'Even so, we'd like another word.'

'It's not convenient.'

'Very well. Maybe later. You've got a builder in?'

'Scott. We have very little to do with him while he's working,' Jocasta said.

'You've used him before?'

'He's done odd jobs for us and he's always proved reliable.'

'You don't know a builder called George?'

Both of them shook their heads.

Gerry looked at Search. 'When you were interviewed before, you were asked about a purple sheet.'

'And I said I didn't possess such a thing.'

'We've spoken to the former owner of this house, Mrs Wallace, and she said she left bedding of that description here when she moved out.'

'She did leave the furnishings, yes. But I'm not aware of a purple sheet.'

'She thinks it was in the attic. Would you mind if we had a look to see if it's still there? Or shall I send some officers round with a search warrant?'

Search looked horrified, and Jocasta scowled.

'I really don't want policemen crawling all over the house,' she said haughtily. There was a long silence. Then she obviously decided that Gerry's determination was a match for her own. Besides, he had the law on his side.

'Very well,' she said with a heavy sigh. 'I'll show you the attic staircase, and you can have a look for yourselves.'

Without another word, she led them up the main staircase and onto a wide landing. The floorboards were dark oak and uneven and the doors either side were equally old. There were oil paintings on the wall, landscapes and family portraits. Wesley wondered if they'd once belonged to Mrs Wallace; Quentin Search didn't seem the type to go in for that sort of thing.

At the end of the landing, they arrived at a small door that led to a set of bare, narrow steps.

'It's not locked,' Jocasta said before leaving them there.

Wesley went first, ducking his head to get through the low doorway. When he reached the top of the stairs, he opened the door in front of him. The attic, as he'd expected, was filled with junk. Old chairs and chests of drawers, a broken rocking horse, battered packing cases, empty picture frames; the collected detritus of a hundred years or more. He began to search through the drawers while Gerry stood looking around. He was just despairing of finding anything useful when he heard the DCI's voice.

'Bingo.'

He swung round and saw that Gerry had opened a dome-topped trunk and was staring down at its contents, grinning.

'Look at this, Wes.'

The trunk contained a sheet identical to the one the body had been wrapped in. Wesley put on a pair of crime-scene gloves and pulled it out carefully.

'Only one,' said Gerry. 'Mrs Miller said the Wallaces bought a pair. When I was a kid, nobody had duvets. They used blankets and sheets – one top and one bottom – so it looks like one's missing. And I think we can guess what happened to it.'

'Which means the killer had access to this attic.'

When they broke the news to Search and Jocasta, the couple could barely conceal their anger.

'This is ridiculous,' fumed Jocasta. 'We had nothing to do with anybody's death.'

'It's police persecution,' said Search. 'I warn you, we'll take legal advice.'

Wesley and Gerry left the house, his words ringing in their ears. They would leave the search to others.

They were making their way across the courtyard when they heard a voice behind them.

'You're the policemen.' The words sounded like an accusation.

They turned round to see a fragile-looking young woman with long blonde hair and a pretty elfin face. She wore a white T-shirt and a purple skirt.

'I need to talk to you.'

'What about?' Wesley said gently.

'My mother. That body you found after the cliff collapsed. I think it could be her. And if it is, I think my father might have killed her.'

Wesley and Gerry looked at each other.

'In that case, you'd better make a statement, love,' said Gerry.

163

27

Ginevra Search gave a new statement to a very nice female police officer, a tall young woman with straight dark hair and a smart trouser suit who wrote down the details of her brief encounter with Maggie Beattie, who'd called at the Hall during her father and Jocasta's absence. The officer, DC Trish Walton, listened carefully to what she had to say and took a swab from the inside of her mouth. DNA for comparison, she said. They needed it to eliminate the possibility that the body they'd found belonged to her mother. Ginevra told DC Walton that she knew nothing about any purple sheet and that she'd always believed her mother was travelling abroad. It was only now that she was starting to wonder whether that wasn't true.

Her father had insisted that the marriage had been in difficulties for a while before her mother walked out, and that his affair with his new assistant, Jocasta, had been the last straw that had driven her to leave and seek a new life.

Ginevra admitted that she and her mother had never been close. Kiara had been a selfish woman, interested only in herself and having frequent affairs. She'd said on several occasions that having a child had been a grave mistake, and her daughter hadn't been at all surprised when she'd failed to keep in contact while she was on her travels.

And her mother wasn't the only person who'd abandoned her. Edith, her father's former assistant, had gone too, which somehow she found much harder to understand. She'd always thought Edith was her friend; perhaps the only person who'd truly cared about her when Kiara had been too busy with her own concerns to pay her any attention. But when Edith's elderly mother had fallen ill, Edith had left to look after her. All the people she'd ever cared for had vanished from her life in the end.

Jocasta had replaced Edith as her father's personal assistant, and had been at the Hall, and frequently in her father's bed, at the time her mother left. If the body in the sheet did turn out to belong to her mother, Jocasta must have been complicit in what had happened. Ginevra told DC Walton that the police shouldn't believe a word the woman said.

She needed to get away from the house, so she walked to the far side of the island in a daze. She rarely left the island these days; for a while now she'd found the prospect of crossing the causeway to the mainland positively frightening. She liked it best when the tide was in; when the island was cut off so nobody else could access her private world.

The only place she ever encountered strangers was in the Hanging Monk. She often went there alone after drinking some of Quentin's whisky for courage. The landlord had accused her of being drunk, but he didn't understand that she needed something to dull the pain, to make the misery go away. Having no contact with the outside world, she didn't know anyone who could supply her with drugs, so she made do with alcohol. Anything to reach oblivion. Anything to forget.

Her one pleasure, if you could call it that, was immersing herself in the history of the island. Not her father's brand of history with its magic and crazy legends, but the real history. The priory where the monks had spent years in prayerful silence, and the necromancer, Elias Anselmo, who'd lived in the Hall after the priory was destroyed by Henry VIII's lackeys. She'd seen the evidence of Anselmo's attempts to contact spirits: the faint pentagram on the floor and the remnants of his rituals, still there after more than four centuries. Her father used the legends to make money, but Ginevra suspected there might be a grain of truth in the stories; that Elias Anselmo really had held power over life and death.

It was a fine evening, and as she walked, she remembered Edith telling her how the lumps and bumps in the earth near the church concealed the foundations of the ancient priory. Over the past few days, fences had been erected, and she'd been told that some archaeologists would be starting work there soon. Edith would have loved that as much as her father hated it.

She reached a field that sloped gently down to a small shingle beach. She sat down on the damp grass and stared out to sea, thinking of the monks who'd once lived here and wondering if their spirits still haunted the island. Then she closed her eyes and made a solemn vow. If it did turn out that her father was responsible for ending her mother's life, she would make sure he paid the price.

Trish Walton rushed into the incident room that was being set up in an empty holiday cottage, one of the small cluster of buildings that had been home to the lighthouse keepers in the days before automation. She looked pleased with herself, something Wesley found surprising. Trish normally worked quietly and efficiently in the background rather than grabbing the limelight, and his instincts told him that she'd got hold of something good.

'Well? What did Ginevra Search have to say for herself?' Gerry sounded impatient for news.

'She said her mother left home around a year ago and severed all contact with her and her father, although Quentin Search claimed that he'd had a phone call from her sometime after she'd left to say that she wasn't intending to come home and that she wanted a divorce.'

'She didn't want to speak to her daughter?'

'I think the relationship was pretty distant. According to Ginevra, her parents had never got on, but the last straw was Search's affair with his personal assistant at the time – Jocasta Adams; now his partner. Ginevra had no reason to doubt her father's explanation, but since the body in the purple sheet turned up, she's started to wonder whether her mother didn't choose to leave after all. She suspects her father might have killed her.'

'So she told us.'

Gerry looked at Wesley. 'Our body could well belong to Kiara Search. The letter K on the ring certainly fits. And the sheet did come from the Hall.'

'But until we get the DNA results back, we've no reason to believe that Kiara Search is dead.'

'I took a sample like you said, sir,' said Trish. 'I'll send it to the lab.'

'We should get it fast-tracked.' Gerry made a note. 'I'll authorise it.'

'We've already had a look in the attic,' said Wesley. 'But maybe we should get a search warrant for the whole place.'

Gerry hesitated, his initial enthusiasm turning to caution. 'Let's wait for the DNA results first, and if it turns out to be Kiara, we'll go through the place like a dose of salts. But until those dental records turn up, we can't rule out the possibility that our body belongs to Deidre Charlton.' He turned to Trish. 'I know Kiara's supposed to have gone travelling, but does anyone know what countries she was visiting?'

'Afraid not.'

'Might be worth checking whether there's any evidence she's moved back to this country: bank accounts, electoral register, car ownership, tax records, all the usual. If it turns out she's alive and well, we don't want to start a wild goose chase.'

Trish nodded. 'Will do,' she said before hurrying off.

'It's time we had another word with Quentin Search,' said Wesley.

Gerry levered himself out of his seat. 'Just what I was going to suggest. He's been accused of doing away with his missus and we've got an unidentified body.' He grinned. 'So it'd be rude not to.'

As they walked to the Hall, a stiff breeze was blowing over the island and the sky had turned a dark battleship grey. But the rain held off. When they arrived at their destination, Wesley noticed that there was still no sign of the builder's van. Gerry had asked one of the team to ask Scott whether he knew anything about the sheet, but that would have to wait until he returned.

Once again it was Jocasta who answered the door, pressing her narrow lips together into a disapproving slit.

'We've told you everything we know.'

'We've had some new information and we really need to speak to Mr Search again.'

Without a word, she led the way to Search's study, where he was typing into a laptop. When he saw them, he shut the lid with a bang.

'This is getting ridiculous.'

Gerry came straight to the point. 'We need to confirm the whereabouts of your estranged wife, Kiara Search.'

'She's abroad. Last I heard she was in Switzerland.'

'Your daughter hasn't spoken to her since she left a year ago.'

'That's because they didn't get on. Fought like cat and dog. They might be mother and daughter, but there was a distinct clash of personalities. Besides, Kiara was never the maternal type. Even when Ginevra was a baby, she wanted little to do with her.'

'Your daughter thinks you might have killed her.'

'I can assure you she left entirely of her own accord. Even left me a note saying why.'

'That's right,' said Jocasta, who had lingered in the doorway. 'Quentin and I were having an affair, so she decided there was no point in staying. She thought it was holding her back. It's as simple as that.'

'Abandoning her daughter?' said Wesley. Coming from a close and loving family, he found the relationships at Coffin Hall difficult to understand.

'Kiara wanted to lead her own life, and presumably that's what she's doing.'

'When exactly did you last hear from Kiara, Mr Search?' Wesley asked.

'I had a call from her around six months ago asking

how the divorce was progressing. She said she was in Switzerland, but she'd met someone, a man, and she was planning to move on. Look, I can assure you I didn't kill her and wrap her in a hideous purple sheet.' The man looked faintly amused at the idea. 'I really have no idea who that body belongs to, but I promise you it isn't Kiara. And before you ask, I didn't see that woman who died in the churchyard. And you can't prove I did.'

'Have you still got the note your wife wrote when she left you?'

He hesitated. 'I have it somewhere.' He glanced nervously at Jocasta and opened the bottom drawer of his desk. After rummaging around for a few moments, he produced an envelope and handed it to Wesley.

Wesley opened it and read the letter inside, Gerry looking over his shoulder.

I'm leaving because I can't stand being in this awful place any longer. I can't stand your obsession with this house and what happened in it and I won't play second fiddle to that woman any longer.

What she had to say about Jocasta was hardly flattering and she went on to demand a divorce, saying she intended to cut off all contact. Ginevra wasn't mentioned once.

'You can take it with you if you like,' said Search, sounding bored. 'I have no use for it.'

'By the way,' said Wesley, 'what was Kiara's name before you married?'

'Lambert. Why?'

'The body in the sheet was wearing a ring engraved with the initials KL.'

'There must be lots of people with those initials. And my ex-wife didn't wear rings. Didn't like them.'

170

Gerry gave Wesley's arm a nudge. Until they had more evidence, such as a positive DNA match between the body in the sheet and Ginevra Search, they'd have to put their suspicions on hold.

As he pointed out as they walked back to the incident room, you couldn't arrest someone for possessing an offensive personality. 'More's the pity,' he added with a mischievous grin.

28

A message was waiting for Gerry when they reached the incident room. It was the news they'd been waiting for. Deidre Charlton's dentist in London had been traced, and he'd confirmed her husband's claim that she'd had several expensive implants. The body in the purple sheet didn't belong to Deidre. But they weren't exactly back to square one. Kiara Search was another possible candidate, and he wasn't sure whether to believe Quentin's claim about her dislike of rings.

His phone rang, and after a short conversation he looked up. 'That was Rachel. She's over at Jack Beattie's bungalow in Cranton. The search team have been going through the place and she says they've found something.'

'What?'

'A shrine, she says. I told her we'd get over there. I want to see where the victim lived for myself.'

'Me too.' Wesley suddenly felt unsure of himself. 'Can we walk to the car park on the mainland?'

Gerry saw the apprehensive look on the inspector's face. 'We'll have to buy you a pair of sea legs, Wes. I'll take you out on the *Rosie May* again when we've got some free time. Acclimatisation, that's what you need. Mind over matter.'

'Thanks, Gerry. I'll think about it.'

'Let's go then.' He looked at his watch. 'Tide's not due in for another couple of hours, so we should be fine.'

The light was starting to fade when they arrived at the little dormer bungalow Jack Beattie had shared with his late wife. It was on the landward side of the small village of Cranton, three miles down the coast between Midton and Millicombe, situated near the little parish church and almost the furthest house from the sea. Rachel met them on the doorstep and Wesley saw a look of concern on her face.

'How's Jack?' was his first question.

She pressed her lips together in disapproval and leaned towards him. 'If your wife died, would you give all her things away to a charity shop before her body's even cold?' she said in a whisper.

Wesley glanced at Gerry, hoping he hadn't heard. He didn't need any painful reminder of Kathy's death. 'No,' he whispered back. 'But different people react in different ways. Perhaps he didn't want to see her things around because they'd be a constant reminder of what happened.'

Rachel looked sceptical. 'I had to stop his sister loading up her car. I told her we needed to look through everything first.'

'Perhaps she thought she was doing her brother a favour,' said Wesley. 'How are the search team getting on?'

'They've been going through the victim's things, but they haven't found anything significant yet. Are we still treating the husband as a possible suspect?'

It was Gerry who answered. 'He was in the pub, but his fellow ringers said he left them to visit the toilet a couple of times and he was in there a while. Told them he has a bit

173

of prostate trouble. It's unlikely that he killed his wife, but not impossible. Let's have a look at this shrine then, Rach.'

She led the way into the house. In the small beige living room dotted with vases of fresh flowers, Jack Beattie was being looked after by a family liaison officer called Donna, a motherly middle-aged detective constable who was normally based in Dukesbridge. Out of politeness Gerry and Wesley stopped to have a word, assuring him that they were doing everything they could to find his wife's killer. Jack looked as though he'd hardly taken in what they had to say.

Out in the hallway, Donna told them that Matt Evans and Julia Partridge had been round on behalf of the northern bell-ringers to see how he was. They seemed a nice couple and they'd brought flowers, she said approvingly.

'Anyone else?'

'The vicar from the local church where Jack rings the bells paid a visit, and the Reverend Charlie popped in too. And Jack's sister, Sue, has been bustling round making cups of tea. I get the impression she's a bit of a busybody. I don't think she approved of Maggie's, er ... interests. You'll see what I mean when you go upstairs,' she added with a knowing look that stopped short of a wink.

Rachel led the way up the narrow staircase leading to the room in the roof space. The stair carpet looked new and barely worn. When she reached the top, she opened the door with a flourish. 'Welcome to the Quentin Search Suite.'

As soon as they stepped inside, they understood what she meant. The place was filled with Search's books. Different editions of the same books filled shelves that took up two walls. Every inch of spare wall space was occupied by posters advertising his books and talks, including his coming symposium in Tradington. A life-sized cardboard figure of the author, probably a piece of bookshop publicity, watched from the far end of the room, gazing unseeingly in the direction of the desk beneath the dormer window. The figure reminded Wesley of a wizard from a storybook, with his long grey hair and his enveloping dark cloak. The magician, the all-wise magus. The sight brought on an involuntary shudder, and he resisted the temptation to turn the thing round so that it wasn't staring at him disapprovingly.

On the desk sat a laptop computer and a printer, alongside a heap of notebooks and computer printouts.

'This computer needs to go to Scientific Support,' said Gerry. 'Bag it up, will you, Rach. Get it over to Tom. He owes me a favour.'

Wesley sifted through the printouts. Most of them were about Search and his theories. Aliens. Atlantis. Ancient civilisations with origins in outer space. And more recently, the lost land of Lyonesse, which according to Search was situated locally, St Rumon's Island being the only remaining part of that prosperous, extensive and fertile land left above water.

He began to flick through the notebooks. It seemed that Maggie had had theories of her own about the origins of the West Country and the influence of magic on the locality, particularly the power of herbs to conjure and quell storms. He recognised various things he'd been told about by Della: the strange civilisations, the island people, 'the dry ones', and their sinister enemies from the sea. In one of the drawers he found a thin manuscript, only a few chapters. Maggie Beattie's book hadn't progressed very far. He had a quick scan through it, but there was nothing that stood out as relevant. He gave it to one of the DCs and told them to look for anything interesting, but he wasn't getting his hopes up.

They left the room and the cardboard Quentin Search's unsettling gaze and went back downstairs. One of the DCs who'd been examining Maggie's things was waiting for them in the Hall. He shut the door to the lounge before he spoke.

'We've found a bag with a book inside. And you'll never guess whose name's in the book. Deidre Charlton.'

Gerry raised his eyebrows. 'Well, we know she isn't our body in the sheet. But I'd still like to know whether she's connected to our latest victim.'

'Me too,' said Wesley with feeling.

Journal of the Reverend Thomas Nescombe

February 1574

Elias Anselmo left me as soon as he had completed his work of destruction. How could I trust Anne after what he had said? And how could I love the child she carried?

She swore to me that she had never lain with Anselmo, and yet I had seen her that night kneeling before him. I wished to believe her, but his words about being responsible for her happy condition still rang in my ears. I could barely bring myself to speak to her, and the servants must have noticed the coldness between us and the tears my wife shed. As a Christian, I knew I should forgive her weakness. And yet I could not. She had betrayed me, and the child she bore would be the living proof.

That summer night last June I had seen my wife summon a storm. And now, on this grey winter day, the storm blew again. In my imagination, this time it was being summoned by the coming babe, as Anne's agonies began. The maid was sent to summon the village midwife.

Battling against the wind, I set off to the church to pray for her safe delivery, spending the night in that place where the poor prior once held sway before the father of my wife's child sent him to the gallows. I told myself that I must rid my heart of this bitterness. I must forgive.

As I looked upon the child in the cradle the next morning, a healthy boy, I searched for Anselmo's features, but I could detect no resemblance.

29

The book found amongst Maggie Beattie's possessions was brought to the incident room in the lighthouse cottage. As soon as it arrived, Wesley and Gerry donned their crime-scene gloves and pulled it from its protective bag.

It turned out to be a foxed paperback novel with a lurid cover showing a glamorous woman in a skimpy red Tudor-style dress with a neckline that left little to the imagination. She was in a clinch with a muscular young man against a background that resembled Hampton Court. One glance at the preliminary pages told them that it had been published in the 1960s. Practically a museum piece, Gerry observed cheerfully. It was entitled *The Isle of Murder*, by an author called Peregrine Falstaff – and sure enough, the name handwritten in bold capitals at the top right-hand corner of the title page was Deidre Charlton.

'How did Maggie Beattie get hold of it?' Gerry addressed his question to Wesley, who was staring at the book as though he expected it to hold the answer to both the cases they were investigating. 'Did Maggie know Deidre? And if she did, is it relevant?'

'Jack says he never heard his wife mention a Deidre. He did say she used to be an avid reader before she became fixated with Quentin Search, and she bought a lot of books second-hand. There are two possibilities. Either Maggie knew Deidre, who gave her the book. Or Deidre donated it to a charity shop or jumble sale where Maggie happened to buy it.' Wesley thought for a moment. 'I'd like to know what that book's about.'

Gerry looked sceptical. 'Think it might contain a clue?'

'It's a long shot, but who knows? I'll ask Pam,' said Wesley. 'She reads quickly and she's always looking for a new book.' He turned the paperback over and scanned the blurb on the back cover. Then he passed it to Gerry. 'Read that.'

Gerry's eyebrows shot up in surprise. 'Bit close to home,' he said.

Neil checked his phone and found another attack on his reputation by Quentin Search on Facebook. This time Dr Neil Watson was a narrow-minded bigot, hardly the way he would have described himself. Search referred to him as 'the confidence trickster in charge of the county's archaeological establishment', and the post ended with the message *Come and hear the truth they don't want you to discover,* followed by details of Search's Tradington symposium.

Neil decided to ignore it in the hope that Search would give up once he'd sold enough tickets. Besides, if he didn't hurry, he'd be late for his appointment with Colin Bowman at the mortuary in Tradmouth.

He'd arranged to meet the facial reconstruction expert from the university there, even though it was out of hours. She was a young woman with cropped blonde hair and an array of piercings, whose solemn manner seemed appropriate to the surroundings; and she made it quite clear that she was doing him a big favour. Without much ado, the unidentified corpse was taken from its fridge and the head was photographed from all angles and measurements taken with various lasers. It seemed to take a long time, but they needed to be thorough.

With any luck, he'd soon be able to send Wesley an image of the unknown woman's face. Then they might be able to give her a name.

So far the investigation into the backgrounds of the northern bell-ringers had produced nothing. Apart from a couple of minor traffic offences, they appeared to be a law-abiding bunch. 'More's the pity,' said Gerry, who'd been hoping for scandalous revelations. There was no hint of any of them having been acquainted with either of the Beatties before they arrived on St Rumon's Island. Jack Beattie was just an enthusiastic local ringer who'd done them a favour by making up the numbers.

As for Maggie, she'd probably tagged along because of Quentin Search. Search and Jocasta Adams had said they'd never seen her, but Wesley wasn't sure whether to believe them. But then, after Search's treatment of Neil, he knew his judgement might be biased.

The team had searched the Hall, but apart from the bedding in the attic, nothing had been found. Wesley asked them if they'd come across a cellar, but the officers had been told that the house didn't have one.

As yet, nothing had been found to link the occupants of Coffin Hall with either the body in the sheet or Maggie Beattie. Gerry hadn't been able to hide his disappointment.

Wesley was at his desk, going through statements from various witnesses, when he heard Paul Johnson's voice. 'Can I have a word?'

'Course you can, Paul. What can I do for you?'

'I've been looking for Kiara Search in official records. The only bank account we know about is a joint one with her husband, but her bank cards haven't been used for a year. Mind you, she might have other accounts, and if she's gone abroad ...'

'We don't even know what country she's in, so it'll take time for the various authorities to trace her, but keep trying.'

Paul paused. 'Her maiden name was Lambert. KL. The ring. It fits with her being the victim.'

'I know, but we're waiting to find out whether the daughter's DNA is a match, then we'll know for sure. Thanks, Paul. How are the wedding arrangements going?'

Wesley saw Paul's cheeks redden. 'Trish's mum's been doing all the hard work, so all I've got to do is turn up sober and on time. You've got the date in your diary, I hope. You and Mrs Peterson.'

'We're looking forward to it,' Wesley replied. 'And I know the DCI is too.'

Paul shuffled his feet. 'He told me it was about time I made an honest woman of Trish.'

Wesley laughed. 'Typical.'

He looked at the window and saw that it was almost dark outside. They'd been so engrossed in the case that he'd lost track of time. He found himself hoping that the next day would bring the breakthrough they were waiting for.

30

It was almost ten o'clock when Wesley arrived home, and the first thing he did was hand Pam the paperback found amongst Maggie Beattie's possessions, explaining how he came to have it and asking for her opinion, providing she had the time to read it. In the meantime, one of the civilian investigators on the team had volunteered to read Maggie Beattie's manuscript. Gerry said the woman deserved a medal if she managed to finish it, short as it was.

Pam flicked through the pages of the paperback. 'It's hardly *War and Peace*, so it shouldn't take me long,' she said. 'You say it was found amongst the belongings of the woman who was in my mother's creative writing group?'

'Yes. But I'd prefer it if you didn't mention it to Della. Just read through it and tell me what it's about.'

'No problem,' said Pam, depositing the book on the kitchen table. 'Is Gerry going to pay me for helping the police with their enquiries? Maybe informer's rates?'

Wesley laughed and gave her a hug just as Michael and Amelia entered the kitchen, followed as usual by the dog, Sherlock, a canine of uncertain ancestry whom Wesley had adopted following one of his cases. Sherlock was now firmly part of the family, adored by the children and tolerated by Pam, who'd ended up doing most of the walks and clearing-up duty.

'Get a room,' said Michael, wrinkling his nose in disgust at his parents' embrace.

'Shouldn't you be in bed?'

'It's the weekend tomorrow. No school.'

The lad was growing up too fast, and Amelia wasn't far behind. Wesley felt a sudden twinge of sadness at the real-isation that their innocent childhood years would soon be over, and then they'd be at the mercy of peer pressure and a world he knew from experience to be wicked.

His thoughts were interrupted by his phone's ringtone. It was Neil, and he took the call in the hall.

'Wes, just wanted to tell you the facial reconstruction's under way and should be finished soon.'

'Great,' Wesley said, suddenly hopeful that the case was about to move forward.

'I'll be on St Rumon's Island tomorrow. I've promised to have a look at the test pits the Millicombe Archaeological Society are digging on the site of the old priory. Our commercial dig at the Dukesbridge site's proved a bit disap-pointing. Just the foundations of some nineteenth-century farm buildings so far. I'd hoped we'd find some medieval or even earlier stuff underneath, but . . . Anyway, the priory will make a nice change. Unless Quentin Search organises a protest.'

'He's at his symposium this weekend.'

'That should keep him out of my hair. Might see you on the island then?'

Wesley said he probably would, as he'd be based there for the foreseeable future, and the incident room didn't close over the weekend; not with a murder to investigate.

When the call was over, he joined Pam in the living room.

'I've been thinking about that woman buried on the island,' she said as he sat down. 'Someone at work told me she used to know Deidre Charlton, the woman whose name's in that book you gave me. She went to school with her.'

This caught Wesley's attention. 'Did she say anything interesting?'

'Only that Deidre was always one for the boys – and that she hated Devon and couldn't wait to move away. Didn't her lover kill her before killing himself?'

'That's one theory.' Wesley didn't mention Greg Dearlove's suspicion that his brother might still be alive. Or that dental records had now proved that the body on St Rumon's Island wasn't Deidre. He had a sudden desire to change the subject. He wanted to escape work for just a few hours.

'One of our teaching assistants has tickets for Quentin Search's symposium,' Pam continued. 'Personally I think Search's books are a load of rubbish. The man's a total fraud.'

'You're not wrong there,' he said. But he was afraid that Search might be more than just a fraud. If his daughter's suspicions were proved right, he might also be a murderer.

The following morning, Wesley kept checking his phone for a message from Neil about the results of the facial reconstruction. But he should have known these things took time. Besides, it was Saturday; a working day for the murder team but a day of leisure for most.

He was surprised to receive a call from Pam at midday. The kids were out – Amelia at ballet and Michael at

185

football – so she'd spent all morning reading the book he'd given her. She'd done a speed-reading course while she'd been studying English at university, so it hadn't taken her long.

'What's the verdict?' he asked.

'It's not very good.' He heard a note of amusement in her voice. 'Far too many adjectives and adverbs and flowery descriptions.'

'Ignore the literary merit, what's it about?'

'It's set in the sixteenth century and is about a woman called Paloma Rome, whose wicked parents arrange her marriage. She hates the man they've chosen, who, predictably, turns out to be a wrong 'un and keeps her prisoner. One day she meets a handsome young stonemason who's working on the local church, and they fall in love. They have a few steamy scenes together, then she leaves various pieces of evidence around to suggest that she's been murdered because she's afraid the wicked husband will come after her. The stonemason confesses to her murder before faking his own death. Then they meet up, run away together and live happily ever after under new identities in London, where he works on Westminster Abbey and Queen Elizabeth I's palaces. It's sort of *Romeo and Juliet* without the tragic ending. Not a bad story, I suppose, if you're into romance. Is that any use to you?'

'I'm not sure.' It appeared to be pure romantic fantasy and Maggie had probably picked it up in a second-hand shop. And yet the plot seemed all too familiar. He thanked Pam for making the effort to read it and said he'd see her later before heading for Gerry's office.

When he told Gerry about the story found among Maggie Beattie's possessions, the DCI listened with interest, glad of the distraction from his budget forms. 'Does it ring any bells?'

'It does, Wes. Do you think Greg Dearlove could be right and Bryan's still alive? Could he have killed Deidre then faked his own death?'

'There's been no word from Barbara since we spoke to her, but the similarities to the plot can't be ignored, don't you think?'

Gerry sighed. 'We thought it was a clear-cut case at the time, and now there might be a link with our latest victim. Did Maggie Beattie know Deidre? Could she have been in on whatever went on? And if Bryan has returned from the dead, could he have killed her to stop her talking?'

This was something they hadn't considered and Wesley had to admit that it was a possibility. Which meant they needed to find Bryan, but that might be easier said than done.

Gerry thought for a while, turning his pen over and over in his fingers. 'If Bryan Dearlove does turn out to be alive, it's possible the confession to Deidre's murder was made up and she's been with him all this time.'

'The story has definite similarities. The affair; the lover confessing to the woman's murder before faking his own death. What if they got the idea from the book? If they did, it means that Deidre might still be alive as well. Pam works with someone who knew Deidre. She said she always yearned to get away from Devon.'

'Then she could be anywhere. Same goes for Kiara Search.'

'And we're wasting valuable time looking for a connection with our body in the sheet.'

Gerry leaned forward. 'Don't be hard on yourself, Wes. The book might have nothing to do with it.'

187

Before Wesley could comment, his phone told him he had a message. It was from Neil, saying he'd called in a favour and telling him to look at the attachment. His fingers became clumsy as he scrabbled to find out what it was.

He stared at the phone for a few seconds before passing it to Gerry.

'What's this?'

'The computerised facial reconstruction of the body in the sheet. Neil arranged it with the university. They've been quicker than I expected, but then I don't understand all the mysteries of technology. What do you think?'

Wesley returned to his desk to fetch his laptop so the image would be easier to see. He and Gerry both studied the enlarged face. They hadn't seen a photograph of Ginevra Search's missing mother, but the woman in the picture was nothing like he'd imagined Search's wife to look. Her face was rather plain, with small eyes, straight brown hair, a large nose and a prominent chin. She was no beauty. And she didn't resemble anyone who'd featured in the case so far.

31

As if on cue, Gerry's phone rang and he switched on the speaker so that Wesley could hear what was being said. It was the lab, telling them there was no DNA match between Ginevra Search and the mystery body.

'So now we can rule out Kiara Search,' said Gerry. 'It looks as though we're back to square one.'

'At least we now know what the victim looked like,' said Wesley.

'That's something. We'd better get this picture circulated. Somebody must know who she is.'

'Well we know who she isn't.' Wesley began to count them off on his fingers. 'She isn't Carl Shultz's long-lost half sister. Nor is she Kiara Search, née Lambert. And she's not Deidre Charlton as we first suspected. I'll ask the press office to give this picture to the local TV news and social media. Then we'll show it to everyone on St Rumon's Island, and if we have no luck, we'll show it to all the people who've stayed there over the past couple of years.'

'Someone must be missing her. No man is an island. Who said that?'

'"No man is an island, entire of itself". John Donne. He lived around the time Elias Anselmo lived at Coffin Hall.'

Gerry rolled his eyes. 'I can always rely on you for a spot of culture, Wes. I've heard from Tom in Scientific Support, too. Nothing very interesting on Maggie Beattie's computer apart from the book she's writing and a load of stuff about Quentin Search and his theories. Talking of Search, let's go and rattle his cage. And we can show the picture to Ginevra while we're there. You never know, she might recognise the woman.'

Their route across the island to Coffin Hall took them past the church, where blue-and-white crime-scene tape still fluttered around the place Maggie Beattie's body had been found. Wesley could see activity in the distance. A group of people standing in the field beyond the church. He recognised Neil among them, with Dave standing along-side in his distinctive hat. Neil appeared to be addressing the assembled group – probably briefing the amateur archaeologists before the excavation began. Wesley hoped Quentin Search wouldn't attempt to interfere.

Gerry interrupted his thoughts. 'Aren't they ringing the bells today?'

'Yes, they're supposed to resume today but I heard that Jack Beattie's changed his mind about taking part so they're waiting until they can get a replacement from amongst the local ringers.'

'Well, it's OK with me, provided they still feel up to it.'

As they passed the church, they saw the Reverend Charlie emerging from the porch, her hair blowing about in the stiff breeze. As soon as she saw them, she waved. 'Chief Inspector, Inspector. Just the people I wanted to see. Have there been any developments?'

Wesley could see the anxiety on her face. A shocking crime had intruded into her world and she needed to see things set right. He took out his phone, brought up the facial reconstruction and passed it to her. 'Do you recognise this woman?'

She shook her head. 'No. Why? Who is she?'

'She's the woman whose body you found.'

Charlie looked shocked as she stared at the phone. 'Poor woman. It seems all the more real when you know what someone looks like, doesn't it? I'm sorry I can't help you, but I haven't been here long, so ...'

'Thanks anyway.'

They were about to carry on walking when she spoke again. 'I visited Jack Beattie again this morning.' She glanced in the direction of Coffin Hall, just visible in the distance behind a copse of trees. 'I believe poor Maggie was obsessed with Quentin Search's books.' She lowered her voice. 'I know it's not very Christian of me to say so, but if you ask me, Search isn't a nice man. There's something about him – a terrible arrogance.'

'We've met him,' said Gerry.

'Then you'll know what I mean.' She took a deep breath, as though she was trying to banish the image of the dead woman's face from her mind. 'I'm just going to have a word with the northern ringers – see how they're faring. In the circumstances, Matt Evans and his wife have decided to abandon their champing for the time being and have moved to a B&B in Midton. It's not straightforward to replace Jack, apparently, because a lot of Devon towers only do call changes – whatever that means – and they need someone who's able to ring their methods. It's such a shame, because they really wanted to ring their peals on the island, and Matt loved the idea of champing. Perhaps when all this has blown over, I'll make it a regular thing for visitors. Bring in some much-needed funds for the church.'

'Great idea,' said Gerry.

They said their farewells and walked on. The wind had grown stronger and they pulled their coats close to keep out the chill. Wesley hoped the weather would soon improve. But unlike in his parents' native Trinidad, the only thing that was predictable about the Devon weather was that it couldn't be predicted.

When they arrived at the Hall, the builder's van was outside again. They hadn't been told exactly what Scott Helivant was doing there, but a house that age was bound to need a lot of maintenance. All attempts to trace a builder called George had failed, suggesting he was no longer working. And when Scott had been spoken to, he'd denied all knowledge of a purple sheet. He was there to do his job, not to poke around among his employer's personal possessions.

Gerry knocked on the door and Ginevra answered, saying she'd seen them arrive from her bedroom window.

'Good news, love,' said Gerry gently. 'We've had the DNA results back and that body we found definitely isn't your mum.'

'Oh.' She didn't look as pleased by the news as Wesley would have expected.

'Is your dad in? Or Jocasta?'

Ginevra shook her head. 'They're in Tradington. The symposium starts today. My father's been having another go at that archaeologist, Dr Watson, on social media, but he's only doing it to sell tickets. He says controversy brings in the cash,' she said with a cynicism Wesley hadn't seen in her before. 'If I was Dr Watson, I'd sue for slander – or is it libel?'

'He's a friend of mine and I doubt if he could pay for the lawyers,' said Wesley.

'Unlike my father, who's got tame ones at his beck and call. He's such a bastard,' she added under her breath. 'What did you want to see him about?'

Wesley knew he should have remembered that the symposium was starting that day, but he put it down to brain overload. He caught Gerry's eye as he produced his phone. 'I was going to ask your father if he recognised this woman.'

'I wouldn't ask him anything. You won't get a straight answer out of him.'

'Have you ever seen her before?'

He handed her the phone and, like the Reverend Charlie before her, she studied it closely. Then a look of recognition appeared on her face.

'This looks like Edith.'

'Who?'

'She was my father's assistant before Jocasta came on the scene – his dogsbody really: admin, housekeeping, whatever he could think of. And as soon as he found out she used to be a teacher, he asked her to give me some tuition so he didn't have to send me to school. I kicked up a fuss at first because I wanted to live a normal life and I couldn't stand the thought of being stuck in this mausoleum seeing nobody my own age. But I ended up spending most of my time with Edith and I got really close to her. She was easy to talk to if you know what I mean.'

'I know,' said Wesley. 'Why did Edith leave the Hall?'

'She had to look after her elderly mother, who hadn't been given long to live.'

'When was that?'

'About eighteen months ago.' Wesley saw tears forming in her eyes. She wiped them away with the back of her hand.

'When did you last hear from her?'

She thought for a moment. 'We spoke on the phone regularly, then around a year ago she called to tell me her mother had just passed away. She promised to keep in touch, but I never heard from her again. I tried her number but there was no answer.'

'How did your father get on with her?'

'As long as she kept me out of trouble, he wasn't bothered. Edith didn't treat me like a nuisance like my own mother did. Kiara was a waste of space and I wasn't sorry when she walked out on my father.' Her hand went to her mouth. 'Does that sound terrible?'

'No.' Wesley's answer was honest. He knew from his own children that teenagers needed a sympathetic ear, and it sounded as though Edith had provided that in Ginevra's case.

There was a long silence before she spoke again. 'After Edith left, I went to the local college hoping to do my A levels, but ... '

'What happened?'

'I had a breakdown,' she said simply. 'I was really hurt when Edith didn't answer her phone when I tried to call her. Even she let me down,' she added bitterly.

'I'm so sorry, Ginevra,' said Wesley gently. 'There's no easy way to say this, but this face is a computerised reconstruction. It belongs to that body found on the beach. I'm afraid you couldn't contact Edith because she was dead.'

Journal of the Reverend Thomas Nescombe

July 1574

A wet nurse was hired from the village of Midton and the child thrives. My wife named him Thomas after me, yet I cannot bring myself to look at him. She is sorely distressed by my coldness and claims she does not know the reason for it, but I cannot help my feelings on the matter. The boy is not mine but is the product of my wife's adultery with a man known as a follower of the Devil. A betrayer who was responsible for the terrible death of a saintly man. I pray and pray over the matter yet I still cannot forgive.

I no longer share Anne's bed, but last night she came to me weeping.

'You have been so cold towards me since our son was born. You will not even speak to me.'

'There is nothing to say.'

'But there is. There is a confession I must make.' She knelt by the bed on the hard floorboards.

At last, I thought, she is about to admit the truth. But her words were not as I expected.

'You are a man of God, so I was ashamed to tell you. Our son was brought about by magic.'

195

'What foolishness is this?' I snapped.

She bowed her head. 'We had been married three years with no sign of a child. Then I heard talk that Elias Anselmo had certain powers. I visited him and underwent rituals.'

I could contain my fury no longer. 'Rituals that involved you lying with him.'

'No,' she cried. 'You are mistaken. I did no such thing. He performed magic in his cellar, then when I thought I was with child he told me to take herbs to the cliff and offer them to the sea to raise the land of Lyonesse. He gave me words to chant. There was a storm, but the lost land did not appear.'

I heard the ring of truth in her words. And yet my pride would not let me acknowledge my error.

'I resorted to summoning spirits to help me in my plight. Can you forgive me?'

I did not know what to say.

32

They needed to find out everything they could about Edith Craven. All they knew was that she had left Quentin Search's employment eighteen months ago to care for her dying mother. She'd called Ginevra around six months later to say that her mother had passed away, but after that Ginevra had heard nothing further from the woman who had become a trusted figure to the vulnerable teenager.

Ginevra was clearly upset about Edith, but at the same time Wesley detected a fresh confidence in the girl, as though being treated as an important witness had distracted her from her troubles. She told them that Edith had left the Hall on Bonfire Night, and that she'd seen bright fireworks on the mainland as she'd watched her put her luggage into the boot of a taxi. She'd promised to keep in regular touch, and for a while she'd kept her word.

'Did you have her address?'

Ginevra shook her head. 'There was no need because we always spoke on the phone, although she didn't have a mobile, just a landline.' She gave a sad smile. 'She was a bit old-fashioned that way. I should have asked for her address but I never got round to it. I never thought ... ' She fell silent, her eyes glassy with tears.

'Did she live here in the house when she worked for your father?'

'Yes. He wanted her on call. Although she went off to visit her mother from time to time.' A tear trickled down her cheek. 'Who on earth would want to kill Edith? I don't understand. She always stood up for me and she never harmed anyone in her life.'

'That's what we're trying to find out, love,' said Gerry. 'Is there anything else you can tell us? Anything at all? Who else was around at the time Edith left?'

Ginevra considered the question. 'My father and Kiara – she hated being called Mother. Not Jocasta – she arrived a few weeks later to take Edith's job.' She frowned, trying to remember.

'Scott the builder?'

'He's been here on and off for a while, but I can't be sure whether he was here at the time Edith left.' She took a tissue from her pocket to wipe her eyes.

Gerry gave Wesley a small nod. It was time they left the girl alone with her thoughts and grief. They had to speak to Quentin Search again as a matter of urgency. But Scott the builder might have known Edith Craven too. And he was there on the premises, so it was a good place to start.

When DC Rob Carter approached Rachel's desk, she hoped he was about to tell her something interesting that would distract her from her paperwork.

'I've been checking out those bell-ringers, Sarge. The ones from up north.' He placed a printout on the desk in front of her. 'They led us to believe that none of them had any connection with the area, but this one was brought up in Neston.'

Rachel studied the printout. 'He moved up to Cheshire when he was ten,' she said, disappointed.

'It's still a connection. Want to talk to him? He's still staying in that cottage on the island.'

Rachel reread the details. 'Eddie Culpepper, aged twenty-six, IT professional, boyfriend of one of the other ringers, Ruth Selby. I can't see him as an obvious suspect, but you're right, Rob. We should have a word.' She gave him an encouraging smile.

The young DC walked away. He used to irritate her, but since his partner's death, the spark had gone out of his eyes. Once he would have crowed with triumph at spotting a possible lead. Now, though, his shoulders were hunched, and as Rachel watched him return to his desk, she felt sad.

'Mr Helivant?'

The builder swung round, startled, a plaster-caked bucket in his hand. When he saw Wesley and Gerry standing there, he put the bucket in his van and rearranged his features into an expression of helpful co-operation.

'Bloody hell, you gave me a fright. What can I do for you?'

'We think you might be able to help us.'

'I've already given a statement. I've never seen that sheet before in my life. I just do my job, pack up and go home, and that's what I'm about to do now.'

'Do you remember a woman who used to work here – Edith Craven? She was Mr Search's assistant and left his employment eighteen months ago.' Wesley produced the picture on his phone and held it in front of Scott's face. The builder's hands were filthy with plaster dust, so Wesley didn't want him to touch it. Scott peered at it for a while before answering.

'It could be her. On the other hand, it could be a lot of people. I didn't have much to do with her; only saw her around, if you know what I mean.'

'You didn't talk to her?'

'No. Can't help you. Sorry.' He didn't sound very sorry, but his answer wasn't particularly surprising. It was unlikely that he would have had much contact with Search's assistant.

'And you don't know anything about Maggie Beattie, the woman who died in the churchyard?'

'A policeman's already been round asking the same question, and I'll tell you what I told him. I saw her and I told her Quentin wasn't here, but that was it. She left and I don't know what she did after that. But it's a terrible thing to happen,' he added. 'You're not safe anywhere nowadays.'

'Thank you, Mr Helivant,' said Wesley. 'We might want to talk to you again.'

'No problem.'

He had the feeling that the builder had been lying to them.

33

Gerry burst into the incident room like a human hurricane, Wesley following in his wake.

'We've got an ID for our body in the sheet,' he announced to the assembled officers. 'She was a Miss Edith Craven, who was employed as Quentin Search's assistant-cum-dogsbody at Coffin Hall. She worked there for about three years before leaving eighteen months ago to look after her dying mum. Ginevra Search was in regular touch with her for six months after she left, then all contact suddenly ceased. I think we can guess why, can't we? She was buried here on the island in a sheet from the Hall, so either she went back there for some reason without Ginevra being aware of it, or her body was brought over and dumped there.'

Trish Walton raised her hand. 'Can we rule Ginevra out, sir?' she asked.

'I'm pretty sure she knows nothing about it. But we can't yet say the same about her father,' said Wesley. 'We need to find out more about Edith Craven as a matter of urgency. We haven't got an address for her yet, so we need that asap.' He looked at Paul Johnson. 'Paul, will you go over to Tradington and see if you can find Search. Ask him for chapter and verse on Edith. And don't let him fob you off.'

Paul grinned. 'I won't, sir.'

Wesley followed the DCI into his temporary office. 'Do you think we should regard Search as our number one suspect?'

'Don't you, Wes?'

'It would please Neil no end if we arrested him.'

'You can't arrest someone for conning people with made-up fairy tales and insulting archaeologists.'

'If we could, Search would be in for a long stretch,' said Wesley with a laugh. Then he remembered something. 'To change the subject, Mrs Wallace, the hall's previous owner, said she used to employ a builder called George.'

'We haven't managed to trace him yet, but it was such a long time ago that I can't see how it's relevant.'

'I just thought he might be someone else who had access to the house and the sheet.'

'If he hasn't worked at the Hall since the Wallaces' day, I can't see him bumping off Edith Craven, can you? But I suppose we should leave no stone unturned.'

Before Wesley could answer, Rachel rushed in, She had news. Rob Carter had discovered that Eddie Culpepper, one of the bell-ringers, had links with the area he hadn't mentioned in his statement.

'Why would he hide the fact that he'd lived round here?' she asked. 'What if it wasn't the first time he'd met Maggie Beattie?'

'Good question, Rach,' said Gerry with an approving nod.

The quest to find out everything they could about Edith Craven had begun. Ginevra thought she was living in Dukesbridge, so the electoral register was being scoured and owners of rental properties were being contacted, as were local estate agents in case Edith had decided to move house after her mother's death.

Paul Johnson looked crestfallen when he returned to the incident room. When he'd arrived at Tradington Hall, where the symposium was being held, there'd been no sign of Quentin Search or Jocasta Adams, although the audience had still been milling around, chattering about the talk they'd just heard. The place was filled with publicity material: stands piled with Search's books manned by earnest young people in black. They'd been doing a roaring trade.

Paul had been told by a woman who was tidying the stage that the Searches had gone off to Exeter to meet someone from his publicity team and that they might be back later.

'Anyone would think they're trying to avoid us,' was Gerry's instant reply when Paul broke the news. 'Keep trying. We're legally entitled to make a nuisance of ourselves and we really need to speak to him again.'

Trish Walton had spent a long time on the phone to taxi companies, asking whether any of their drivers remembered picking up a fare from Coffin Island on 5 November the year before last. And if so, had the passenger made a return journey six months later? It was a long time ago, but she imagined the journey would stick in the driver's mind, as they'd need to be aware of the tides. She'd received various promises to make enquiries, but was warned it might take time so she'd have to be patient.

In the meantime, Gerry wanted to speak to Eddie Culpepper. Wesley pointed out that as the young man had left Devon when he was ten years old, he might not have thought his connection to the area was relevant.

'Even so, Wes, I don't like it when people don't tell us the truth, the whole truth and nothing but the truth.'

'Unfortunately that's an occupational hazard in our job.'

'True, but honest bell-ringers aren't supposed to tell us porkies.'

Wesley knew better than to argue. Once the DCI had an idea in his head, it was hard to shift it. But before he could arrange to speak to Eddie Culpepper, a message came through from Tradington. Quentin Search was back.

Search might have managed to intimidate Neil, even though Neil's pride would make him deny it, but he couldn't intimidate a pair of senior police officers. Gerry claimed that he'd eaten worse than Search for breakfast and he wasn't going to let him slip through his fingers this time. He sent a local uniform round to order him to stay put until he and Wesley could get there.

When they arrived, they found Search pacing impatiently to and fro in a side room off the main hall.

'You've chosen an awkward time,' he said as the two detectives were shown in by a thin young man in a black T-shirt with an image of Search's latest book cover emblazoned on the front.

'Sorry, sir,' said Gerry. 'But we are investigating two murders.' He nodded to Wesley, who held out his phone. 'Do you recognise this woman?'

Search took the phone in his fingertips as though he feared it was contaminated and studied it for a few moments.

His bored expression became a puzzled frown. 'It looks like Edith, my former assistant. Where did you get this?'

'It's a computerised reconstruction of the face of the woman found wrapped in that purple sheet from your attic,' said Wesley, watching Search's face carefully. For the first time, the man appeared to be lost for words.

'I ... I don't know what to say. It's impossible. Edith left my employment around eighteen months ago to care for her elderly mother. I believe Ginevra kept in touch with her for a while.'

'Your daughter told us Edith broke off all contact about a year ago.'

'She never mentioned that to me.' Search slumped into the nearest chair. He looked like a man in shock.

'When did you last see Edith?'

'On the day she left. She took a taxi to Dukesbridge.'

'She must have left a forwarding address.'

He shrugged. 'Ginevra might have it. To tell the truth, I was annoyed with Edith. She left me at a most inconvenient time. I needed my manuscript typed, you see. She let me down.'

'Her mother was ill.' Gerry's words came out in a growl.

'I'm sure she could have got someone else to look after her – or put her in a home.'

Gerry and Wesley looked at each other.

'Did she ever return to the island after her mother passed away?'

'Not as far as I know. She had no reason to. Jocasta had taken over her job by then. Ginevra might know more.'

'Why's that?' Wesley asked.

'She really liked Edith – became very upset when she left.'

'How do you think Edith ended up buried on the island?' Gerry asked.

Search shook his head. 'It's a mystery to me. As far as I was concerned, she left me and I soon found a replacement. Fortunately Ginevra was old enough not to need a tutor by then.'

'Did Jocasta ever meet her predecessor?'

Search's cheeks turned red. 'No. She never met Edith. She knows nothing.'

'Your wife was living at the Hall when Edith worked for you?'

'Yes.'

'How did the two women get on?'

'They didn't have much to do with each other.'

'But Edith was close to your daughter?'

'Kiara had her own life and took very little interest in what Ginevra got up to. I'm afraid my ex-wife didn't have a maternal bone in her body.'

'And you definitely haven't seen Edith since she left your employment eighteen months ago.'

'That's right. Look, it's terrible news, but I've told you everything I know.' Search made a show of looking at his watch. 'Now if you'll excuse me, I have an audience waiting.'

Wesley knew when they were being dismissed.

'Believe him?' Gerry asked as they pushed open the heavy doors leading to the outside world.

'Not sure.'

'Mind you, I can't think why he'd want to kill her, can you?'

'Unless she knew something incriminating about him. Unless Ginevra's right and her mother is dead and she's just not been found yet. What's next?'

'We need to speak to Eddie Culpepper.'

34

Eddie Culpepper and his fiancée, Ruth Selby, were staying in one of the island's holiday cottages, and Wesley and Gerry spoke to the couple in the bland but comfortable lounge.

They took the sofa while Culpepper perched nervously on the edge of one of the armchairs. Ruth asked if anyone wanted coffee. When they declined politely, she looked disappointed and sat on the arm of Eddie's armchair.

'I've already made a statement and I really can't add anything more,' he began before the detectives had a chance to speak.

'We asked if anyone had connections with this area, and you failed to mention that you were brought up in Neston,' said Wesley pleasantly.

For a few seconds Culpepper's eyes widened, and Wesley wondered whether this was panic at being found out or surprise that something so trivial should bring about a visit from the police.

'I . . . I didn't think it was important. I thought you meant the island.'

'Which was it?' said Gerry sharply.

'Both, I suppose. '

'So it wasn't a deliberate lie?' said Wesley, playing good cop.

'Of course not. My family moved to Cheshire when I was ten. I don't remember much about Devon, so I didn't think it was worth mentioning. I'd never met Maggie Beattie before we came here.'

There was something honest about the young man's protestations, and Wesley felt some sympathy for him. 'Do you still know people down here? Relatives, for instance?' If there was a connection with the Beatties, however tenuous, he wanted to know about it.

'My dad has a cousin in Tavistock,' Eddie said. 'But he's a lot older than me. He's married with kids and we haven't seen them for years.' He paused. 'And there's an aunt – my mother's cousin, actually, although they're not in contact very often. Mum always calls her "the maiden aunt". You know, the sort that Jane Austen wrote about.'

Wesley smiled. 'I didn't think they made them like that any more.'

'They probably don't. It's just my mum's little joke. She says she regrets not keeping in touch more with the Craven side of the family and she suggested that I should look her up while I'm down here and introduce her to Ruth, since we're getting married in six months' time. But I'm afraid I've been busy, so I haven't got round to it yet.' He smiled. 'Family duty and all that.'

'You said Craven.'

'That was my mum's maiden name.'

Gerry leaned forward. 'What are your relatives' names?'

'There was an Aunt Mary my mum used to mention, but she died about a year ago. Her daughter, Mum's cousin, is called Edith.'

Wesley heard a sharp intake of breath from Gerry.

'Was she a teacher?'

'That's right.' Eddie looked surprised, as though Wesley had made a lucky guess. 'I remember Mum saying she taught in a private school for a few years. Then it closed down and she went to work for a writer, but she had to give up her job because her mother was very ill. She wrote to Mum to tell her that Mary had died.'

There was a long silence while Wesley selected the photo of the facial reconstruction on his phone and passed it to Eddie.

'Could this be Edith?'

The young man studied the image, a slight frown on his face as though he was concentrating hard. Eventually he looked up. 'I haven't seen her since I was small, but it could be her.' He passed the phone back to Wesley. 'Why?'

'Do you remember the storm on Monday night – the first night you spent on the island?'

'Of course. It broke the flagpole on top of the church tower.'

'It also brought down a section of the cliff.'

'Yes, it disturbed some burials. The police came round asking questions.'

'Two of the burials dated back centuries. But one was a woman who died around a year ago. According to our pathologist, she was murdered, then buried on the edge of the churchyard in a shallow grave.'

Eddie looked puzzled. 'I don't see what it's got to do with us.'

'The picture I showed you is a computer reconstruction of the victim's face, and we have reason to believe that her name was Edith Craven. I'm really sorry, Eddie, but I think it could be your relative.'

The young man gasped. 'You must have got it wrong. Who'd want to kill somebody like Auntie Edith?'

'When was the last time your mother or anyone in your family had any contact with her?'

He thought for a while. 'Like I said, she wrote to Mum to say her mother had died. I think that must have been around a year ago.' He closed his eyes as though he was trying to remember something. After a few seconds, they flicked open again. 'Come to think of it, Mum did mention that she didn't have a Christmas card from Edith last year. But the post was very bad so she just assumed it had got lost.'

'So your mother hasn't heard from her for over a year?'

Eddie nodded. 'That's right.'

Wesley and Gerry looked at each other. It was all starting to fit together. 'Do you have Edith's address?'

'Yes, Mum gave it to me when she suggested I pay her a visit.' Eddie consulted his phone and recited an address in Dukesbridge.

'Did Edith tell your mum much about her job with the author?'

'Oh yes. She liked working as his assistant. I think there was a teenage daughter too, but to be honest, I didn't take that much interest.'

'You didn't know the job was on St Rumon's Island?'

He raised his eyebrows in surprise. 'Was it? I assumed it was near where she lived. My mum would probably be able to tell you more.'

'We may need to speak to you again. When are you planning to leave?'

'Not until next week. The Reverend Charlie said we can do our last two peals at St Petroc's on the mainland if we'd rather not ring at St Rumon's, but I think Matt would rather we carry on here if possible, providing we can find someone to replace Jack. After that we're planning to ring with a few local bands. They do some mean call changes around here.'

'I'll take your word for it. You're really dedicated, aren't you?' said Gerry.

Eddie gave a weak smile. 'Ringing's quite addictive when you get into it. We've had other outings – did Norfolk last year.'

'Keeps you off the streets, I suppose,' Gerry said cheerfully. Then his face became solemn. 'Look, we're sorry about your auntie. Must have come as a shock.'

'You can say that again. I should call my mum – she'll need to know.'

'Of course. Unless you'd prefer us to do it. We'd like to speak to her anyway.'

'No. It'd be better coming from me.'

When they all stood up, Wesley touched Eddie's sleeve. 'Death always comes as a shock,' he said. 'Even when it's expected. But this ... Take care, won't you.'

'Where to now?' Gerry said once they were outside.

'Edith Craven's address. With any luck, we'll find some answers there.'

35

Wesley and Gerry drove straight to the address Eddie
Culpepper had given them. Secretly Wesley hoped Ginevra
had made a mistake with the ID and the door would be
opened to them by a puzzled Edith, wondering what on
earth the police were doing on her doorstep.

The flat was in a low-rise modern block overlooking
the river and Dukesbridge's main car park, not far from
the library and the tourist information office. Gerry, ever
resourceful, gained access to the communal hallway by
trying a number of flats and claiming he had a delivery.
As soon as someone buzzed them into the building, they
made straight for Flat 13 at the end of a corridor on the
ground floor.

'Unlucky for some,' Gerry said as he rapped on the door.

'Wonder if anyone has a spare key,' said Wesley.

'No need for that,' said Gerry, pulling on his
crime-scene gloves.

Wesley knew what was coming next, so he looked round
to make sure nobody was watching. Many years ago, Gerry
had acquired a set of skeleton keys, claiming they'd been
a gift from a grateful housebreaker. Wesley had been
shocked at first. But over the years he'd come to realise that

they came in very useful on occasions. As long as the chief super didn't find out.

It only took Gerry half a minute to unlock the door, and when they walked in to the flat, the air was still and stale, as though nobody had lived there for a while. They went from room to room, calling out Miss Craven's name in case they'd got it all wrong and they found the woman cowering in a corner, shocked by the intrusion of two male strangers.

But the place was empty, and it looked as though it had been for a good while. Everything was neat and tidy; a place for everything and everything in its place, as Gerry put it. In some ways it looked as though the occupant had recently stepped out to do some shopping or visit one of the neighbouring flats, but a layer of dust coated every surface and when they reached the kitchen it was clear that nobody had been in there for a very long time.

The unsliced loaf on the wooden bread board was green with mould, and a half-finished cup of something next to the draining board was similarly coated. Wesley put on his crime-scene gloves before opening the fridge, where he found the contents covered with green fur.

'Takes a while to grow penicillin like that, Wes,' said Gerry.

They made their way to the bedroom. Whereas everywhere else hinted at the occupier of the flat being fastidious, here the duvet was askew and one of the pillows had been thrown to the foot of the bed. Wesley left everything *in situ*, but studied the pillow carefully without disturbing it.

'Feathers,' he whispered to Gerry, who grasped his meaning immediately and took his mobile phone from his pocket. 'Colin found a feather in the dead woman's airway.'

'I'm calling the crime-scene people. We need this flat sealed off and examined.' Once Gerry had made the call, he spoke again. 'Why waste time, Wes? Now we're here, let's have a word with the neighbours.'

Wesley nodded. If there'd been any doubt before, he knew now that they were on the right track. Someone had killed Miss Edith Craven, possibly here in the flat. Then they had taken her to Coffin Island and buried her in a shallow grave.

They started with the flats on the same corridor. There was no answer from two of them, but the door of the one adjacent to Miss Craven's was opened by an elderly gentleman. He was tall, with a shock of silver hair and a military bearing. Unexpectedly, he was cradling a white Persian cat in his arms, reminding Wesley of a Bond villain. He introduced himself as Major Eric Fowler, then invited the detectives in and offered them tea.

'We'd like to ask you about your neighbour, Miss Craven,' said Wesley once they were settled in the spick-and-span living room. Here everything was arranged with military precision, making Edith Craven's flat look positively homely.

'Why? What's she done? Somehow I can't see her as the criminal type, although appearances can be deceptive,' Major Fowler said with a smile playing on his lips. 'Not that I know the lady well. She moved in eighteen months ago to care for old Mrs Craven, who'd lived here a number of years. I've always found Edith a very pleasant woman. Quiet. The perfect neighbour, I suppose.'

'When was the last time you saw her?'

'She tootled off on a world cruise a couple of weeks after her mother's funeral and I haven't seen her since.' His eyes narrowed. 'I take it she's not safely sailing the seven seas and dining at the captain's table, or you wouldn't be here.'

The man was sharp, and there was no point dressing up the reality in euphemisms or tactful words.

'We believe Miss Craven has been murdered.'

Wesley saw a look of horrified disbelief on the Major's face.

'What happened? Was she killed on her travels? A street robbery? The poor woman was hardly the type to go around dripping with jewellery or laden with Rolex watches, so who would want to do such a thing?'

'We think she might have been killed closer to home; possibly even in her flat. Her body was found on an island nearby.'

'St Rumon's Island? I saw on the local news that they'd found an unidentified body there, but I never connected...' The Major sank into his armchair. 'I really can't believe she was killed here. Surely someone would have heard something.' He pointed to the hearing aid he was wearing. 'Although I run into technical difficulties from time to time. One of the trials of old age.'

'What about your other neighbours? Do you know them well?'

'Not very neighbourly, and out at work all day. Young professionals, I believe they're called. You see them going out in their running gear after work. Nothing wrong with a brisk walk, that's what I say.'

'Did any of them have much to do with Miss Craven?'

He shook his head. 'Dear me, no. I was the only one Edith passed the time of day with. Nice lady. I was quite sad when she went off travelling.' He paused. 'She used to work for an author, you know.'

'Quentin Search.'

'That's the chap. She lived in, but when her mother became too frail to care for herself, she left to come back here. She told me she'd enjoyed her job – and I think there was a member of the family she was fond of.'

'Quentin Search's daughter?'

'Might have been.' He frowned. 'To be honest, I was very surprised when Edith went off without saying anything to me. We'd always been on friendly terms. Not that we lived in each other's pockets, of course. Just invited each other in for the occasional cup of tea.'

'When was the last time you saw her?'

The Major considered the question for a few moments. 'I think it was on a Sunday. I was on my way to church, and we passed in the corridor and exchanged a few words about the weather.'

'She didn't mention that she was going on a cruise?'

'No, although she had said she was keen to go on more holidays now that she had no ties and while she was still fit enough. I told her to go for it. You only live once.'

'Then how did you find out that was where she'd gone?' Wesley watched the Major closely, eager to hear his answer.

There was a long silence while the man closed his eyes, his forehead furrowed in concentration. Eventually his eyes flicked open and he raised a finger. 'The workman. He told me. He said she'd gone off on a world cruise and she wanted some jobs doing while she was away. Nice young chap.'

'Do you know his name?' Wesley held his breath, awaiting the answer. If it was the one he expected, he'd found a link.

'I saw his van parked outside. It had a name on it, but my eyes are the same as my ears – not what they were, sadly. He asked me if I needed anything doing.' A smile spread across his lined face. 'I think he gave me his business card. Bear with me.'

He disappeared into another room, and Wesley and Gerry waited in silence for him to return.

It seemed an age before the Major came back holding a small rectangular card. He gave it to Gerry, who read it with a look of triumph on his face before passing it to Wesley.

'Scott Helivant. Always knew he was a wrong 'un.'

'Did you?' said Wesley, giving the DCI a sideways look.

Gerry went out into the corridor to set things in motion, leaving Wesley to thank the Major for his help. His gratitude was sincere. For the first time since the Reverend Charlie found the body on the beach on St Rumon's Island, he felt optimistic.

The second coat of lime plaster, the float coat, had just gone onto the wall of the old stables. Quentin Search planned to transform the building into an exhibition space, but for now it was a building site and it was hard to imagine it as anything else. The skim coat would go on next, and then it would be a matter of leaving the plaster to dry before it could be painted.

Plastering took considerable skill, a skill Scott Helivant had learned at an early age from his father, who'd been a tough teacher, sometimes a frightening one; far stricter than the teachers he'd known at school – when he'd bothered to go in. Scott had never seen the point of school.

While he'd been learning from his father, he'd been terrified of getting anything wrong. Once his father had punched him for making a mess of the scratch coat, the first layer to go on the wall. Since then, Scott had made sure there were no more mistakes.

He needed to clear up his things. If he didn't hurry, he'd miss the tide and wouldn't be able to get the van back over to the mainland. The last thing he wanted was to be stuck on the island.

He heard a voice and looked round.

Ten minutes later, a body was lying on the cold cobbles of the stable floor with its head stuck in the bucket of solidifying plaster.

Journal of the Reverend Thomas Nescombe

October 1574

The summer is gone and the storms have returned. I am reconciled with my wife, who continues to swear that she never had carnal knowledge of another man. I now believe her, especially as all who see the babe say that he resembles me greatly. And yet, as a man of the cloth, it is hard to forget that my own son might have come about through evil spells. But could such a good thing ever come out of evil? I do not have the answer to that question.

It pleased me greatly when Talitha Sellars came into my little household as nursemaid to young Thomas. She has a clear affection for the child, who appears to return it with wide, toothless grins each time she enters the room. When Anne picks him up, he cries bitterly, but Talitha has only to touch his tiny hand and he calms straight away. It is as though the girl possesses some magic trick, and it is wonderful to see.

Today my wife left the house without telling anybody in the household where she was bound. I thought nothing of this until I heard the maid saying she'd seen her mistress near St Rumon's Hall.

219

I do not wish her to go there again or to have further dealings with Elias Anselmo.

36

Ginevra Search needed a distraction to numb the pain of Edith's death, so she went over to watch the archaeologists. She'd expected a dig to be more exciting. The Indiana Jones films made it look positively thrilling, but the reality involved lots of people squatting beside a series of small square holes in the muddy field behind the church, scraping at the soil with trowels. Every so often one of them would take something they'd found over to show to a man who appeared to be offering advice. Apart from that, it was like watching the plaster dry in the old stables.

The man in charge looked as she'd expected an archaeologist to look. She knew his name was Dr Neil Watson and that he'd been the target of her father's spiteful campaign of defamation. He had long fair hair and an attractive, intelligent face; he wasn't bad-looking even though he was a bit old. He went from hole to hole to chat with the volunteers as though he was genuinely interested. No superiority, no pulling rank, and even though she'd never exchanged a word with him, she found herself liking him. Or perhaps this was because he was the person her father had appointed as his unwitting arch-enemy; the academic world that scoffed at his crazy theories made flesh.

The suspicion that her father had been responsible for Edith's death was developing into a certainty. What if Edith had returned to the house to see her and Quentin had killed her because she'd seen something she wasn't supposed to see? Perhaps he'd murdered Kiara, and Edith had either witnessed it or stumbled across something incriminating. What if Jocasta had been in on it too? What if that was what bound them together?

After a few minutes she'd seen enough of the excavation, and she knew Quentin and Jocasta were safely in Tradington, spouting nonsense and basking in the adoration of his fans, so she began to walk back to the Hall, glancing to her right as she passed the church. There were no bells today. To her surprise, she'd enjoyed hearing them, a cheerful sound on the island where the only birdsong was the screeching of seagulls. Anything that gave the place some life was welcome.

When she arrived in the courtyard, she saw that Scott's van was still there. She wasn't sure how she felt about the builder. Like Dr Watson, he was far too old for her, but she'd noticed the way he looked at her. She'd heard he was married, but he'd never mentioned his wife during all the time she'd stood there watching him work for want of anything better to do.

The back doors of the van were wide open, which meant Scott couldn't be far away. Any minute now he'd come out of the stables to fetch some messy piece of equipment. He'd told her all about plastering, how it wasn't just a skill, it was almost an art. He'd told her about the different coats needed for a perfect finish and the different kinds of plaster. He'd made it sound interesting.

She entered the house and made for her room, intending

to read. But after ten minutes her book lost its appeal and she felt the need for some company, any company, so she went outside and approached the open door to the stables. When she walked into the building, she saw that one wall had been finished, a perfect, flawless sea of off-white. The others were still rough, awaiting their finishing coat. There was no sign of Scott. She called his name, but there was no answer.

She wandered further into the building, looking round, and called Scott's name again. As she reached the old stalls where horses had once been kept, she spotted something on the floor. A shoe; a scruffy old trainer with a leg attached to it. Suddenly frightened, she approached cautiously.

When she was little, she'd visited a circus where she'd seen a clown run around the ring with his head in a bucket. Everyone had laughed. But this was no laughing matter. This bucket had been full of wet plaster, and it had dried around Scott Helivant's head.

Ginevra stared in fascination for a few moments before letting out a scream.

Wesley climbed into the driver's seat and tried the number again. But again it went to voicemail.

'I've called the number on Scott Helivant's business card a few times, but he's not answering,' he said, looking across at Gerry in the passenger seat.

'You can't answer phones when you're up to your elbows in plaster.'

'Is it worth going over to the island in case he's there? And we should really speak to Eddie Culpepper again; tell him what we found at his aunt's address.'

'I think that'll keep. It's more urgent that we speak to Helivant.'

Wesley knew Gerry was right. Scott Helivant had told Major Fowler that Edith had gone off on a world cruise, possibly to stop him asking too many questions about her absence. And he had spoken to Maggie Beattie before she was killed.

'Motive?'

'Not sure yet. But if we look hard enough, we're bound to find one. Think about it, Wes. He's been around a while, doing odd jobs for Search, so he had access to that sheet. And if we rule out Search and Jocasta for Maggie Beattie's murder, because they were both in Tradington – and Mrs Wallace and her daughter, Sarah Rowdon, because, to be honest, I can't see them murdering anybody – that leaves us with Scott Helivant.'

'We haven't spoken to the cleaner yet.'

'She's away for a few weeks, visiting her daughter in Newcastle who's just had a baby. Besides, I've yet to meet a homicidal cleaning lady. Let's get going.'

But before Wesley could start the engine, his phone rang. When he answered, there was silence on the other end of the line.

'Hello?'

'Is that Inspector Peterson?' The voice was faint, as though the speaker was whispering – or in shock.

'Speaking. Who's that?' He hadn't recognised the call-er's number.

'Ginevra. Do you remember me?'

'Of course I do,' he said. She sounded frightened, and he wanted to encourage her to talk. 'What can I do for you, Ginevra?' he asked, turning on the speaker so Gerry could hear what was being said.

'I've found a body. It's horrible.'

'OK. I need you to keep calm and tell me everything. Take your time.'

'It's Scott. The builder. He's ...'

'Is he dead?'

'Yes. I don't know what to do.'

'Do you know the lighthouse?'

'Yes.'

'We're using one of the cottages there as a temporary incident room. If you go over there and tell any of the officers there what you told me, they'll help you. OK? And we'll be with you in twenty minutes.'

Once Ginevra had ended the call, Wesley started the car.

'So our builder's dead and he was about to become our new prime suspect.' Gerry sounded despondent. 'You never asked her how. Was it a heart attack, or was he decapitated with a plastering trowel?'

'She sounded frightened. I didn't want to make her go into the details. Whoever she sees at the incident room will report back soon enough.'

Gerry grunted his agreement and Wesley began to drive. After their visit to Major Eric Fowler, he'd begun to feel as though they'd finally found a viable suspect in Scott Helivant. But now it seemed they'd have to think again.

37

The tide was in, so they parked in Midton and took the police launch over to the island. A team had been sent to Edith Craven's flat, which was now being treated as a crime scene. Resources were stretched, and Wesley found himself hoping that Scott Helivant's death would turn out to be an unfortunate accident.

There were signs of police activity when they reached Coffin Hall.

'When Quentin and Jocasta get back, they'll be in for a shock,' Gerry observed as they walked across the courtyard.

Gerry collared a CSI who'd just emerged from the stables. The mask she was wearing meant they couldn't see her face. But her body language suggested she'd witnessed something unpleasant.

'What can you tell us?' said Wesley.

She stopped and pulled down her mask. 'It looks like someone dunked his head in a bucket of lime plaster and held him down. It's caustic, so even if he wasn't asphyxiated ... ' She didn't need to finish her sentence. They understood. 'Horrible way to go,' she added with a shake of her head.

'We can rule out suicide, then?'

She nodded again and hurried away, just as Colin Bowman appeared carrying the bag containing the tools of his trade.

'You're keeping me busy,' he said breezily.

Wesley suspected he wouldn't look so cheerful once he'd seen what was waiting for him in the stables.

'According to the CSI we've just spoken to, it's not a pretty sight.'

'Death rarely is,' said Colin. 'I'd better take a look.'

The three men struggled into their white crime-scene suits and Gerry led the way into the building. He'd been unusually quiet, as though the CSI's observations had shocked him into silence. With Gerry, that took a lot.

One wall of the stable block was immaculately plastered, but the rest was unfinished. Scott had died before he could complete his work. Wesley avoided looking too closely at the body sprawled on the floor. The victim lay on his front, his head inside the large bucket of plaster, now dried solid. He'd obviously put up a struggle, as there were multiple splashes on the flagstones.

'I'll never think of getting plastered in the same way again,' said Gerry, recovering the irreverent sense of humour that had lightened the mood at many a gruesome scene. 'Poor sod.'

'We need to check on everyone's whereabouts,' said Wesley. 'I'll ask Rach to make a start.'

'What are you thinking, Wes?' Gerry asked once he'd finished the call.

Wesley didn't answer for a few moments. The thought of what the man had gone through was too much to bear. 'I suspected he had something to do with Edith Craven's murder, but now . . .'

227

'That's not to say he was innocent. This might be a case of revenge.'

'But nobody knew he was a suspect. Certainly not Eddie Culpepper, the nephew – or Jack Beattie, for that matter.'

They left Colin to his work and walked out into the fresh air. It was a pleasant spring day, with a fresh breeze blowing wispy clouds across the blue sky. Like everywhere else on the island, the gentle beat of the waves could be heard like soothing background music. After a while, you didn't even notice it was there.

The CSIs were examining Scott's van, bagging up anything the killer might have touched. Wesley and Gerry waited in the courtyard, watching the activity going on around them and saying little. Eventually Colin appeared in the doorway of the stable block, his face more serious than usual.

'Well, Colin. What's the verdict?' Gerry sounded impatient.

'It looks as though someone came up behind him, grabbed hold of his shoulders and shoved his head in the bucket. That stuff burns, so he must have been in agony. There are signs that he fought for his life as best he could, but his assailant probably had the advantage of surprise.' The pathologist hesitated. 'I'll do the post-mortem first thing tomorrow if that's OK. The plaster will need to be chipped away from the face. Not that he'll be recognisable when we do.' He shuddered. Wesley had never seen him so affected by a violent death before – but this one was particularly unpleasant.

They started to walk back to the incident room, relieved to get away from the scene of the crime.

'I think we need to speak to Quentin Search again. It

happened on his property, so he's involved whether he likes it or not,' said Wesley.

'You're right, Wes. Edith Craven worked for him and Maggie Beattie was a big fan, so he's the connection between two suspicious deaths – three if you count Scott Helivant. In my opinion, he could be in this up to his neck.'

'Only we left him in Tradington, half an hour's drive away, getting ready for his next talk. Unless we can prove he slipped back here somehow, he's got a perfect alibi for this murder. Even he can't be in two places at once.'

'Didn't I hear that a magician lived in that Hall at one time?'

'Quentin Search is no magician. According to Neil, he's a con man.'

'You've got to admit Neil's biased.'

'Just because he's biased doesn't mean he's wrong.'

'Talk of the devil . . . '

They were passing the church on the south side, where the excavation was taking place. They'd chosen that way instinctively, avoiding the place where Maggie Beattie's body had been found, still separated from the rest of the churchyard by a barrier of police tape. They could see Neil talking to a tall man, both examining something too small for Wesley to see from that distance. They were deep in conversation, and he wished he could go over and see what they'd found. But the murder investigation took priority.

When they reached the lighthouse cottage, the incident room was buzzing with activity. As soon as Rachel saw them, she stood up and hurried over.

'Everyone's whereabouts are being checked and I've been looking into Scott Helivant's background. He took

229

over the business from his father.' She paused. 'The father's name is George.'

Wesley and Gerry looked at each other. 'Mrs Wallace did say the George she employed had a young man helping him. Could that have been Scott?'

'Highly possible,' said Gerry. 'Where can we find George now?'

'He's in a nursing home on the outskirts of Millicombe,' said Rachel. 'I rang the manager. She's expecting us.'

'Is Scott married?'

'Separated. No kids. His wife, Kylie, left him four months ago to live with another bloke in Tradmouth. I've traced her to a flat above the chippy in Harbour Street.'

'She'll have to be told. I'll get someone to break the news then I'd like to speak to her myself. I'd better speak to the dad first, though.' He looked at his watch. 'Then me and Wes can pay a call on Mrs Scott – pick up some fish and chips while we're at it.'

'Sounds like a plan,' said Wesley.

Rachel returned to her desk looking a little deflated. Wesley knew Gerry's intentions were good, but he could tell she was longing to get back to the challenges she'd faced before going on maternity leave. Perhaps he'd have a word with the boss – when the time was right. In the meantime, they had bad news to break.

Journal of the Reverend Thomas Nescombe

March 1575

Young Thomas grows and thrives. He gives me such joy, and all my misgivings as to his parentage are gone, for he is so like me in appearance. And yet Anne seems more distant than ever, and when she watches Talitha with the child, I sense coldness there. She tells me she loves our son, yet she seems not to know how to speak and play with the infant, whereas Talitha does so with a naturalness that is sweet to witness. Thomas loves his nursemaid, and I fear what would happen were a young man to pay court to Talitha and lure her away with the promise of marriage and children of her own.

I have overheard gossip that Anne has been seen visiting the Hall, but when I ask her if this is true, she denies it. I know not whether to believe her. There should not be so much mistrust between husband and wife.

Yesterday I suggested that she visit her sister in Tradmouth and stay there while Talitha cares for the babe. She flew into a fury at my words and left the house in the darkness. I feared there was a storm brewing, so I followed her. But she was nowhere to be found and she did not return until dawn.

*

Talitha is sick and Thomas cries for her in the night. I know not what ails the girl and I called a physician from the town of Dukesbridge to attend her. He brought leeches and herbs, but she is still sick unto death.

I sent for her father, who came right away and wept to see his daughter so gravely ill. I asked Anne to attend to the sickbed herself, but she said she would not as she now has the child to care for.

38

Over the past couple of hours, Neil had noticed a great increase in police activity, and he wondered whether something else had happened; another death perhaps. In case he didn't bump into Wesley later that day, he'd contact him that evening to find out what was going on.

The test pits were producing exciting finds and the enthusiasm of the amateur archaeologists from the Millicombe Archaeological Society was infectious. The members ranged from students to pensioners, and all worked with gusto. Neil and Dave were only meant to be there to share their expertise, but it hadn't been long before they were getting their hands dirty with the rest.

He was about to check what the test pit nearest the church had produced when his phone rang. It was Margaret, the bone specialist, calling from her lab at the university. He was surprised that she was working on a Saturday, but he knew from experience that she'd never been able to resist a mystery.

'Neil, I have news,' she began. He could hear the excitement in her voice.

'Don't keep me in suspense.'

'You know those bones you sent me – the ones from St Rumon's Island. Two male skeletons.'

'What about them?'

'I thought you'd like to know that the individuals didn't die naturally. Their necks were broken. All the indications are that they were hanged.'

Neil fell silent for a few moments while he took in the news. 'That would explain why they were buried outside the churchyard boundary. In unhallowed ground.'

'That makes sense,' said Margaret. 'I've sent samples off for carbon dating. It will be interesting to know when they died.'

'Brilliant. Thanks, Margaret. You're a star.'

Once he'd ended the call, he told Dave that he was going off in search of the Reverend Charlie. There was something he needed to ask her.

In the summer months, Millicombe was packed with visitors. With its quaint harbour, picturesque cottages and sandy beaches, it was a magnet for tourists, especially the well-heeled kind. The majority of the houses were second homes, which made finding staff for the local shops and restaurants a challenge, not to mention a crew for the lifeboat. Gerry described it as a Devonshire Disneyland. Wesley thought he wasn't far wrong.

Just outside the town stood a large Victorian villa. At one time it had been the holiday home of a wealthy industrialist from the Midlands, but now a large sign announced that it was the Millicombe Court Nursing Home.

'Bet it's expensive,' Gerry whispered as Wesley rang the doorbell. 'Must be a lot of money in the building trade.'

Before Wesley could reply, the door was opened by a slim Asian girl with a carer's overall, a friendly smile and a name badge telling them her name was Meera. When they held up their warrant cards, her smile disappeared.

'We'd like to speak to George Helivant,' said Wesley. 'I'm afraid we have some bad news for him, so if one of the staff would like to be present when we . . . '

Meera seemed to understand. 'Is it a death in the family?'

'You've got it in one, love,' said Gerry. 'How is he?'

'He has severe mobility problems, but mentally he's very sharp.'

This meant he would understand the full horror of what had happened to his son, which in Wesley's opinion made the situation worse.

Meera hesitated, and Wesley wondered whether there was something she wasn't sharing with them. 'I'd prefer it if someone else went in with you,' she said. 'I'll fetch the manager.'

'Why's that?' asked Gerry.

'George is a difficult man,' she replied reluctantly. She looked at Wesley. 'To be honest, he's quite racist. Just thought I'd better warn you.'

'Thanks,' said Wesley. His eyes met hers in understanding. 'Does he have many visitors?'

'Only his son. He doesn't come very often, and his visits always seem to end in a row.'

'Is that Scott?'

'Yes. George only has the one son that I know of.'

'What about his wife?'

'I believe she died some years ago. I'll fetch the manager.'

Meera disappeared down the corridor and returned with a middle-aged woman in a navy blue suit. She looked severe at first glance, but her smile was warm and it spread to her grey eyes.

'I believe you're here to see George. Meera said you had bad news.'

'I'm afraid his son died earlier today. Perhaps you'd like to be there when we tell him.'

'I'm sorry to hear that.' The smile vanished and she looked at them sharply. 'They don't send a couple of senior detectives to report a natural death.'

'You're quite right, love,' said Gerry. 'Scott Helivant was murdered.'

The woman nodded. 'In that case, you'd better leave it to me to tell him. Perhaps if you wait there ... '

As the manager bustled off down the corridor, Meera offered tea, which Gerry accepted gratefully. When she came back with two mugs, he thanked her. 'You're a life-saver, love. I'm spitting feathers.' He sipped at the brew, savouring every mouthful, before speaking again. 'I know George isn't your favourite resident, but you obviously know him better than we do. How do you think he'll take it?'

She sighed. 'If you ask me, George is a bully. He likes to think he's a hard man, and if I were you, I'd be straight with him.'

'Thanks,' said Wesley, wondering whether she was right. As far as he was concerned, the death of a child was the worst thing anybody could possibly face.

They'd just finished their tea when the manager returned, and they followed her to George's room at the end of a long corridor. As they entered, a thickset, bald man watched them from his wheelchair by the window. His clothes were baggy and looked as though they belonged to a bigger man – unless their owner had lost a great deal of weight since their purchase. Small, watchful eyes peered out from the loose flesh of his face. He looked like a malevolent gnome.

The manager took a seat on the bed. She obviously intended to stay, but the detectives didn't mind.

Wesley, having received a hostile glare when he walked in, decided to leave the initial questioning to Gerry. The man's manner made him wonder whether he'd had encounters with the police in the past.

'We're sorry for your loss,' Gerry began.

George made a noise that sounded like a grunt.

'We'd like to ask a few questions if you're feeling up to it.'

He turned his head away. 'I don't know nothing.'

'When did you last see Scott?'

'Must be a month ago. Maybe more.'

Gerry went on to ask about Scott's life and relationships, but George denied knowing much about them, although he did know about his separation. 'That bitch Kylie left him for a bloke from the fishing boats. I told Scott he should have given her a good hiding.'

Wesley and Gerry exchanged a glance. Meera had been spot on. George Helivant wasn't a nice person.

'We understand you did some work at Coffin Hall before you retired,' said Wesley, trying hard not to let his feelings show.

George looked at him as though he was something unpleasant he'd trodden in, and addressed his answer to Gerry. 'It was called St Rumon's House in those days. The old woman who lived there needed a wall rebuilding. Real lady she was. Then a poncey author bought the place. He found my phone number with the things the old lady left behind and got in touch because he wanted some plastering doing. I'd had my accident by then, so Scott did the job. Said he was a snotty bastard. And that wife of his . . . Kiara, her name was.' He gave a snort. 'Lady Muck.'

'So Scott took over your business?' said Wesley.

'I taught him everything he knew. But what thanks did I

get? I fell off a roof four years ago, hurt my spine and lost the use of my legs, so he shoves me in this place as soon as he can and tells me I'm no use to him.' George sniffed, as though he'd just remembered why they were there, and looked at the manager accusingly. '*She* said it was suspicious. Does that mean someone did him in?'

The woman obviously hadn't been able to bring herself to go into detail, and she gave Wesley an apologetic look. It was up to them.

'He was found at Coffin Hall. We're treating his death as murder.' Normally Gerry wouldn't have been so blunt, but George didn't seem the sensitive type.

'Well it's got nothing to do with me.' The old man nodded towards the manager. 'This lot have had me banged up here for four years. Might as well be in Parkhurst.'

'Now, George, you don't really mean that,' said the manager sweetly.

'Don't I? Look, I don't know nothing about Scott or who he got on the wrong side of. Might have been anyone. Might have been that stuck-up wife of his. I told him he could do better. Hope that fisherman she's shacked up with drowns.'

Gerry gave Wesley a nod. They'd learned all they could from George Helivant for now.

'I'm sorry for your loss, Mr Helivant,' said Wesley as they moved towards the door.

'Piss off,' was the reply.

39

It was almost 6.30 when they set off back to the incident room.

'What did you think?' Gerry asked as Wesley started the car.

'He doesn't like the police.'

'I don't think he likes anyone. Male, female, black, white. An equal opportunities hater. Wonder what makes someone like that.'

'Some people would say he had an unhappy childhood.'

'I've known lots of people with terrible families who didn't turn out like George Helivant. In my opinion, some people are just born like that.'

'"Some are Born to sweet delight. Some are Born to Endless Night."'

'Did you just make that up?'

'No,' said Wesley with a smile. 'William Blake did. I feel sorry for the poor woman George married – Scott's mother.'

'I'd like to know how she died. And I want to find out more about George. I suspect he's had criminal connections at one time, and that could be relevant.'

Gerry took out his phone, and after a short conversation, he told Wesley to pull into a lay-by.

When Wesley killed the engine, Gerry twisted round to face him. 'Right, Wes. It probably won't surprise you to learn that George Helivant's got a record. Grievous bodily harm. Actual bodily harm. Affray. Drunk and disorderly. Domestic violence. His wife, Sheila, died eighteen years ago. Accident. Fell down the stairs. Or was she pushed?'

'So Scott was brought up by George from an impressionable age. Anything known about him?'

'Nothing. Either he kept his nose clean or he was never found out.'

'Well he obviously upset someone.'

'I reckon we can cross his dad off our list of suspects. Even if he wasn't in a wheelchair, that place is as secure as Parkhurst, and there's no way anyone could escape without being noticed.' Gerry glanced at his watch. 'Have we got time to see Scott's wife?'

Wesley shook his head. 'She's already been informed, and I reckon our visit can wait till morning. I vote we go home. Colin's arranged Scott's post-mortem for first thing tomorrow. Great way to spend a Sunday morning, eh.'

Wesley dropped Gerry off at his house on the quayside and saw Alison come out to meet him. She greeted him with a cheerful peck on the cheek and led him indoors. Wesley sat for a few moments outside the house, pleased to see this evidence of the DCI's new domestic happiness. He hoped it would last.

When he arrived home, he saw Neil's car parked in the drive and hurried indoors, looking forward to a distraction from the world of murder. The visit to George Helivant had left a nasty taste in his mouth and he wanted to forget it.

Pam opened the door. 'Neil's arrived. I said he could stay for dinner and sleep in the spare room if he didn't fancy another night in his tent. He turned down my offer.' She smiled. 'You have to admire his dedication.'

'Rather him than me.'

'Hard day?'

Wesley nodded. He didn't feel inclined to talk about Scott Helivant's gruesome death. There were some things you didn't want to bring home. He was glad Pam had dinner ready, because he was hungry and knew he wouldn't be able to concentrate on what Neil had to tell him on an empty stomach.

'What's new?' he asked as they enjoyed a cup of tea in the living room. As Neil intended to drive, Pam had delayed bringing out the wine bottle.

'I've been on St Rumon's Island all day giving the Millicombe Archaeological Society the benefit of my wisdom, such as it is, and lending a hand with their test pits. It made a nice change from boring commercial digs. I'm going to try to arrange a proper excavation on the island. The priory's a fascinating site, and if I can get some funding, I can involve the community, not to mention the university.'

'Good luck.'

'And there's something else. You'll love this, Wes.' Neil sprawled on the sofa, making himself completely at home. 'Those skeletons that came down with the landslip – two men. According to Margaret at the lab, their necks were broken, and she thought they'd been hanged. Which explains why they were buried outside the churchyard.'

'Criminals, then?'

'You could be hanged for all sorts at one time. Margaret's sent samples off for radiocarbon dating.'

'Let me know the results, won't you?' This was just what Wesley needed to help him forget the day's events.

'Of course. And Charlie's offered me free access to the church records. The originals are in the archives in Exeter, but they were copied before they were sent over, so I won't have to add to Annabel's workload.'

'How is Annabel?' Pam asked. She'd been listening with interest, and she couldn't help enquiring about Neil's love life.

'Fine. We're going to Suffolk next month. I want to have a look at Sutton Hoo.'

'And she's happy with that?' Pam had realised long ago that for Neil, archaeology took precedence above everything else; it was one of the reasons their embryonic relationship at university had withered after a few short weeks.

'We're booked into a nice hotel in Lavenham. Interesting building. Old coaching inn.'

'It would be,' she said, catching Wesley's eye. She imagined Neil would spend a good deal of the time examining the historic fabric of the building.

There was a short silence before Neil spoke again. 'I'm thinking of going over to Tradington to listen to one of Quentin Search's talks, you know.'

'Why would you do that?'

'I fancy standing at the back of the hall like the spectre at the feast and asking awkward questions to get him rattled and hopefully expose him as the charlatan he is.'

'That's wicked,' said Pam with a mischievous grin.

'Tempting, though. He's used me for free publicity, so why shouldn't I put the argument for the other side?'

'Are you serious?' Wesley asked, worried that his friend might risk being arrested for a public order offence if Search was feeling vindictive enough to make a complaint.

'Probably not. I wouldn't waste my precious time on a man like him.' Neil frowned as though he was trying to remember something. 'One of our amateur diggers said something today that might interest you. He saw a van driving across the causeway and said it was a builder he wanted a word with. Wasn't the builder at the Hall killed? Isn't that why all the cops were buzzing around the place?'

'Yes.'

'I spoke to him, you know. I went up there to have a word with Quentin Search, and the builder told me he wasn't there.'

'So this man at your dig knew Scott Helivant?' The case had just intruded on Wesley's evening, but it was something he couldn't ignore. 'Will he be there tomorrow?'

'That's the plan.'

'What's his name?'

'Bill. He's a retired dentist.'

'Can you tell him I'd like a word?'

Neil shrugged. 'If you want. You don't think he's the killer, do you? Anyone less like a murderer I've yet to meet.'

'Murderers come in all shapes and sizes. You'd be surprised,' said Wesley with a smile.

40

Sunday morning was meant to be a time of leisure: breakfast in bed with the papers; maybe church or a visit to a
garden centre. But crime was no respecter of weekends, so
for Wesley and Gerry it was just another working day.

Wesley felt the need for some exercise after a few days
spent sitting at desks or in the driving seat, so he walked
down to the centre of Tradmouth and met Gerry outside
the mortuary entrance. Colin was expecting them.

They'd braced themselves for an unpleasant experience.
They knew the plaster would have been chipped away from
Scott Helivant's head to reveal something terrible beneath.
As they stood behind the screen, Wesley could hardly
bear to watch.

Colin, as usual, kept up the commentary. 'The flesh of
the face has been badly burned away by the caustic lime
plaster. He's certainly in no state to be identified by a friend
or relative.'

Wesley took a peep. As he'd expected, the head was a
mass of reddened pulp. He looked away again.

'The bruising around the shoulders indicates that he
was attacked from behind and held down in the plaster.
He struggled for a while, but mercifully his death would

have been fairly quick. It's a horrible way to go, gentlemen, and I hope you find whoever did this as soon as possible.' Colin, normally so detached and matter-of-fact about his work, sounded positively emotional.

'Anything else you can tell us?' Gerry asked.

'He was a healthy specimen. And he looked after his teeth. No fillings, so we won't be able to get an ID from his dental records. We'll have to rely on DNA.'

'There's a father. We'll get a sample from him,' said Gerry.

'Good.' Colin paused. 'His hands are remarkably soft for a tradesman.'

'I suppose he wore gloves much of the time,' said Gerry.

'Fingerprints any use to you?'

'He hasn't got a criminal record, so nothing's on file.'

'But somewhere along the way he obviously made a dangerous enemy.'

Wesley and Gerry couldn't argue with that. Whoever had killed Scott Helivant was ruthless and had no pity for his victim.

'Could a woman have done it, or are we looking for a man?' Wesley asked.

Colin thought for a while. 'If he was taken unawares and panic rendered him helpless, I wouldn't rule a woman out. Mind you, whoever killed him must have been wearing protective gloves, or they'd have run the risk of being burned themselves – unless they washed the stuff off immediately.'

'There's a water supply near where he was discovered. A tap. It's been checked for prints, but nothing was found.'

Colin completed the post-mortem in uncharacteristic silence, then, as usual, the two detectives were invited for tea and biscuits. But this time the atmosphere was subdued.

'This is one of the nastiest murders I've dealt with in my

245

career,' Colin said as he poured the tea through the little silver strainer he had once told them had belonged to his grandmother.

'We know he had dealings with the woman who was buried in the purple sheet,' said Wesley. 'According to her neighbour, he did some building work for her.'

'So there's a connection.'

'We were going to talk to him about it, but he was killed before we had a chance.'

'Unfortunate. I saw the facial reconstruction that Neil's colleague from the university created. And I believe she's been identified.'

'Her name was Edith Craven, and she once worked for the author Quentin Search, who owns the house where Scott Helivant died.'

'Is Search a suspect for the latest murder?'

Gerry shook his head. 'He says he was in Tradington around the time it must have happened.'

'And nobody can be in two places at once. Strange about the connection, though.'

'My thoughts exactly, Colin.'

Wesley thought the boss sounded despondent, and he was glad when the conversation turned to more pleasant things: families, and the holidays they had planned for later in the year – work permitting.

Once the tea was finished, the detectives left the mortuary and walked out into the spring sunshine. The bells of St Margaret's were ringing as they headed for Scott Helivant's estranged wife's flat above the chip shop in Harbour Street. At one time Gerry had sung in the choir at St Margaret's, in spite of Joyce's disapproval. He still helped them out occasionally, but with his work commitments it wasn't always easy.

The sound of the bells reminded Wesley of the ringers at St Rumon's. Eddie, Edith Craven's relative, had broken the bad news to his mother, and she was travelling down to Devon. Wesley wasn't sure whether to treat Eddie as a suspect. Apart from his relationship with Edith, he'd been on the island when Scott was killed. And he was young and strong; a fit man who could easily have overcome the slightly built builder if he'd taken him by surprise. He was definitely on the list of people they wanted to speak to again. But as for a motive, he couldn't think of one.

Before their visit to Scott's wife, they called in at the station to see whether anything new had come in since the previous night. Most of the team were in the incident room on St Rumon's Island, which meant many of the desks were empty. But Rob Carter was at his usual place by the window. Wesley walked over to join him.

'Hi, Rob. How's it going?'

'Something's come in from the CSIs,' he said, rooting through the paperwork on his desk. He produced a printed email and handed it to Wesley.

'Interesting,' Wesley said once he'd read it. 'No prints found in the victim's van.'

'Probably wore gloves.'

That was one explanation, although Wesley found it hard to believe he'd wear them all the time. Perhaps it was relevant – or perhaps not.

'I've got a job for you, Rob. Something to get you out of the office. I need someone to take a DNA swab from an elderly man in a nursing home on the outskirts of Millicombe. He's the victim's father, and we just need the sample for confirmation of identity.'

247

'No problem.' Rob seemed to perk up a little at the prospect of a drive over to Millicombe in the sunshine.

'Just one thing. He's not the easiest of men to deal with, so be tactful. Oh, and I should mention that he doesn't like the police.'

For the first time in a while, Rob smiled. 'Thanks for the warning.'

'Best of luck.'

Gerry had been checking messages in his office, and he emerged zipping up his old anorak. 'Right, Wes. Next stop the flat above the chippy. Hope we don't get there to find someone's been battered.'

Wesley groaned at the boss's terrible joke, and was pleased to see that Rob joined in.

It was only a short distance to Harbour Street. The streets were Sunday quiet, but in a couple of weeks' time they'd be teeming with holidaymakers enjoying the spring half-term break. The chippy was shut, but there was a door next to the entrance giving access to the flat above. Wesley rang the doorbell and waited.

It seemed an age before the door was opened by a man wearing pyjamas that resembled shorts and a T-shirt. Leisure wear for all occasions, even opening the door to a couple of police officers. 'Yeah?'

He was good-looking in a rugged kind of way, with wavy dark hair, and his tanned complexion suggested he spent much of his time out of doors.

They showed him their warrant cards. 'We're here to see Mrs Helivant. Kylie Helivant. It's about her husband.'

The man suddenly bristled with righteous anger. 'A policeman came over to say he'd had an accident. To be honest, I'm shedding no tears for him. Treated her like dirt, he did. And he was always trying to make trouble for us.'

'And you are . . . ?'

'Ashley Smith. So what happened?'

It was Gerry who answered. 'He was murdered.'

Ashley looked stunned and swore under his breath. 'Well it wasn't me and it wasn't Kylie. She was working at the salon all yesterday.'

'Where were you yesterday?'

'I'm a fisherman. I was out on the boat. You can check.'

'We need to speak to Kylie. Is she in?'

Ashley stood to one side. 'Yeah. You'd better come up. That Scott made her life a misery, but it'll still come as a shock.'

They were directed up a narrow uncarpeted staircase to the flat above, where they were relieved to find Kylie Helivant out of bed though still in her dressing gown, which she pulled tightly across her body as soon as the strangers entered the room. She was a thin, pale woman with long blonde hair, although the dark roots peeping through showed that her chosen shade wasn't the one nature had given her.

Ashley broke the news that two detectives wanted to speak to her with commendable gentleness, sitting close to her and holding her hand. Kylie sat and listened, her eyes widening a little when they went into the details of Scott's death. She didn't seem upset. She just looked shocked.

'I'm sorry for your loss, Mrs Helivant,' said Wesley.

She looked him in the eye. There were no tears; no signs of grief. 'I won't lie, Inspector, I'm not sorry he's dead. Scott was a horrible person. He was all sweetness and light with his customers, and he could make old ladies and lonely people think he was a saint, but that was all an act. He used to have it off with women he worked for, but he didn't like me working because he wanted me at his beck and call. He was out for himself and what he could get out of people, and he used to come home and boast about it. I fell for his charm at first, but as soon as I discovered the real Scott, I started making plans to get out.' She looked at Ashley adoringly. 'Meeting Ashley was the best thing that could have happened. I've no regrets.'

'If Scott kept you on such a short rein, how did you two meet?' Gerry asked, genuinely interested.

Ashley lowered his eyes as though he was reliving a happy memory. 'I'd just come off the boat and she was walking along the embankment. She wasn't looking where she was going and she bumped into me. Fate, I suppose.' The couple exchanged a smile.

'I'm sorry to have to ask this, love,' said Gerry. 'But where were you yesterday?'

'At work. Snippers and Curls. Ask anyone there. Is that when Scott . . . ?'

'Yes. He was doing a job on St Rumon's Island when he was attacked. Someone dunked his head in a bucket of plaster.'

'You reap what you sow, Chief Inspector,' she said, straightening her back. 'I learned that at Sunday school. The way he treated people was going to catch up with him sooner or later.'

'You say he was out for what he could get. What exactly did he do?' Wesley asked.

'He used to take deposits from people – quite a lot of money sometimes. At first he'd make excuses for not turning up. He was so convincing, he could have won a bloody Oscar. Then he stopped taking their calls. He never gave them his real address, of course. Sometimes he'd deliberately cause damage and turn up offering to put things right – the Good Samaritan act, he called that. Then he'd get in with elderly people who had a bit of money and tell them a sob story. He had a cash-flow problem and needed to borrow a few thousand – just for a week or so, then he'd pay them back. They never saw the money again, of course, and if anyone tried to find him, he'd disappear.'

'The man was immoral,' Ashley muttered.

'I'm surprised he didn't come to the attention of the police – or at least the small claims courts.'

'Like I said, he had the gift of the gab. He could talk his way out of anything.'

'Except murder,' said Gerry. 'Someone clearly took exception to his activities.'

'What was his relationship with the Search family at Coffin Hall like?' Wesley asked.

Kylie shrugged. 'He didn't mention them much – only said they had a big house that would keep him in work.'

'Our officers have been to the address we had for him, but they found it was a derelict garage,' Gerry said. 'What's his real address, love?'

Kylie recited an address in Neston, a flashy apartment near the river. Wesley made a call to the station to get someone over there right away.

'Would you have a list of his customers?'

'It would be on his phone. Have you found it?'

'Our crime-scene people are still looking for it.'

'He kept everything on his phone. Never wrote anything down.'

'Didn't want to leave a paper trail. And I don't think he liked to trouble the taxman,' said Ashley.

'He told me it was a pay-as-you-go phone. Untraceable,' Kylie added. 'Said if he didn't want the punters to find him, they wouldn't. Look, it's terrible the way he died, but I didn't have anything to do with it and neither did Ashley.'

'What about any relatives who might have taken exception to his behaviour towards you?' Wesley asked.

She looked at Ashley, who gave her a nod. She was to tell them everything. 'There's my mum. She's widowed and she's just had a new hip. Then there's my sister and her husband, but they both work and they've got three kids, so they're always busy. I've got cousins, but they're in South Wales and I can't imagine any of them coming down here to take revenge on my behalf. My best friend from school is on holiday in the Maldives, but that's it really. And now I'm settled here with Ashley, why would anyone need to hurt Scott anyway? I've moved on.'

Gerry looked at Wesley. Kylie had a point. She had a new life, and neither she nor Ashley had an interest in ruining it. Unless there was something they weren't saying.

'How did Scott react when you left him?' Wesley asked. 'Surely he didn't just accept it?'

'I knew he'd kick off, so I left one day while he was out on a job. He went round to my mother's and made threats, but luckily my brother-in-law was there at the time and he chucked him out. He found out about Ashley somehow – don't know how – but I told my mum to say we'd gone abroad. I'd taken my passport along with all my things and they told him I was in Spain, which suited me fine.'

'What if you were spotted? Surely you're taking a risk working in a salon.'

She gave Ashley a nervous glance. 'I wasn't going to let Scott keep controlling my life. Anyway, Ashley's a fisherman. The men he works with are great, and they're big lads who can take care of themselves. If Scott did make trouble . . . '

She didn't need to finish her sentence. They understood. The close-knit fishing community would look after their own.

'But he never found me, so there was no need.' She looked at Ashley again, and Wesley saw tears in her eyes; tears of relief. 'At last I feel safe. And I've got my job now, so I'm getting my life sorted. Why would I risk going to jail for murder?'

Gerry stood up. 'Thanks, love. I won't ask you to identify the body. We'll do that by DNA. You've met Scott's father, I take it?'

They saw her shudder. 'Only the once, and that was enough. George isn't a nice man. Like father like son. No wonder Scott's brother got away. Can't blame him.'

'Brother?' There'd been no mention of a sibling before, so this was news.

'Scott had a younger brother who moved to Australia when he was seventeen. Probably moved to the other side of the world to get away from his brute of a father.'

'You've never met him?'

She shook her head. 'I don't even know his first name. Scott never talked about him.'

'He should be told.'

'I've no idea where he is. I don't know what part of Australia he lives in – or even if he's still alive. The only thing Scott told me is that he changed his name from Helivant because he hated their father so much, but I don't know what he changed it to. Sorry,' she added with another glance at Ashley. Wesley thought she was telling the truth, but he couldn't be absolutely sure.

'Thanks, love. We'll be in touch,' said Gerry as Ashley showed them to the door.

'Do you think the brother's relevant?' Wesley asked as they walked back to the station.

'That's what we need to find out. But if we don't even know his name or whereabouts he lives, it'll be like looking for a needle in a haystack.'

Wesley took out his phone. 'I'll text Rob. If he's still with George Helivant, he can ask him about his other son. Funny he hasn't been mentioned before.'

'A lot of families have a relative nobody talks about. George and Scott might have cut him off because he's an honest, upstanding member of society.'

Wesley knew the boss was joking. But he suspected he could be right.

An hour later, Rob arrived in the incident room. When he appeared in the doorway of Gerry's office, it was obvious from his expression that he had news.

'I've just seen George Helivant, he began. 'I took the swab and it's been sent off to the lab.'

'Thanks, Rob. That should give us a definitive ID. Anything else?'

'I asked him about his other son like you asked, and he denied having one. Said Scott was an only child. But there was something about the way he said it. Bitter, if you know what I mean.'

'I think he's a very bitter man,' said Wesley.

'You can say that again. When I was leaving, I got

chatting to one of the carers. Meera, nice girl.' Rob paused, as though he was about to make a great revelation. 'I asked her whether she'd heard anything about George having another son, and she told me that once, when he was in a particularly foul mood, she was helping him get dressed and he started swearing at her. He was shouting so it was hard to make out what he was saying, but she thought it was something like "You're as useless as that effing Craig." There's no Craig on the staff and he'd never mentioned the name before.'

'So it's possible that Scott's brother is called Craig,' said Wesley, thinking it was a long shot. Craig could be anyone; maybe someone who'd worked for him in the building trade. 'I've got another job for you, Rob. Tomorrow morning first thing, can you check with immigration and get a list of all the Craigs who've travelled here from Australia over the past few months?'

Rob looked eager to tackle his Herculean task. Wesley, however, wasn't sure whether he'd just sent him on a wild goose chase.

Journal of the Reverend Thomas Nescombe

March 1575

Talitha Sellars is dead. I watched with her father as she breathed her last after hours of agony, her fragile body undergoing the most terrible spasms as her back arched in a manner most unnatural. The physician suspects poison. But who would wish to poison such a good and gentle girl?

When I tried to offer a few words of comfort to our maid, who was weeping, she told me that two days ago while I was at the church, Elias Anselmo visited the house and spoke to Talitha. The maid saw him giving her a small vial. Then he left swiftly, as though he did not wish to be seen, not knowing the maid had witnessed all.

I went to the Hanging Monk, where Talitha lay in a rough coffin, surrounded by her grieving family. I took her father aside and told him what I'd heard. He nodded grimly and said he knew what must be done.

Elias Anselmo swore he was innocent; that the vial he gave Talitha contained only valerian, a harmless remedy to aid sleep. His story was not believed, and today they hanged him upon a gallows hastily built by Jed the carpenter, who took great pleasure in his work.

A hooded cloak concealed Anselmo's features, as though he was too ashamed to show his face as he was dragged to his end by the villagers, many of whom had never set eyes on him because of his reclusive habits but were only too aware of his sinister reputation. I am a man of God who believes in forgiveness, but the sin of ending that lovely girl's life had to be punished. It is said that his servant has fled the island, but I know nothing of the man, for like his master, he never attended my church.

Anselmo's body was buried in unhallowed ground outside the churchyard, away from the place where the good people of the village are laid to rest. Thus the life of the island's magus ended ignominiously. He was a killer and deserved his fate.

Anne has been with Thomas constantly. She watches him so closely that on occasions I fear for her sanity. She has left our bed and sleeps beside him at night, and when he tries to run off, as children will, she brings him back to her side.

She refuses to engage another nursemaid, and I fear this is a mistake.

41

When Gerry arrived at the station on Monday morning, he found a message waiting for him on his desk. *Call Barbara Dearlove. Urgent.*

He made the call and after a short conversation turned to Wesley, who'd been listening carefully.

'Someone tried to break into Barbara's cottage last night. Let's go and see what's going on.'

'Surely we can leave it to uniform.'

'If there's a chance Bryan Dearlove's still alive as his brother believes and he was involved with Deidre Charlton's murder, I'd like to deal with it myself. Who knows, we might find a connection to Edith Craven and Scott Helivant.'

They took one of the pool cars, and when they arrived in Bereton, Barbara was waiting for them at the door. She looked anxious.

'Whoever was in the garden tried the patio door. I haven't touched it. I thought you'd want to test it for fingerprints.'

'Thanks, love. We'll send our CSIs round,' said Gerry. 'Fan of crime dramas on TV, are you?'

Barbara smiled. She was suddenly more relaxed. 'Guilty as charged. I never miss an episode of *Midsomer Murders*.

You don't think that letter I received was right, do you? You don't think Bryan's come back from the dead?'

Wesley was about to say no; that it had probably been an opportunist thief trying to break in. Then he remembered Greg Dearlove's certainty that the strange phone call he received had been made by his brother.

'Just make sure all your doors are kept locked,' he said.

She nodded vigorously. 'I will.'

'By the way, have you ever used a builder called Scott Helivant?'

'I don't think so. Why do you ask?'

They didn't answer the question.

As they were leaving the cottage, Wesley said what was on his mind. 'I'd like someone to revisit Edith's flat in Dukesbridge and have another word with the Major.'

'About Scott Helivant?'

'As a builder he'd be in and out of people's houses so he might have seen something; maybe that's why he was silenced. I think we should ask Steven Charlton whether Scott ever did any work at his house while Deidre was at home. We might have been approaching this from the wrong angle.'

Rachel and Paul went to Dukesbridge to interview the Major again. They reported back that as witnesses went, he was perfect: unimaginative, matter-of-fact and concise. However, as far as he knew, Edith Craven had never mentioned a Bryan Dearlove or a Deidre Charlton. A call to Steven Charlton told them that he and Deidre had never had any dealings with Scott Helivant. They'd drawn another blank.

Even if Bryan had killed his lover, Deidre Charlton,

Wesley couldn't see any possible connection with Scott Helivant, Maggie Beattie or Edith Craven. There was only one person who was linked to all three of them and that was Quentin Search, but according to the officer who'd gone over to Tradington to check his alibi for the time of Scott's murder, nobody had seen him leave the symposium. Gerry reckoned that if he'd left straight after they'd spoken to him, he could have made it back to the island. Closer enquiries would have to be carried out.

Gerry wanted to see what was happening in the incident room on St Rumon's Island, so Wesley went with him, saying he needed to speak to a retired dentist who might have had dealings with Scott Helivant.

It was high tide, but he survived the short voyage by closing his eyes and thinking happy thoughts: getting home; putting his feet up with a glass of wine; the uninterrupted Sunday dinners he'd be able to enjoy once the case was wrapped up; the short holiday he and Pam were planning in northern Spain while his parents came from London to look after Michael and Amelia. By the time he reached the island, he was feeling quite chilled.

The local amateur archaeologists had been working with Neil over the weekend, but some retired members of the group were carrying on during the week while Neil resumed his duties on the Dukesbridge site. Gerry decided to delay his return to the incident room so that he could hear what the retired dentist had to say, and the two detectives walked through the churchyard to the site of the dig. On Neil's advice, more test pits had been created, some revealing sections of stone walls, and Wesley picked his way across the uneven ground, aware that he was wearing the wrong shoes for the terrain.

'We're looking for Bill,' he said to a man in his late sixties with little hair and a healthy tan; the type people meant when they talked about 'active retired'. He was kneeling on the edge of one of the pits with a clipboard, sketching the contents: stone flags that had once formed part of a floor.

'You've found him. How can I help you?' Bill's movements were sprightly as he rose from his kneeling mat and straightened his back.

'I'm a friend of Neil Watson's,' Wesley began. 'He said you might be able to help me.' It was only then that he showed his ID, and the man raised his eyebrows in surprise.

'I hope you haven't come to arrest me,' he half joked.

'Not at all. We're investigating the murder of a builder who was working at the manor house on this island – Coffin Hall.'

'Some officers have already been round asking everyone at the dig whether we saw anything suspicious, but nobody had. And that includes me, I'm afraid. Sorry I can't be of help.'

'I understand the name Scott Helivant means something to you.'

'Er, yes. I did mention to someone that I'd seen his van and I wanted a word. But I never got round to following it up.'

'Why did you want to speak to him?'

Bill's manner had changed as soon as Scott's name was mentioned. He was definitely on his guard.

'It's not for myself, it's for a neighbour. An elderly lady. She's in her eighties and her husband died last year after a long spell in a nursing home. My wife and I look out for her.'

'That's kind of you,' said Wesley. 'What did you want to talk to him about?'

'He owes her money. He said he'd see to her roof and took a deposit of a thousand pounds, ostensibly for materials. He even drove her to the bank to get the cash out. After she'd handed the money over, she never saw him again. I've been trying to get in touch with him on her behalf. He answered his phone the first couple of times and made some excuses – first he said he'd been ill, then he said he'd broken his leg playing football, and then his child had been rushed to hospital. He was very convincing. When I kept ringing, he obviously recognised my number and stopped answering. I left messages for him, but he never called back.'

'Do you know where he lived?'

'There was an address on the quote my neighbour was given, but when I went round there I found it was a derelict garage on the edge of Neston. Nobody in the houses nearby had heard of him.'

It seemed Scott had made a habit of using the garage as an address of convenience. They were still waiting to see what the officers found at the address Kylie had given them, but they'd heard nothing yet.

'So when you saw his van, you went to the Hall to confront him?' It was the first time Gerry had spoken, and Bill looked at him curiously, as though he'd only just noticed he was there.

'No. I didn't.'

'Why's that? I would have done.'

'Because I'm not stupid. After my visit to Neston, I'd concluded that he was a con man, semi if not downright criminal. I'm not used to dealing with people like that.'

'So what did you plan to do?'

'I called Trading Standards. Told them where they could

find him.' He shook his head sadly. 'They said they'd take action but they couldn't respond quickly because they were short-staffed. I didn't hear anything after that. Then your officers came round asking questions and I heard that Scott Helivant was dead. I knew nothing about what had happened, so I thought it best to keep out of it.'

'We'll check with Trading Standards,' said Gerry.

'Please do. They'll confirm what I said.'

'You should really have told us about this sooner,' said Wesley.

'I realise that now. But I don't see how it could have made much difference.'

'We'd have known about your neighbour.'

'If you're thinking she has relatives who'd want to take revenge, you're wrong. Poor Mrs Wentworth is all alone in the world. That's why my wife and I keep an eye on her. I'll give you her address so she can confirm everything I've told you.' He paused. 'Scott Helivant was a bad man, Inspector. But I'm not saying he deserved to be murdered.'

42

Wesley judged that Rachel would be the ideal person to speak to Mrs Wentworth. When they reached the incident room, he told her what Bill had said and she pursed her lips in disapproval.

'How can anyone do that to a vulnerable old lady? It's wicked.'

She fell silent, and Wesley wondered whether the thought that Scott Helivant had deserved his fate had passed through her mind. Only she hadn't seen the body and stood there watching the post-mortem. Nobody really deserved an end like that.

As soon as he reached his desk, he received a call from Eddie Culpepper to say that his parents had just arrived from up north to deal with the formalities associated with Edith Craven's death. Wesley called the number Eddie gave for them and his father answered, saying that he might have important information and he wanted to speak to the investigating officers face to face.

Half an hour later, Wesley and Gerry were sitting in the lounge at the Star Hotel, the long-established coaching inn on Dukesbridge's main street where the Culpeppers were staying. Wesley had expected them to be conventional suburban types, and he was surprised to discover that Mrs Culpepper had purple hair and a T-shirt advertising the virtues of a heavy rock band. Mr Culpepper, in biker jacket and frayed jeans, had long grey hair drawn back into a ponytail. They were well-spoken and polite, and they seemed genuinely upset about Edith.

'I'm sorry we have to meet under such sad circumstances,' Wesley began.

'Thank you, Inspector. We wanted to talk to you about Edith. You've searched her flat, I believe?'

'Our team have.'

'But you haven't spoken to her bank?'

Wesley looked at Gerry. 'Our team didn't find any bank correspondence in her flat. We're in the process of contacting all the local banks to see whether she had accounts with them.'

Mr Culpepper shook his head. 'I know her mother left her a tidy sum, so it must be somewhere. Have you asked the man she worked for, Quentin Search?'

'Why him in particular?' Wesley asked.

It was Mrs Culpepper who answered the question. 'She mentioned in the last letter we received from her, the one she sent to tell us her mother had died, that she'd been getting her financial affairs in order and that she'd contacted the solicitor Mr Search used. I sent her a condolence card, but I never heard from her again after that. I feel guilty that I didn't make more effort to keep in touch and make sure she was all right. It's not that we didn't want to, but we've been really busy lately.' She looked embarrassed. 'Her usual card didn't arrive last Christmas but I put that down to the post. We asked Eddie to pop round to her address while he was down here, but ... '

'We didn't take much notice of this financial business at the time,' Culpepper said, looking at his wife. 'She was hardly a millionaire.'

'No.' Mrs Culpepper pushed her hair behind her ears and sat up straight, as though she was about to say something important. 'Edith always said how good Quentin Search was to her, but I couldn't help wondering what was in it for him. Maybe I'm being cynical, but I've seen him being interviewed on TV and he didn't look the philanthropic type to me.'

'I don't suppose you know the name of the solicitor she saw?'

'Since we found out about her death, we've been doing a bit of research,' Mr Culpepper said proudly. 'We phoned round and eventually found him. His name's Lionel Graves and his office is in Neston. We called him, and it turns out we're the main beneficiaries of her will. He sent a copy over.'

Mrs Culpepper produced a sheaf of papers from her capacious shoulder bag. 'You can read it if you like.' She pushed the papers across the low coffee table to Wesley.

It seemed that Mr and Mrs Culpepper had inherited the bulk of Edith's estate. There were a few bequests to charities, but one name got an unexpected mention. *In the event of my death, the loan of ten thousand pounds to my builder, Scott Helivant, should be repaid in full to my cousin Mrs Ingrid Culpepper named above.*

'Do you know anything about this Scott Helivant, Inspector?' Mrs Culpepper asked. 'Edith never mentioned him in her letters, but she must have trusted him if she lent him all that money.'

'Oh yes, we know about him all right,' said Gerry. 'I don't

know whether Eddie told you, but Scott Helivant was found murdered at Quentin Search's house on Saturday.'

The Culpeppers looked stunned.

'Well it's got nothing to do with us,' said Mr Culpepper defensively. 'Even if he refused to pay up, who'd kill someone over ten grand?'

'People have been murdered for a lot less than that,' said Gerry. 'You'd be surprised.'

The Culpeppers suddenly looked worried. 'We've only just arrived down here. And we can prove it. We saw some friends yesterday – they'll vouch for us.'

'Thank you, Mr Culpepper. We'll leave that for the time being,' said Wesley, calming the waters. 'Can I ask you a question? Do the initials KL mean anything to you?' This was a mystery he'd wanted to clear up for a while.

'KL?'

'It was engraved on a gold ring we found on Edith's finger.'

Mrs Culpepper nodded as realisation dawned. 'Of course. It stands for Katherine Langham, Edith's grandmother on the other side of the family. It must have belonged to her.'

'Thanks. We've been wondering about that.'

'Have you any idea who killed my cousin?' she asked.

'No, I'm afraid we don't,' said Gerry. 'But we'll find them. I promise you that.'

Journal of the Reverend Thomas Nescombe

August 1575

Anne visited her sister in Tradmouth in May and has not returned. I have not set eyes on my son for three months and this grieves me sorely. I wrote to my wife to beg her to return but she does not reply. However, a messenger arrived today bearing a strange missive from my brother-in-law, the man who would be Mayor of Tradmouth one day. He says he would speak with me on the subject of my wife and he will visit in a week's time. It is a matter he does not wish his own wife, Elizabeth, to hear for fear that she should disclose all to her sister. The child is well, he says, but Anne will not leave him, even in the care of Elizabeth or her servants.

The Hall was shut up for several months after Anselmo's hanging, but word has it that a relative of his has taken possession, although he has not yet been seen. I walked by the Hall yesterday and saw a man at the window. He looked very like Anselmo, but I told myself I was mistaken.

Then last night a most singular event occurred. A knock came upon the door as I was preparing for bed. I went downstairs and unbolted it, thinking it would be one of my flock in need of help. When it opened, I was faced with a cloaked figure, the hood pulled over his face despite the warmth of the night.

'What do you want, my friend?' I asked, for I took the person for a traveller in need. Then he lowered the hood and I stood open-mouthed in horror, for I was face to face with a dead man. A man I had seen swinging on the gallows not four months since.

43

'Can we rule out the Culpeppers?' Wesley asked as they made their way back to St Rumon's Island. He was pretty sure the answer would be yes. They'd been up north when Scott died and had been eager to offer witnesses to confirm it. Besides, he liked the family. Not that this meant anything. There had been times he'd taken a liking to people who'd turned out to be killers. But maybe not killers who disposed of their victims in such a brutal way.

'Yes, I think we can cross them off our little list, Wes. But we'll certainly check where they were around the time Colin estimates Edith was killed. Can't be too careful, as my old mum used to say.'

They'd sent one of the DCs to interview Lionel Graves, the solicitor, but they weren't expecting to learn much from him. Drawing up a will was a routine process, and he'd have just been obeying Edith's instructions.

The tide was out, so they walked across to the island, Gerry grumbling about missing his boat trip. Wesley seized the chance to share his thoughts.

'If Scott Helivant was a con man who thought nothing of ripping off vulnerable people, he must have made a lot of enemies over the years.'

'Agreed. But there's something we haven't considered,' said Gerry. 'Scott was elusive, giving false addresses to his customers and all that. Is it possible he had a business partner; someone behind the scenes we don't know about?'

'We know he worked with his father for a while, but he's in no fit state to go round murdering anyone. And I think we can rule out his wife, Kylie.' Wesley thought for a moment. 'There's one customer of Scott's we haven't managed to speak to since his body was found, and that's Quentin Search. Scott did a lot of work for him. Search can't be stupid, so can we assume that Scott didn't rip him off like he did the other people we've heard about?'

'Why would he deal with Search honestly when he was in the habit of conning everyone else?'

'I can think of two explanations. Either Search is in on the con too, or Scott wanted access to Coffin Hall for some reason. His father worked there before his accident. Didn't he rebuild a wall for Mrs Wallace? Let's go and talk to Search again.'

As they were walking towards Coffin Hall, Gerry had a call from the lab. There was a DNA match between George Helivant and the body in the plaster. Now that the victim's identity had been officially confirmed, they could release his name to the media and appeal for anyone who'd had dealings with him to come forward.

'Mind you,' Gerry grunted. 'If the killer's been ripped off by the victim, he'd be daft to draw attention to himself.'

'Have they finished searching Scott's address yet?'

As if on cue, Gerry's phone rang. It was the search team. They'd gone to the address Kylie had given them but had found nothing incriminating: no business records or bank details and no sign of Scott's missing phone. The place was as clean as a bishop's conscience, the officer said. If there was any evidence of Scott's dubious dealings, he kept it elsewhere. If Quentin Search was slippery, Scott Helivant could give an eel a run for its money. One step ahead of his customers; two steps ahead of the police and Trading Standards. But why, Wesley asked himself, had he treated Quentin Search so differently from his other clients?

As they reached the courtyard of Coffin Hall, Ginevra Search came hurtling towards them, running as though she was fleeing some fearsome monster. Wesley stopped and waited for her to reach them. Gerry prodded him in the back, indicating that he should move on because they were in a hurry to speak to the owner of the house. But Search's daughter looked as though she had something important to say.

'Have you found out who killed Scott yet?' she began, breathless.

'We're still working on it. We need to speak to your father again.'

Ginevra leaned forward so that her face was close to Wesley's. 'If he told you he was in Tradington when Scott was killed, he was lying.'

'What makes you say that?'

'I was upstairs in my room and I think I heard some-one come in.'

'How do you know it was your father?'

'I heard a key in the door and only family have keys. It must have been him or Jocasta.'

'Not Scott?'

She shook her head.

'Did you tell the officer who came round to take your statement?'

She looked flustered. 'I didn't hear anything more after the door opened, so I wasn't sure.'

'Are you saying this because you want to get your dad into trouble?' Gerry butted in with characteristic bluntness.

Ginevra didn't answer for a few moments, and Wesley suspected that Gerry might have got it right.

Then leaned forward, almost spitting out the words. 'OK, I admit I hate Quentin and that woman, but I'm sure one of them was here when Scott was killed.'

Wesley took out his phone and brought up the website advertising the symposium. He passed it to Gerry, pointing to a particular entry.

'Well, well,' said Gerry. 'He kept that one quiet. Get on to Traffic and see if his car was caught on camera heading this way.'

While Wesley was making the call, the DCI turned to Ginevra. 'Is your dad in, love? We need a word.'

'He's in, but he's getting ready to go away tonight. He's got a tour of bookshops and libraries in the north to publicise his book.' She didn't sound as though she approved. 'You should be arresting him, not letting him go swanning round the country staying in flashy hotels and pretending to be nice to his fans.'

'We've no evidence against him, and until we get some . . . I'm sorry.' Gerry sounded as though he meant it. 'By the way, Edith Craven's relatives have come down from up north to deal with her affairs. I thought you'd like to know.'

Ginevra's anger suddenly turned to sadness. She sniffed and bowed her head. 'Thanks.'

273

'Did Edith have much to do with Scott when she worked here?' Wesley asked.

'I saw her talking to him occasionally. And I think he agreed to do some work in her flat when she left to move back in with her mother. Why?'

'You don't know anything about her lending him a large sum of money?'

Ginevra frowned. 'No, of course not. Why would she do that?'

Wesley caught Gerry's eye. He felt they had a lot more to learn about the relationship between Edith and Scott, a relationship that had resulted in her making him a sizeable loan, but Ginevra wasn't the right person to ask. Her father, on the other hand, might know more about what had gone on in his house.

'What did you think of Scott?'

'I always thought there was something false about him. He was smarmy, too anxious to please, and I didn't like him. Is that an awful thing to say about someone who's just been murdered?'

'We prefer people to be honest with us,' said Wesley.

'And he was screwing my mother.'

'You know that for a fact?' said Gerry, glancing at Wesley. This was something new.

'Well I didn't actually catch them at it, but I knew the signs.' She tilted her head to one side. 'Have you seen the cellar?'

The question took Wesley and Gerry by surprise.

'Your father told our officers there wasn't one.'

'He lied.'

'Why didn't you say anything about it before?'

'Nobody asked me. I thought he would have told you.'

'So what's down there?' Gerry asked.

'Go and look for yourself. He's obsessed with Elias Anselmo, who used to live here hundreds of years ago. A necromancer, he called himself. I was always told it was too dangerous to go down there, but I know for a fact that my father got Scott to knock a wall down in the cellar, and that's when he found the room.' She hesitated. 'You don't think my mother could be buried down there?'

'There's no evidence that she's come to any harm.'

'If Scott or my father killed her, they'd be careful not to leave any evidence. You still haven't found her, have you?'

'If she's travelling abroad, these things take time. When did Scott do this work?'

'A couple of years ago, I think.'

'Not around the time your mother disappeared?'

She shook her head. 'No, I'm sure it was before that. But what if my father paid him to dig her grave ready for when he decided to get rid of her? What if he paid him to kill her?'

'We really need to speak to your father again,' said Wesley.

'He's in his study. You should just catch him before him and the bitch set off on their book tour.'

'Where are you going now?' Wesley was reluctant to abandon the girl in such an emotional state.

'To the Monk. I need a drink.'

'I'd like you to make a statement first.'

Wesley knew that Rachel had just returned to the incident room after taking a statement from Mrs Wentworth, Bill the archaeologist's elderly neighbour, so he told Ginevra to go over there. He trusted Rachel to assess the situation and provide a sympathetic ear.

He watched Search's daughter walk away, not sure how

far they could trust what she said. Edith's death and her father's relationship with Jocasta had hit her hard, and he couldn't help feeling sorry for her. If she was telling the truth about the cellar, there might be forensic evidence down there. But first they needed to corner Quentin Search and ask some awkward questions.

They were greeted at the door – although greeted wasn't the word Wesley would have used – by Jocasta, who scowled as she told them that Quentin was working and couldn't be disturbed. Nobody was allowed to disrupt the author's train of thought while he was writing.

'We can get a warrant if necessary – or we can arrest him on suspicion of murder. Would you prefer that?' Gerry said with threatening sweetness.

Jocasta knew she'd met her match. She stood aside, seething with fury.

'Can you show us the way, love?' said Gerry, pushing his luck. 'We wouldn't want to get lost.'

'When are you going to leave us alone?' she muttered.

'When we've finished. By the way, where were you when Scott Helivant was murdered?'

'We were in Tradington. You spoke to Quentin there yourself. Don't tell me you've forgotten.' She rolled her eyes, pleased with herself.

'We estimate that one of you could have left soon after that and made it back here in time to dispose of Scott.'

'Nonsense. After seeing you, he delivered a talk. Hundreds of witnesses. I was there too.'

'According to the programme on the website, you then did a speech entitled "We need to talk about historians", but there was a three-hour gap between you and your husband's talks..'

276

Wesley noticed her cheeks turn slightly red. 'That's right. But Quentin was in the audience when I spoke. He'll tell you.'

'I hope you're right,' said Gerry, an edge of threat still in his voice.

When they reached the study at the end of a panelled corridor, Jocasta knocked on the door and waited.

The words 'Come in' reminded Wesley of a headmaster summoning a recalcitrant pupil into his office. As soon as Jocasta opened the door, Gerry stepped into the room before she could announce them.

'Mr Search. We need another word.'

'Professor Search. And I'm busy.' He gave Wesley a killing look. The man clearly hadn't forgotten his association with Neil. 'I've already given a statement about my builder's death to one of your officers. Tragic though it is, it had nothing to do with me. I wasn't even here.'

'You weren't giving a talk at that particular time, so you could easily have made it here and back to Tradington. Are there any witnesses who actually saw you there?'

'Er, possibly not. I wanted to collect my thoughts, so I went for a walk in the grounds. The symposium, preparing the talks and putting the programme together, required a great deal of concentration, so I felt the need to have some time to myself.'

Wesley glanced at Jocasta, who was hovering by the door. 'Ms Adams told us that you were in the audience when she spoke.'

Search gave her an insincere smile. 'It's all right, darling. I'll deal with this.'

Wesley could tell from her face that she resented her dismissal, and she hesitated for a few moments before leaving them alone.

'I didn't want Jocasta to hear that I hadn't been in to hear her talk. A little white lie to spare her feelings. She'd been rather nervous, so she said she'd appreciate my opinion, and I told her she'd done well. The truth was that I sat out of sight at the back and sneaked out of the hall after the session started. It was a small deception, but as I said, I needed a break from the intensity of the weekend. I'm sure you understand,' he added with the sincerity of a dodgy quiz show host.

'It's a pity nobody can vouch for you,' said Gerry.

'I wasn't aware I'd need an alibi or I would have arranged to be observed. Now if that's all ...'

'We haven't finished yet, Mr Search. Your daughter told us that your wife, Kiara, had a relationship with Scott Helivant.'

'That's nonsense. Ginevra sometimes has problems distinguishing reality from her fantasies.'

'Why did you lie to my officers and tell them there was no cellar here?'

Wesley watched Search's face and saw that the question had taken him by surprise.

'I knew there was nothing of interest to them down there.' Search was clearly doing his best to sound casual. 'I didn't see the point in prolonging the intrusion.'

'So you lied.'

'I wouldn't put it quite like that. I thought I'd save them a fruitless search.'

'Ginevra also told us Scott did some work in your cellar some time ago. We'd like to have a look down there – maybe get a forensic team in.'

Search rose to his feet. He looked angry – and possibly frightened, although he was trying his best to hide it.

'That's out of the question. The house is very old and the steps are dangerous. I admit I asked Scott to have a quick look, but he said it would require a structural engineer to assess the work involved and it's one of those things you keep putting off,' he added with an insincere smile.

'So you've never been down there?'

'I looked when I first bought the house, but when I saw how hazardous it was, I locked the door and forgot all about it.'

Wesley caught Gerry's eye. 'So why did you want a wall knocking down?'

For once Quentin Search was lost for an answer.

Gerry turned to Wesley. 'Inspector Peterson, can you ring Sarah Rowdon and ask her what state the cellar was in when her mother lived here?'

'Of course, sir,' said Wesley formally, wanting to show Search they were doing everything by the book.

But before he could make the call, his phone rang. It was Traffic with an answer to his earlier enquiry. When he'd finished speaking, he took a deep breath and faced Quentin Search. 'Mr Search, your car was caught on camera just outside Midton, heading for the island, at two o'clock on the day of Scott Helivant's murder. You came back here.'

Search sank into his chair, opening and closing his mouth like a fish. Wesley looked at Gerry, who gave him a nod. He'd allow him the pleasure of making the arrest.

'Quentin Search, I'm arresting you on suspicion of the murder of Scott Helivant.'

Once he'd been cautioned, Search rushed to the study door and began shouting. 'Jocasta! Call Lionel Graves! Tell him I've been arrested for murder!'

'Tell him you're being taken to Tradmouth,' said Wesley. 'And let him know we'd like to ask him some more questions while he's there. We need to find out more about Edith Craven.'

44

Fortunately the tide was out so Quentin Search could be picked up by a patrol car, which Gerry reckoned gave them a psychological advantage. A boat trip wouldn't have made the same statement. Wesley and Gerry didn't follow immediately, because Gerry wanted to make the suspect sweat for a while.

'Now he's been arrested we can have a nosy down the cellar,' he said, rubbing his hands together in anticipation. 'I didn't believe it's dangerous, do you?'

'I called Sarah Rowdon to check, and according to her, what Search told us is nonsense. The cellar's in good condition, and consists of a single room with an impressive vaulted ceiling – it was where the prior used to store his wine. I'm pretty sure Search said it was dangerous because there's something down there he doesn't want us to see. If Scott knocked a wall down, it must have been because Search found out there was another space down there. The room Ginevra mentioned.'

'Or he wanted to hide something – like a body. There's only one way to find out. How do we get down there?'

Ginevra timed her entrance well. And she looked pleased with herself. 'I saw my father going off in a police car. Have you arrested him?'

'We've taken him in for questioning, love,' said Gerry. 'Did you give a statement to Sergeant Tracey like I asked?'

She nodded.

'We want to take a look in that cellar.'

'It's kept locked.'

'That won't be a problem. Can you show us the way?'

Ginevra's body appeared to stiffen. 'I'll show you, but I'm not going down there. It's an evil place.'

The entrance to the cellar was a small door set in an outside wall, easily missed unless you were looking for it. The stone steps were well worn by centuries of monastic feet traipsing up and down to fetch wine and other victuals. As Wesley gazed into the dark void, he experienced an unexpected shudder of fear, but told himself it was just a cellar; an ordinary underground storage room like so many others he'd seen.

Gerry had flicked on the light switch at the top of the steps so they could see where they were going. Sarah Rowdon had been right about the impressive stone vaulted ceiling, and Wesley's first thought was that Neil would love to see it; the only intact part of the priory complex apart from the pub and the church itself.

The room was empty, but he spotted a wooden door set into the far wall that looked fairly recent. Sarah had spoken of a single room, but the presence of a doorway suggested that there was another room beyond it with an entrance that had been created since her time at the Hall.

Gerry went ahead. When he opened the door, it scraped on the floor, making a sound like a low scream. He felt inside the entrance for another light switch but couldn't find one, so they turned on their phone torches as they stood in the doorway.

'Bloody hell.' Gerry Heffernan rarely swore, but on this occasion it seemed appropriate.

'I think we've found where Elias Anselmo practised his magic,' said Wesley.

'He's the bloke Quentin Search has been wittering on about, isn't he?'

'That's right. The Magus of Coffin Island, he calls him. See the pentagram on the floor. This must be where he performed his rituals.'

'You don't think Search drew it himself?'

'I wouldn't rule out the possibility if he wanted evidence to back up his theories. Although according to Neil, Anselmo definitely lived here and he was known as a magician. He's reputed to have conjured the spirits of Lyonesse and brewed up storms – although why anyone would want to do that, I've no idea,' Wesley added with a smile.

He stepped into the room to make a closer examination. The pentagram was faint, as though it had been there for centuries, and there were arcane symbols painted on it but he had no idea of their meaning. Sweeping his torch around the room, he could see niches containing the burned-out stubs of candles, and rusted wall brackets supporting lanterns coated in dust and grime.

'Someone's been using this place for nefarious purposes, Wes,' Gerry said. 'Perhaps Quentin Search dances naked down here before he sacrifices virgins?'

'What a thought,' said Wesley. 'No. I think Search is all talk. Mrs Wallace and Sarah Rowdon didn't know about this second cellar, so it must have been sealed up, maybe centuries ago. Search researched the history of the house, so he knew this room existed. It was just a case of knocking through a wall to find it, and that's where Scott came in.'

'He knew the secret.'

Wesley spotted something out of place: a section of wall in the far corner where the mortar between the bricks looked considerably fresher than in other places. He shone his torch downwards. In one particular area there appeared to be dark splashes on the stone floor.

'See that, Gerry? What does that look like to you?'

'Let's get the CSIs down here.'

Wesley hurried out of the cellar to make the call.

45

The sight of Quentin Search being driven off in a patrol car lifted Neil's spirits. He'd returned to the island, leaving Dave in charge of winding up the Dukesbridge dig, and after an adequate lunch of beer and sandwiches he had been coming out of the Hanging Monk with Bill and two other retired amateur diggers when they spotted the car driving slowly past towards the causeway. Neil hadn't been able to resist giving Search a little wave as they passed, a petty, cheeky gesture that gave him immense satisfaction.

The Reverend Charlie had called him before lunch to say that she'd found the records he wanted, and he promised to pop into the church as soon as he'd eaten. He'd also had an excited call from Annabel to say that she'd located the originals in the archives and found some old papers hidden inside the binding, possibly dating from the late sixteenth century. She hadn't had time to examine them, but they were available for Neil to look at any time he wanted. And did he fancy going for a pizza when he got back to Exeter? He'd told her his answer was yes and that he'd be back as soon as he could.

Before heading to the church, he couldn't resist looking at the test pits and the plastic trays of finds stacked beneath a little green gazebo set up by the church wall. Some of the pits were proving very productive and had been expanded, under Neil's supervision, into small rectangular trenches containing medieval pottery, coins, writing implements used in the monks' scriptorium and more worked stone, including an elaborately carved ceiling boss. Neil suspected that the St Rumon's Priory site might turn out to be of national importance and he felt rather pleased with himself.

He knew he'd feel even more satisfied if he could find the real story behind the two skeletons that had tumbled onto the beach after the landslip. That morning he'd received a text from the lab saying that they dated from between the second half of the sixteenth century and the first quarter of the seventeenth century. This encompassed the Elizabethan age; the time of Elias Anselmo. Was it possible the bones had some connection with Quentin Search's obsession? If so, he and Search would have an interest in common after all. It all depended on what the Reverend Charlie had discovered.

As he walked into the church, he saw the bell-ringers making for the door leading to the tower, chatting amongst themselves. He waited until they were out of sight before seeking out Charlie in the vestry, where he found her seated at a desk in front of her laptop.

She looked up as he entered, switched the computer off and sat back in her chair. He saw that she'd kicked her shoes off. 'I'm working on my sermon for Sunday. But come in and take a pew. I'll be glad of a break,' she said.

'I see your ringers are back.'

'I did offer them the use of another church, but they want to finish their peals here and they've managed to recruit another experienced ringer from Whitely to replace Jack Beattie. They're dedicating their remaining two peals to Maggie Beattie and they're ringing them both today. They told me that when they complete their challenge, it'll be down on record that they're ringing in her memory.'

'Nice.'

'I thought so.' She reached across the desk and retrieved a file. 'I've got those copies of the burial register you wanted. And I think I've found what you're looking for.' She opened the file and handed the contents to Neil. 'The fifth entry down.'

'"Elias Anselmo. Dead by hanging. Buried outside the confines of holy ground."' Neil looked up. 'The famous Elias Anselmo.'

'Wonder what he did to deserve his punishment?'

'Any hint in the records?'

Charlie shook her head.

'In the past, criminals were often buried at crossroads to confuse their restless spirits,' Neil said.

'I can't think of any suitable crossroads on this island, so I presume they made do with the next best thing. The vicar at the time was called Nescombe. In those days, the incumbent of a country parish often spent his life there, but he was only here three years. There's a Thomas Nescombe in the baptismal records the previous year, and I presume that's his son, as there's no record of any other family of that name, so there must have been a wife. Wonder what happened to the family. There's nothing in the death records.'

'I'd like to find out why Elias Anselmo was hanged. My ... er, friend is searching the archives in Exeter for any reference.' Neil was never quite sure how to refer to Annabel; 'partner' seemed too permanent, 'girlfriend' too young.

'I'm curious too, so let me know what they find, won't you. And I'm sorry I haven't had time to take more interest in the dig, but with five parishes to look after and that terrible murder, I've had my hands full.'

'The Millicombe Archaeological Society have been finding some amazing things, so I'm planning to organise a proper excavation ... with your permission, of course. It's on church land after all.'

'Of course. Permission granted.'

'If it turns out to be as important as I think, it'll put St Rumon's on the archaeological map.

'That would be wonderful. I'm so glad the body I found and this latest terrible murder haven't interfered with the society's activities.'

'Me too. Talking of terrible murders, did you ever meet that builder who was found dead at Coffin Hall?'

'I saw his van passing occasionally, but I never met him.' Charlie went back to studying the file. 'I was intrigued by this entry a few months after the one we've been looking at,' she said, turning a couple of pages. 'Same name. Elias Anselmo. It's an unusual name, so maybe it's his son.'

Neil took the file from her. There it was, five months after the first entry. *Elias Anselmo. Dead by hanging. Buried outside the confines of holy ground.*

'It's identical. It must be his son – or maybe another relative. Nobody dies twice.'

He stared at the entry. 'Could this be the second body?'

Charlie shrugged her shoulders. 'Anything's possible.'

*

As Wesley and Gerry walked back to the mainland across the causeway, the church bells began to ring again. Not even the death of Maggie Beattie had deterred Matt Evans and his dedicated band of ringers. The CSIs had been called out to examine Coffin Hall's cellar. Now it was a matter of waiting for them to report back on what, if anything, they'd found down there.

As soon as Quentin Search had been taken away in the patrol car, Jocasta Adams had called the solicitor and told him to get over to Tradmouth police station. Wesley listened in while she made the call and thought she sounded like a lady of the manor ordering a servant to clear up in the drawing room. It was obvious she was used to giving commands, and he suspected she was the power behind Quentin Search's recent success.

When the CSIs had arrived and traipsed down into the cellar with their equipment, Jocasta could barely contain her fury. But the police had the law on their side, and Gerry was satisfied that as the couple had been taken by surprise, they hadn't had an opportunity to destroy any evidence.

Once they'd picked up their car in Midton, Wesley drove back to Tradmouth, where Search was waiting for them in one of the interview rooms; not the most comfortable one, but not the grimmest either. They wanted him fairly relaxed, and they both suspected that without the formidable presence of Jocasta, he might prove more co-operative.

Search looked pale under the harsh fluorescent strip lights in the interview room. Wesley thought he seemed ten years older as he sat fidgeting with the plastic cup that had until recently held a liquid that claimed to be coffee from the machine out in the corridor. His arrogance and bluster had disappeared. He looked like a broken man.

Before Wesley and Gerry could take their seats, Lionel Graves arrived. He wasn't one of the usual briefs who turned up at the station when someone had been arrested, so they hadn't met him before, and Wesley immediately got the impression he was out of his depth. He was a tall, thin man with receding hair and a harassed expression who was probably more at home handling wills and house purchases than defending murder suspects. Wesley almost felt sorry for him.

They left Graves to confer with his client for a while, and when they returned to the room, Search wasn't looking particularly confident.

Gerry switched on the recording machine and gave a smile that would have put a crocodile to shame.

'Now, Mr Search, you employed Scott Helivant to carry out building work in your stables.'

Wesley knew the technique. Start with the simple things.

'I'm planning to make the stables into a centre for research into the paranormal history of the island. There's a great deal of interest in the subject. The success of my symposium proved that.'

'How long had Mr Helivant been working there?'

'Three weeks.'

'And you'd used his services before at Coffin Hall?'

'That's right.'

'What exactly had he done there?'

Search was beginning to relax. These were the easy questions. The difficult ones would come later.

'He'd done general plastering work for us and a few repairs to the roof. It's an old house and it needs a lot of maintenance by someone who knows what they're doing.'

So far, so straightforward. Gerry gave Wesley a nudge. It was his turn.

'What was your relationship with Scott Helivant?'

Search glanced at his solicitor, who'd suddenly become alert, like a meerkat on watch. 'He was a builder and I employed him to do a job. That's all. We didn't have a relationship other than that.'

'Did he have a relationship with your wife, Kiara?'

The hands that had been fidgeting with the plastic cup froze. The question had clearly hit a nerve. 'Not that I know of.'

Wesley and Gerry exchanged a glance. They knew a lie when they heard it.

'What about your former assistant, Edith Craven? Did she have much to do with Scott?'

Search glanced at Graves. 'They seemed to be on amicable terms, but I wouldn't say it went further than that. I remember her asking once whether he was reliable, because she mentioned that she needed work doing on her mother's flat in Dukesbridge. This was shortly before she left and the subject never arose again, so I don't know whether she employed him or not.'

'Edith was close to your daughter.'

'Ginevra seemed to get on well with her,' Search said casually.

'Let's talk about Kiara,' said Wesley. 'Was Scott working at the Hall at the time she walked out?'

Search pondered the question for a few moments. 'Probably. There's always a lot to do in a house like Coffin Hall.'

'He knocked down a section of wall in your cellar, I believe.'

Search hesitated. 'My research into the history of the house suggested that there might be another room down

291

there that had been sealed up at some point. Around two years ago, I asked Scott to knock an entrance through the wall.'

'We've seen your cellar. And the pentagram.'

Search nodded. 'I was excited to discover it, as you can imagine.'

'Why did you lie to my officers and tell them there was no cellar? Then you told us it was too dangerous to search, which it clearly isn't.'

'Because I didn't want a horde of policemen down there destroying priceless artefacts, that's why.'

'You said you'd found out about the second room through your research. It features in your book, I believe.'

'It was where Elias Anselmo carried out his spells and experiments in the sixteenth century. His laboratory, if you like.'

'We noticed a section of wall in there where the mortar looks newer than the rest. Was Scott responsible for that?'

Search shook his head. 'As far as I know he knocked the opening in the wall and installed the door. That's all.'

'So you've never noticed the new mortar in the pentagram room?'

Search looked unsure of himself. 'Maybe he noticed some crumbling mortar that needed replacing. I'm a busy man. I couldn't watch him all the time, but I would never have given permission for anything that would interfere with the important historical fabric of the chamber.'

Wesley suspected this was another lie. Work had definitely been carried out in that cellar. And when the CSIs had done their bit, they'd know what Search had been hiding from them.

When the phone call came, Gerry left the room to

take it. A few minutes later, he returned wearing a grim expression.

He sat down and leaned forward so his face was only a couple of feet away from the suspect's. 'Mr Search, have you or anybody in your household had an accident in the cellar?'

Wesley saw that Lionel Graves was looking very worried.

'I don't think so. Why?'

'Our forensic people have carried out an examination of the room. Can you explain why my team found traces of blood on the floor?'

Search's eyes widened. He looked terrified. So did his solicitor, who leaned over and whispered, 'Say no comment' in his ear, loud enough for Gerry and Wesley to hear clearly.

Search opted to accept legal advice. 'No comment.'

'Did you know about the blood?'

'No comment.'

'Does the presence of the blood in that cellar have anything to do with you?'

Search looked as though he was longing to give an answer, probably a denial, but Lionel Graves shook his head.

'No comment.'

'Who does the blood belong to?' Wesley asked, taking over the pressure. At a signal from Gerry, he straightened his back, ready to ask the question. 'We still haven't managed to locate your wife, Kiara. Did Edith Craven come back to Coffin Hall after her mother died, maybe to see Ginevra? Did she stumble on something you didn't want her to see? Was she killed because she found out that you'd murdered your wife?'

'No comment.'

'Why did you kill Maggie Beattie? Did she witness something she shouldn't have done when she came to the Hall in the hope of speaking to you?'

'I didn't kill her. I never even saw her. I was signing books in Exeter at the time she died.' The man's face was becoming redder.

'But you sneaked back when Scott was killed, so maybe you did the same on that occasion. We'll be making enquiries to see whether that was possible.'

'You do that.'

'Did you kill Scott Helivant because he knew something that might incriminate you? Was he blackmailing you for some reason?'

'No.'

'Why did you come back to the house around the time he died then lie about it?'

Search didn't answer for a few moments. Then he seemed to make a decision. 'Very well, I admit I came back. I needed to pick up some notes for my next talk and I didn't think it worth mentioning because I didn't see anything ... apart from Scott's van parked outside. I swear I didn't go anywhere near the stables. I don't think you appreciate the importance of my seminar and the book tour. I only lied because I didn't want the police harassing me at a crucial time in my new book's publication.'

'We only have your word for that.'

Search shot out of his chair and banged his fist on the table in front of him. 'You can't prove a thing!' he shouted, finally losing control. And as he began to rant about persecution and police harassment, Lionel Graves looked as though he'd rather be anywhere else.

*

Did they really have enough to charge Quentin Search? At that moment it was all supposition; nothing yet that would provide a watertight case to present to the Crown Prosecution Service. Samples of the blood in the cellar had been sent off for DNA analysis, but that would take time and the clock was ticking.

Search had no real alibi for Scott's murder, but they'd reinterviewed everyone at the bookshop, and his alibi for the time of Maggie Beattie's death still seemed solid. However, Gerry was confident that it was only a matter of time before they obtained a confession.

They left the custody sergeant to escort a still protesting Search to a cell, and were about to make their way upstairs to the CID office when Gerry saw Lionel Graves in the foyer, about to leave through the automatic glass doors.

'Mr Graves, can I have a word?' The DCI turned and walked down the staircase to join the solicitor. Wesley followed.

'If this is about Professor Search . . .'

'No, it's about another client of yours. Her name was mentioned in the interview room – Edith Craven.'

'What about her?'

'You drew up her will.'

'That's right.'

'The will mentioned Scott Helivant owing her ten thousand pounds. Do you know what the loan was for?'

Graves paused as though he was gathering his thoughts. 'When Miss Craven came to my office to make her will, I did enquire, and she told me that the young man had got into financial difficulties through no fault of his own – a leg injury that had prevented him working for a while. He had dependants – a sick wife and an invalid father,

I believe – and he needed a short-term loan.' There was another pause. 'I was a little concerned, but I agreed to the insertion of a clause to ensure that the money would be paid back into her estate.'

'But it wasn't.'

'Until her body was discovered, there was no reason to think she was dead.'

'Did you have any dealings with Scott Helivant yourself?'

'No. But I was aware that he'd done work at Coffin Hall for Professor Search.' Graves pursed his lips in disapproval. 'I was very much afraid that he'd taken advantage of Miss Craven's good nature. But one can't protect people from their own naïvety, can one?'

Wesley looked at the boss. The solicitor was probably spot on.

Journal of the Reverend Thomas Nescombe

Elias Anselmo stepped forward and smiled at my shock.

'You should thank me, Reverend, for it is I who saved a guilty one from the gallows.'

Amazement had rendered me speechless. But as I regained my senses, the words stumbled from my mouth. 'I saw you die.'

'You saw a man die – a man who knew that his death was much deserved. My servant, Ralph, was once my fellow novice at the priory. We were both unsuited to the monastic life, but unlike me, Ralph proved to be a cowardly, avaricious man who took his thirty pieces of silver to betray our prior.'

'But that was your doing.'

'I let the village think that in the knowledge that one day the truth would emerge. It was Brother Ralph who sent the prior to the hangman, but he repented of his wickedness soon afterwards and lived in penitence as my servant. The man was wretched and offered to take my place on the gallows.'

'And you allowed him to make such a sacrifice?' I said, amazed.

'You must understand that he knew I was innocent of

the girl's death. He could not let me suffer for a crime I did not commit.'

'What will you do?'

'I will live secretly in the Hall until I can leave the island by night at low tide. I trust you will not betray me.'

'I swear I will say nothing. But where will you go?'

'It is best you do not know.'

As we spoke, I regretted my doubts and suspicions of the man I had so misjudged. And yet he had allowed the guilty brother to go to the gallows in his place, which I suppose was a kind of murder, even though the man had gone willingly to his death.

Before Anselmo left my house, he leaned towards me and whispered in my ear the true identity of the one responsible for Talitha's terrible death.

Maybe I am a fool for not realising the truth earlier, but I shall pray for wisdom and guidance.

46

Wesley left Gerry at Tradmouth police station and returned to St Rumon's Island. He needed to speak to Jocasta Adams. She'd been living at Coffin Hall since Edith had left to care for her mother, and in his opinion she was bound to know more about their discoveries in the cellar than she was admitting.

But first he called in at the incident room to see whether anything new had come in from Forensics. As soon as he walked in, Rob Carter stood up to greet him with the news that there was nothing from the lab yet about the bloodstains in the cellar, even though the samples had been labelled urgent.

'Sounds like something out of a horror film,' said Rob. 'Black magic in an old cellar. Forensics reckon the bloodstains aren't that old. Think Quentin Search was conducting rituals down there? Human sacrifice?'

Wesley felt he had to shoot the DC's colourful theories down in flames. 'Sounds a bit far-fetched. Although we can't rule anything out at this stage,' he added.

When Rob returned to his desk, Wesley checked his messages. One was from Pam saying she had a parents' evening that night. If he was going to be home late, she'd have to ask Della to babysit. He put off replying for the moment and called Gerry's phone. The DCI answered at once with the news that he'd seen the chief super and she'd authorised more time to question Search.

'Gerry, I want to find out what's behind that newly pointed wall in the cellar. I'm going to ask Neil if any of his geophysics equipment will be of use.'

There was a silence on the other end of the line. Wesley could almost hear the boss doing the calculations in his head. 'OK, Wes. If it helps us nail Search, go for it. Are you thinking what I'm thinking? The missing wife?'

That was exactly what Wesley had been thinking. Ginevra's mother had gone on her travels around a year ago, a few months after Jocasta arrived. But in view of what had been found in the cellar, he had a strong feeling that she might not have left home after all. He called Pam back to say he'd be late home. But, he added optimistically, they hoped to have the case wrapped up soon. It was a half-truth, but he thought it was what she wanted to hear.

Then he called Neil. 'Have you got any equipment that might tell us what's behind a wall?'

'I think I might have just the thing,' Neil answered. 'I'm at the office in Exeter and I know where to lay my hands on it. Do you want me to bring it over?'

'Thanks. I'll meet you at the Hall.' If Neil's equipment found nothing, it would save him bringing the CSIs in.

An hour and a half later, Jocasta Adams looked displeased as she opened the door to admit Wesley, and when she saw that he was accompanied by a grinning Dr Watson, the scourge of her husband's reputation, she could barely conceal her fury.

'Which way to the cellar?' Neil asked cheerfully. Wesley could tell he was enjoying the situation.

'I'll show you,' he said, giving Jocasta an apologetic look.

Neil didn't start work at once. He was too busy looking round and studying the pentagram on the floor. He circled the room, examining the niches, and when he shone his torch obliquely at the walls, Wesley saw carvings he hadn't noticed before. Crude pictures of humans and animals and names he recognised as ancient demons along with other, more unfamiliar names.

'I knew all about Elias Anselmo, of course,' said Neil. 'But I'm surprised this place has been preserved untouched for more than four hundred years.'

'It was sealed up for centuries and only rediscovered a couple of years ago.'

'Quentin Search must have thought all his birthdays had come at once when he found this,' said Neil as he set up the equipment. Wesley's eyes were drawn to the blood splashes on the floor. He needed the DNA results, but he had to be patient.

He left Neil to his task and climbed the cellar steps in search of Jocasta, wondering how she'd taken Quentin's arrest.

She was in the drawing room, making notes on a manuscript, and greeted Wesley with a frown.

'When are you going to release Quentin?' she asked.

'He's still being questioned,' Wesley said. 'I'd like to ask you a few questions, if I may.'

'I've already told the police everything I know.' There was defiance in her voice.

'Can you remember all the jobs Scott did in this house after you arrived?'

She sighed. 'If Quentin needed something doing, he called Scott in. I don't see how that's relevant to his death.'

'He did some work in the cellar.'

'Did he? I don't concern myself with that sort of thing.'

'We found traces of blood down there.'

'I wouldn't know anything about that,' she said quickly. 'I really can't help you.'

'Bear with me. About Scott . . . '

'I never took much notice of him. He used to say hello, but I ignored him. You know what builders are like.'

'I believe some of them have had a certain reputation in the past,' Wesley admitted grudgingly. He never liked to stereotype people, and he'd met many honest and upright builders over the course of his life. 'When you arrived at Coffin Hall to replace Edith Craven, Kiara Search was still here?'

'Yes, though she and Quentin led separate lives. It didn't surprise me when she left. Quentin said she'd been restless for some time. Wanderlust, he called it.'

'Did you actually see her go?'

'At that time I often returned to my flat at weekends. When I came back one morning, she was gone.'

'Can you recall the exact date she left?'

'Not off the top of my head. It was May last year, I think. Why?'

'When did you last see Scott?'

'He arrived on Saturday morning, just before Quentin and I left for Tradington. I never saw him again after that.' She stood up. 'That's all I can tell you,' she said impatiently. 'So if you don't mind, I have things to do.'

'Just one more thing. Did Scott always come to work here on his own? He didn't have anyone else helping him?'

Jocasta sat down again. 'He was usually on his own. But I did see him with someone else a couple of days ago.'

'Who?'

'I only saw him from a distance coming out of the stables.' A look of distaste passed across her face. 'He was wearing a hoodie, so I couldn't see his face.'

Wesley's heart began to beat a little faster. This was something new. 'Anything else?'

Jocasta shook her head. 'He was around the same height as Scott, and was wearing the same sort of clothes Scott always wore underneath his overalls. I thought it *was* Scott at first, but then I saw him coming out afterwards.'

'Was this the day Scott was murdered?'

She thought for a moment. 'It might have been. Yes, I think it probably was.'

'Why didn't you tell us this before?'

'I didn't think it was important. I've had rather a lot on my mind since you arrested Quentin.' It sounded like a barbed criticism.

'Did this person see you?'

'No. I'm sure they didn't.'

He was about to ask her if she'd make another statement when Neil burst into the room, his muddy boots leaving marks on the large Turkish rug that covered most of the flagged floor. Jocasta didn't look pleased.

'Wes, can I have a word?'

Wesley followed him out into the hall. He knew Neil well enough to know that he had news.

'There's a cavity behind that newly pointed section of wall. Can't see inside, of course, but it's possible something's been walled up in there. Something or someone.'

The chief super's budget would be blown, but this

couldn't be ignored. Wesley took out his phone and asked for a forensic team to get to the Hall asap. Then he called Gerry to tell him what was happening, and the DCI said he'd come over as soon as he could get away. Wesley himself would have liked to stay while the forensic team dismantled a section of the cellar wall, but he had other things to do back at the incident room. Besides, he'd be alerted soon enough if anything unusual turned up.

The CSIs worked under Neil's supervision, because he wanted to make sure they didn't damage the historic fabric of the building. They created a small hole before inserting a camera, a version of a medical endoscope that he had acquired to investigate curious cavities in the ground or inside historic buildings. He watched the computer screen in silence as the CSIs operated the flexible cable with the camera and light on the end.

'You've got something,' he said as a bone came into view. 'Looks like a spine. And it's topped by a skull.'

'Almost certainly human remains,' said the woman in charge of the CSIs, her manner calm and professional. 'We need to enlarge the hole to get them out.'

The CSIs were happy to let Neil take the lead, advising how best to achieve their aim. He supervised as another stone was chipped out. Then another. Eventually the cavity was revealed, along with a crouched body inside; little more than a skeleton now, with desiccated flesh clinging to the bones and short hair sprouting from the grinning skull. Whoever this was had been shoved into the hole and sealed in. Neil hoped he or she had been dead when it happened.

While the photographers went about their work, he took out his phone and broke the news to Wesley before calling Colin Bowman. This was something the pathologist needed to see.

47

Wesley called Pam to tell her what had happened and to say he'd be home later than he'd first thought.

'What the hell's been going on there?' she said. 'I knew some people call it Coffin Island, but this is ridiculous.'

'I'll be back as soon as I can,' he promised. 'Kids OK?'

'I think so. Michael doesn't say much.'

'Hopefully he'll grow out of that.' He said he had to go. He was needed at Coffin Hall.

When he arrived, there was no sign of Gerry, but a constable was standing outside, checking everyone in and out, and he wondered how Jocasta was taking the new development. As he was handed his forensic suit, he was told that she was in the drawing room. But seeing Ginevra was more of a priority, because there was every possibility that the remains in the cellar belonged to her missing mother, and he wanted to prepare her for the worst.

He called Rachel's number. She was at the incident room and answered at once.

'I've heard about the human remains in the cellar,' she began. 'Do you need me there?'

'Please. I want to speak to Search's daughter.'

'You're thinking it's her mother?'

'Exactly.'

While he was waiting for Rachel in the courtyard, Colin Bowman breezed in. He asked the same question as Pam. What on earth had been going on? Wesley wished he knew the answer.

As Colin disappeared into the house, Wesley received a call from Gerry to say he was on his way, and as soon as he'd put his phone back in his pocket, Rachel appeared. First they had a word with Jocasta, who appeared to be irritated by the news rather than horrified. 'If there were human remains in that cellar,' she said, 'they've been there for hundreds of years. This has nothing to do with us.'

Wesley didn't feel inclined to contradict her. Instead he asked where they could find Ginevra, and they were pointed in the direction of her bedroom on the first floor.

When Rachel knocked on the door, Ginevra asked who it was. Wesley suspected that if it had been Jocasta, the girl would have told her to get lost, but it seemed the police were welcome.

They found her sitting on her bed, propped up against the pillows with a book in her hand. As soon as they entered, she jumped up.

'You've found something in the cellar. It's my mother, isn't it?'

'I'm afraid we don't know yet,' said Rachel softly. 'We'll need to carry out tests.'

'My father killed her,' Ginevra said bitterly. 'And that bitch Jocasta was here when she disappeared, so she must have had something to do with it.'

'She says she was at her flat in Neston at the time your mother left.'

'She's lying. It's obvious.'

Wesley didn't feel happy about leaving Ginevra alone, so Rachel requested the services of a family liaison officer. The girl needed someone there to support her.

They arrived downstairs just as the bones were being taken away to the mortuary after being examined and photographed *in situ*. A grim-faced Colin announced that the remains appeared to be female and that he couldn't give a cause of death until he'd made a more thorough examination.

As for Jocasta, she'd been told to stay put. She needed to answer some questions. But that could wait till the morning. Tomorrow would be another busy day.

That evening Barbara Dearlove found it difficult to concentrate on the crime drama playing on the TV. Since she'd received the letter she now knew had been sent by her brother-in-law, Greg, she'd been living in dread of something happening to stop her rebuilding her life.

She'd become used to not having Bryan around, although she'd never quite come to terms with the fact that the dull, respectable solicitor she'd married was capable of anything so adventurous as having an affair, stealing a large sum of money from his firm, killing his mistress and then drowning himself. It still seemed surreal, like the plot of an opera or a lurid TV thriller. And yet it had happened.

She'd spoken to Greg on the phone and he'd been apologetic, even though he still insisted that it was his brother's voice he'd heard before the call was cut off. It crossed her mind that he blamed her in some way for driving Bryan to such lengths and his anonymous letter was a form of twisted revenge. What she couldn't deal with was the possibility that Greg was right and Bryan was alive and out there lurking somewhere in the shadows. The very thought made her shudder.

The evening was cold for early May, so she switched the central heating on. Bryan would have accused her of wasting money, and she'd often wondered whether he'd been so petty and penny-pinching with Deidre Charlton. Or had she seen another side to him?

She was convinced that stealing the money from the firm had been Deidre's idea, because the Bryan she knew would have been far too timid to do such a thing. He'd claimed in his suicide note that after Deidre had got her hands on the money, she'd threatened to leave him because he'd ceased to be useful to her, and that was when he'd lost control and killed her. He'd said he couldn't bear the thought of life without her or the disgrace he'd have to endure if he came home to face the music. Of course, this might all have been a lie. But at that moment she didn't want to think about it.

It was ten o'clock and the TV news had just started. Bad news as usual. She switched off the TV and went into the kitchen to pour herself a glass of red wine; drinking in bed while reading a good crime novel was an indulgence Bryan would definitely have disapproved of.

She'd just taken a glass out of the cupboard when she heard a quiet knocking on the patio doors at the far end of the room. There was no moon that night, so when she looked out of the window above the sink, she could only see her own frightened reflection staring back. When she heard another knock on the glass, she wished she'd found someone to mend the security light that had given up the ghost a few months ago. The doors were a pair of long black mirrors and she couldn't see who or what was on the other side. But the kitchen light was on, so whoever it was could see her.

It suddenly occurred to her that she'd feel more confident with some kind of weapon. She opened a drawer and took out a rolling pin, weighing it in her hand, assessing its potential as a defence against attack.

'Who's there?' she shouted, trying to hide her fear as she walked slowly to the patio doors. Then she saw a distorted face pressed against the glass and let out a shriek. In spite of the beard and the close-cropped hair, it was a familiar face; one she'd thought she'd never see again in this life.

'Barbara. It's me. Let me in.' The voice was muffled by the double glazing, but she recognised it at once.

'Go away. Leave me alone,' she shouted back.

'Please, Barbara. I want to explain.'

She put the rolling pin down on the worktop, within easy reach should she need it. Her instinct was to call the police straight away. Then curiosity got the better of her and she unlocked the door and stood back. He stepped into the kitchen, closing the door behind him to keep the heat in. Waste not, want not had always been his favourite saying.

48

Wesley and Gerry made an early start on Tuesday morning. There was a lot to do, including resuming their interview with Quentin Search. The CSIs had calculated that the mortar in the cellar had only been in place between the stones for a year or two, which meant Mrs Wallace and Sarah Rowdon were definitely out of the frame and Quentin Search had shot to the top of their suspect list. The skeleton was female, and Search's wife hadn't been heard from for close to a year, so it didn't need a detective with the abilities of Sherlock Holmes to reach the obvious conclusion.

They met at the station and walked to the mortuary, eager to hear what Colin had to say. The remains on the table had been laid out neatly. Last time they'd seen the half-mummified body it had been crouched in a foetal position. Now they could see that the woman had been tall in life – around five feet ten. Wesley wished he'd thought to obtain a full description of Kiara Search.

They watched while Colin made a thorough examination of the body, removing samples carefully for DNA analysis. He worked in uncharacteristic silence for a while before looking up, ready to deliver his verdict.

'This woman was aged around fifty, and there are no obvious signs of disease. Good teeth apart from a few amalgam fillings in the back molars. There are indications that she was stabbed with a sharp implement of some kind, so it's definitely another murder, I'm afraid.' He pointed to a bag lying on a stainless-steel trolley nearby. It appeared to contain filthy rags; tattered and half rotted away but still identifiable. 'That's her clothing. A T-shirt of some kind. Jeans. Trainers too. Once your forensic people clean them up a bit, we'll see exactly what she was wearing when she died. Any thoughts about who she is? There was no ID with her.'

'We've got a good idea,' said Gerry. He sounded confident, even a little smug.

But Wesley feared his optimism might prove to be premature. The clothing didn't fit with the mental picture he'd built up of Kiara Search, although he knew he could be wrong. 'We should wait for the DNA results. We already have the sample Ginevra gave us. If this is her mother . . .'

'Who else would it be?' said Gerry. 'Man bumps off his wife and walls up her body in the cellar. He probably got Scott Helivant to do it and Scott was blackmailing him. That's why he kept him on to do work for him. Then Scott became too greedy so he had to die.'

'What about Edith Craven and Maggie Beattie?'

'They stumbled over something. It's obvious, Wes.'

'Search couldn't have killed Maggie.'

Gerry rolled his eyes, exasperated. 'Maybe he got Scott to do it. No doubt we'll find out once we put more pressure on him. I want Jocasta brought in too.'

They told Colin they wouldn't stay for refreshments this

time. Their chief suspect was waiting back at the station and the clock was ticking.

The pathologist looked disappointed. 'Next time then,' he said, raising a gloved hand in farewell.

'Hopefully we've got our man, so it might be a while,' said Gerry cheerfully. Much as they enjoyed Colin's company, the last thing they wanted was another murder.

Spending the previous night in a cell hadn't crushed Quentin Search's spirits. He was wearing a grey tracksuit and a defiant expression.

'I'm suing for wrongful arrest,' were his first words.

'Good luck with that,' was Gerry's reply. 'We've found human remains in your cellar. A woman.'

'The body was sealed behind a wall,' said Wesley. 'In the room with the pentagram. Is it your wife, Mr Search?'

Search's astonishment looked genuine, although Wesley knew that some people were better at acting than others. 'That's nonsense. I didn't kill Kiara.' He paused. 'Besides, I'd never have desecrated that room. It's where Elias Anselmo conducted his rituals. A sacred space.'

'An appropriate burial place then?' said Wesley, watching Search's face closely.

'You don't understand. It's not something I'd ever have done.'

'Are you absolutely sure the body is that of Kiara Search?' Lionel Graves asked. It was a good question and one they couldn't in all honesty answer until the DNA results came back.

'How tall is your wife?' Wesley asked.

Search shrugged. 'Average. Five feet five – maybe five six.'

'Not tall? Five ten?'

'I'm five ten and she's certainly smaller than me.'

'What was she wearing when you last saw her?'

'I don't remember exactly. But it would have been something expensive. She loved clothes; spent a fortune on them.' He sounded as though he disapproved of her extravagance.

'Not jeans, T-shirt and trainers?'

Search shook his head. 'She wouldn't be seen dead in that sort of thing.'

Lionel Graves gave him a warning look.

Gerry stood up, suspending the interview pending further enquiries. They needed to ask Ginevra about her mother. That way they would be guaranteed to learn the truth.

The call from Barbara Dearlove came through to the incident room because the caller had asked to speak to DI Peterson. As Wesley was otherwise engaged, it was Rachel who answered. At first it wasn't easy to hear what Barbara was saying because she was speaking in a whisper as though she didn't want to be overheard. Rachel asked her what was wrong.

'He came back last night. Turned up out of the blue, staring at me through my patio doors.'

'Who are we talking about, Barbara?' Rachel asked gently.

'*Him.* Bryan. My husband.'

Rachel frowned. 'You mean he's still alive?'

'That's right. I let him sleep in the spare room last night and he's in the bathroom at the moment, but I don't want him to know I'm calling you. I'm scared.'

Rachel remembered that the man was a self-confessed thief and murderer. And now it looked as though he'd faked his own death to escape justice. 'Right, Barbara, this is what I want you to do,' she said. Hopefully they'd arrest and charge at least one killer that day.

A patrol car was sent over to Bereton to bring Bryan Dearlove in. He didn't put up any resistance when the officers made the arrest, bowing his head in resignation and putting his hands out to receive the cuffs. The only thing he said was that he'd never killed anyone and the theft from his firm had been Deidre's idea and he'd just gone along with it because he'd been dazzled by her. He might have been a stupid fool, but he was no killer.

Wesley was keen to interview the man, but first he needed to go to St Rumon's Island to speak to Ginevra Search again. He called Rachel and asked her to meet him at the Hall.

The tide was out, and as he was walking over to the island, he was struck by the silence. No bells. Then he remembered that the northern ringers had now completed their challenge and Gerry had told them they were free to continue their tour of Devon towers but to leave their details in case the police wanted to talk to them again. Only Eddie Culpepper had stayed behind, with his parents, who were putting Edith Craven's affairs in order and arranging her funeral.

Rachel was waiting for him in the courtyard. Scott Helivant's van was no longer there, having been taken away to the police garage for forensic examination.

'We've brought Bryan Dearlove in,' was the first thing Wesley said when they met. 'It'll be interesting to hear what he has to say for himself.'

She hesitated for a moment. 'You don't think Deidre could be the woman in the cellar?'

'How would Dearlove have got access to the house? I know he rented a cottage on the island for a short break, presumably with Deidre, but sneaking into a stranger's cellar and walling up a body...'

Rachel had to acknowledge that he had a point.

'Besides, he says he never harmed Deidre; he says she's still alive and well.'

'Where?'

'Last heard of in sunny Spain. Hopefully we'll learn the full story in due course. And once we speak to Ginevra, we'll know whether Quentin Search has been lying to us about Kiara. There's not much love lost between her and her father, so I think we can trust her to tell the truth.'

'She never got on with her mum either, by all accounts. Poor girl. I feel sorry for her.'

'Me too. I get the impression that Edith was the only one who ever had time for her.'

Ginevra wasn't at the Hall, but they found her in the Hanging Monk, sitting alone in a corner with a glass of soda water on the table in front of her. Wesley was glad she wasn't seeking solace in the bottle.

'I didn't want to be on my own at the Hall,' she said as they sat down. 'Not with all those forensic people going up and down to the cellar.

'Isn't Jocasta there?'

She shook her head. 'She's gone back to her flat in Neston. If my father's charged, I can see her packing her Louis Vuitton bags and leaving. She's always had an eye for the main chance. It's fine to be shacked up with a bestselling author, but it wouldn't suit her to be tied to a convicted murderer. Can you imagine her queuing up outside the prison at visiting time with the wives of all the armed robbers and sex offenders? Unless she was in on it. Unless she helped my father dispose of my mother's body. In which case, she'll be inside too,' she said with a satisfied nod.

'If she had anything to do with what happened, we'll find out,' said Wesley. 'In the meantime, we've got a few questions to ask you about your mother. How tall is she?'

'Average. Around five five, I think. Not tall, not short.'

Rachel glanced at Wesley. This seemed to confirm what Quentin Search had told them. But they needed more. 'Did she usually dress in jeans and trainers?'

Ginevra shook her head. 'Never. If she wore trousers, they had to be white. She spent a fortune in posh boutiques in Exeter and Tradmouth. My father used to complain that she was extravagant, even though most of it was her money before his book sales took off and he started making a fortune from his nonsense.'

'When your mother disappeared, what happened to her clothes?'

Ginevra frowned. 'A couple of days after she left, I sneaked into her bedroom and looked in her wardrobe. All her clothes had gone, and when I asked my father, he said she'd taken them with her. But maybe he got rid of them to make it look that way.'

'You say it was her money?'

'She had a big inheritance from her grandfather. She had a secret bank account so my father couldn't get his hands on it. He wasn't pleased about that.'

It seemed Quentin Search had told them the truth about Kiara's height and choice of clothes. Wesley didn't know whether to tell Ginevra that the body in the cellar wall was unlikely to be her mother. In the end, he decided to leave it until the DNA results confirmed the matter once and for all.

As they stood up to leave, his phone rang. It was Gerry; he wanted Wesley over in Tradmouth right away.

49

Gerry asked Trish Walton and Rob Carter to interview Bryan Dearlove while he and Wesley watched from the observation room next door. Trish played the sympathetic role while Rob asked the tough questions. Gerry thought they made a good team.

It seemed Bryan was in a confessional mood. 'I worked with Deidre,' he began. 'And I became infatuated with her. It was the sex to start with. It was exciting. Like being a teenager again. Then Deidre pointed out how easy it would be to divert money from the firm's client account. Big money: house deposits and that sort of thing. But she said we should wait until the time was right, until a few big deposits came in and she could work her magic. She was brilliant with computers and technology.'

'Whose idea was it to disappear?'

'Deidre got the idea from the plot of a book she'd read. We bought ourselves a couple of fake passports from a bloke in a pub, then she cleaned out the client account, transferred the money to a new account she'd opened, and immediately withdrew it and put it in another one so it couldn't be traced. She did it just before the weekend so it wouldn't be discovered until Monday morning, then she went abroad under her new name. A couple of days later, as arranged, I posted a confession to Barbara saying that I'd killed Deidre during an argument and I couldn't live with myself.

'Once I'd posted it, I went out sailing and abandoned the yacht. I left my normal dinghy in place so it would look as though I couldn't have escaped that way, but I'd stowed an extra dinghy on board to get me ashore. I booked into a hotel in Lyme Regis, dyed my hair and grew a beard, and a couple of days later I took a flight to Spain with my new passport to join Deidre. We thought no one would come looking for us if everyone believed we were both dead. We'd escape our former lives and make a fresh start in the sun with new identities. We rented a lovely little place in Ronda, in Andalusia. Beautiful spot. Just like paradise. '

'And now you've come back. What went wrong?' Trish asked.

Bryan looked more embarrassed than repentant.

'I thought living with Deidre would be bliss, but it turned out she was hard work; what they call high maintenance. She ordered me about and criticised everything I did, and eventually I found myself longing to be back with Barbara again, just for a bit of peace. It all seemed so exciting at first, but I decided I'd rather come home and face the consequences than live like that. I tried to ring my brother, but I lost my nerve.'

Wesley could see that Trish was trying hard to keep a straight face. Bryan Dearlove's romantic adventure had backfired. Better the devil you know . . .

'Then I met someone in a bar in Spain. She was also from around here, funnily enough.'

'You began a relationship with her?'

A faraway look appeared in Bryan's eyes. 'Oh no. She was way out of my league. She'd left her husband in Devon. She said he was an author and he'd been screwing his new assistant.'

Gerry jumped up and left the observation room, and Wesley followed. They needed to talk to Bryan themselves. They burst into the interview room and announced their presence for the recording machine.

'What was this woman called?' was Gerry's first question.

Bryan looked startled. 'Kiara. Why?'

'Kiara Search?'

'No. Kiara Lambert. I felt sorry for her. She said she'd been a selfish bitch and she didn't think her daughter wanted anything to do with her.'

'And she's in Spain?'

'Yes, in Ronda, where me and Deidre rented a house.'

'Did she tell you anything else?'

'Only that she'd done some unforgivable things and she could never go back. What'll happen to me?'

'You'll be charged with theft and perverting the course of justice. And when we find Deidre Charlton, she'll be facing the same charges. What name's she using?'

'Paloma. Paloma Rome.'

Wesley recalled the book Pam had read and smiled to himself. 'Of course.

Gerry turned to him. 'Get on to Rach, will you, Wes. Tell her to break the news to Ginevra Search that her mum's still alive. And ask the Spanish police to track her down as soon as possible – and the same goes for Deidre Charlton, alias Paloma Rome.'

*

321

For a change, they'd just witnessed a pleasant development in the case, and they'd soon be able to tell Ginevra that her mother was still alive. Although Kiara's previously cold relationship with her daughter probably ruled out a happy reunion.

All this meant that Quentin Search could no longer be suspected of murdering his wife. But there were the other murders to take into account. Someone had killed Edith Craven, Maggie Beattie and Scott Helivant, and Search was the only person all three victims had in common. Besides, there was the question of the unidentified body in his cellar. The chief super had granted an extension so that he could be questioned further. Gerry was convinced they'd get him to crack sooner or later. Wesley wasn't so sure.

When they returned to the incident room, they were told that Rachel was at the Hall speaking to Ginevra. Wesley was tempted to call her, but he didn't want to butt in on what might be an emotional interview. Kiara's return from the dead would be a lot for Ginevra to take in.

He sat down at his desk and began to sort through the messages that had come in during his absence. They'd now ruled out the possibility that the bones in the cellar belonged to Kiara Search, although the DNA results hadn't yet come in. But there was one interesting message that he took over to Gerry's desk.

'Here's a list of men named Craig who've flown to the UK from Australia recently. I asked Rob to sort them by age and when they arrived. There isn't one called Craig Helivant.'

'That's that then. The brother's not here.'

'Unless he came via another country – took a flight to Amsterdam, for instance, and then one to the UK.'

'That'll be like looking for a needle in a haystack. Why couldn't he have a name like ... Tiberius, or Septimus?'

'I can't see George Helivant going in for Latin names somehow, but I have got an idea.'

Wesley went outside to make the calls. The sun had come out and he felt a sudden urge to discover what was happening at the priory dig. Then he told himself there was no reason why he shouldn't walk over there while he was waiting for people to call him back.

When he arrived, he found Neil chatting to a few retired volunteers who were expanding one of the test pits into a bona fide trench.

Neil seemed delighted to see him. 'I couldn't resist popping over from Dukesbridge to see how the Millicombe Archaeology Society are progressing. I suspect we've located the site of the scriptorium. And we found some gaming counters. The monks obviously liked to enjoy themselves when the prior's back was turned. It was a Benedictine priory – one of the smaller houses. *Labore est orare.* Work is prayer, according to St Benedict.'

'Then their whole way of life was destroyed,' said Wesley, looking around.

Before Neil could reply, Wesley's phone rang. When he heard what the officer on the other end of the line had to say, he said his goodbyes to Neil and hurried back to the incident room. This was something he hadn't expected at all.

50

George Helivant's marriage had taken place back in the 1970s, but the details were readily available when DC Trish Walton made the enquiry. George had married a Sheila Vernon and they had had two sons, Scott and Craig. Craig was the younger by only a year.

When Wesley asked Trish to check the list of passengers again, she hit the jackpot. A Craig Vernon, born in Devon and exactly the right age to be Scott's brother, had flown from Sydney to Heathrow eight days ago. Wesley felt a thrill of triumph that his hunch had paid off, but now it was a case of finding the missing brother and asking him some questions.

His phone rang again. This time it was the lab. The DNA results for the body in the cellar had come back. He made for the side office, where Gerry was deep in his hated paperwork, and switched on his phone's speaker so the DCI could hear.

'There's no familial match with Ginevra Search,' said the voice at the other end. 'There is, however, a familial match for another sample you sent over a few days ago.' There was a pause, as though the woman on the other end of the line was consulting her records. 'A Carl Shultz.'

Gerry was leaning forward, looking puzzled.

'Could it be his missing half-sister?' Wesley asked.

'That would fit.'

'Looks like we've found Karen Liden,' Wesley said once the call was finished. 'Is Shultz still at the Castle Hotel?'

'I believe so. But how on earth did Karen end up behind a wall in the cellar of Coffin Hall? There's something here we're missing.'

'We never really took Carl's missing persons report seriously, did we?' Wesley sounded as though he regretted the omission.

'Because there was no evidence she'd come to any harm,' said Gerry. 'If people choose to move and lose touch with their long-lost relatives, that's their business. We can't blame ourselves. We were in the middle of a murder inquiry, and once the DNA proved she hadn't been buried in that purple sheet, we had to drop it or the chief super would have had my guts.'

Wesley smiled sympathetically. 'I realise that, Gerry, but now we need to find out how Karen Liden was linked to the Searches.' He paused. 'And we have to speak to Quentin Search again to see if he knows how she ended up in his cellar.'

'You're right there, Wes. We also need to step up the search for Craig Vernon, or should I say Helivant.'

'We know he was in the UK when Maggie Beattie died, but could he have been involved in the killings of Karen Liden and Edith Craven?'

Gerry thought for a moment. 'I suppose it's possible if he came over on a previous occasion but I can't see it myself. You didn't mention his brother. Fratricide. Didn't they teach you about Cain and Abel in Sunday school?'

'The Helivants don't seem to have been a happy family.'

'With George as a father, I'd say they were bloody miserable. Dysfunctional, they call it nowadays. If Scott wasn't dead, I'd be bringing him in for questioning.'

Wesley nodded. He'd been thinking exactly the same. They were as sure as they could be that Scott conned Edith Craven out of ten grand and killed her so he'd never have to pay it back. He probably hadn't known that Edith had put that clause in her will. And even if he had, Wesley couldn't see the Culpeppers having much luck getting the money back.

Had he done something similar to Karen Liden, the widowed ex-teacher who'd moved to an area where she knew nobody? Had he been systematically cheating people out of their money and then disposing of them if they asked too many questions? Could one of his victims have taken the law into their own hands and plunged his head into a bucket of lime plaster? And had Maggie Beattie died because she'd witnessed something she shouldn't?

'Let's go and see Carl; break the bad news,' said Gerry, rising slowly from his chair. 'We'd better start making a real effort to trace Karen's last known movements. She must have had a bank account. Let's get it examined.'

Wesley gave the orders. Now they knew the latest victim's identity, it was a case of discovering everything they could about her life. He had always been taught that to learn how someone had died, you had to find out how they had lived.

51

When Quentin Search was asked whether he recognised the name Karen Liden and shown her photograph, he said he'd never heard of her and, as far as he could recollect, had never met her. When he was told that her body had been found in his cellar, his reaction was one of puzzled amazement. It was nothing to do with him, he said, though Scott had spent a lot of time down there doing goodness knows what. Trish and Rob, who were conducting the interview, were inclined to believe him.

A quick call to the hotel confirmed that Carl Shultz was still in residence. Wesley had wondered whether he might have postponed his mission to find Karen in order to explore more of the country. However, Tradmouth was as pleasant a place to stay as any. In the holiday season, the visitors flooded in.

Gerry seemed more harassed than usual. The chief super had been nagging him again about the budget for the investigation, something he could have done without. In the end, Wesley decided to take Rachel with him to break the bad news to Carl.

'I see the archaeologists are still at work on the island,' she said as they walked side by side along the exposed causeway towards the mainland car park.

'It's just a preliminary investigation at the moment, but Neil's planning to organise a proper excavation later in the year.'

'Ever wish you'd followed in Neil's footsteps?'

'Sometimes. Out in the fresh air with nothing to worry about except the past. No recent corpses and nobody expecting you to build up a case for the CPS to take to court.'

She stopped. 'You sound as though you mean it.' Her words were serious, as though she'd suddenly realised that she might one day lose him as a colleague.

Wesley shook his head. 'It's just this case. I keep feeling there's something obvious we're missing.'

'I think we're nearly there. We just need a bit of luck, that's all.' Rachel had always been a realist.

On the journey to Tradmouth, they chatted about Rachel's family, little Freddie, and Nigel's latest plans for the farm. The proposed excavation of the old priory wasn't mentioned again.

They parked at the police station and walked the short distance to the hotel. Someone had called ahead and Carl had arranged to meet them in the lounge, where they found him sipping coffee and looking nervous. The officer who'd spoken to him had said there'd been a development in the case, but it was up to Wesley and Rachel to outline the details.

Carl stood up as soon as he spotted them.

'I understand something's happened. Have you found Karen? Can I see her?'

'It's best if we sit down,' said Rachel. Once they were settled, she broke the news. Carl sat stunned for a few moments. Then he began asking questions they couldn't yet answer.

'We're doing our best to find out who was responsible,' said Wesley. He offered to bring Carl another drink: coffee, or something stronger for the shock. Carl opted for bourbon, and Wesley went to the bar, leaving the American with Rachel.

When he came back with the drink, he heard Rachel asking whether Karen had ever mentioned having building work done. The answer was no. But Carl said he did have something to tell them; something they were sure to be interested in.

'After we last spoke, Inspector, I assumed the police had lost interest so I took things into my own hands and hired a private eye.'

Wesley was stung by the implied criticism and was about to point out that they'd had three murders to deal with, but he stayed silent and listened.

'My investigator went to Karen's address and spoke with the neighbours. They said she'd needed some plastering work done but the man she'd employed had let her down. He'd taken a thousand pounds for materials, then never turned up. Kept making excuses: said he had an emergency on some island. She was angry and said she was going to track him down. After that, they didn't see her for a while, and then they noticed a van outside her house, so they thought he'd arrived to do the work at last. My investigator spoke to the current owners of the house, who said no plastering had been done recently. In fact they had to get someone in to do it when they moved in.'

'Did the van have a name on?'

'They didn't notice. But there's more. The house was put on the market a few weeks later. It went through a real estate agent and the neighbours gave the investigator the name of the company on the board. He went to their office and they told him that a Mr Helivant had dealt with the sale on behalf of the vendor, Mrs Liden, who had just emigrated to New Zealand. He was in possession of the keys and the deeds and she had signed all the relevant papers, so it seemed to be above board.'

Rachel and Wesley looked at each other. 'So the estate agent never actually spoke to Karen? This Mr Helivant dealt with everything.'

'That's right. He told the real estate agent and the lawyer that he was her nephew and she'd asked him to manage the sale. He seemed genuine, and like I said, he had all the paperwork.'

'Which he could have found in her house if he'd taken her keys,' said Wesley. 'And he could easily have forged her signature. When was this?'

'Just under two years ago. Around the time she stopped replying to my messages. Do you think he murdered her for her house? If so, you should lock him up, nephew or no nephew.'

'First of all, we don't believe he was her nephew,' said Rachel. 'And we would lock him up, but I'm afraid he's dead. He was murdered.'

'Well I had nothing to do with it,' Shultz said.

'Are you planning to stay here so we can keep you updated?'

'You bet. Looks like I'm the only person Karen had in the world. I should be here to arrange the funeral.'

Wesley could see tears forming in the man's eyes and felt desperately sorry for him. To discover you had a sister you hadn't known existed and then for her to be lost to you before you could even meet was bad enough. To find out she'd been murdered and cheated out of her property made things even worse.

'Of course,' said Rachel. 'We'll keep you informed. We're sorry for bringing such awful news. If there's anything you need ...'

'Another bourbon would be good.'

Wesley went to fetch the drink and Shultz downed it in one. They felt bad about leaving him, but they had things to do.

As soon as they'd left the hotel, Wesley's phone rang. It was the incident room. When the call was over, he turned to Rachel.

'They've got Scott's bank details. His account was cleared out around the time of his death. And this is the interesting bit. The balance of over three hundred thousand pounds was transferred to an account that was opened in Switzerland in the name of Craig Helivant.'

'That's it then. We're looking for Craig.'

'There's more. We found large payments into Scott's account from the sale of Karen Liden's house and several from accounts in Edith Craven's name. He obviously got hold of her details and had been milking her accounts ever since. There are smaller sums too, mostly in the hundreds or low thousands, from other people; probably payments for building work that never happened. We'd better get someone to speak to them, if they're still alive.' It wasn't like Wesley to be so pessimistic, but the situation was beginning to look bad. 'Karen Liden knew he was working on an island, and there aren't many islands around here, so I think she went to St Rumon's Island to confront him. She tracked him down to the Hall, where he killed her and walled up her body in the cellar he was working on. Then

331

he took her ID and keys and pulled the scam with the house sale. As for the others, including Edith, he charmed his marks and selected the ones with no relatives to kick up a fuss.'

'What about Maggie Beattie? Where does she come into all this?'

Wesley considered the question for a few moments. 'I think she witnessed something she shouldn't have when she went up to Coffin Hall. I think she was collateral damage. I can't come up with any other explanation.'

Rachel nodded slowly. 'There must be a lot of people out there who'd want to kill Scott Helivant, and I don't think we can rule out Carl Shultz as a suspect. His investigator identified Scott, and it wouldn't have been difficult for Shultz to find him.'

Wesley was reluctant to countenance the possibility. He felt a great deal of sympathy for Carl Shultz. He even liked the man.

'I suppose we should check his alibi for the time of Scott's death.'

He took a deep breath before returning the Castle Hotel. Some things couldn't be avoided.

Journal of the Reverend Thomas Nescombe

August 1575

I cannot rid myself of grief. Nor of guilt that I did not realise the truth earlier. I repent of my naïve stupidity. How could I have been so blind? I have knelt on the hard stone floor before the altar begging forgiveness and seeking guidance.

I agreed to say nothing; to allow Anselmo to escape the island unnoticed and begin another life. Whether he continued with his ungodly magic, I cared not, because he had once been a holy brother and I trusted the Lord would restore him to the path of righteousness in time.

But last night, my hopes were destroyed. I awoke at midnight to the sound of a large angry crowd, and when I looked from my chamber window, I saw they carried flaming torches and were led by Cuthbert Sellars, Talitha's father. I opened the window and asked their business, and Sellars called up to me.

'The Devil is restored to life, but he shall not escape death a second time. We go to the Hall and thence to the gallows.'

The gallows still stood where they had been built, and I knew I must prevent this. Yet it is a hard task for one man to stop a crowd determined on what they consider to be justice.

I dressed swiftly and ran after them, but by the time I reached the Hall, they had broken down the door. I saw them descend the cellar steps, unstoppable like a human wave, and a few minutes later they dragged Anselmo roughly out of his hiding place with jeers of triumph.

They pushed me aside, and even when I clung to Cuthbert Sellars' arm, he would not listen. Anselmo was dragged to the gallows and I was stunned at the swiftness of his death. I knelt and wept. Yet if I had managed to convince Sellars and his followers of the truth, I would have condemned another; someone closer to me than Elias Anselmo.

The mob refused my offer to give Anselmo Christian burial. He was Satan's man and his soul was now in Hell, they said. I knew then that I had to leave St Rumon's Island.

52

Neil was looking forward to returning to his Exeter flat after his camping adventure, and he decided to call Annabel about the arrangements for their meal that evening. His team had almost finished at the disappointingly unproductive Dukesbridge site and some of the trenches had already been backfilled, awaiting the diggers that would soon begin work on the new housing estate.

He was also looking forward to next weekend, when he'd promised to meet the volunteers at St Rumon's Island again. He was excited by the prospect of a full excavation of the priory site. It was just a question of finalising the arrangements with the university, arranging funding and fitting it in alongside his other commitments.

Annabel answered her phone after one ring. She sounded glad to hear his voice, which was a good sign.

'I was about to call you. You know I found those papers hidden in the binding of the St Rumon's church registers? Well, I've examined them and they seem to be pages from some sort of journal.'

'You've read them?'

'Couldn't resist. It appears to have been written by

a clergyman, and it describes the man who owns the Hall as a necromancer and a friend of Satan, but the most interesting bit is when the vicar's wife goes over to the dark side and starts hanging around with this Elias Anselmo.'

'I've seen what's left of his laboratory in the cellar of the Hall, complete with pentagram on the floor.'

'I'd love to see it.'

'Can't arrange that at the moment, I'm afraid, because Wesley's taped it off as a crime scene. Fancy that pizza tonight? There's that nice little Italian round the corner.'

'Eight o'clock at yours then. And in the meantime I'll scan the journal and send it over. I warn you, it's not what I was expecting.'

'Can't wait,' said Neil before ending the call. His back was aching and he suspected he was getting too old for camping out. It wasn't only the meal with Annabel he was looking forward to – it was a night in his own bed.

When Kylie Helivant arrived home from work, she found three envelopes on the doormat. She carried them into the lounge before flopping down on the puffy leather armchair Ashley had found in the charity shop and brought back in his mate's van. The van had been used to carry fish to local restaurants, and a fishy odour still lingered around the chair. But Kylie didn't care. She'd been on her feet in the salon all day and she needed the rest.

She shuffled the envelopes and found that two were addressed to Ashley. They looked as though they might be from the taxman, so she put them to one side before turning her attention to the third. It was a circular advertising a furniture sale. Even at sale prices, the goods on offer were out of her financial reach for the moment. The break-up with Scott had left her skint, as he'd transferred all the money from their joint account, including a small inheritance from her grandfather, into a new account in his own name. She could have gone to a solicitor and fought for it, but her estranged husband scared her, and the less she had to do with him the better. She told herself that she'd soon get established at the salon, and with all the expensive restaurants around the area needing fresh local fish, Ashley would be making a decent living. They would hardly be millionaires, but she was hopeful that better days were coming.

The sound of her phone ringing made her jump. It was a number she didn't recognise, and she answered with a tentative hello.

'Am I speaking to Mrs Kylie Helivant?' a female voice asked. She relaxed. It was probably a scam call, and she was about to tell the caller to get lost when the woman spoke again. 'This is Devonshire Life Assurance. I'm calling to inform you that we've had an application to insure your life.'

'An application? I don't understand.'

The woman lowered her voice. 'I might be a bit out of order here, but we had your phone number on file from a previous policy you held.'

'That's right. I remember.'

'It's just that I thought I'd better check whether you were aware of this application.'

'I'm not aware of any application. I really don't know what you're talking about.'

'So you didn't know that your life has recently

337

been insured for half a million pounds with a Craig Vernon-Helivant as the beneficiary?'

Kylie's mouth fell open. 'No. I didn't know.'

Shultz's alibi for the time of Scott Helivant's murder had been checked, and to Wesley's relief, it turned out that he'd been at the hotel, drinking coffee in the lounge, something the staff were happy to confirm.

Then Wesley took a call that raised all sorts of fresh possibilities. It was something he needed to discuss with Gerry.

'You look worried, Wes. What is it? Tell Uncle Gerry.'

'I've just taken a call from Kylie Helivant, Scott's estranged wife – or should I say widow? Someone from Devonshire Life Insurance rang her wanting to check whether she was aware that her life's just been insured for half a million pounds. I called the company, and they told me that if Kylie dies, the money goes to Craig Vernon-Helivant.'

Gerry stood up, sending his chair skittering back. 'Do you think the brothers were working on a scam together, and the policy was in Craig's name so Scott wouldn't fall under suspicion when Kylie died?'

'If that's the case, Kylie's in danger. I've warned her to be careful, but Ashley's going to be out on the fishing boat all night, so she'll be on her own in that flat. He doesn't arrive back in the harbour until the morning.'

Gerry sighed. 'In an ideal world, I'd get someone to stay with her – make sure she's safe. But we're short-staffed, so ...'

'She knows not to open the door to anyone she isn't expecting, and she says her mother's coming to spend the night. And of course the insurance company won't pay out if the beneficiary of the policy is convicted of her murder.'

'Unless he makes it seem like a convincing accident. Has Kylie ever met Craig?'

'She says not.'

'So she doesn't even know what he looks like.'

'She says he wasn't invited to her wedding. Mind you, neither was George. It was a little register office do, she said. I need to speak to George again – ask him what he knows about Craig being here.'

'He'll lie. Blood's thicker than water and people lie for their kids even in the most chaotic of families. Talking of families, what are we doing about Carl Shultz?'

'He's in the clear. He was having an innocent coffee at the Castle Hotel and he couldn't possibly have got to St Rumon's Island unless he had a time machine.'

'You look relieved.'

'I am. I feel sorry for Shultz, finding his sister like that, then his hopes being dashed.'

'You're too soft, Wes.'

Wesley smiled. 'You've had your moments.'

Gerry didn't look convinced. 'Scott was the builder from hell, but who else knew what he was up to?'

'We've got officers contacting all the people who paid money into his bank account. Although some probably paid in cash. They've spoken to four women who said Scott took a large deposit for materials then never turned up to do the work, and they couldn't contact him. There were three other people we couldn't get hold of,' Wesley added ominously. 'I've told the team to dig deeper. If there are more victims ... If they made a fuss or Scott thought he could get more money out of them somehow, he might have regarded them as disposable – like Karen Liden.' He shuddered. 'I can't help worrying about Kylie.'

'Me too. If this Craig's at large, she needs to be on the alert. And we don't really know what he looks like. The photo the Australian authorities sent over isn't much use. He's got a bushy beard and dark hair. He might have shaved off the beard, dyed his hair and changed his appearance completely since it was taken.'

'I'm going to speak to George Helivant. We need to know whether Craig has visited him, and if he won't talk, then Meera, the carer, might know something. I suspect nothing much gets past her.'

Gerry nodded slowly. 'You'll arrive at the nursing home around teatime. Hope you don't mind the smell of cabbage.'

'I'll take Rob.'

'Good idea.'

Half an hour later, Wesley and Rob arrived at the nursing home. Meera opened the door to them.

'If you've come to see George, you're out of luck,' she said before they could explain why they were there. 'An ambulance took him to hospital a couple of hours ago. His heart.' She looked round as though she was afraid of being overheard. 'Actually, I wasn't sure he had one.' Her eyes glowed with mischief. If anything happened to George Helivant, Wesley suspected he wouldn't be greatly missed.

'You might be able to help us,' said Wesley. 'George told us he only had one son.'

'That's right – the one you asked about before. The one who died.'

'We've discovered that he has another son who's been living in Australia. His name's Craig.'

She nodded in understanding. 'So that's who he meant.'

'Yes. And we think he returned to the UK recently. Has George had any new visitors over the past couple of weeks?'

'Apart from you, you mean.' She shook her head. 'No son from Australia has visited while I've been on duty. And if I wasn't here, I'm sure one of the staff would have mentioned it. You can have a look at the visitors' book if you like. People are supposed to sign in, although they don't always bother.' She reached for a large leather-bound volume on the hall stand, and Wesley flicked through it. Scott had last visited his father two months ago, but Craig's name didn't feature, either as Helivant or Vernon.

They were about to leave when Meera spoke again. 'George said something odd before he was taken to hospital. He said his son should do something about "that bitch Kylie". He said he should wring her neck. Or if he couldn't, he should get someone else to do it.'

'Charming,' said Rob.

'Trouble is, I think he meant it.'

Ashley had kissed Kylie goodbye. A long, passionate kiss before he set off to spend another night at sea. She would have loved to see him off, to stand on the quayside and watch the boat disappearing into the darkness until the lights vanished into the vast, heaving waters beyond the mouth of the River Trad, but he'd told her to stay inside. At least it was calm that night. She worried when it was stormy.

She looked out of the flat window at the sliver of water she could see through a narrow gap between the buildings opposite, which had been enough for the letting agent to describe the property as having a river view so they could hike up the rent. There was a full moon, but she wasn't sure whether this was a good omen or bad. She wondered whether the natural superstition of fisherfolk was rubbing off on her.

Her mother hadn't arrived as promised. She'd called to say she'd be late because she'd been held up by some minor domestic difficulty; something to do with the dog being sick. When Kylie told her to hurry, her mother said that if she made sure all the doors and windows were locked, she'd be fine.

She sat down and switched on the TV. Beneath the sound of the presenters' babble, she could hear the murmur of voices below in the chip shop as the aroma of frying drifted upwards. She found the sounds of life comforting. From the window she could see a steady stream of people approaching the shop and going in. Some of Ashley's catch would be on sale in there, she thought with a frisson of pride. But the real money was made by selling the more expensive kinds of fish to Tradmouth's posh restaurants. Kylie had looked at the prices on the menus outside and couldn't imagine how anyone could afford to spend that amount on a meal.

She felt more relaxed now that the chip shop was open and she knew people were down there getting on with the normal business of life. For the short time she'd been with Scott, nothing had seemed normal. He'd stopped her working in the job she loved. He'd tried to control her, and she'd lost all power over any money that came into the house. He had never even allowed her to see bank statements, and as she was no longer working, he'd closed her account. Marrying Scott had been a massive mistake, but Ashley was different. Now she had a new account for the money she earned at the salon, and Ashley liked to talk about her working day and laugh about the local gossip. She felt safe with him.

She closed the curtains and made herself comfortable. But if she'd gone back to the window and looked out at the street, she would have seen a hooded figure standing in the doorway of the clothes shop opposite.

53

Wesley felt uneasy as he made his way home that evening. The connection between Karen Liden and Edith Craven was Scott Helivant and possibly his elusive brother. Maggie Beattie's death was still a mystery, although it was possible that she'd had some contact with Scott during her visit to Quentin Search's house. But Scott was dead and Craig, the shadowy figure who might provide the solution to everything, couldn't be found. The problem occupied his mind as he walked, but he tried to put it out of his mind as soon as he turned the corner into his street.

He was surprised to find Neil there when he arrived home. When they'd spoken earlier, his friend had said he was returning to Exeter that night to have a meal with Annabel. It seemed his plans had changed.

Before he could ask Neil about this, Sherlock came hurtling out of the kitchen to greet him. He bent down to stroke the dog, whose tail was wagging like a windscreen wiper in a storm, and felt a rough tongue licking his hands.

'Someone's pleased to see you,' said Neil.

'We didn't expect you tonight. Thought you were in Exeter with Annabel and a large pizza.'

'Annabel had a call from her mum. She's not well, so our

pizza evening's been postponed. But Pam's stepped into the breach. She said I could stay here tonight.'

'That's what spare rooms are for,' said Wesley. 'The St Rumon's Island dig seems to be going well.'

'I've told the volunteers that I'll take some geophys equipment over there this weekend so we'll get a better idea of exactly what's there. And I've had a good look at the demolished section of the church. The Millicombe volunteers are really excited and I reckon it'll keep the university and local archaeology groups occupied for a few seasons. The Reverend Charlie's very keen too. Got anyone for your murders yet?'

Wesley hesitated, surprised at the sudden change of subject. 'We're getting closer to making an arrest,' he said with a confidence he didn't feel.

'I think Quentin Search did it. The latest body was found in his cellar and I've heard Maggie Beattie was obsessed with him. He must be guilty. Can't think why you haven't carted him off in handcuffs.'

'But we can't charge anyone unless we have enough evidence to stand up at a trial,' said Wesley. 'The Crown Prosecution Service tend to be a bit funny about that sort of thing. Are you still having trouble with him on social media?'

'Not for a few days. Maybe he's seen the error of his ways.'

Wesley noticed that Neil was holding a cardboard file. 'What's that?'

'Annabel emailed me over a copy of something she found in the archives along with the old church registers from St Rumon's. I printed it out – thought it might provide a spot of after-dinner entertainment for you.'

'Where's Pam?'

'Picking Amelia up from drama club. She won't be long. I've been helping with the dinner. Chopping veg and peeling spuds. It'll be ready as soon as Pam gets back. And I've fed Sherlock. And I've opened a tin of cat food for Moriarty.'

'Wow.' Wesley was impressed. Annabel had obviously been a good influence on his friend. 'Let's have a look at what you've brought me then.' He took the file from Neil. His head had been buzzing with the case all day and he needed something to take his mind off it.

'I was saving it until after we'd eaten.'

'Nothing to stop us making a start, is there?'

Neil answered with a shrug of his shoulders, and after making themselves comfortable in the living room, Wesley began to read, Neil leaning over to point out the juiciest bits.

'Looks like poor Thomas Nescombe led a miserable life,' Neil said after a while. 'See this bit about Elias Anselmo – he's the so-called magus Quentin Search goes on about. I was wondering whether he actually existed until I read this.'

'He existed all right. And he lured the vicar's wife into his activities. This is a better story than any fantasies Quentin Search could think up, and it explains what we found in the cellar. It was sealed up until Search got a builder to break through the wall and found Anselmo's ... I suppose you could call it his laboratory. After making a discovery like that, it's not surprising he became fixated with it.'

'Or saw it as a perfect money-making opportunity,' said Neil.

Wesley smiled. 'That as well.'

They heard the sound of Pam's key in the door, and a few moments later Amelia bounced into the room with Michael behind her, hanging back, solemn. But his eyes lit up when he saw Neil, who asked him how his day had been.

Soon they were sitting around the kitchen table eating Neil's offering. Sausages, carrots, peas and boiled potatoes. Hardly cordon bleu, but the kids covered the sausages with a blanket of ketchup and devoured the lot before going upstairs to tackle their homework. Maths in Michael's case, so neither Wesley nor Neil could be much help.

Pam had marking to do, so she retreated to the dining room, saying she'd expect a glass of wine to be waiting for her when she'd finished. This meant that after loading the dishwasher and clearing up in the kitchen, Neil and Wesley were left to continue reading the journal.

An hour later, Pam burst into the room to find that Wesley had forgotten all about her glass of wine. Neil got up to fetch it, because Wesley's mind was on other things. He now knew the names of the two sixteenth-century skeletons found after the landslip. And he knew why Elias Anselmo's name appeared twice in St Rumon's burial register. Better still, the story was starting to make him see his own case from a whole new angle.

54

Kylie Helivant's mother had arrived late but she'd left early, even though Kylie had begged her to stay as they'd arranged. She'd insisted that she had to get back for the dog. The poor little thing, a spoilt French bulldog, couldn't possibly be left on his own for the night. When Kylie suggested that she fetch him and bring him back to the flat, the answer was no. Fritzy didn't like strange places. Besides, Kylie would be fine as long as she didn't answer the door to strangers.

Kylie heard the downstairs door bang shut as her mother left. The dog had taken precedence over her daughter's safety. Her own mother had let her down and she felt like bursting into tears.

She didn't feel like watching TV because she knew she wouldn't be able to concentrate on what was happening on the screen. Her mind was in turmoil as she peeped through a gap in the curtains. Late-night drinkers were coming and going, buying chips after closing time. She watched them for a while, comforted by the proximity of everyday life. Then she decided that the best thing to do was to go to bed.

Kylie had never been one for reading at bedtime, but she couldn't sleep so she reached for the doorstop bestseller on

Ashley's bedside table. It was a thriller, with a lurid cover featuring a shadowy figure hidden in a doorway. She put it back; the figure reminded her too much of Scott. But, she told herself, Scott was dead. Soon, as his legal wife, she'd have to arrange his funeral. If it had been up to her, she would have disposed of him on the municipal tip, but she supposed appearances had to be maintained, even under the circumstances.

It was the warning she'd received from the police that worried her, along with the fact that Scott's brother, Craig, might be in the area. If anything happened to her, Craig would be entitled to claim his brother's money, including the money that Scott had transferred into his own account; money that rightfully belonged to her. Craig had every reason to want her dead, and in her imagination, he was a shadowy figure who might be lurking in any dark space, around any corner. He might even be hiding somewhere in the flat.

When Kylie was a child, she used to search her bedroom for monsters before she went to sleep: under the bed, in the wardrobe and behind the tall chest of drawers in the corner. Now, for the first time in more than two decades, she felt the need to do it again. She got out of bed and checked the flat, opening every cupboard, looking behind every piece of furniture capable of concealing a living human body. Lastly she looked under the bed, finding nothing there but a box containing her shoes and a layer of dust. The place was empty. She could sleep soundly. But she knew she wouldn't. When you thought someone wanted to kill you, you could never truly relax.

She told herself firmly that Craig would never find her. And once Ashley came home in the morning, she'd be safe.

*

As soon as Wesley finished reading the journal, Neil asked his opinion. Wesley didn't answer. Instead he said he had to make a call.

When he called Gerry's phone, a female voice answered. The woman had a strong Liverpool accent like Gerry's.

'Is that Alison?' he began.

'Yeah. Is that Wesley? Your name came up on Dad's caller display. How are you?' She sounded as though she was getting ready for a pleasant chat. Wesley wished he could oblige, but he had a feeling that if he was right, they needed to act quickly.

'Sorry, Alison, but is your dad there?'

'He's just stuffing his face with toast. Do you want to speak to him?' Again she sounded as though she had all the time in the world.

'Can you fetch him and tell him it's very important? Tell him I think I know the killer's identity . . . and what they're going to do next.'

Alison hesitated. Then she gave a nervous giggle. 'Sounds like one of those detective programmes on the telly. Hang on. I'll get him.

Kylie slept like a cat, half awake, half asleep; superficially relaxed but on the alert and ready to spring up at the slightest sound.

The chip shop customers had drifted away by half eleven and she'd heard the shutters go down on the shopfront. By half past midnight the street was silent; empty of vehicles and people. She closed her eyes, telling herself she'd be useless at work the following day if she didn't manage to get some proper sleep, and Mrs Johnson was booked in for blonde highlights – a complicated job she couldn't risk getting wrong.

As she lay there, her hand reached out to the empty space beside her in the bed. She recalled the nights she'd lain next to Scott, wishing he wasn't there and plotting and planning how she'd kill him; thinking of the best way to get away with murder.

A sound from downstairs made her eyelids flick open. It sounded like the front door next to the chip shop, but only Ashley, herself and the letting agent had keys. She hauled herself into a sitting position and listened. She was sure she heard the door closing, gently, stealthily, and for a moment she wondered whether Ashley had returned to port because of some problem or other; the boat's engine, perhaps. She told herself he was creeping about because he didn't want to wake her. He was thoughtful like that.

She decided to call out his name, to let him know she was awake. 'Ashley? That you?'

But there was no reply. Just a distant creak. The fifth stair always did that. Perhaps he hadn't heard her. Then she heard a scraping noise, as though a clawed animal was pawing at the flat door. This wasn't someone with a key. It was someone picking the lock. She grabbed her phone from the bedside table and with shaking fingers began to dial 999.

But then the door burst open and a rough hand snatched the phone from her. The intruder stamped on it before grabbing her hair, forcing her head back and putting a bottle to her lips. She began to swallow automatically, something that tasted like wine. She tried to close her mouth, but it was useless. He held her firmly as he rammed the neck of the bottle between her teeth. After a while, she began to feel weak and helpless, and though she tried her best to fight back, her limbs refused to obey.

Then her weakness turned to dizziness. And the dizziness turned to oblivion.

Gerry thought Wesley's new theory sounded interesting, but surely it could wait until morning. He'd just had his supper and was about to turn in for the night.

Wesley tried to conceal his frustration. 'OK, there wasn't anyone available to keep a watch on her flat, but I'm going to ask a patrol car to go round and check.'

'If you think so, Wes.' Wesley could hear the DCI yawning loudly on the other end of the line. 'I'm off for my kip.'

But before Wesley could call the patrol to make the request, his phone rang. It was a message to say that there'd been an aborted 999 call from Kylie Helivant's mobile number. His heart was beating fast as he rang Gerry back. The boss wouldn't be pleased, but that couldn't be helped.

As soon as he heard the news, Gerry's attitude changed. 'Get that patrol car over there fast. I'll meet you at the flat. Hope the chippy's still open,' he added.

They found Kylie's flat in darkness, the door ajar and the place empty. Wesley could see signs of a struggle in the bedroom and the broken phone on the floor. And he feared they might be too late.

55

All patrols were on the lookout for Kylie, possibly in the company of a man who may or may not have a beard. It was the early hours of the morning and the streets were empty, which should have made their job easier. But there was no sign of the woman they were looking for.

Wesley and Gerry made for the quayside, where the lights lining the embankment were reflected in the water, small globes of brightness on the rippling tide. The moored boats bobbed in the moonlight beside the pontoons, but there was no hint of life aboard any of them. The only sign of movement was a solitary water taxi skimming over the river, and Gerry stood watching it, seemingly mesmerised.

'She must be out there somewhere,' he said quietly, as though he was talking to himself.

'He could have driven her somewhere inland.'

'No, Wes. A car or van would be caught on CCTV. He's on foot, but how did he get her out of that flat?'

Wesley's phone rang and the sudden sound breaking the silence of the night made him jump. A patrol had spotted a man wheeling a large holdall along the quiet section of the embankment near the Marina Hotel. He'd probably just disembarked from one of the moored boats, but the officer thought he'd better call it in. Just in case. Wesley asked him to describe the man.

'Dark, with a beard. Average height. Average build. Walking along the embankment as though he knows where he's going. He's making for the road behind the hotel that leads to the gates of the naval college boatyard.'

'We're on our way,' said Wesley.

The nightly walk up the hill from work had done wonders for Wesley's fitness levels, and he began to run, conscious of Gerry panting behind him, trying to keep up.

The embankment was unfenced at that point, and as Wesley rushed along, he glanced to his right. There was a ten-foot drop down to the river, so he called back to Gerry to take care. The breathless answer was 'You're supposed to be a detective, not the health and safety police.'

Wesley ignored the quip and sped up. If the bearded stranger was just a yachtsman who had nothing to do with the case, they were in for a minor embarrassment. On the other hand, if it turned out to be Craig Vernon – also known as Craig Helivant – he feared that when they opened the holdall, they would find Kylie. Although it was unlikely she'd still be breathing.

They dashed past the entrance to the hotel car park and up the steep street behind the building. Wesley knew that if they carried on to the end they'd arrive at a tall security fence with gates leading to the boatyard; property of the Royal Navy and out of bounds to the public. If they turned right there, they'd meet a dead end with a long drop down to the water.

They reached the gates, and when they turned the corner, they saw a figure leaning over to gaze into the inky depths below. Beside his feet lay a huge holdall, large

354

enough to contain a human body. Wesley heard the running footsteps of the officers who'd been on lookout, and he saw Gerry spin round and hold up his hand. Don't come any closer. If the man chose, he could kick the holdall and it would drop straight into the river.

As Wesley watched, the shadowy figure squatted down and began to unzip the holdall. Once it was open, he hauled something out. Something, large, heavy and recognisably human.

Kylie.

Gerry signalled the officers forward but put his finger to his lips. Kylie wasn't moving. She might be dead. But if she was still alive, they couldn't risk the man panicking and tipping her into the river.

Wesley moved fast, his focus on the woman lying on the cobbles. The man had hold of her outstretched arms, ready to drag her over the edge, but Wesley swooped and grabbed her legs, holding on fast until the officers could reach them. Kylie's assailant's instant reaction was to pull her away in a split-second tug-of-war. Then, realising he was outnumbered, he dropped her, sending Wesley staggering back until he almost lost his balance and fell into the choppy water himself.

Wesley dropped to his knees beside Kylie and felt for a pulse while the other officers pursued the assailant back down the road. To his relief the pulse was there, weak but unmistakable, and he spoke to her, willing her to wake up. As Gerry called for an ambulance, she began to stir.

'Is she alive?' Gerry sounded anxious.

'Yes. But I think she's been given something.'

'Keep an eye on her.'

When Wesley looked up, he saw that the man had been

cornered in front of the securely locked gates leading to the naval college boatyard. He turned and shook the gates frantically, seeking an escape, but they held fast as two constables closed in on him. Then suddenly he evaded them by darting towards the river and vanishing from sight with a splash. He'd taken the only means of escape left to him.

Gerry was on the phone as soon as the man hit the water. He needed the police launch there fast, and the lifeboat too; belt and braces. Then he turned to the constables. 'Anyone fancy a swim?'

Wesley saw them glance down at the churning river and shake their heads. He leaned over the railing. In the moonlight he could see something moving in the water. It might have been a seal – they often came this far up the river – but it lacked that animal's sleek elegance, so he concluded that it was a swimmer, fully clothed and struggling towards a dinghy moored some distance away.

They watched, helpless, hoping the lifeboat wouldn't be long. Then they heard the reassuring sound of the approaching ambulance siren. Help was on its way for Kylie at least. By the time the paramedics reached her, she was regaining consciousness, groaning and opening her eyes, puzzled and confused. The detectives didn't try to ask any questions. Learning the details of her ordeal could wait until she was safe and recovering.

As the ambulance left, the inshore lifeboat, a fast RIB, sped up. Gerry had been watching the swimmer, who was now in difficulties, weighed down by his clothes as he tried to stay afloat. The lifeboat crew hauled him from the water and he slumped onto the deck like a landed fish. Gerry called out to them to take him to the nearest

356

pontoon, where he and Wesley would meet them, along with a police car.

Twenty minutes later, the lifeboat discharged its human cargo, wrapped in a silver thermal blanket and sopping wet. Another ambulance had already arrived and the paramedics were waiting to check the prisoner over. But Gerry was taking no chances. The handcuffs were put on as soon as their quarry stumbled ashore.

As the man entered the brightly lit ambulance, Wesley had a good view of him for the first time. He was surprised to see his beard dangling off, attached only at one temple, and something dark was trickling down his cheeks – hair dye, possibly. He kept his head bowed as though he was trying to hide his face from the two watching detectives.

'Look at me,' Wesley called out.

The man stared down at the floor as if he hadn't heard.

'Look at me,' Wesley repeated.

This time the man turned his face towards him slowly and reluctantly, refusing to meet his eyes.

Before he could stop himself, Wesley shouted, 'I know who you are.'

As soon as Neil had shown him the journal, everything had started to fit together. And now he allowed himself a moment of satisfaction. He'd got it right.

56

Once the paramedics had given the prisoner the all-clear, he was taken to the police station in a patrol car, hand-cuffed and escorted by two large constables. The hospital had been called for an update on Kylie's condition; the doctor who was treating her suspected that she'd been drugged, possibly with something like Rohypnol, but she was improving. Ashley had been contacted on the boat's radio, and he would dash to her bedside as soon as he arrived back in port.

Wesley looked at his watch. It was 3.30 in the morning, so questioning could wait. They didn't want some clever defence lawyer saying that they'd deprived a half-drowned suspect of rest in order to elicit a confession. Besides, the killer was safe in the cells. He wasn't going anywhere. Not this time.

When Wesley arrived home, he let himself in quietly and crept up the stairs. He remembered that Neil was in the spare room, so he couldn't sneak in there to avoid disturbing Pam. But when he slipped into bed, hoping he wouldn't wake her, she turned over and opened her eyes.

'Everything OK?'

'We've just made an arrest in the St Rumon's Island case.'

'Congratulations.'

She turned over again and appeared to go to sleep. But Wesley lay awake until morning, unable to switch off his brain. When they got up, Pam didn't ask him about the case; she'd sensed that he didn't want to talk about it just yet.

He and Gerry planned to begin the questioning straight after the morning briefing. There was a definite mood of festivity in the CID office, but Gerry told them to hold their horses until they were ready to charge the suspect. Only then would they all go to the Tradmouth Arms for a proper celebration. The wide grin on his face as he said it told the assembled officers that he felt pretty confident.

The prisoner had been brought up from the cells and was waiting for them in the grimmest interview room the station had to offer. The windowless space had bottle-green walls and smelled of sweat and fear, and Gerry liked to use it on occasions like this.

The prisoner, dry now after his midnight swim, was wearing a pale grey tracksuit. The beard had gone and his hair was several shades lighter, almost the same as when Wesley had last seen it, although traces of dark dye remained in places. The duty solicitor, a young man in a crumpled suit who looked as though he was recovering from a heavy night, sat beside him. His expression and demeanour said he'd rather be somewhere else.

'Well, Scott,' said Gerry. 'Are you going to tell us how you've achieved this remarkable trick? Not many people come back from the dead.'

'No comment.'

'Who was it who died with their head in that bucket of lime plaster? The DNA is a match to your father, so I'm guessing it was your brother, Craig. When he arrived here from Australia, did he have any idea you were planning to kill him?'

'No comment.'

'Did he let you know he was coming back to the UK or did he just turn up? My guess is that you invited him over, saying you wanted to be reconciled. The emotional reunion. And he fell for it. Am I right?'

Again Scott said, 'No comment.' But a momentary change in his expression told Wesley that he'd probably guessed right.

'Did your father know he was back?'

'My dad hated Craig. He said he was soft – said he was no son of his.'

'DNA proved he was,' said Wesley. 'How many people have you killed, Scott?'

'No comment.'

The solicitor was looking uncomfortable.

'Let me put this to you,' Wesley said, catching Gerry's eye. 'You killed a woman called Karen Liden because you'd run off with her money and she came after you. You then sold her house, pocketing the proceeds. You were doing work in the cellar at Coffin Hall at the time, so it was a convenient place to dispose of her body. Then there was Edith Craven. You tried to swindle her as well, and when she guessed what you were up to, you decided to kill her too. You wrapped her in a sheet you'd found at Coffin Hall and buried her on the edge of the churchyard. If it hadn't been for that landslip, she might never have been found. Am I right so far?'

'I never touched the Craven woman. And you can't prove I did.'

'Her neighbour saw you at her flat.'

'I went there to give her a quote.'

'Intending to take her money and vanish. You told the neighbour she'd gone on a cruise, but that was a lie. You'd killed her.'

'I told you, I never touched her.'

'You gave her a sob story and she lent you money. If she died, you wouldn't have to pay it back.'

The suspect's eyes widened. He suddenly looked like a cornered animal. 'No comment.'

Gerry took over. 'Maggie Beattie – I think she saw you when she went to the Hall to find Quentin Search. I think she witnessed something you didn't want anyone to see.'

'No comment.'

'Did she see you with Craig? It's my guess that he didn't have a beard at that point. Did you persuade him to shave it off because it didn't fit in with your plan? I think underneath all that facial hair he looked a lot like you, and if Maggie told anyone she'd seen you together, it would ruin your plans. Did she speak to you? Maybe she commented on how alike you were. Did she ask if you were twins?'

'No comment.'

'I think the resemblance between you and Craig gave you the idea. You'd been squirrelling away the money you'd swindled off your customers and you were planning to kill your estranged wife for a large amount of insurance. You needed to disappear and you intended to assume Craig's identity after you'd transferred all the money into Swiss bank accounts in his name. You killed your own brother in a horrible way because if everyone believed you'd been murdered, nobody would come after you. You'd frame Craig for the crime and we'd be chasing a ghost.'

'No comment.'

'You pushed his head into a bucket of caustic lime plaster. It not only killed him but had the added advantage of making him unrecognisable.'

The solicitor looked horrified as Scott Helivant smirked and repeated, 'No comment.'

They knew they wouldn't get a confession, but now that they knew what they were looking for, they would amass enough forensic evidence to get a conviction. Scott Helivant was a dangerous man who thought nothing of disposing of innocent people for financial gain.

The breakthrough came when two sets of prints were found at his address: his own and the dead man's. Most of Craig's were found in the spare room, suggesting he'd been staying with his brother since his arrival in the UK, unaware of what was in store for him. By a stroke of luck, his prints were on record in Australia because he'd been convicted of a traffic offence. Scott had been careful to wipe his van clean of prints, which had been suspicious in itself, but the comparison with the Australian prints sealed it. Craig was the victim. Scott, whose prints hadn't been on record, had taken his brother's identity.

By six o'clock, he'd been charged with the murder of Craig Vernon and the attempted murder of Kylie Helivant. He was told that further charges would follow. That evening, the team celebrated in the Tradmouth Arms. Gerry bought the first round and Alison joined him from his waterfront cottage a few yards away. Father and daughter looked happy, and Wesley felt glad for them.

The following morning, Wesley awoke with a hangover. Pam put a strong coffee under his nose and ordered him to drink it. Neil was still installed in the spare room but hadn't yet emerged into the light. Wesley realised that he had every reason to thank his friend, because if he hadn't found out about Elias Anselmo's deception, he might never have realised the truth about Scott Helivant so quickly. He would have got there eventually, of course, but more people might have lost their lives in the meantime – in particular, Kylie, who was recovering from her ordeal in Ashley's care.

When he arrived in the CID office at 8.30, most of the team looked as tired as he felt. He'd left the pub at 10 p.m., but many had stayed longer. He made straight for Gerry's office, where he found the DCI with his eyes closed, taking a short nap. As soon as he heard Wesley enter the room, his eyes flicked open and he smiled.

'Just the paperwork to complete now, Wes. And the file for the CPS.'

'Aren't you forgetting something? We might have got him for the attempt on Kylie's life, but he's still denying having anything to do with the murders of Karen Liden, Edith Craven and Maggie Beattie.'

Gerry looked puzzled. 'You can't think we've got the wrong man, surely?'

'No, but . . . '

'The forensic evidence is bound to confirm his guilt. I know the lab sometimes takes its time, but they usually come up trumps in the end. And he's under arrest for Kylie and Craig, so he won't be going anywhere.'

'I hope you're right.'

Wesley slumped down on Gerry's visitor's chair. 'I'd like to see the victims' relatives – tell them we've made an arrest. And you never know, maybe one of them will provide us with the crucial piece of the jigsaw.'

Gerry nodded slowly. 'You go. Take Rach with you.'

Wesley looked beyond the glass front of Gerry's office at the wide window beyond. He could see blue sky with small fluffy clouds. Meeting with the bereaved relatives wouldn't be easy, but at least it was a nice day to be out of the office.

But first they called on Kylie, and they found Ashley hovering over her like a mother hen. If she'd made the wrong choice when she married Scott, it seemed she'd now rectified the situation.

Ashley didn't move from her side all the way through the informal interview, and Wesley's instincts told him that she'd be all right from now on. She'd been through a lot and he wished her well.

'Is there anything you've remembered that might help us?' said Rachel gently. 'Anything you've forgotten to mention?'

Kylie looked at Ashley for support, then closed her eyes as though she was thinking.

Within seconds, she'd opened them again. 'When Scott's apartment was searched, did they look in the garage underneath?'

Rachel glanced at Wesley. 'I presume so.'

'Did they find the safe?'

'Nobody mentioned a safe,' said Wesley.

'It's hidden behind a wooden panel on the back wall. He thought I didn't know about it, but I was standing by the door once when he was getting the van out and I saw him put something in there.'

Wesley excused himself and went out of the room to make a call.

57

It was an hour before the officers who'd been sent to Scott's address reported back. They'd found a safe hidden behind what appeared to be a rectangle of bricks in the garage allocated to his apartment. On closer examination, the bricks turned out to be painted on a sheet of plywood. It had been very well done and it had fooled the team who'd made the initial visit.

The safe contained a lot of material. Names and bank details, accounts with payments from Edith Craven and several others, plus details of the sale of Karen Liden's house, the proceeds of which had gone into one of Scott's accounts. He'd received large sums of money for work that presumably had never been started, let alone completed, together with some anonymous payments. There were payments from Quentin Search too, although these seemed quite reasonable. All the people who'd paid Scott for work that had never been carried out would be traced and interviewed. If he had chosen to use his considerable financial skills honestly, he would have made a good living. But as it was, he'd chosen the dark side.

Wesley imagined it had suited Scott to be the semi-permanent handyman at Coffin Hall and keep in with the man who provided him with access to the ancient building. There was a possibility that alarmed him: the thought that Scott might have used the Hall as his personal cemetery, and that if he'd preyed on people who were alone in the world – people with nobody to report them missing – he might have been getting away with murder for years. He gave Rob, Paul and Trish the task of tracing the names from the hidden safe, but he dreaded what they might discover.

Along with details of Scott's murky financial dealings, the safe also contained some letters but, after a quick glance, Gerry reckoned these were of no importance, so they were placed in the evidence store. The important thing was that they accumulate enough evidence against Scott to charge him, and the DCI spent the rest of the day with the chief super and the CPS, determined that justice would be done.

It wasn't long before they had the answers they'd been waiting for. The DNA results that had been fast-tracked at great cost to Gerry's budget came through. Traces of Scott's DNA had been found on both Karen Liden's and Craig's clothing. Traces were also found on the spade used to kill Maggie Beattie. None had been found at Edith Craven's murder scene, but Gerry dismissed that by saying Scott had probably worn gloves.

All this meant they now had enough to charge Scott Helivant and make those charges stick.

The paperwork needed to be completed, but Wesley had more important things to do. First he took Rachel with him to visit Carl Shultz and let him know they were about to charge Scott. Then they headed over to the hotel in Dukesbridge where Eddie Culpepper and his parents were staying while they cleared out Edith Craven's flat and dealt with the administration surrounding her death.

They chatted to the Culpeppers for a while about Edith and her annual news bulletins from the south-west. Unfortunately, they hadn't been in the habit of keeping her Christmas letters, but they did recall certain things about her work in Quentin Search's household; things they'd found quite touching. Wesley said nothing to Rachel about the idea that was forming in his head, nagging away at him like a stone in his shoe.

Jack Beattie needed to be informed that they'd arrested someone for his wife's murder, but he'd gone to stay with his sister in Newton Abbot, so they decided to delegate the task to someone else in the team. Rachel observed that at least Jack was being looked after.

Wesley called the CID office. George Helivant would need to be informed and asked just how much he'd known about Scott's activities. Ten minutes later, Rob Carter called him back. He'd spoken to the manager of the home, who'd told him that George had passed away earlier that afternoon. They'd been trying to get in touch with Scott to let him know.

There was one more visit Wesley wanted to make, but when he called Gerry, the DCI asked him to hang on until he could join him, because this was one interview he didn't want to miss. It had never been too difficult to lure the boss away from his paperwork, and when Rachel returned to Tradmouth, Wesley got a lift to Midton from a patrol car and waited for Gerry in the car park so they could walk over the causeway together.

When Quentin Search opened the door, he didn't look pleased to see them. But his former arrogance had disappeared, and Wesley realised that he hadn't yet been told that he was off the hook. Wesley broke the news about Scott's arrest and saw a look of sheer relief pass across Search's face.

'I have some news as well, Inspector,' the man said. 'My wife's back. The Spanish police traced her and told her the police here wanted to speak to her.'

'We know. We discovered her whereabouts from someone unconnected with the case.'

'She's not pleased about it, I can tell you. She says she'll be going back as soon as all this is cleared up.'

It wasn't easy to tell how Search felt about this new development as he led them into the hallway. There was no sign of Jocasta, but to Wesley's surprise, Ginevra appeared at the top of the stairs. She was wearing a long pale green dress in a floaty fabric and there was a wreath of spring flowers on her head. He thought she looked like a May queen – or a sacrifice from some pagan ritual.

As soon as she saw Wesley, she hurried down the stairs, lifting her skirt daintily to avoid tripping over. Her father kept his gaze focused on the ground.

'My mother's back. She's here.' The girl didn't exactly sound delighted about the prodigal's return.

Wesley turned to Search. 'Did you know where she was all along?'

'No, of course not. All this has come as a complete surprise to me, I assure you.'

'Where's Jocasta?'

'In Neston, at her flat. She thought that under the circumstances ... '

At that moment, a woman appeared at the top of the staircase and descended with the elegance of a catwalk model. She was slim and tanned, with dark hair, and she bore a marked resemblance to Ginevra. Wesley knew at once that this was Kiara Search, the woman who'd left Coffin Hall a year ago, destination unknown.

'I hope this won't take long,' she said in a monotone.

'Thank you for coming back,' said Wesley.'

'I had no inclination to go on the run.' Her lips twitched upwards in an ironic smile. 'So I thought I'd get it over with. Although I don't see how I can help you.'

Wesley noticed that Ginevra had turned her back on her mother.

Gerry took a deep breath. 'We thought you might be dead.'

'As you can see, I'm very much alive.'

'You knew Scott Helivant?'

Wesley thought he could detect a blush beneath her layer of foundation. 'Yes.'

'He's just been charged with four murders and an attempted murder, as well as multiple charges of theft and fraud.'

Kiara stood in stunned silence for a few seconds. 'I can't believe that of Scott. He seemed so ... ' she searched for a suitable word, 'lovely.'

'He buried one of his victims in the cellar while you were living here. Do you know anything about that?'

'I know he did some work down there, but I had no idea ... That's horrible.' She turned away so Wesley couldn't read her expression. The news was shocking, but he thought there was something theatrical about her reaction, almost as though she'd already known what they were going to say. But he had to acknowledge that his imagination might be working overtime again.

When they left the house, he looked back and saw

Ginevra standing some distance from her mother. He'd hoped that if one good thing came out of this case, it would be that mother and daughter would be reunited. As far as he was concerned, family was important. But it seemed the relationship between Kiara and Ginevra had been damaged beyond repair.

Journal of the Reverend Thomas Nescombe

May 1576

It is less than a year since I left the island, soon after that terrible night, and I have now taken a living up north, well away from St Rumon's Island and also away from Anne.

On the night Anselmo visited my house, he revealed all to me, swearing he spoke only the truth. He told me the unfortunate Talitha was poisoned because of my son's love for his nursemaid. The child's rejection of his own mother brought about a terrible envy that gnawed away at my wife's soul until she could bear it no longer. She visited Anselmo requesting valerian to aid her sleep, but during her visit she had stolen poison from his workshop. He noticed it was missing later, but to his shame, he thought nothing of it. Then he heard about the girl and knew what Anne had done.

'But you were seen handing the potion to Talitha,' I told him.

He smiled sadly. 'A harmless sleeping draught only. I gave the girl no poison, I swear.'

I felt tears welling in my eyes. How could I have been so mistaken? How could I not have understood that Elias Anselmo had no reason to kill sweet Talitha Sellars? How did I not notice that my own wife harboured murderous resentment against the girl she thought had taken her place in Thomas's life – and perhaps even in my bed? How could I not have anticipated that her intense hatred would drive her to murder?

Her sister writes to me regularly and says Anne is not well. As fortune would have it, my Thomas is cared for well by his aunt in Tradmouth, whose husband now serves as mayor. Anne's obsession has faded, and nobody has guessed the truth of what she did.

Before I left the island, I sought out Anselmo's rough grave outside the churchyard near the clifftop and said a prayer of blessing. I hope he now rests in peace.

58

Neil didn't stay in the Petersons' spare room that night. He drove back to Exeter to see Annabel, and Wesley didn't know whether to be glad or sorry. Perhaps a quiet night with the family after the CID celebrations at the Tradmouth Arms the previous night was just what he needed.

He arrived home at a reasonable time and Pam greeted him at the front door, bursting with news. 'It turns out that one of the women I teach with knows someone who's a friend of Barbara Dearlove.'

'Oh yes?'

'Well,' she continued, leaning forward in gossip mode, 'apparently Barbara's husband came back and she chucked him out.'

This was old news to Wesley, but he let her carry on.

'She's started divorce proceedings. She thinks the husband's mistress, Deidre Charlton – the one whose name was in that book – is still in Spain. Didn't everyone think Bryan killed her?'

Wesley nodded. 'That's what we were led to believe. Bryan Dearlove caused us and his poor wife no end of trouble, but he's not going to get away with it. He'll be facing a prison sentence. What's for dinner?' It was hardly surprising that Barbara wouldn't take her errant husband back after what he'd done. But Dearlove's deception had nothing to do with the recent murders, so it was something Wesley didn't have to think about at that moment.

The children joined them to eat, Michael steering the conversation towards murder. 'Is it true there was a serial killer on Coffin Island? Did you catch him, Dad?' The boy's dark brown eyes lit up with prurient curiosity.

'No comment,' said Wesley with a grin. Then he felt mean. 'I'll tell you all about it another time,' he promised.

'By the way,' said Pam as Wesley began to clear away the dishes, 'my mum wants to come over on the bank holiday weekend. Your parents will be here and so will your sister and her family. Della says all her friends are going away and she's angling for an invitation. Shall I put her off?'

A picture flashed through Wesley's mind: Ginevra Search and her mother reunited but still keeping their distance. Pam was Della's only daughter. It wasn't up to him to separate them, especially when his own family were using the time to get together.

'No. We should invite her.'

Pam rolled her eyes. It seemed she'd been hoping for a different answer.

The following day everything was wrapped up, apart from the inevitable paperwork. Wesley was at his desk ploughing through forms when Paul Johnson appeared holding an evidence bag that contained some papers.

'You know that safe at Scott Helivant's place where we found details of all his scams?'

'What about it?'

'There were some letters in there, but we were looking for evidence of Scott's scams, not his love life, so the boss didn't think they were relevant.'

Wesley looked up, suddenly interested.

'Trish decided to get them out of the evidence store and take a look,' Paul continued. 'There are no signatures, but she thought you should see them just in case they're important.'

Wesley took the letters from him and began to read.

When he'd finished, he took them into Gerry's office. He wanted his boss's opinion.

Wesley had hoped he'd seen the last of Coffin Hall. The house held too many bad memories: a hidden body and murderous deceit. However, after what he'd just discovered, another visit couldn't be avoided.

He took Rachel with him, and when he asked to see Mrs Search, Kiara appeared. She looked angry about the intrusion.

'What is it, Inspector? I've already given a statement.'

'We didn't know whether you'd still be here.'

'I've as much right to be here as Quentin. But I'm returning to Spain tomorrow.'

Wesley stepped forward. 'We discovered letters hidden in a safe on Scott Helivant's premises. We believe they were written by you to Scott.'

'Why would I write to him?'

'We've read them, Mrs Search,' said Rachel. 'You mention this house and your husband. We can bring in a handwriting expert if necessary.'

'They must be forgeries.'

'I don't think so,' said Wesley. 'I think you and Scott were lovers and he kept the letters in order to blackmail you. He doesn't strike me as the sentimental type.'

Her face reddened. 'This is ridiculous.'

'What was your relationship with Edith Craven?'

'She was my husband's assistant. I had no relationship with her.' Her words were defiant.

'Did Scott try to blackmail you about your affair? There were no payments from you into his account. Maybe you paid him in cash.'

'Nonsense.' She appeared to relax a little and Wesley knew he'd got it wrong.

He thought for a moment. 'I don't think it *was* about your affair; I don't think you'd have been too bothered about your husband finding out. No, I think Scott had something else on you. Something a lot worse. Was that why you left? Was that why you went somewhere Scott couldn't get to you?'

She pulled herself up to her full height, defiant and dignified. 'You can't prove anything.'

'Scott's already been charged with several murders and other offences, so he'll have nothing to lose by telling the truth. I think it's strange that the one murder he's denied committing is Edith Craven's. Did *you* kill her?'

Wesley noticed that Ginevra had emerged from the drawing room and was standing perfectly still, as though she'd been turned to stone by an evil spell. He didn't like doing this in front of her, but he felt he had no choice.

'I think you quarrelled with Edith,' he continued. 'Was it over the way you were behaving with Scott? Or was it because she thought you were neglecting your daughter? I've spoken to Edith's relatives and, according to them, she was very fond of Genevra and she'd even started to regard

376

her as the daughter she'd never had. It was natural that she'd want to look after her interests.'

'That's right, she did,' Ginevra whispered. She stepped forward, glaring at her mother. 'I could tell her anything and she always listened. She kept in touch when she went off to care for her mum, but then she suddenly stopped. I never understood why until I found out she was dead.'

Wesley saw Rachel move closer to the girl, ready to comfort her if what she was about to hear became too upsetting.

'Were you jealous of Edith, Kiara?'

Kiara gave a derisive snort. 'That's absurd. Why would I be jealous of *her*?'

'Did Edith catch you with Scott?'

She didn't answer.

'What happened when Edith died? Did she phone to say that her mother had passed away and she wanted to return and take up her former job?'

Kiara looked away. 'She should have kept her nose out of other people's business.'

'Did you go to her flat to tell her that coming back was out of the question? Did she threaten to appeal directly to Quentin?'

It was clear from the look on Kiara's face that he'd hit a nerve.

'Did you lose your temper and kill her?'

Tears welled in Kiara's eyes as her uncaring mask began to crumble. She started to speak in shaky gasps. 'It was an accident . . . I didn't mean to . . . '

Wesley leaned forward. 'What happened?'

'Yes, what happened? I need to know,' said Ginevra, her hands clenched tight, trying to control her emotions.

Kiara swallowed hard, avoiding her daughter's horrified

gaze. 'I answered the house phone and it was Edith. Quentin was out but she said she wanted to speak to him because she wanted her old job back. I told her she'd been replaced, but I could tell she wasn't going to give up. She said she was concerned for Ginevra's welfare and she wanted to discuss the matter with Quentin face to face. I told her he wasn't available, but if she'd let me have her address, I'd pass on the message.'

'But you didn't?'

'I thought that if I spoke to her myself, I could clear up the matter once and for all, but when I got there, she said she'd only speak to Quentin. I decided it was time I told her a few home truths. I said she wasn't wanted and I wouldn't put up with her interference in my family any more. But she stood her ground and said the decision was up to Quentin and Ginevra. When she threatened to tell everyone about me and Scott, I laughed and told her she was pathetic. That's when she started going on about how I'd neglected my own daughter and damaged her emotionally. She had no right to lecture me like that.'

'What happened then?'

'I lost my temper. I called her a frustrated spinster who'd latched onto someone else's child because she didn't have any of her own and I told her that the way I treated my daughter was my business, not hers. She said she'd rather discuss it with Quentin. She stayed really calm, which made me even more furious. Maybe if she'd shouted back ... but she just stood there with this smug look on her face, and I ...'

She was crying now, tears rolling down her face, leaving her cheeks stained with grey tracks of mascara. Wesley waited for her to continue.

378

She wiped her eyes with a tissue and took a deep, shuddering breath. 'She told me to go, then she left the room. I was so angry I followed her into the bedroom and gave her a shove. She lost her balance and fell onto the bed. Then she just lay there, staring up at me. Judging me in that holier-than-thou way of hers. That's when I lost control. I picked up a pillow and pressed it down on her smug, self-righteous face and I kept pressing down until she wasn't moving any more. I couldn't stop myself.' She began to sob. 'I didn't mean to kill her. It was an accident, a moment of madness. When I realised what I'd done, I was horrified. You have to believe me. I didn't mean to ...'

'How did you dispose of her body?' Wesley asked once she'd composed herself a little.

'I didn't know what to do, but after a while I called Scott. He pretended he was doing some work at the flat so he could take her away in his van. He even told the neighbour she'd gone away so nobody would come looking for her. We found an old sheet in the attic and Scott buried her. We thought she'd never be found.'

'But Scott saw it as a business opportunity, didn't he? If there's one thing he loved, it was money, and he tried to blackmail you about what had happened. That's why you skipped the country. No Kiara, no money.'

'I didn't intend to kill her. I swear.' Kiara reached for her daughter with a pleading look in her eyes.

Ginevra stepped away from her. 'Edith cared for me. You've only ever cared about yourself.' Her words came out as a cry of pain.

Rachel put her arm around the girl's shoulders, and Ginevra started to sob uncontrollably.

*

It was low tide, so the patrol car summoned from the mainland arrived swiftly. As Kiara was led away, Quentin Search came out of his study at the back of the house, where he'd been out of earshot of the raised voices and unaware of the drama that had just been played out. Rachel told him what had happened, but he made no attempt to comfort his daughter. Theirs wasn't that sort of relationship. He did at least reach out his hand to touch her shoulder when she announced that she was going up to her room.

'Will you be all right?' Wesley asked as she passed him. He was concerned for the girl.

Ginevra stopped and took a deep, shuddering breath, straightening her back. 'Yes, I'm OK. It's just a shock, that's all.'

'Do you need anyone to be with you?'

She gave him a sad smile. 'No thanks. I just want to leave here. Maybe go back to college. I've been thinking about it since I found out Edith was dead. I reckon I owe it to her to make a new start. It's what she would have told me to do.'

'Tell us if you need anything,' said Rachel, who'd been hovering at the girl's side like a guardian angel. 'We can get you help if you want it.' She handed her a card with her contact details.

'Thanks, but I'll be OK,' Ginevra said with a brave smile. 'Now I know that Edith didn't abandon me on purpose, I can start facing the world again.'

When Wesley and Rachel left Coffin Hall for what they hoped would be the last time, Wesley looked back. He was sure he could see a pale face at one of the first-floor windows. A cadaverous figure with long grey hair; a figure that looked very much like the mental picture he'd formed of Elias Anselmo. But he told himself it was probably his imagination.

A few days later, the investigation was wrapped up, barring the paperwork. The chief super hadn't given Gerry too much of a hard time over exceeding the budget, and Scott Helivant and Kiara Search were awaiting trial.

As Scott was being led down to the cells to await transfer to the prison where he'd be held on remand until he faced the court, he passed Kiara in the corridor and Wesley saw their eyes meet. Scott gave her a rueful smile, but she looked away, as though he was a part of her life she wanted to forget.

There was one more thing Wesley needed to do, and that was to bring Carl Shultz up to date with the outcome of the investigation. He met him in the lounge of the Castle Hotel, and Carl told him sadly that he was returning to the States the following day. He thanked Wesley with tears forming in his eyes, and Wesley wished that he could have done something to help. He told himself that bringing Scott to justice was enough. But it didn't feel that way.

That evening, he arrived home at a reasonable time to discover that they had a visitor. When he saw Della installed on the sofa with a glass of white wine in her hand, his heart sank. After the events of the past weeks, he'd been hoping for a peaceful evening.

'You'll never guess, Wesley,' she began as soon as he entered the room. 'It's all over social media. Quentin Search has announced that he's working on a new book, *The Hall of Evil*. Didn't you see him being interviewed on TV last night?'

'I was otherwise engaged,' said Wesley sharply. He'd had enough of Quentin Search and his household to last a lifetime.

'He's writing his own account of those awful murders and he claims that everything that happened was caused by evil forces in the house. According to him, the killer was controlled by influences beyond his control – and that the evil even spread to his own wife.'

'I'd like to see them try that defence in court.'

Wesley left the room, angry that Search was intending to cash in on the misery his estranged wife and Scott had caused. He knew that if he stayed with Della any longer, he'd say something he'd regret.

He was glad when Neil rang to say that he was in the Tradmouth Arms. Did Wesley have time for a swift half? He had something to tell him. Bring Pam too.

Wesley smiled to himself. It was perfect timing for once. Della was there, so she could make herself useful by babysitting. And as the kids had already eaten, he and Pam could pick up a takeaway on the way back. Make a night of it.

They left the house before Della could raise any objections, giggling at their neat escape as they rushed down the hill into the town.

When they reached the pub, Neil was waiting in the lounge bar looking uncharacteristically sheepish.

'I've got some good news,' he began as they settled down with their drinks. 'The Dartmoor community dig's going ahead, so that'll keep Michael out of mischief during the summer holidays. The even better news is that I've managed to arrange a full training dig with the university on St Rumon's Island in the autumn term. The Millicombe Archaeological Society will be involved too, as they've done the initial work. The Reverend Charlie's thrilled – says she might join in.'

'That's great.'

'Quentin Search won't be pleased,' said Pam. 'But it serves him right for giving you a hard time.'

Wesley wondered whether to tell his friend about Search's latest project, but he decided against it. He'd seen the fallout from Scott's crimes and witnessed Carl Shultz's grief for the sister he'd never met, and he wanted to think about something else.

'I haven't told you my third piece of news,' said Neil nervously.

'What's that?' said Pam, draining her glass.

'I'm getting engaged.'

'What?' Wesley and Pam said in unison.

'Me and Annabel. She told me it was time she made an honest man of me.'

For once, both the Petersons were lost for words.

'When's the wedding?' Pam asked once they'd recovered from the shock.

'One step at a time.'

Something in Neil's tone made Wesley suspect that they'd be waiting a while for their invitation.

They were summoned home by a call from Della. She was meeting someone later that evening. She didn't specify who it was, but Pam suspected it was one of her online dates.

As they walked back, they passed a bookshop with a display in the window; numerous copies of the book Quentin Search had been publicising at his symposium. The shop was shut but a lifesized cardboard figure of Search had been left outside.

There was a rubbish skip outside an empty shop over the

road and all of a sudden Wesley had an urge to do something completely out of character.

'What on earth are you doing?' Pam said with a giggle as he picked up the figure and tossed it into the skip.

'I'm avenging the honour of the archaeological community,' he said, linking his arm through hers, 'Think of it as Neil's engagement present.'

Author's Note

All books begin with a germ of an idea that grows over months and sometimes years until it develops into a plot. In the case of *Coffin Island*, the initial idea came to me when I read about the legend of Lyonesse in a book of local tales I picked up in Devon a couple of years ago.

I had already heard the name Lyonesse in connection with the legend of King Arthur, but I didn't know the details of the story. It is said that Lyonesse lies beneath the waves off the south-west coast of England between Land's End and the Scilly Isles, and that it was once inhabited by hard-working people and contained a great number of parish churches. Eventually, however, it was engulfed by the sea like that other famous lost land, Atlantis. The Anglo-Saxon Chronicle contains a reference to a great sea flood doing much harm at Martinmas (11 November) 1099. However, Domesday Book (completed 1086) makes no reference to any land or villages in this particular location.

Some believe that the island of St Michael's Mount, home to a church and a priory and connected to the mainland at low tide via a causeway, is a remnant of the lost land, and it is said that the remains of a forest still exist beneath the sea round about. There is a tale that a female relative of a local vicar was told in a dream to stand on Land's End and scatter a concoction of herbs into the sea in order to raise the lost land complete with its inhabitants. Unfortunately, nothing happened. As Devon and Cornwall lie across a geological fault line, it is possible that some cataclysmic event accounts for the disappearance of great swathes of land during the so-called Dark Ages, much earlier than the legends suggest, but this is conjecture and we may never know the truth.

St Rumon's Island exists only in my imagination, but it was inspired by three islands I've visited in the past: St Michael's Mount off Cornwall, Burgh Island off south Devon and Holy Island in Northumberland. All three are accessible at low tide via a causeway.

St Michael's Mount and Holy Island were the locations of monastic houses, and the monks of old must have considered their isolation conducive to spiritual contemplation. The monasteries were dissolved on the orders of Henry VIII in the 1530s and the monks sent away. Several abbots and priors defied the king's commissioners and denied the king's supremacy over the church. For this, some were punished by hanging, including Adam Sedbergh, abbot of Jervaulx in Yorkshire, and Richard Whiting, abbot of Glastonbury. A number of monks from the Charterhouse in London also paid this penalty for their 'treason'. Not showing unquestioning obedience to Henry was a very dangerous business. The monastery buildings and lands were usually sold off to the king's supporters, but some of the churches were repurposed as cathedrals or parish churches. However, many other monastic buildings fell into disrepair and were used as a source of construction materials by local people.

In the historical sections of this book, my vicar, Thomas Nescombe, is married. After the Reformation, clergy were allowed to marry, although when Henry's elder daughter, Mary I (better known as Bloody Mary), came to the throne in 1553, she returned England to the Catholic faith, which meant that all married clergy had to hide their wives away until she was succeeded by her half-sister, Elizabeth, in 1558 and the Protestant faith was restored.

Elizabeth's astrological and scientific adviser, John Dee, chose her coronation date and advised on England's voyages of discovery. He took an interest in the occult and attempted to contact spirits and angels. He was also a respected astronomer and mathematician. To modern eyes, Dee's blend of science and magic might seem strange and contradictory, but in those distant days it wasn't considered unusual.

As for my fictitious Quentin Search, a mixture of magic, legend and conspiracy theories never fails to be popular and controversial (as some bestselling novels over the past years have proved). But as with certain novels about strange lost codes, people occasionally find it difficult to separate fact from fiction!

I felt I had to add some bell-ringers to the mix. I have rung bells at my local church for some time now (although, starting as an adult, I'm not very accomplished, unlike my fellow ringers who began as teenagers). I couldn't resist putting some ringers on St Rumon's Island to ring a number of peals lasting approximately three hours each, and I took inspiration from our own tower captain and his family, who go on an annual trip to the island of Lundy (off the north Devon coast) to ring the bells there.

Finally I'd like to thank my editor, Hannah Wann, and

my agent, Euan Thorneycroft. And I mustn't forget Matt Evans and Julia Partridge, who won an auction to raise funds for my granddaughter's school. Lastly, I'd also like to give a huge thank you to Sarah Rowdon, who donated the use of her name for Young Lives vs Cancer.